MW01435814

DEMON BASTARDS

By Clinton Williams

First Edition

Biographical Publishing Company
Prospect, Connecticut

Demon Bastards

First Edition

Published by:

John R. Guevin
Biographical Publishing Company
95 Sycamore Drive
Prospect, CT 06712-1493

Phone: 203-758-3661 Fax: 253-793-2618
e-mail: biopub@aol.com

Editing and proofreading by:

Christy Phillippe
The Versatile Pen

First Printing 2013

PRINTED IN THE UNITED STATES OF AMERICA

Publisher's Cataloging-in-Publication Data

Williams, Clinton.
Demon Bastards / by Clinton Williams.
1st ed.
p. cm.
ISBN 1929882890 (alk. Paper)
13-Digit ISBN 9781929882892
1. Title. 2. Fiction 3. Action. 4. Adventure. 5. Occult. 6. Supernatural
FIC002000 - Fiction/Action & Adventure
FIC024000 - Fiction/Occult & Supernatural
FIC031020 - Fiction/Thrillers/Historical
Dewey Decimal Classification: 813 American Fiction
Library of Congress Control Number: 2013935124

Chapter 1

Stretching out on his reclining chair, Lemuel's six-foot frame held a healthy two hundred pounds, with no flab anywhere. His appearance revealed a young man, but he was much older. With curly black hair extending past his neck, it often possessed a shining glow, eliciting admiration from everyone. With a black beard on his brown face, it brought out exquisite details to his facial features, specifically entrancing dark brown eyes, giving his appearance an angelic demeanor.

He reclined back in his chair even more with a worried expression. People were becoming suspicious because of his perpetual youth. He would have to move soon. He had been moving from place to place most of his life, though he never enjoyed it. He hated moving because of losing friends. He grew attached to people, and dreaded leaving without a word.

Lemuel felt exhausted. He had fallen asleep in the chair many times before, and knew this would be one of those times. He felt tired from the deep thoughts he contemplated. With eyes slowly closing, he fell asleep with thoughts of leaving on his mind...

Lemuel found himself standing in a void place. He gazed around and saw nothing but white light. With shock he wondered if he had died, when suddenly he heard a bellowing voice above.

Looking up, he gazed on a giant golden throne. It consisted of solid gold light, with a giant Divine Being sitting on it. The Divinity's glory appeared astounding, as vibrant lights shined out.

Lemuel fell prone while trembling with fear.

"Who do you think I am, Lemuel?" a deep voice bellowed out.

Lemuel answered with a trembling voice, "You are God."

The Deity continued with His awe-inspiring voice, "That is My title, but do you know My name?"

Lemuel stuttered nervously as he said, "You- You- You're Yahweh."

The Almighty One appeared pleased as He said, "That is one of My names. I have many names, each one glorifying a wonderful quality I possess."

Bright light from the Supreme Being faded slightly as a hurt tone crept into His Celestial Voice. "The reason I have called you here is to answer My question. Why have you decided to abandon mankind by turning your back on them in their time of need? The end of their civilization has drawn near, and you abandoned them."

"May that never happen!" Lemuel exclaimed fervently.

The Omniscient One shook His head sadly as He said, "It happened when you ceased trying to rescue mankind from the evil plots of Lucifer and his son."

Lemuel replied in frustration, "I've tried to help mankind for many years, but I've grown weary. I just want to keep hidden and live my life in peace. Besides, it's impossible to save mankind because of their sins."

Sighing with exasperation, the Celestial Being said, "There has not been a sinless human since the fall of Adam and Eve. All humanity inherited sin from them. You have known this for a long time. Why have you abandoned them?"

Lemuel replied again, "Before, I thought I might be able to find at least some humans who were not sinners, who would be worthy of life, but after all these years I still haven't found one. I've become so discouraged with mankind I've given up on them. I just want to live my life in as much peace as I can."

The Spiritual Deity said with certainty, "At this time you will not find a sinless human. All have sinned because of their inherited imperfections. The only ones who may have a chance at becoming sinless someday are the ones who do not become followers of Lucifer and his son. Since human society is near the end, you must alert them about Lucifer and his son in order to save as many as possible."

Lemuel felt disheartened as he said, "I've been making plots against the devil's son for many years, but he always bounces back in one way or another. How can I defeat someone I'm not allowed to harm physically?"

After a moment of silence, the Supreme Being said with encouragement, "You can defeat Lucifer and his son by publishing to the world their actual existence. Most people do not know who Lucifer's son is, but you can let the world know. In so doing you will save many."

Lemuel then asked, "Why am I the only one here with You in

this emptiness?"

The Almighty One laughed as He said, "You think you are alone because My glorious light outshines everything in the universe. I will back up so you may see."

Lemuel watched with astonishment as the Creator streaked away on His throne. Looking around with wide-eyed wonder, Lemuel observed all the different colors of the universe crash toward him like lights on a gigantic wave, cascading around him in a colorful mist of twinkling stars.

Suddenly a myriad of spiritual beings materialized around him singing. They sang a song so beautiful it brought tears of love to Lemuel's eyes. It was the most beautiful song he had ever heard. He did not recognize the words, but he knew the meaning innately. He opened his mouth and praised God with pure joy, along with the other creatures. They swayed together in perfect harmony as they sang praises to the Holy One. He felt astonished while singing in a language he had never spoken, with more love than he had ever experienced. All he wanted to do was praise and glorify the Lord with song. Nothing else mattered. His obsessive love for Yahweh intermingled with the song he sang.

Suddenly Lemuel felt an awesome power levitate him above the colorful congregation, and then with incredible speed he was hurtled faster than light past the stars. In the blink of an eye, he found himself floating above the earth. With curiosity he examined the bluish oceans, white clouds, and distinguishable continents. He examined it all as he felt the supernatural power pull him toward the earth with relentless energy.

President Cain sat in his office, feeling invigorated with power. He felt pride when thinking of the millions of people he ruled over, and millions more he influenced. As the most powerful man on earth, he felt exalted with prestige, and he often fantasized about what was to come. In times of solitude, he daydreamed of ruling the entire world. Sometimes when dwelling on his accomplishments, he savored memories of his rise to power. It had been nothing short of a miraculous journey, a journey helped by his stately appearance—and his secret spiritual ally.

Physically he was handsome. Standing six feet, six inches in height, he looked slim at two hundred pounds. He took pride in the snow-white hair on his head, which befitted his exalted station. He also possessed distinguishable sapphire-colored eyes that adorned his face like two precious jewels. His clean-shaven features were sharply defined, with a long, narrow nose, pointy chin, high cheekbones, and paper-thin lips. His youthful appearance depicted him as being the youngest American president ever.

More importantly, his public personality portrayed a kind, peace-loving man who felt the deepest concern for all humanity. His private personality contrasted dramatically with his public one. In reality greediness guided every decision as egotistical, self-centered thoughts flowed through his mind, causing selfish cravings for complete control. He craved power over individuals and nations. He yearned to rule the world with an iron fist, so he often devised subtle plots in order to accomplish that ultimate goal. Through blackmail, threats, and schemes, he already controlled many of the world's nations. He wanted more.

There was a persistent knock on his door. It reminded him of a woodpecker's insistent hammering.

He stood up with reluctance. Then, smiling mischievously, he sauntered over to the door with a swagger in his gait, wondering who would dare interrupt his noonday fantasy. Beside the door, he briefly licked his lips with anticipation. He looked forward to scolding the intruder. He opened the door, only to look disappointingly into the darting eyes of his nervous secret service agent, Clarence Sexton.

Sweat beaded on Clarence's forehead, and his breath came in quick gasps. He walked into the room without permission, directly to Cain's desk. He snatched up a crystal decanter and pulled the lid off. He guzzled the expensive wine with deep gulps, his facial gestures mutely proclaiming his agitation and ravenous thirst.

At fifty years of age, Clarence appeared ten years older than his true age. Being shorter and heftier than Cain, he looked like a corrupt monk with a bald head. His devilish personality loved the carnal life and the wicked desires that accompanied it.

He reminded Cain of a drunken derelict. As he continued watching Clarence greedily gulp the wine down, the more nauseated the president became.

"If only Clarence had some manners," he mumbled with disgust.

Anger crept in his voice as he asked, "What do you want now, Clarence?"After reluctantly placing the crystal decanter back on the desk, he walked over to Cain, and handed him a well-known smut tabloid while pointing with quick motions at it. After a few seconds of pointing at the magazine erratically, he found his voice and yelled with alarm, "Mr President, look at this! They're saying you're the devil's son! Look, Mr. President, look on the front cover. There's a caricature of you smiling with canine teeth, forked tongue hanging out lewdly. You're gazing lustfully over a miniaturized earth. Right above the goatlike horns protruding from your head, it says in bold red letters, 'PRESIDENT IS THE DEVIL'S SON!'"

After reading the article, Cain walked over to the desk and placed the magazine on it. Cleverly concealing his anger, he walked over to the window and stared out. He then spoke in a deceitfully polite voice, "Please tell me who wrote this."

"You'll not believe it!" Clarence exclaimed with an admiring undercurrent. "It was Lemuel! You know the one, the smart one we can't catch. He's—"

"Silence!" Cain screamed.

His unexpected outburst silenced Clarence immediately.

Cain turned around with smoldering eyes while continuing to scream at Clarence. "I've been trying to get you to find him from the day I hired you, but it appears you're too incompetent to find him yourself! Well, no more Mr. Nice Guy! Find him now, or pay the ultimate price!"

Clarence felt bewildered as he searched for the proper words. He wondered if Cain had lost his mind. He had never witnessed Cain exhibit such anger before. He stared at him mutely, with mouth half-open in astonishment.

After ten seconds of eerie silence, Cain screamed with even more impatience, "Did you hear me, idiot? Bring him to me alive—immediately! That means now!"

Clarence recovered and became indignant, as hurt seeped through his words. "You didn't have to scream at me, Cain! I've already called the magazine to try to get his address, but they said they can't give it because of the privacy laws. It's not my fault that—"

Cain shut him up in mid-sentence with an upward jerk of his arm. He extended it out with the palm facing Clarence. He bent his fingers around like claws, and moved them back and forth in clutching motions while whispering alien chants.

Within seconds of Cain's odd behavior, Clarence began choking. Grabbing at his neck, he frantically attempted to pry the invisible fingers from it. Desperately he formed begging words as his mouth opened and closed with distraught, futile attempts, but no words would come. His eyes opened wide with terror as life seeped away.

After staggering with panic into the furniture, he fell on the floor and flopped like a fish on dry land. His mouth continued to open and close, silently pleading for Cain to stop.

Cain gazed down at him condescendingly as terror ran rampant in Clarence's heart, smothering any hope of living another day.

Cain spoke with an unnatural calmness, which veiled his rising temper. "You shouldn't have interrupted my noonday meditation. You shouldn't have forced your way into my office. You should have requested politely some of my wine. Most importantly, you should have brought Lemuel to me. You should have gotten your Mexican crime buddy to force the editor to give you the info you needed. Sure, it's against the law, but that's what they do—they break the law!"

With mocking tones of regret, he continued while shaking his head with pretended sadness. "How can I save Clarence, my best friend? How? He doesn't deserve to be saved, but I would if I knew how, so how..."

His sarcasm faded away in Clarence's oxygen-starved brain, as darkness slowly shrouded the light he saw. His flopping ceased as he twitched with spasms on the floor. With blood-speckled saliva rolling down his chin, he knew Cain had lost his mind. More importantly, his terrified mind knew his last moment of life twitched away, as his oxygen-deprived brain crossed over the boundary of consciousness, into a pitch-dark place.

Clarence sat on the floor in his personal room at the White House. His throat felt sore from what had happened earlier, but he felt grateful to be alive. He regained consciousness sprawled out on the floor, as if someone had tossed him aside like a broken doll.

After what happened, he knew without a doubt Cain's mind flirted with insanity. They did have problems occasionally, but nothing compared to what had transpired earlier. He knew Cain had almost killed him. He'd lost consciousness before Cain stopped choking him with the unseen fingers.

"Perhaps he really is the devil's son," Clarence whispered hoarsely as fear filled him. "How else could he have choked me without touching me?" Clarence felt despondent and emotionally drained from the traumatic ordeal, so he tried not to think about it.

After his fear subsided, he regained some of his composure. Standing up, he walked over to the phone and picked it up. He needed the aid of his Mexican connection, just as Cain had suggested. Dialing the number, he waited with agitation as the ringing seemed to go on forever. Eventually he heard the pick-up on the other end.

"Hello, Mr Hernandez?" Clarence asked politely.

"Yeah," Hernandez said with casual indifference.

"Mr Hernandez, this is Clarence. It looks like I'm going to need your assistance. Could you come by so we can discuss it in private?"

"Yeah, but I'll need your help, too. Maybe we can make a deal," Hernandez said.

Since Clarence knew about some of Hernandez's illegal activities, he knew he could order him to help, but he wanted to stay on Hernandez's good side. "Sure, Mr. Hernandez, just come on down about nine tonight, that should give you plenty of time to get ready."

"I'll be there, Clarence," Hernandez said with a reassuring tone.

"Great! See ya around nine, then," Clarence said eagerly before hanging up. Clarence walked over to his couch and fell back, exhausted. He could not sleep, so he began doing deep-breathing exercises. "It's been a stressful day," he mumbled miserably.

After a few moments of controlled breathing, his mind descended into a state of meditation. He found out long ago it helped relieve stress. Eventually he dozed off from exhaustion.

Clarence woke up to a loud pounding on his door.

"Clarence? Are you there? It's me, Hernandez. I'm leaving if you don't answer."

"Don't leave, Hernandez!" Clarence cried, still half-asleep. He jumped up, disoriented, and stumbled over to the door, opening it swiftly.

With a worried expression on his face, Hernandez asked with concern, "Are you alright, Clarence? I've been knocking for a few minutes now. I thought maybe you had a heart attack."

Clarence chuckled nervously as he let Hernandez in. He then closed the door as he examined his criminal friend up close. Clarence felt amazement every time he saw him. At seven feet tall and three hundred pounds, Hernandez appeared like a giant, especially in comparison to the average Mexican. He also possessed the deepest voice Clarence had ever heard. Except for those two oddities, he looked like the typical Mexican.

"Let me look at you for a moment," Clarence said with affection.

Hernandez had worked his way up into becoming leader of a crime family. At only thirty-five years of age, Clarence knew him to be a conniving man. He knew to be cautious around him since Hernandez was so shrewd.

Uttering his words with the utmost respect, Clarence said, "Mr. Hernandez, please have a seat in my chair. Would you like a glass of wine?"

"Don't mind if I do!" Hernandez exclaimed with a smile, as his huge body sank into the well-cushioned chair.

Gazing at Clarence, Hernandez became suspicious when he poured him a glass of wine with nervous hands. With suspicion he said, "Clarence, I'll pass on the drink. I'm a busy man, so let's get to the point."

Clarence breathed a sigh of relief, "Of course, Mr. Hernandez. I know you're a busy man, and I don't feel like being sociable, either. I'm truly sorry for taking up your time, but I have no one else I can trust. I also know you can handle this delicate situation."

Hernandez sighed as he said, "Please, Clarence, save the sweet talk. What do you want?"

Clarence chuckled nervously as he said, "Of course, Mr. Hernandez, please forgive me. Right to the point, well, where do I start?"

After an impatient grimace from Hernandez, he quickly regained his composure and said, "It seems a man somewhere has been spreading accusations about the president. I need you to find out where he lives, apprehend him, and bring him back to me alive."

He emphasized *alive*, hoping Hernandez understood.

He continued with an enthusiastic tone, "I don't know where this man lives, but I do have his name, and I know the magazine editor who has his address, so I want you to force the editor to give up the address."

Hernandez smiled as he squinted his eyes suspiciously. He then said, "No problem, but I'll need a favor from you. You need to get those FBI men off my ass. They've been following me for months now. I can't even take a leak at a public restroom without them following me in. Can you get them to stop?"

Clarence exclaimed with a relieved smile on his face, "No problem, Mr. Hernandez! I can do that, but since I'm sort of pressed for time, you get started now, and I'll do the same."

"Deal!" Hernandez said in agreement. Taking the information he needed from Clarence, he left without a word.

(PAST)

Planted on a planet called Earth, the garden's beautiful colors were like a sparkling kaleidoscopic gem in comparison to its dismal surroundings.

The garden's large variety of trees was beautiful with their assorted colors, which appeared to intermingle from a distance. Unique shrubs and flowers draped the grounds like a velvety carpet. Blooming floral displays shimmered in the sunlight with waves of colorful hues and appeared to vibrate with the scented breezes.

Wonderful smells accompanied the living waves of fluctuating colors. Scents of vibrant life rose throughout the garden on perfumed vapors, clinging tenaciously to the crisp, clean air.

The garden also thrived as a musical paradise, with nature's unique sounds echoing throughout it. Musical sounds orchestrated by the wind, with a band consisting of rustling trees and snapping twigs, joined by singers consisting of buzzing insects, melodic birds, and other musically inclined creatures.

Within the garden two humans lived. Their names were Adam and Eve, and they were the first of their kind. They lived on the pinnacle of perfect happiness within their growing paradise. With absolute freedom they did whatever their hearts desired, save one exception: They were forbidden to eat from the Tree of Knowledge.

During their blissful days they eagerly devoted time clearing away weeds and planting seeds. Often they ran through the garden with eagerness, plucking up unwanted plants. They sometimes made a game of their horticultural work by leaping joyfully throughout it.

Wherever they were, animals often found an infectious urge to join them in their celebration of life. Shouts of unabated delight often punctuated their work because of their frolicking with the creatures they came in contact with.

To them life felt blissfully captivating. They never experienced sadness, depression, rage, or any negative emotion. Their hearts overflowed with abundant love, happiness, and curiosity. They lived a perfect life. They did not know how old they were, since age was irrelevant. They knew deep down in their hearts their perfect lives would never end.

They planned on cultivating their beautiful garden forever. With tender loving care they intended to extend the boundaries until it eventually covered the world.

They would need help caring for it because the garden appeared to grow a little larger every day. It grew independently, like a living entity. The creatures around them reproduced, so they assumed their Father of the Wind would also give them children to help them. Offspring also meant more living beings to celebrate life with, so they eagerly anticipated sharing their lives with their progeny. They planned on celebrating life on earth forever, with lots of love and happiness.

Chapter 2

At 11 p.m. Eastern time, Hernandez and his crew of three rode around the outskirts of Jackson, Kentucky, in a black van they stole at the Lexington airport. They considered it a perfect vehicle for a kidnapping.

They searched for the home of Lemuel. They searched diligently for it with eyes open like goldfish, becoming more perplexed with each passing moment.

Hernandez searched with frustration for the name of the gravel road the magazine editor gave him, to no avail. The more he searched, the more confused he became. As he drove recklessly down another road, he felt more lost than ever. Since most of the gravel roads did not have signs, he drove down every one. Since he searched all day, and it had been dark for a while, Hernandez grew exhausted and irritated. Knowing his crew felt exhausted also, he decided to give up and start again the next day.

Right before he gave the order, he drove by a white, wooden two-story house. The numbers on the mailbox matched a set of numbers in his memory. "Gotcha!" he exclaimed triumphantly, with a big smile brightening his face.

Since Lemuel had no neighbors, and the country road appeared deserted, Hernandez decided to leave their vehicle on the road. They would be in and out in a flash, or so he reasoned. Stopping near Lemuel's home, he turned his headlights off and signaled for quiet with fingers to his lips. Whispering softly, he ordered, "Okay, guys, this is it! We go in, grab him, tie him up, and dump him in our van. Any questions?"

No one said anything. They had kidnapped before.

With Hernandez leading the way, they stepped out of the vehicle, closing their doors quietly.

After Hernandez flattened all the tires on Lemuel's vehicle with a pocket knife, he ran to the steps and crept up them with his men close behind.

At the front door, he picked the lock while whispering excitedly,

"Ready?"

They agreed with nervous nods.

With anticipation, Hernandez led the way into the dark home.

As Lemuel sat in his study, he kept thinking about more ways on how to alert the world that President Cain was the son of the devil. Since he had used one method by publishing his findings in a major tabloid, he could not use that method again. He needed more legitimate sources for getting his message out. He knew the vast majority of people would not believe a tabloid. They would read it, laugh about it, and think it was a big joke.

Suddenly he heard hateful words piercing the silence downstairs. Just frantic whispers, but his ears were more attuned than ordinary human ones. He stood up cautiously and with fear backed up to the wall. His mind raced through different escape plans, but his body would not cooperate. His heart pumped fast and furious, and his stomach felt like butterflies were beating their wings frantically within it. He continued to stare intensely at the study door, unable to shift his fearful gaze from it. He felt like an innocent deer hypnotized by the glare of bright headlights.

"Check upstairs, *puta*!"

Lemuel heard it clearly, though it was just a low whisper. Sinister intentions seeped from the muttering words, while undertones of wickedness saturated the whispering voice. Like an insulting slap, it snapped him out of his petrified state.

He ran over to the window and raised it up with an efficient flick of his wrist. He looked toward the study door one more time. He could hear footsteps on the stairway slowly creeping up the stairs. As the sound drew closer, it reminded him of a tiger stalking, with bloodlust in its eyes.

Forcing his gaze back out the open window, he looked out into the night. Swallowing his fear, he bravely dove out into the darkness, rolling around in the air like an Olympic diver. As soon as he hit the ground, he continued rolling to redistribute his weight. He rolled like an agile cat, landing on his feet firmly in a squat.

Standing up, he quickly looked around with frightened eyes. He painstakingly surveyed the surrounding area, searching for intruders who might have been left outside. He saw no one, but observed the intruders' black van, and noticed all four of his tires flattened.

Anguish grew in his heart, and a silent scream of agony filled his mind. He sprinted toward the two-lane paved road that lay a mile away. He ran as fast as he could. He ran with a silent scream shrieking in his mind.

With stretched lips over grinding teeth, he ran. With clenched facial muscles, he ran. With arms jerking back and forth, he ran. With nostrils flaring open for air, he ran. As a bitter copper taste filled his mouth, he ran. Even when his heart felt ready to burst, he ran. He ran through the silent screams and physical infirmities.

He eventually made it to the paved road. With a sweat-drenched body, his heart palpitated dangerously fast against his chest. With burning sensations, his lungs wheezed, starving for air. He bent over to help catch his breath. As his oxygen-starved lungs continued to consume large amounts of air, his fluttering heart regulated its beat back to normal. Saliva dribbled past dry lips, so he spit, attempting to get rid of the copper taste that saturated his taste buds. Staying in a bent position for a few moments, he fed his lungs, regulated his heart, and spit until he heard the faint slamming of a front door.

Quickly rising up, he stared down the gravel road, but the darkness hindered his perfect vision. Turning around, he looked in both directions along the paved road, but he saw with despair, no traffic. He felt no surprise. Late night in Eastern Kentucky existed the perfect components for solitude.

In the distance he heard the faint sound of a van starting up. He knew it was the one he had seen near his home. Soon they would be heading in his direction. He knew he needed to hide. With a resolve to escape, his mind became obsessed with finding concealment as he jogged alongside the paved road.

He heard the van come closer as an occasional stone thrown by a tire hit against its metal body with a metallic *ping*, so he increased his speed until he sprinted again. As soon as he heard the van near the paved road, he dived, scraping his arms against the hard ground while sliding.

He lay there motionless, breathing with fast breaths. He dared not move a muscle. He lay there as if transfixed by nature. He felt himself become part of the ground. Shock encompassed his body, as he felt like he was sinking in quicksand.

He heard the van pull off the gravel road. In a stalking way it turned right on the paved road and headed in his direction. It crept by as if expecting to see him beside the road at any time. He continued lying there patiently, even after the mechanical humming sounds of the van were long gone. He did not move an inch.

Croaking frogs and fluctuating chirps of crickets put him into a deep state of meditation. All his fears, memories, and thoughts dissolved into oblivion. His body felt heavy, like lead, and he felt himself slowly losing consciousness...

They found him! With a rope tied around his ankles, they drug him along the paved road with their van at top speed. Lemuel felt as if his body were on fire as his clothes and skin shredded unmercifully under the friction. He tried to scream as torturous pain filled every crevice of his brain, but no scream came. His vocal cords felt paralyzed with shock.

He gave up the futile attempt to scream, realizing his physical body was doomed. Acceptance filled his psyche, so he welcomed the gruesome death, even embraced it while envisioning God's glory, knowing he would see Him soon.

He gazed up, expecting to see God waiting for him with loving, open arms. What he saw instead brought absolute terror! In the sky he saw a beautiful angel of light plunging down at him, brandishing a flaming sword. Behind the angel a fiery lake of molten lava bubbled in the sky, unfolding itself like a scroll being opened, filling the sky.

The horror of it took his breath away. With terror, he tried to scream through the insanity of it all, with every ounce of strength left in his mangled body.

Cain stood beside an open window in his personal quarters at the White House. He gazed curiously into the night sky. The view appeared beautiful since there were no clouds to hide the sparkling stars. The night air felt crisp, invigorating him. He continued gazing on the thousands of sparkling stars, when he caught sight of a falling one. It appeared close, and it plunged closer with every second. He watched, fascinated, until it flew directly toward the open window. He screamed in fearful surprise while raising his arms up, shielding his face.

Instead of crashing into him, the ball of light stopped suddenly outside his window. It appeared to be the size of a basketball and made of solid light. It materialized into a laughing, spiritual creature made of thick, yellow light.

"You're so easy to scare," Lucifer said with a hearty laugh. "You should have seen yourself. You would've even laughed."

The more Lucifer laughed, the more angry Cain became. After a moment of patiently listening to the laughter, Cain finally shouted, "Shut up! Just shut up!"

The laughter ceased immediately.

Lucifer then asked with an ominous voice, "Did you just tell me to shut up?"

Fear gripped Cain's heart when he remembered whom he spoke to. "Please forgive me, Father. I've been having it rough lately. My enemy's attempting to ruin my reputation with a magazine."

Lucifer frowned even more with anger.

Cain bowed his head meekly while saying, "Please forgive me."

Lucifer brightened. "I'm glad you've remembered your station. If I want to laugh, be happy and laugh with me, but never tell me to shut up again. The day you do will be the day I punish you. Do you understand?"

Cain agreed compliantly as he said, "Yes, Father, I understand. It will never happen again."

Lucifer smiled, then said with excitement, "I've come this night with good news. Your dream of ruling the world will soon come to fruition. I want you to begin preparations tomorrow for invading Syria."

Warning flags began waving in Cain's mind. He did not trust Lucifer, and there was no one in the universe he feared more. With a deceitful smile, he said, "Father, that's good news, but I'm not ready for any major invasions at this time. Please give me a couple of years to build up my military forces even stronger."

Lucifer spat out, "I'm warning you. Obey me if you want to rule the world."

Cain replied nervously, "I'm sorry, Father, but I want to make sure there's no chance in losing. Please allow me to gain control of this world on my own. I don't want to owe anyone, especially you."

"I see. You think I'll abandon you in your time of need. No wonder you're shaking like a leaf in a windstorm." Lucifer chuckled as he continued, "I promise to help you as long as you stay loyal and obey me. If you obey my orders, I'll make you the king of this world. All I ask in return is for you to require all people to worship me as a god. What will it be? Do you want an opportunity to become what you've always wanted?"

Cain thought about it for a moment. The offer was tempting. It would catapult him to the status of world leader faster than his own plan. And after he became the world's king, he would use all his earthly power to destroy Lucifer. After he was the king of the world, he would not be satisfied until he himself became Earth's god. The planet then would not big enough for him and Lucifer. With a cunning smile, he said, "Thank you, Father. I'll obey. I'll begin the preparations for invading Syria tomorrow."

Lucifer smiled with exuberance. "Great! I'll go now. The pope's expecting a message from me over his Ham radio. Good-bye."

He then dematerialized as his thick body of light faded away.

(PAST)

Lucifer sat in his small ship among his large multitude of angelic followers, each with their own ship made of translucent light. They floated in a tactical formation near the part of the universe known as heaven.

They gathered together to wreak havoc on heaven. They realized they would be unable to kill any spiritual creatures because of the indestructible nature of their immortal bodies, but they would destroy their mansions, which were constructed with assorted lights. They felt determined to destroy every translucent building in the city. They wanted the city to become battle-scarred in order to cause unrest and dissidence among its inhabitants, thereby influencing more spiritual creatures to join them in their rebellion against God.

Lucifer felt jealous over Adam and Eve, the new physical creation called humans. God appeared to have more love for them than for the spiritual creatures that had been around much longer. Lucifer also craved the glory and praise God received from all the intelligent creatures. He knew if he could turn most of them against God, then God would abscond to the farthest part of the universe, leaving him as sole ruler. He would then be the "New God."

In a colorful assortment of bright lights, their translucent vessels continued to hover with grace near the border of heaven. Lucifer sat in the lead, with excitement flowing through his thick body of light. After building up his courage into a crazed obsession, he screamed for his followers to attack. Leading the way bravely, he zoomed across the border with his loyal followers close behind.

Soon they arrived on the threshold of the heavenly city with its glorious specks of colorful lights shimmering everywhere, filling the celestial sky. Zooming past the thick walls of light, they spread out.

They each chose a different mansion to destroy and hovered above it. After everyone flew to their designated places, Lucifer ordered them to fire at will.

They all fired their destructive beams, focusing on the colorful buildings of light. After a minute, the buildings changed from their unique colors to a bright red, then blue, then they vibrated intensely before disintegrating with a loud explosion, leaving the baffled occupants surrounded by puffs of black smoke.

The rebels then moved to their next set of buildings in an orderly formation. Soon the heavenly sky became full of a different array of translucent ships.

Over Lucifer's ravings, another voice boomed out deeply with authority, "This is Michael. I command you to cease and desist from this atrocity! If you don't, we'll fire on your ships."

Lucifer knew they were vastly outnumbered, and he knew they would lose in a battle. To fight back would be futile. He also knew he needed more time in order to scar the city enough to win more recruits, so with a bold resolve he screamed, "Don't fight back! Use your shields for protection and continue destroying the mansions. Be brave. We'll prevail in the end!"

Without hesitation, the rebel force activated their invisible force-fields, and continued firing on the buildings with a tenacious resolve, surprising even Lucifer with their determination.

With regret, Michael saw his order disobeyed flagrantly as the rebels intensified their efforts. With resignation, he ordered his forces, "Attack now! Attack their ships until they're destroyed. After their shields are destroyed, focus your tractor beams on the rebels so they can't escape by materializing elsewhere. As soon as you apprehend them, bind them with fetters they can't escape from."

Since Michael's forces outnumbered the rebels, squads of them conglomerated around each rebel vessel and concentrated their lasers on them.

Since the rebels had their force-fields up, the air around their ships cackled with static as their shields dispersed the laser beams.

All the while the rebels continued destroying the mansions without mercy.

After around a third of the buildings had been decimated with wispy black smoke lingering behind, Lucifer laughed with eager anticipation while observing large desolate tracts of emptiness on the heavenly streets. His laugh was cut short as the rebel force-fields finally became compromised from the enemies' beams of unrelenting light.

Their shields fluctuated even more intensely with static, and their power waned under the destructive laser beams of Michael's force.

The second-in-command of the rebels screamed, "Sir, our shields are buckling under their onslaught! Permission to escape."

Lucifer's eyebrows tightened in a thoughtful grimace. He needed more time. He wanted to destroy at least half the city, so with a sarcastic chuckle he retorted, "Where can we escape to, Baal? No, there's nowhere we can go to hide from God. Just continue firing on the city. Maybe we'll get lucky and destroy at least half the city before we're brought down, then we'll be able to recruit even more of heaven's citizens."

Soon their shields malfunctioned with loud, sputtering sounds, leaving the rebels defenseless.

Michael's forces refocused their destructive beams on the power source of the rebel ships, turning them into blue-hot ships of destruction. The rebels inside the small capsules screamed with intense pain before their ships disintegrated from the extreme heat.

Before each ship was zapped out of existence, a beam of light immediately restrained the rebel pilot. After they all were apprehended, they were gently lowered to the ground.

Michael walked over to the defiant Lucifer and asked sadly, "How could you attack your own species? Why have you rebelled against your Father?"

Suddenly the sky was filled with a great, golden throne. Michael and his followers bowed before the heavenly image, to the One who oozed waves of pure love and holiness. He consisted of a light shining so brightly, it was difficult for anyone to open their eyes wide.

God said with disappointment to Lucifer, "I have heard your argument and your boasting, and I am here to refute your accusations. I love you more than you will ever know, and you have broken My heart. I now regret the day I created you, but I will not change the past. Since you are so interested in receiving the worship of others, your punishment, and the punishment of your followers, will be an incarceration on Earth. None will be allowed to leave except for an occasional update to Me. All will stay there to see exactly how many humans you can convert to your side, then we will see whose way is better. The only restrictions are that you cannot harm them or kill them without My permission. Nor can you force them to do anything against their will. Now go, evil ones. Go, go, go..."

The demons' shackles of light disappeared, and they found

themselves plunged toward the Earth at speeds faster than light. They screamed with shrieking terror as their whole lives appeared to flash quickly by.

Chapter 3

Joseph sat in his office, troubled. He should have been performing his religious duties for that morning, but instead he read the article in the tabloid about the American president being the devil's son. Since he associated publicly with the president, the article caused him concern. He did not want the president's tarnished image to damage his own.

Cain had called, reassuring him with confidence that everything was under control. He had people in Kentucky looking for the man who had written the slanderous article. He then berated the pope for not trusting him.

Joseph still felt apprehensive over the entire situation. The president should have called back with the good news. The slanderous propaganda put a wrinkle in Joseph's intricate plan of ruling the world.

He reluctantly allowed Cain to berate him in order to deceive him into thinking that political power made him the most powerful man on earth, but Joseph knew better. He knew religious power influenced more people than Cain's political power ever would. He knew Cain would someday find out who the *real* leader in the world was.

Born on 9-9-1962 C.E., in St. Louis, Missouri, he was the only pope who had originated from America. People speculated that the "nines" in his birthday meant a variety of fantastical things, but Joseph figured the nines were more coincidental than anything else, though they had been beneficial in his rise to power. Because of them, it made it easier for him to accidentally stumble on a scientific formula that aliens used. Joseph found that the nines were the key root number they used to communicate in their language.

They communicated with him over a Ham radio in a code similar to Morse code. It took him several years to break their numerical code, but with dogged determination, he deciphered it at age eighteen. Since then, they had communicated with him at least once a month. It was they who had guided him to greatness. They gave him crucial information, and he used it shrewdly.

Whenever he thought about it, he became proud. He influenced more people than the United States had in citizens! Like Cain, he relished dwelling on his accomplishments. After becoming baptized at a local Catholic church in St. Louis, his astronomical rise to power became phenomenal in the ranks of the Catholic hierarchy. He soon became priest, then bishop, then archbishop, then cardinal, and then, in a relatively short amount of time, the pope.

In his fifties, he looked his age. With Jewish blood coursing through his veins, he felt handsome with a large nose, gray hair, bushy eyebrows, and dark brown eyes, which usually twinkled mischievously. He felt disappointment over his small size since he only stood at five foot, four inches in height, and he weighed a mere 120 pounds, but he comforted himself by knowing his other attributes made up for his physical flaws.

Through blackmail, threats, bribes, and conniving plots, he controlled most of the religious leaders of the world, and he knew after he had them all under his control, he would control their converts, thus making him the true leader of the world. He felt sure he would control them all soon. The more he thought about it, the more power-hungry he became. He would not allow a president, or any other leader in the world, to block his goal of becoming the most powerful man on earth. He felt sure his alien friends would continue aiding him in reaching that ultimate goal.

Right before the scream escaped his lips, Lemuel awoke with his eyes open. He stared into the sky, feeling his heart palpitate erratically. With his mouth open, it appeared frozen in a silent scream. Sweat covered his shocked body. He caught a breath with a deep gasp, and then shook his head to shake off the lingering sleep. After several more deep gasps, oxygen filled his lungs, and his heart rate returned to normal.

Somehow he had turned over on his back while asleep. It was dawn, and he heard the crowing roosters in the distance. Raising his stiff upper body into a sitting position, he took his swollen hand and ran fingers through his hair, plucking off grass, dirt, and small pebbles.

He wondered how he looked, and he softly chuckled to himself at the thought of it, until memories of the night before, along with the hellish nightmare he'd had, filled his mind. He felt relieved he was not really being dragged along the road. He especially felt relieved the sky was not becoming a lake of fire.

"Thank God it was just a nightmare," he mumbled to himself.

He stood up and stumbled awkwardly toward his best friend's

home. Professor James White lived in Jackson, Kentucky. James taught at a college there as a professor of religion. They discussed religion over many a cup of coffee at the local restaurant. Lemuel knew it to be at least five miles to Jackson from where he started walking, but he felt sure James would help him after he arrived. With determination, he increased his pace, walking with brisk, long strides.

After two hours of walking, Lemuel finally stumbled up the steps to his friend's home. He walked up to the door, exhausted, and knocked impatiently. "James! Let me in!"

After a moment of silence, he pleaded desperately while banging his head against the door. "Please, James, let me in! I need to talk to you now!"

Suddenly a frightened voice called from inside, "Who is it?" Lemuel sighed with relief as he said, "It's me, James. It's Lemuel."

The door opened quickly with James grabbing him by the shirt and swinging him into the house, shutting the door with lightning speed.

Without hesitation James said, "Quick, man, anyone could be watching! Don't say a word! Follow me!"

He led Lemuel down the hall, mumbling incoherently under his breath. His darting eyes moved from side to side, as if he was on constant alert. Finally he led Lemuel into a private library. Inside the room, James walked over to a bookcase. He chose the Bible from it, and the bookcase slowly moved, revealing a secret passage behind it. Darting inside, James turned the light on and motioned for Lemuel to follow.

Lemuel followed at a safe distance, fearful the demented professor would snatch him up again. He knew him well, and he knew something vexed him. He wondered about his strange behavior as they walked down the passageway.

James came to an old door and fumbled nervously for his keys. After he found the one he wanted, he attempted to penetrate the keyhole with shaking hands, but he kept missing, which in turn caused him more impatience. Finally he placed the key in, and both heard the lock mechanism click open. Opening the door, James hurried through it while beckoning Lemuel to follow.

Lemuel stood in the passageway, speechless with astonishment. He felt bewildered with James's eccentric behavior.

With urgency James cried, "Hurry up, Lemuel, we don't have much time!"

Lemuel walked in and was immediately amazed at all he saw as he glanced around with curious eyes. He never knew about the safe room, or the technology James possessed at his fingertips. He observed a large computer covering part of a wall, and office machines he did not recognize were placed around the room. In the middle of the room sat a large desk, with a chair placed behind it. "James, I never knew you had so much technical stuff," he said with awe.

James shut the door loudly and turned around with a relieved smile on his face. He appeared more rational as he said with modesty, "It's always good to keep abreast of technology, especially if one is a professor such as myself."

The carefree way in which he said these words soothed Lemuel's nerves. He exhaled with a sigh of relief, thankful James had not, in fact, lost his mind. He hoped his saneness would remain.

At sixty-five, with grayish-white hair, James looked his age as he walked over to a large chair behind the desk. He pulled it out and flopped his five-foot-six-inch frame in it with exhaustion. Pointing to a smaller chair, he said with his Southern accent, "Boy, I'm tired. Have a chair and rest with me."

Suddenly the phone rang out, startling them both with the abruptness of its unexpected ring. Their eyes opened wide in alarm as it continued ringing.

Lemuel grew irritated and inquired with a hint of sarcastic impatience, "Well, James, are you going to answer it or just let it keep ringing?"

James refocused his eyes and picked up the phone nervously. Looking at the phone with dread on his face, he forced himself to say the word, "Hello?"

Hernandez's deep voice became obscene with drawn-out, erotic breaths. He spoke lewdly, "Hello, sweet cheeks."

James swallowed in terror with a silent gulp. Trying to hide his humiliation, he demanded with a fearful stutter, "W-w-what do you want?"

Hernandez laughed hideously, causing James to hold the phone from his ear with trembling fear. "You know what I want, sweet cheeks! I'll get it soon if you don't hand him over now!"

After the laughter stopped, James brought the phone back to his ear and said courageously, "He's not here! Don't you understand English? I told you I'd get in touch with you as soon as he showed up, so leave me the hell alone!"

Hernandez's voice became more aggressive as he threatened James louder, "Damn you, sweet cheeks! We've been watching your place. We know he's there! Soon it'll be time to pay with your sweet cheeks! Do you hear me? Soon it'll be time to pay with..."

James let the phone slide from his fingers, not even bothering to put it back on the cradle. Terror took over his voice. His lips moved, but only gasps came out.

Lemuel became concerned. It appeared James was suffering from a heart attack. "Are you alright? Are you having a heart attack?"

After no answer, Lemuel rushed over and began beating on his chest. "Breathe, James, breathe!" he kept yelling with fear.

The chest beating brought James back to reality. "Oh my God," he said with terror. "It was them! They know you're here! They're going to rape us both!"

Right after he finished talking, both heard the splintering sounds of metal against wood. The sound was unmistakable.

"Someone's taking an ax to the upstairs door!" they both yelled.

James's eyes were terror-stricken as he moaned, "They're going to rape us, they're going to rape us, they're going to..."

With trembling lips, he continued emitting groans of terror, which sent Lemuel plunging into his own depths of horror.

James's hysterics grew worse and showed Lemuel the futility of going into a panic. With self-control, he halted his own downward spiral by taking controlled breaths. With a redundant chant, he muttered to himself, "Be calm, be calm, be calm..."

James became even more irrational as disgusting images of being raped sent him into a deeper state of terror, a terror he could not escape from. His sanity slipped away, and hyperventilation became his technique for breathing.

After Lemuel regained control of himself, he worked patiently at calming James down with a soothing voice. "It's okay, James. We'll escape before they find us. Please calm down. Breathe slow and deep. That's it, slow and deep, slow and deep, slow and..."

James screamed out with irritation, "Stop saying 'slow and deep'! Are you trying to scare me to death?"

Lemuel then began chanting, "Be calm, be calm, be calm..."

James followed his instructions and relaxed enough to respond in a rational way, "Yes, I do feel better now. Thank you, Lemuel."

Lemuel exhaled with relief as he said with a smile, "You're welcome, James, and I understand. I went into a panic myself, but we need to leave now."

James nodded his head in agreement. "Of course, you're right, we need to leave, but first we have to get some of my research. Look over there," he said while pointing. "We'll load it on that cart."

Lemuel saw the cart James pointed at. It was only waist-high with a top shelf, middle shelf, and bottom shelf. With James telling him what to take, they loaded the shelves with computer disks and papers.

After a few moments of packing, James finally led the way out of the room with Lemuel pushing the cart. James led him through a hallway and down a ramp, all the while listening to the destruction of furniture, glass, and other items above. James finally came to a large metal door. Pointing at it, he said with pride, "My secret tunnel!" He opened the door and led the way down a short tunnel while exclaiming, "This tunnel leads to the basement of the college. I've had it installed with my own savings."

They soon arrived at another door. It possessed a miniature computer console on the wall beside it. James pushed in a numbered code, and the door made a clicking noise. He then opened the door, and they walked through.

Before Lemuel could examine the basement, which was filled with all sorts of odds and ends, James motioned for him to continue following him as he led him to the stairway.

James then said breathlessly, "Let's get this cart up the stairs together since it will be easier. You pull and I'll get behind it and push. I'll also make sure nothing drops off. We'll get it up to the first floor. My RV's in the school parking lot. Let's hurry. We need to get out of this Godforsaken town as soon as possible! He'll soon figure out we're gone."

Lemuel felt amazed as he wondered how James could have been so organized for such a quick escape. He never knew about the safe room, equipment, or tunnel. He wondered what other secrets James hid as they worked toward getting the cart up the stairway.

After they wrestled the cart up the stairs, they made it to the first floor gasping for air.

James felt anxious to leave, so with long strides he led Lemuel through the main hallway. The students greeted them, but they were in such a hurry they never even noticed.

Quickly arriving at the RV, Lemuel observed it appeared new with an assortment of bright colors painted all around. It was long and consisted of six rooms: kitchen, living room, office, bathroom, and two bedrooms. Each room was enclosed with partitions of walls and doors, thus giving privacy to each. They came fully equipped with their own unique furniture, appliances, and other things the rooms required.

Before they unloaded the cart completely, James jumped in the driver's seat. With impatience he started the RV and began racing the motor. The roaring of the motor agitated Lemuel as James screamed over it, "Finish up quick, son, we have to leave now!"

Lemuel jumped in with the last armload of equipment.

Before the door shut, James quickly shifted the gear into DRIVE, almost knocking Lemuel down with the forward momentum.

After Lemuel recovered, he yelled at James, "You're forgetting about the cart!"

"No time!" James shouted as he drove toward the main road, kicking up gravel and leaving a lingering cloud of dust and exhaust fumes behind.

President Cain lay in bed at the White House with a sleeping twenty-one-year-old intern whose duties consisted of aiding the president. The night before he had ravished her, then allowed her to sleep with him.

He had just finished talking with different leaders of the Highway Departments of Kentucky, Tennessee, Arkansas, and Texas, and he felt pleased with the results. He found out earlier that morning what vehicle Lemuel and his accomplice had fled in. He then ordered the Highway Departments in every state to hand over information from video cameras they possessed along their highways. With the information he received, he narrowed the search down and felt positive Lemuel had headed to Mexico, where Cain would be unable to trace him.

Looking over at the black-haired beauty in his bed, he felt the power of conquest surge through his veins like an intoxicating drug. She still slept soundly, so he decided with reluctance that he did not have time for seconds. Besides, he felt sure she was still sore. Earlier he had burst through her hymen and filled her up. She screamed in intense pain at first, but he was a professional lover. After she became accustomed to his immense size, she bucked under him like a wild mare. He remembered her clutching the sheets tightly with both hands as he brought her to several climaxes. The veins on the side of her sweat-streaked neck had appeared to throb along with the climaxes.

He stepped out of bed naked, leaving her and the bloody sheets behind. His confidential maid service would take care of it with no questions asked and no gossip spread. He took a shower and dressed in a comfortable bathrobe. He then went to his office and called Clarence, who still lay half-asleep.

"Hello?" Clarence asked with a groggy voice.

"Hello, Clarence, your old leader here," Cain said jokingly. "Seriously, I'm sorry for cussing you out last night. I just felt upset when you told me Lemuel had escaped from your Mexican connection. I'm sure you understand."

Cain heard him yawn loudly as he said, "Yes, Mr. President, I understand. I know you've been under a lot of stress, especially after I showed you the article accusing you of being the devil's son. Hopefully we can get back to normal now." After another yawn, he exclaimed with a swaggering tone, "Maybe we can go out tonight and party under disguise!"

Cain replied back with a serious voice, "No, Clarence, we can't do that. We have more important things to do than party. I have reliable information that tells us that Lemuel and his accomplice are heading to Mexico. I want you to apprehend them in person. This is not negotiable. I really don't trust your Mexican friend, but you can take him with you. I want to make sure there are no more blunders, so you'll be directly responsible for their capture. I can trust you, can't I?"

Clarence dropped his head in disappointment. He had planned on getting drunk and picking up a male prostitute. "Oh, well, life's a bitch, then you die," he mumbled to himself with resignation.

"Clarence! Snap out of it!" Cain shouted with anger as he asked again, "I can trust you, can't I?"

Clarence sounded unsure, with disappointment filling his voice. "Of course, Cain—uh, I mean, Mr. President—you can trust me, but are you sure you need me to go? It'll take me a few hours to meet up with him in Kentucky. Besides, I know he can do it, plus I have to protect you. I—"

Cain interrupted him rudely, "This isn't negotiable! I want you to personally apprehend Lemuel, and I want you to bring him to me alive. I could care less what you do with the other one. They're going to Mexico in an American-made RV. I've a picture of it, and even the plate number, so you should be able to find them. You must leave now."

Cain wanted him to leave right away. He knew how much Clarence loved Washington, especially the young hustlers who walked the streets. Cain never understood how the same sex could lust after one another. He did not care. His philosophy had always been: to each his own. He would not judge such insignificant matters. His job duties consisted in ruling peoples and nations, and he would rule to the fullest.

With that in mind, he warned with an ominous tone, sending chills down Clarence's spine, "If you don't capture him this time, your life will not be worth the air you breathe."

Clarence held his fear in check as he answered with the most pleasant voice he could fabricate, "Yes, of course, Mr. President, I'll leave now."

(PAST)

In the Garden Of Eden, Eve walked leisurely. Earlier she had finished playing with a wolf who loved to slobber when cuddling. Afterward, she rested until she felt relaxed. She then decided to look for unwanted plants.

She soon found herself beside a tree her Father of the Wind called the Tree of Knowledge, the Forbidden Tree. Around it grew thorns and other unwanted plants. She squatted down and pulled up the unwanted growth with an unbridled enthusiasm.

"Eve'sss..."

Raising her head in surprise, she gazed around for whoever had hissed her name in such a soft way.

"Eve'sss..."

"Huh?" she asked with surprise. "Eve'sss..."

"Who are you? Where are you?" she continued to ask as she looked around, searching for the hissing voice.

"It'sss me'sss, down'sss behind'sss you'sss," the voice hissed smoothly.

Looking back, she saw her favorite red serpent, whom she had named Sassy, staring up at her. Giggles came pouring out—they always did whenever she saw him. Because of his sassy, beady eyes, sassy, pointy face, sassy, flickering tongue, and sassy, hissing voice, it always elicited chuckles from her.

After they subsided, she realized he had just spoken to her, and she became confused. With bewilderment, she said, "I didn't know you could talk."

Sassy flicked his forked tongue quickly as he hissed, "I'sss ate'sss from'sss Tree'sss of'sss Knowledge'sss."

Opening her mouth wide in astonishment, she exclaimed with excitement, "Let's go tell Adam you can talk!"

Looking away from her, Sassy's beady eyes shifted slyly as he hissed, "Okay'sss, but'sss you'sss should'sss eat'sss first'sss from'sss

Tree'sss of'sss Knowledge'sss so'sss you'sss can'sss—"

Eve interrupted with impatience as she said, "I can't, Sassy, our Father of the Wind told us we would die if we ate from that tree."

Jumping up, she began walking toward where she had last seen Adam. She felt eager to tell him as soon as possible about the amazing serpent who could talk. Looking back with excitement, she waved for Sassy while shouting with glee, "Come on, Sassy. Adam will never believe this unless you show up, too!"

"Wait'sss," Sassy hissed out with desperation, "you'sss will'sss not'sss die'sss! You'sss will'sss become'sss wise'sss like'sss god'sss!"

Eve stopped suddenly. Turning around, she gazed into Sassy's beady eyes. With her perfect vision she could see enough to notice his eyes pleading with her to trust him, so with resignation she walked back over to him.

She then looked up at the fruit in the forbidden tree with curiosity. She saw it did appear good for food, because it consisted of a pleasant shape and color. She knew it caused no harm since Sassy survived. She knew it gave wisdom because Sassy could now speak, and she wanted to become wise like a god. She wanted to know everything, so she plucked one off the tree and bit into its moistness.

As the juice dribbled down her chin, she felt Sassy slither around her naked leg. As he slithered up more, she felt chills run up her spine, causing goose bumps to rise all over her skin. As he slithered unhindered between her legs, twitching his tail with excitement, her nipples became perky and her innocence melted with the wet hotness seething inside. Suddenly a new emotion of loathing overwhelmed her senses, overriding her obscene passionate feelings. With a resolve bordering on disgust, she admonished him firmly, "Sassy! Stop that!"

Suddenly Sassy fell off and materialized into a naked man, handsomely irresistible with white, silk-like hair and sapphire-colored eyes. He drew Eve close to his chest with strong arms and whispered with a seductive voice, "I'm not Sassy. My name's Lucifer. You'll conceive my son. He'll lead humans into a better future than what your Father of the Wind has planned."

Eve felt the stranger hold her naked body close to his. Every part of his body excreted intoxicating vapors of pure passion, causing her to crave his touch intensely. When he gently pulled her down, she felt helpless to resist. When his erotic lips found hers, she opened to him eagerly.

Chapter 4

James felt puzzled. Under Lemuel's direction, he continued driving southwest, but he wanted to know where their final destination would be. When he had tried to find out, Lemuel became irritated and explained that he would tell him soon. Because of Lemuel's vague answer, James continued driving past America's terrain in a trancelike state. He overlooked the terrain and vehicles as he formulated questions he wanted to ask. Not only did he want to know where their final destination would be, but also when they would arrive, how long they would have to keep hidden, why the dangerous Mexicans were after them, and how they would survive without any finances.

After hours of continuous driving, he pulled off on a gravel road. The road led to a river that flowed fast with the currents. The RV vibrated as he pulled off the road onto the grass. He drove cautiously to the riverbank and stopped. With exhaustion he said, "This looks like a good place to rest."

Turning the RV off, he stood up and stretched his arms with fatigue while grunting with relief. Glaring at Lemuel, he demanded, "You can now tell me why they're after us, where we're going, and how we're going to live without money."

Lemuel rubbed the temples of his head, as if experiencing a painful headache. After a deep breath, he said with certainty, "I've given it a lot of thought, James.

"It's not going to be easy, but I've decided we'll live in Mexico for a while. We can't get passports because they'll find out where we are. We can drive across the border into Mexico without a passport, though. I have enough money to live on for a while, and I know a man there named Carlos who can make us some fake passports.

"Carlos was introduced to me by my undercover agent, who also happens to be Carlos's son-in-law. Carlos specializes in making false passports, among other illegal activities, and his son-in-law works as a chef at the White House. I've used him to keep Cain under surveillance.

"To answer your other question, those Mexicans are after us because Cain sent them after us."

With frustration James said, "Lemuel, enough's enough. We've almost been kidnapped, and God only knows what else may have happened. Let's just keep a low profile and not incriminate Cain anymore until he's out of office. He'll not have the power to bring us harm then."

Lemuel became irritated with James's childlike reasoning, but he set his irritation aside by replacing it with sympathy. He knew James was mortal, with limited experiences to draw on, but he also knew Cain would never give up. Cain would never relinquish the presidency. He knew they would have to continue eluding Cain while exposing his true identity, and he also needed to find the religious beast. Lemuel swallowed sympathetically as he said, "We can't give up. For the sake of mankind, the world needs to find out who Cain is—and soon."

As Lemuel spoke with James, Joseph sat in his office at the Vatican in Rome. He looked anxiously at his watch and saw the time drawing near for his phone call to Cain.

Once he had transgressed by calling Cain too early. Cain had berated him with shameless vulgarities for disturbing him before the appointed time. He knew then that Cain hated the Jews and he wanted to kill him.

After that incident, Joseph fantasized killing Cain first in a sadistic way. Joseph would not feel one tinge of remorse in killing Cain. He would kill him after his goal of becoming the political world leader reached fruition. Then he would indulge his vengeance by killing all his enemies in a glorious bloodbath, with Cain being at the top of his list.

Looking at his watch again, he decided the time had arrived to call Cain. He would call him by using the video phone designated for high-profile calls. Reaching over, he pressed a button, and with an expression on his face resembling a child being forced to swallow castor oil, he heard the connection dial. After a few moments the screen lit up with the face of Cain staring at him with disgust.

Cain asked sarcastically, "What do you want, Pope Lame Duck?"

Joseph took a deep breath to control his temper. Cain seemed to stay in a perpetual bad mood. He did not want to make it worse. With pretended concern, he said deceitfully, "Mr. President, just wondering if you have found your nemesis yet? You know we can't have him telling the world you're the devil's son. You know such information could ruin our plans of making you the world leader."

Cain retorted back with a red face, "How dare you insinuate that anyone on earth could stop me from being the world leader! If you don't get off your ass soon and convince the religious leaders worldwide to support my policies, I'm going to have a talk with your cardinals, and have your wimpy ass removed! Do you understand, Pope Lame Duck?"

Looking down while clenching his teeth with hidden rage, Joseph mumbled acquiescently, "Yes, I understand, Mr. President."

Cain growled with evil contempt as his index finger pointed closer toward the screen, "Do it, Pope Lame Duck, or face the consequences!"

His image vanished abruptly, leaving only pixel static remaining.

Joseph did not turn his screen off. He sat there, immobilized by malicious thoughts, as fantasies of torturing Cain to death surged through his mind.

Cain felt tense with pent-up sexual energy filling his loins. He decided to visit the wife of one of his chefs who also lived at the White House. He knew her to be young and beautiful. At twenty-six years of age, she appeared younger with straight black hair, and lovely brown eyes. She only weighed one hundred pounds, but she was well proportioned at five feet high. Her breasts were small, but tantalizingly firm, and they were highlighted by her voluptuous thighs and buttocks.

She was married, and faithful with high morals, but her marital status caused him even more excitement.

He soon stood beside her door, and he knew he had arrived at the right time. He knew her husband would be working in the White House kitchen. From the first day he met her, he had wanted her in a sexual way. He had visited her a couple of times before, and he felt sure this would be the day he seduced her. With a fluttering heart, he knocked on her door.

He did not wait long before the door opened. Pamela Robinson gazed up into his eyes with curiosity. He became lost in her dark brown eyes. To him they resembled lovely pools of thick chocolate. Her eyes stirred in him romantic emotions.

"How may I help you, Mr. President?" she asked with a friendly smile.

Her question brought him back to reality, and with his own smile he answered, "Oh, yes, I was just wondering if you could answer a few questions I have concerning your husband's menu."

She continued to smile while saying, "I don't know if I can answer your questions, Mr. President, but please come in."

Without hesitation, he followed her into the living room.

In the living room she motioned toward a plush gray chair. "Please sit down, Mr. President, and make yourself comfortable. Would you like refreshment? Wine? Juice? Soda?"

He wanted to say, "Your love nest," but he controlled his tongue while saying, "No, thank you, but you can just call me Cain. 'Mr. President' sounds so formal."

While sitting down on the couch, she said with a nervous smile, "Okay, Cain, what are your questions?"

He replied with a comical expression on his face, "Right to the point, okay. I wanted to know if you could have your husband serve me more cheeseburgers? I'm tired of all his health food, it tastes so bland."

She giggled nervously while saying, "I know, Mr. Pres—I mean Cain, but I'm sure he's powerless to change it. The dietician creates the menu every week, and he has to prepare what she has on it." Looking at him with empathy, she added with an innocent wink, "Perhaps I could have him sneak you some burgers and other unhealthy food sometimes."

He appeared relieved while saying, "Great! Since you solved that problem, maybe you can solve a romantic problem I have?"

With concern she asked, "How could I possibly help you in that area?"

He replied back with a lick of his lips, "I wanted to know what would happen if a man fell in love with a married woman? Could he ever have an intimate relationship with her?"

She felt uncomfortable with the question as she gazed down modestly. She picked at her dress as if attempting to pull off hidden lint. With a deep breath, she said with a blushing face, "I suppose there are a lot of women who have affairs, but there are also a lot who stay faithful, so I guess it depends on the woman."

Looking away with a forlorn expression, he said with sadness, "Yeah, I guess you're right."

Intrigued by his response, she asked, "Are you in love with a married woman?"

Putting on his saddest deceptive expression, he said, "Yeah, I believe I am."

With pity in her eyes, she asked, "May I ask who this woman is?"

He stood up and walked over to her. Sitting next to her with his leg touching hers, he said with a soothing voice, "I'm in love with you."

She gasped with surprise, leaning away from him. She then exclaimed, "Mr. President! I certainly never encouraged these feelings in any way!" She then began to sidle away from him.

To her chagrin, he kept close to her while reaching over and caressing her leg. With a tongue thick with lust, he said, "I'm sorry, Pam, but I love you. Please don't resist me. You're so sexy to me."

With anger, Pamela said, "Mr. President! Please remove your hand! I love my husband, George, and I'd never betray him. I'm sorry, Mr. President, but I'll have to ask you to leave now."

Cain rose stiffly with self-control. He felt disappointed and surprised she possessed enough strength to resist his arduous advances. It hurt his pride, and it made him even more determined to make her his. His damaged ego would accept nothing less. He felt more determined than ever to wear down her defenses until she became his. He would somehow come up with a plan. Looking at her with a puzzled expression, he asked with pretended confusion, "What just happened? I'm sorry, Pam. I guess stress from my job just got the best of me. Let me make it up to you over a cup of coffee in my private suite. Nothing intimate—just one friend entertaining another."

She felt frightened but said with courageous determination, "I'm afraid not, Mr. President. In fact, I don't think we should see each other alone anymore. If you have any more questions, please wait until my husband returns from work, and then he'll be happy to answer any questions you may have.

Cain smiled with a nod, and hidden frustration. He waved good-bye, then turned and walked toward the door. "You haven't seen the last of me," he mumbled with gritted teeth as he softly closed the door.

Lucifer stood in heaven by God during one of His annual meetings. God's throne towered high above Lucifer like a colossal chair of light. Flashing and flickering intensely, it caused Lucifer to squint his eyes.

God said with a resonant tone, "I see what you been doing, Lucifer. You have convinced your son Cain to start a major war, starting with Syria. I commanded you not to meddle in human affairs. Are you disobeying Me?"

Lucifer said with a shrug of his shoulders, "Lord, I've not

disobeyed. I've not helped my son in any way. I've only made suggestions. It's up to him if he follows them or not."

God asked with curiosity, "Why are you trying to cause a major war on Earth?"

Lucifer looked up with a pitiful expression as he whined, "Lord, all the humans deserve to die. They practice what's wicked, and they have been for thousands of years. They have all followed in Adam and Eve's sinful footsteps. Please, Lord, allow me to destroy them all so You can start over. Maybe the next ones You create will stay faithful to You."

God shook his head sadly as He said, "I will not allow you to destroy them for a multitude of reasons, the most important one being love, something you lost long ago. I have loved them since their beginning, and My love for them has not diminished one iota. I will not allow you to destroy humanity because I know some can be saved from their sins."

Jealousy filled Lucifer as he said, "Lord, they're made of flesh, and they are not worthy of Your love. Their bodies are inferior to spiritual bodies, and they are contaminated with sin. For You to love them would be like falling in love with a disgusting virus. It's not normal."

God's bright aura changed to an intense red as He bellowed out with anger, "Are you saying I am not normal?"

Lucifer fell prone with trembling fear. "Of course not, Lord! You are more normal than all creation. Please forgive me for speaking before thinking."

God sighed with understanding as He said, "I hear you, and up to a certain point, I agree. I am above all physical creation, especially sinful humans, but you keep forgetting My main trait. I am a God of love, and it is My essential essence. I cannot stop loving them because they have taken a wrong turn, and they are now lost. Like a good shepherd, I will find as many lost sheep as I can. Understand?"

Lucifer nodded his head with reluctance as he said, "I understand You love them, Lord, but please continue allowing them to choose the path they want, and do not hinder me from influencing them. The sooner this universe is free from the scourge of humanity, the better off we all will be."

God gazed away with disgust as he said, "You are very shrewd, Lucifer, but I will continue to allow you and your followers to influence humanity. The day you kill them personally will be the day you declare war on Me again.

"Love is the strongest essence in the universe, and it is worth all this turmoil to prove it to you, and to all creation."

(PAST)

Cain labored with boredom, pulling weeds from his thirsty crops on the desolate land God had banished his family to, when Lucifer materialized beside him.

"Hello, Cain," Lucifer exclaimed happily, with features appearing to animate feelings of pride, affection, and love.

Surprised, Cain looked at him and asked, "Who are you?"

Lucifer smiled with deceitful benevolence as he said in his most reassuring voice, "My name's Lucifer, and I'm your father."

Anger filled Cain as he said with a frown, "My father's Adam, and lying's a sin. I've heard of you, and because of your lies my whole family has been banished to this wasteland."

Lucifer said with pretended sadness, "I'm heartbroken over what God has done. He did it over my objections. I don't expect you to believe me at this time, but I hope you can believe I'm your father. Surely you recognize the striking resemblance we share? The color of our hair and eyes are the same. Does Adam or Eve have white hair, or sapphire-colored eyes?"

Adam and Eve possessed black hair and brown eyes, so Cain knew Lucifer spoke the truth. He still wanted Adam to be his father, so with frustration he blurted out, "Even if you're my father, I still wouldn't claim you because you tricked my mother into eating from the forbidden fruit. Because of your lies, you've cheated me and all of humanity out of paradise!"

Lucifer denied Cain's assertion fervently, "No, my son, I wanted everyone to live in paradise for eternity. God's the One who took paradise and eternal life away. I would've kept mankind in paradise forever if it had been my decision to make, but it was not."

"Why have you finally decided to visit me?" Cain asked with bitter suspicion. Lucifer gazed into his eyes as he said, "I have watched you and your brother, Abel. I watched God favor him over you many times with blessings. Because you're my son, His selfish favoritism has brought me much grief. I only want the best for you and mankind, and since God practices favoritism, He's not what's best for humanity. I think you're now at the age where I can work with you. You'll be my living instrument in solving the problems of mankind and bringing them back to

an earthly paradise."

"I don't believe you!" Cain exclaimed boldly.

Lucifer sighed with resignation as he shrugged his shoulders. "At this time your feelings are irrelevant, but since you're my son, I'll attempt to help you. You doubt my motives? Perhaps I can alleviate your doubt. You know God has blessed Abel more than you, so we can start there."

Cain knew that was true. Abel had flourished while Cain languished in destitution. While Cain labored under the hot sun trying to eke out a meager existence, Abel flourished with a large flock of fertile sheep that multiplied in numbers with each passing year. Cain mumbled grudgingly with resignation, "Okay, I believe you. Tell me what I must do to receive God's blessings."

Lucifer shook his head sadly. "God will not bless you because you're my son, and He's a God who practices favoritism. The only one who will bless you is me, if you follow my instructions."

Staring unblinkingly into Cain's eyes, he hesitated a few moments in order to emphasize what he would say next. "Before I can bless you, you must kill Abel and take possession of his large flock. After you've vanquished Abel and taken his possessions, I shall open up the windows of heaven and bestow on you more blessings than you could ever dream of."

Cain considered Lucifer's proposal and came to the realization he was right. He would never become prosperous from the cursed, barren soil. He felt envious of his brother, and he desired to see him perish. He decided then to kill his brother. Looking at Lucifer, he said boldly, "I'll do it if you bless me perpetually."

Lucifer spread his arms as he said, "Come, my son, I'll bless you always"

Cain felt a tantalizing evil seed of greed sprout in his heart as he embraced his true father.

Chapter 5

After a productive day, Clarence, Hernandez, and three of his crew sat in a hotel room in Mexico City.

Cain had ordered them to search Mexico City first, so they did. Not only did they search with their eyes, but they also interviewed a lot of people. After walking down many streets and questioning many people, they happened on a major clue. A taxi driver recognized one of the men, and for some money, he gave them an address. The time drew near to capture Cain's nemesis.

Clarence anxiously questioned Hernandez, "You know what we have to do, right?"

Hernandez brushed away Clarence's question with a wave of his hand, and then answered with irritation, "You worry too much. My men and I are professionals. We know what to do. We'll watch the place for a couple days, then when the time's right, we'll make our move."

Clarence appeared relieved as he exclaimed, "Great, Hernandez! I guess everything will be alright, so I'll leave it in your hands."

Lemuel insisted they reside in a trailer park in Mexico City. He knew it would be easier to keep hidden in one of the heaviest populated cities in the world.

They could live in their RV. They would also have electric, phone, water, and septic services at an inexpensive cost.

They shared the household duties, with James doing the cooking and cleaning, and Lemuel doing the laundry and shopping. With their free time they often had conversations, formulating different plans on how to destroy Cain's reputation and have him impeached.

One day while hanging clothes outside to dry, Lemuel heard the incessant jabbering of some of his neighbors. The Spanish language rose and fell like a melodic crescendo. He felt sure they gossiped about him and James living together. He assumed the locals thought them to be homosexual. The thought of being James's lover caused him to secretly laugh, so he happily waved at those who watched him and performed like a homosexual with effeminate body movements. He felt like a comedian portraying a gay man on stage. Smiling with glee, he enjoyed his silent deceptions. As he heard their laughter grow louder, he knew they were making practical jokes about homosexual men.

As Lemuel hung the last shirt on the line, he heard James shout out with an effeminate accent, "Lemuel dear, I need you."

Because of the intimate way in which James called out to him, he blushed with embarrassment. He acted gay with the Mexican neighbors, but it was just playful diversions, and he thought James knew that. After he finished, he walked into the RV wondering if James was homosexual.

James stood at the doorway to meet him when he walked in, so Lemuel asked without hesitation, "You didn't just call me 'dear,' did you?"

James smiled with a mischievous expression as he said, "Yeah, I did. We've known each other for years, so we can be more than just friends now."

Lemuel did not want to hurt James's feelings, but he refused to delude him. With empathy he said as delicately as he could, "James, I'm really not gay. I was pretending with the neighbors because of all their gossiping. I'm sorry but—"

James interrupted before Lemuel could finish, "Are you stupid? Me calling you 'dear' doesn't mean I want to be your lover! Lighten up. I was just joking, like you were joking with our neighbors. Just because your fans outside think you're gay doesn't mean I do. I just wanted to tell you that Carlos called, and he told me to tell you that our fake passports will be ready in a couple of days. We can then fly to Rome and visit the pope."

Lemuel stared at him with such a surprised expression that James began laughing. Lemuel did not expect the passports so quickly.

James's irresistible laughter caused Lemuel to laugh along with him. They felt relieved they would be leaving Mexico soon.

Joseph sat at the Vatican in the presence of religious leaders from around the world. He arranged the meeting and hoped they would cooperate, but as a precautionary measure he had faithful servants from Rome to aid him with his alternate plan. That devious plot consisted of plastic surgeons helping create an exact duplicate of each religious leader. If any of the religious leaders decided to refuse in cooperating with him, he would replace them with the copy who would obey.

Everyone at the meeting felt gloomy. No one liked the pope, but they felt powerless against him. The majority of political leaders in their respective nations commanded their religious leaders to cooperate as much as possible, as long as it did not threaten the security of their own country. Most of the religious leaders knew that Cain somehow influenced their political leaders, and that he was behind giving the pope even more religious power.

A Buddhist from China was one of the few who felt courageous enough to question the pope's attempt to control them. His political leaders did not trust America, or the president, and since they felt they were just as strong as America, they felt no need to change any of their religious beliefs or policies. They would cooperate for diplomatic reasons, but only if it benefited them. They feared neither the president nor the pope, so the Chinese man cleared his throat and, with a loud tone, asked the pope so everyone could hear, "Your Holiness, what's the meaning of this meeting? If you think you have any say on how to manage my religion, you're mistaken. Buddha has told me how to conduct it, and Buddha I shall follow—not you or anyone else."

Joseph stood behind the podium boiling with rage, but somehow he managed to keep it hidden with cunning self-control. He knew China's religious leaders would be a problem, and he decided right then to replace them. Choosing his words carefully, he said to them, "Gentlemen, you know I've been a reasonable pope, always open to negotiations. I'm always working for the good of mankind, no matter what faith they practice. It hurts me to hear such defiance when I'm only trying to do what's best for everyone." Looking sadly around the room, he said with resignation, "Which brings me to why I called you all here today. I've been personally told by the president of the United States that he's the Messiah. In other words, he's saying he's Jesus."

A loud murmur arose among them all. After a few moments of unabated talk, Joseph interrupted as he said through his microphone, "Gentlemen, please allow me to finish."

After the noise ceased, Joseph said with a worried expression on his face, "Like you, I don't believe the president, but I do believe he'll destroy the whole world if we refuse to have our followers worship him like a god. He has already told me he would." Looking into some of their horrified eyes, he continued, "You know he has the capacity to do that with all the nuclear weapons he has, so I say let's do it his way until we can figure out how to be rid of him. If we don't deceive him into believing we are in agreement with him, I promise he'll open the gates of hell, and this whole world will be completely destroyed by a nuclear carnage. Please give it some serious thought. Talk among yourselves, and then take a vote. I'll be in my office. When the voting is completed, call me."

Leaving the podium with his head down, he appeared ten years older while walking out with all the dignity he could muster.

The Buddhist leader walked up to the podium. He gazed at some of the men's faces while shaking his head with a dubious expression. He then said sadly in English, "Gentlemen, you've heard it yourselves. He has condemned himself, and the president of the United States. You have heard all his plans. Apparently he plans on sharing worldwide power with Cain. We can't allow this, even under the threat of a nuclear holocaust. We must stay true to our religions so our followers may be rewarded in the afterlife."

Clutching his hands tightly behind his back, he walked back and forth behind the podium while reiterating his beliefs. "We can't allow them to control us! We all know that religion is for the benefit of mankind, not just for a few. It's obvious that the pope and the president have gone completely mad! We need to vote against the pope's proposal and immediately tell our political leaders about their devious plans of gaining control of the world through religion."

He then stepped down, giving the rest of them time to discuss it.

The conversations rose to a crescendo of outbursts, as a multitude of different languages blended into a unique tapestry of accents.

The Buddhist knew it would take hours for everyone to reach an agreement...

After hours of bickering, the Buddhist leader yelled in English so the whole congregation could understand, "Everyone who's against the pope's proposal, please raise your hand."

Everyone in the room raised their hand without hesitation.

"Great," the Buddhist exclaimed smugly, "we're all in agreement." Turning to the messenger, he commanded him to call the pope in.

Soon the pope walked in sanctimoniously with his hands clasped in front of him and his head bowed down reverently. He walked over to the Buddhist instigator.

With smug satisfaction, the Chinese Buddhist bellowed out their decision, "We have decided not to go along with your plan. You and the president already have too much worldly power, and it would go against our religious beliefs to worship him. Out of respect for your title, we'll not tell the world of your devious plot, though our political leaders may. Whether they do or not is irrelevant. We've decided from this day onward, you're forbidden to exercise control over us. We refuse to continue being your pawns in any more power plays you, or Cain, or anyone else may happen to formulate."

Slowly raising his head, Joseph stared into the Chinese man's eyes. His own eyes flashed with rage as he yelled, "I can't believe you worthless scum have decided to sacrifice the world because of your own self-interest! Do you people think I'm just a common tramp? Because of your foolish decision, none of you will live to see the next day!" He then screamed out an order.

Suddenly twenty men rushed in covered with black robes, Japanese swords drawn. Locking the door behind them, they rushed among the religious leaders like whirlwinds and began slicing their way through them. Their hungry swords ripped into bodies like a multitude of sickles harvesting wheat full of blood. They slashed their way through the religious leaders in such a ravenous way that blood spewed everywhere.

Pandemonium ensued as screams of panic filled the room. Some attempted to escape. They beat frantically on the locked door, trying to break it down. Some tried to fight back, but whenever they punched or kicked, they could find no material body. The ninjas were quick like lightning. The ninjas stabbed and slashed out huge chunks of flesh from them. The religious leaders could not even touch the ninjas. The professionally trained fighters seemed untouchable, as their nimble bodies appeared to frolic around in a martial arts shuffle.

Joseph laughed insanely as screams of terror and hysterical pleadings bombarded his ears. Red blood splattered against the floor and walls as Joseph screamed with glee above the bloody carnage, "See! See! I warned you all! Now the gates of hell have been opened, and the dogs of war have been unleashed! Their swords have come to feast upon your flesh! Die! Die! Die!"

His laughter echoed with their screams throughout the auditorium, as their blood flowed over the white marble floor, changing its color to a dark red.

Cain felt anxious. He needed some fresh air, so he decided to take a stroll around the White House grounds. Nature's wild essence always put him at ease. As he walked along the path, his large feet crunched fallen brittle leaves, which in turn sent rabbits scurrying from their hiding places and birds shrieking shrill whistles of warning. While turning around a large tree on the rustic path, he nearly walked into Pamela.

She stopped and quickly raised her head in surprise. Gazing into his eyes she said nervously, "I thought I was the only one who walked this path."

"Well, you're not," he said bluntly. He then stared obscenely at her covered breasts and then past her short red dress to her bare legs. "What are you doing out here?" he asked with a husky voice.

"Oh, I decided to take a stroll after lunch, but I need to get back now because my husband will be home soon," she said apprehensively.

Grabbing her by the arm, he said, "Please, don't be in a hurry. Stay here and talk with me for a while."

She attempted to pull away as she said with a frightened voice, "Mr. President, you know this isn't possible! You know I'm a married woman, and I love my husband very much. I shouldn't even be talking with you. Release me now!"

"Not so quick," he said with anticipation, as he pulled her closer to him with one hand on her arm and the other grasping her buttocks.

She whimpered with fear as he pulled her close to his body. She felt through the clothing his hard erection against her. She had been a virgin before marriage, and she had never felt anyone's penis but her husband's. The long length of Cain's sent chills running down her spine as she whimpered more with fear.

"Mmm—you feel so good!" he exclaimed passionately as he rubbed her buttocks with both hands.

She pleaded with tears in her eyes, "Please, Mr. President, don't do this! I love my husband, and I don't want to be with anyone else."

"Too late," he said with an evil tone. "I have you now, and I'm going to make you want me."

She struggled with all her strength while trying to pull away. "Help, somebody help me!" she screamed with terror.

He grabbed her by the shoulders and shook her violently while shouting, "Shut up, bitch!"

When she would not stop, he slapped her across the face with his hand, causing her to scream in pain.

Out of desperation, she kneed him as hard as she could around his genital area, hitting his scrotum with full force.

He bellowed out in intense pain as his hands grasped his aching scrotum. Slowly falling to his knees, he moaned in intense pain.

She jumped back several feet from him, screaming in rage, "If you ever touch me again, I swear I'll kill you! You've also helped me to arrive at my decision. There's no way I'll ever live here again! You're a monster, Mr. President, and someone needs to euthanize you before you hurt anyone else!"

She then turned and ran as fast as she could. She felt absolute terror since he was the most powerful man on earth, and she knew she needed to hide from him. She would catch a jet immediately and go stay with her father, who lived in Mexico. Since her father engaged in illegal activities, she knew the president would never find her there. She would call her husband after she arrived at her father's home.

After a few moments, Cain stood up and dusted himself off. He liked her high spirits, which caused him even more determination to make her his own. He felt disappointment over her escape, but he was determined to never allow that to happen again. Since he knew she would fight back, he would be more cautious around her the next time.

While walking back toward the White House, thoughts of sex and world conquest flashed through his mind. Someday he would rule the whole world, and he would then have any woman he wished.

Carlos sat on the deck of his yacht with his bodyguard, Sanchez. They floated serenely on the Gulf of Mexico. The bright afternoon sun warmed their skin, while a breeze consisting of salty seaweed scents whisked over them. Seagulls flew over their heads, screaming for anything edible.

The yacht floated with the swell of the waves, causing Carlos to feel nauseated. He rarely went boating, but he needed to get out in order to relieve the stress he'd accumulated from his illegal activities. With a large deep-sea fishing pole in hand, he fished with Sanchez. Not only was Sanchez his bodyguard, but he was also his friend, and had been for many years. Carlos took him along whenever he decided to engage in any kind of vacation or recreational activity.

Sanchez laughed with an amazed expression on his face as he observed Carlos's discomfort, "Come on, Carlos, don't tell me you're getting sick again. Why do you insist on doing this if it makes you sick?"

"Because I've spent a lot of money on this yacht, and I'm determined to get some enjoyment from it," Carlos croaked back miserably.

"You'll get used to it," Sanchez said encouragingly.

"I hope it doesn't take too long," Carlos said with a sickly expression.

Sanchez laughed at Carlos's discomfort as he said jokingly, "It'll be worth it, boss. We're sure to catch a fish large enough to pull this yacht around like a kid running with a little red wagon!"

"Hopefully not until I get over this seasickness," Carlos said with a worried expression, causing Sanchez to laugh even more.

Suddenly Carlos's cell phone rang. With dread, Carlos answered it. "Hello?"

"Hello, Dad. This is Pam. I'm on my way home. I'll be coming alone. I just wanted to tell you so you would be home when I arrived."

Carlos became suspicious, "Are you okay? Has your husband hurt you?"

Pamela could barely hold back her tears as she said, "No, Dad, George never hurt me, but the president tried to rape me, and I had to get away. He might succeed if I stick around. We can send for George after I arrive."

Carlos felt rage boil in his heart as he clenched his teeth together. "Damn that bastard! Just for that, I'll make sure he's assassinated before the year's out!" he shouted out furiously.

Pamela became alarmed. She knew how unpredictable her father could be when enraged. She needed to calm him down. "Please, Dad, don't do anything stupid. The president's not worth losing your life over, or being locked up for life. Maybe we can get him in trouble with the law instead, but please don't kill him.

"Promise me you'll not kill him?"

Carlos's heart melted with love for his daughter. He could not deny her request. With reluctance he said, "You know I can't rely on the law, but I promise to leave the president alone. From now on, you'll stay with me in Mexico so I can keep you safe. After you arrive, we'll get your husband and keep him here, as well."

"Thank you, Dad," she said with tears in her eyes. "I'll see you in a couple of hours. Bye for now."

After she disconnected, Carlos looked over at Sanchez. He explained what had happened, with anger punctuating each word.

Sanchez became angry himself as he said, "I think you should have the president killed. I'm positive he's nothing more than a power-hungry, perverted brute who'll not be happy until he rapes every woman he meets. I actually think he'll try to conquer the whole world someday, so you'll be doing the world a favor by having him assassinated."

Carlos felt worried as he said, "You may be right, Sanchez, but I can't have him killed. I promised my daughter I'd not kill him. Please take me home now so we can be there when she arrives."

Sanchez moved over to the motor and started it. It roared to life. "Hold on, Carlos, here we go!" He then revved up the motor, causing the large blades to twirl quickly.

The yacht's bow immediately lifted up as it headed toward the shoreline at breathtaking speed.

Sanchez screamed over the loud noise with a big smile on his face, "I'm going to give you a fun ride before we get back!"

Carlos leaned over the side and began vomiting out a steady stream of pungent tacos and beans he had eaten earlier. He knew it was going to be a long day as he heaved up stomach acid along with the caustic food.

(PAST)

Cain watched with curiosity as mankind's inherited sin stole away their immortality. As the years passed, his patient curiosity evolved into indifference as people grew from infants to old, withered bodies, with death claiming them all.

He remained young. Since Lucifer was his father, Cain was immortal.

Lucifer encouraged the other demons to create their own fleshly bodies with genetic technologies and supernatural powers. They created them, then wrapped them around their spiritual bodies like formfitting jumpsuits. They perfected their human bodies so exquisitely, they could also impregnate women with them.

The human women could not resist the fallen angels' newly formed bodies. Their fleshly creations were perfect in every way. Not only were they stronger, faster, more intelligent, and more beautiful than any mortal human, they also had an irresistible sex appeal exuding from their very pores. It caused erotic pheromones to churn turbulently inside women, like an intoxicating aphrodisiac, causing them to become inebriated with sensuous desires. Because of that, all whom the demons chose they acquired.

The fallen angels' nearly perfect hybrid offspring became famous in all of mankind's endeavors. Genetically superior, they did not grow old or die of disease. They only died through accidents or murders. Stronger, faster, and smarter than their inferior human cousins, they excelled in every endeavor—except reproduction. Like the mule, they could not reproduce.

Cain feared no rivals until the other demonic children came into existence. Since they were his equals in every way, the only advantage Cain possessed over them was the fact of being Lucifer's son, and being around before them. He monopolized on his advantages and formed tentative alliances with most of them, which left him with more political power. All his hybrid peers negotiated with him—all but one. His name was Lemuel.

Cain desired to kill Lemuel, but also the other hybrids in order to rule the world. He would have if Lucifer would have allowed him, but Lucifer had commanded all the hybrids not to kill one another. He did not want to cause the other demons, whom he ruled over, to fight among themselves because of their half human offspring. He did not want a civil war among his demonic legions.

While Cain sat on his throne at Nod, he contemplated devious plots on how to murder Lemuel and the other hybrids without having it traced back to him.

Lucifer suggested banning all moral laws, thereby encouraging mankind to practice corrupt wickedness. According to Lucifer's reasoning, the wicked humans would then run amok, killing many of Cain's hybrid rivals in the process. As long as Cain did not have anyone kill a hybrid personally, he would not be held accountable.

Cain sighed with frustration. He knew the odds of success with Lucifer's plan were next to zero. He had been implementing Lucifer's plan for over a century, and few hybrids had been murdered by humans. At best, it would take thousands of years to have even a tenth of them killed. He needed to implement a more realistic plan, one possessing a better chance for success. Ironically, as he sat contemplating more plots, a knock on his door interrupted his thoughts.

"Enter," he said impatiently.

His minister walked in and bowed submissively while saying, "Master Cain, we've just completed your ark. It's just as large as Noah's, with enough food to last a year. It also has enough room to hold one hundred of your staff, which mostly includes women."

Cain grunted, sending him away with an insipid wave of his hand.

After his minister left, Cain muttered under his breath with discontent, "That boat has been a waste of my time, money, and labor."

Cain did not believe there would be a cataclysmic flood, one exterminating most of mankind, but he refused to allow anyone to possess such a colossal icon as Noah's ark without constructing one himself. His idolatrous subjects would worship it as a god, and perhaps he would lose political power if they made Noah priest of the boat god. Cain would be ready for every political and religious contingency, and if the impossible materialized, and there was a cataclysmic flood, he would be ready for that, too.

He hoped there would be a great flood. It would rid him of all his hybrid rivals. Whether it came or not, Cain was a ruthless survivor. He felt determined to survive at any cost and reach the pinnacle of absolute political power, thereby ruling mankind for eternity. It was his ultimate goal, and he felt determined to accomplish it, no matter how long it took, or what it cost.

Chapter 6

The Mexican morning sun shone through the hotel window, ushering in a promising day for Clarence, Hernandez, and his criminal gang.

"Okay, guys, time to get up," Hernandez grunted sleepily as he got out of bed. "It's a beautiful day to finish our job."

Everyone dressed quickly, and with determination they crowded in the stolen van.

Hernandez drove solemnly to the mansion they had under surveillance. Not saying a word, he prepared mentally for trouble at the home.

After encountering traffic jams and treacherous drivers, they arrived at the estate.

The estate appeared impressive with a style boasting money. It displayed a decorative lawn with neatly trimmed hedges and colorful flower beds. Its two-story white stone mansion possessed a built-on four-car garage on one side and a built-on outdoor pool and patio on the other side. Around the upper part of the mansion hung a white balcony supported by stone arches. A black iron fence enclosed the estate, and though it possessed no gate, it still appeared formidably protected with outdoor cameras and tied guard dogs placed around.

Hernandez drove cautiously down the long drive, parked the van at the estate's parking lot, and jumped out with the rest following his lead.

The restrained guard dogs barked savagely as the group of men walked over to the mansion's front door.

Clarence knocked persistently on the door until a female voice asked in English, "Who's there?"

Clarence answered with a friendly voice as he said, "Ma'am, I'm here to speak with Mr. Carlos."

"Do you have an appointment?" she asked.

"No, but it's imperative I speak with him," Clarence said with impatience.

"That's too bad," the woman said with an uncompromising tone of voice, "because Carlos will not see anyone without an appointment."

Clarence's facial features transformed into a villainous smirk as he nodded at Hernandez.

Without hesitation, Hernandez threw himself forward with his weight crashing through the door, sending wood splinters flying all around as it burst open.

His forward momentum carried him right into Pamela.

After he regained his balance, he gazed at her with a lustful smile. His eyes appeared to caress her small firm breasts, which heaved under her red blouse. They moved down the tight blue skirt that covered her shapely buttocks and thighs. Looking back into her wide-open eyes, he licked his smiling lips obscenely while purring with virile desires.

Pamela stepped back from the demolished door in stunned amazement. His huge size astonished her. After he licked his lips, she screamed with terror.

Without hesitation, he grabbed her by the arm with one hand and slapped her with the other. The slap knocked her unconscious. Letting her drop to the marble floor with disappointment, he withdrew his 357 Magnum, then walked cautiously into the foyer.

Everyone followed close behind with their revolvers drawn.

Suddenly two guards ran out of a room with M-16s spewing a hail of bullets.

Before the intruders could fire back at the armed guards, the hail of bullets caught one of the trespassers, jerking him around like a puppet in the hands of a drunken puppeteer.

Before the guards could shoot anyone else, Hernandez shot them both with lightning-fast reflexes. His bullets threw them against the wall, and as they slowly slid to their deaths, they left behind two gory red streaks.

Hernandez went into action by gaining control of the situation in a quick manner. He pointed to one of his men to search downstairs and the other to search upstairs.

Hernandez and Clarence waited in the foyer as the other two men searched diligently. Suddenly they heard ominous shots breaking the silence, followed by a terrified scream.

Hernandez's man on the second floor came staggering out of a room, holding his hands over his blood-soaked shirt. He moaned in agony as he stumbled over to the white banister. Screaming in distress, he fell over it to the first floor, hitting it with a sickening thud.

Hernandez and his last man watched with disgust as thick, red blood slowly spread around the sprawled-out corpse.

Hernandez ordered his last man to follow as he ran over to the stairway. With weapons drawn, they slowly crept up the stairs. Soon they stood cautiously beside the open door upstairs.

Shouting with determination, Hernandez screamed out, "Carlos, my name's Hernandez. I want no trouble. I'm only here on business. Please let me in so we can discuss this matter like civilized gentlemen."

"You should have gone through the proper channels," an American-accented voice said angrily, "but since you didn't, I'm going to have to kill you!" Suddenly a semiautomatic M-16 rifle rattled off a long spurt, sending bullets whizzing by Hernandez and his man.

When the repetitive gunfire ceased, Carlos reloaded another clip.

Hernandez knew he needed to act fast. Plunging headfirst into the open doorway, he saw Carlos reloading another cartridge.

Carlos raised his head up with surprised disbelief when he saw the immense size of Hernandez.

Hernandez lunged at him. Grabbing ahold of him tightly, he picked Carlos up and threw him down hard, knocking the breath from him. Standing over him, he said smugly, "You should have listened, Carlos. We meant no harm to you or your family."

After Carlos regained his breath, he screamed furiously, "Damn you, wetback Frankenstein! Get the hell out of my home now! Leave or die!"

Hernandez stared down at him while savoring his prideful accomplishment. He smiled as he shouted loudly with satisfaction, "Clarence, we've got him. Come on up and see for yourself."

Clarence soon stood by Hernandez while looking down at Carlos.

Hernandez's chest puffed out with pride as he told Clarence, "He tried to get up, but I wanted you to see him at my feet."

"You were right in doing that," Clarence said with a big smile. "It would be better if we keep him humble so we can get the info we need."

Examining Carlos closely like an alien exhibit, Clarence observed he had straight black hair and brown eyes. He looked a lot like the girl downstairs, which aroused his curiosity even more.

Carlos appeared to be in his mid-fifties, at an average weight and height. Remembering his American accent, Clarence said with certainty, "Carlos, you're a Mexican American. It's obvious by your accent you're an American, probably from California. Also, that girl downstairs can't possibly be just Mexican with her accent. In fact she resembles you so much, I'd say she's your daughter. Tell me, Carlos, what's your real name, and where are you really from?"

With hate-filled eyes staring into Clarence's, Carlos screamed in rage with words seeping out like poison, "Eat shit! Not only that, but you can go to hell, bitch! I'm not scared of you or your asshole Frankenstein! Leave us the hell alone, or you'll all pay!"

Without taking his eyes off Carlos, Hernandez snapped his fingers once, then told his last man, "Go get his daughter. Maybe he'll change his mind after we bring her up."

After the man walked out, he rushed back in screaming with alarm, "She's gone! She's gone!"

Hernandez immediately ordered him to watch Carlos as he and Clarence rushed out of the room over to the stairway banister, and except for the three dead men, he saw the foyer empty.

They looked at each other, dumbfounded, as Carlos laughed hysterically. "What are we going to do with him now?" Clarence asked with a puzzled look on his face.

Hernandez sighed with disappointment as he said, "Torture him first, get as much info as possible, then kill him."

Hernandez regretted having to kill him because he respected Carlos's bravery. He knew under different circumstances they could have been the best of friends.

Clarence smiled with anticipation. He wanted to be the one to torture Carlos. A flush of perverted sexual pleasure colored his cheeks while thinking about it.

A few moments earlier, before Clarence, Hernandez, and the last intruder realized the unconscious girl was gone, Lemuel and James walked in the mansion past the broken-down door. They were there to pick up their fake passports. When they saw Pamela lying on the floor and dead bodies strewn all around, they decided to leave immediately.

Lemuel had picked the unconscious girl off the floor, and with James following close behind, rushed out to the taxi, ordering the taxi driver to take them home as fast as possible.

In the RV, they woke her up with smelling salts in order to find out what happened.

She woke up disoriented. When she came to her senses, she recognized Lemuel as being her father's client, and she moaned with terror as memories of what had happened earlier assailed her mind.

"Let me go! I have to warn Dad!" she screamed as she rose up to leave.

"It's too late," Lemuel said with sympathy. "If your dad's still alive, they probably have him somewhere else by now. There were dead bodies everywhere, so we didn't stay around to find out. All we can do now is alert the police."

"We can't!" she protested in anguish. "My dad told me to never get the police involved with any of his problems. Besides, I can't allow the president of the United States to find me, and if you get the police involved, they're sure to question me. Then it would just be a matter of time before Cain found me."

Lemuel asked with puzzlement, "Why are you hiding from the president?" Grief-stricken, she put her head against his chest, and with a deep sigh, said, "My husband works for him. He's the head chef. I'm running because Cain tried to rape me!" She wept uncontrollably as tears ran down her cheeks.

Lemuel knew then she was the wife of his spy at the White House. He tried to comfort her as best he could with gentle strokes down her black hair. Finally her cries slowed to sniffles, and Lemuel told her with encouragement, "We're on the run from the president, too, so you can trust us. We'll protect you."

Pamela looked up as she pleaded, "We have to save my husband, George. He's still in Washington, and I'm afraid Cain will hurt him."

Lemuel said adamantly, "We can't. It's too dangerous. He probably has your phone tapped, and your husband incarcerated already. We'll not be able to save your husband now."

With anguish she exclaimed, "No! I'll not leave George to that monster! I'm twenty-six and old enough to take care of myself. You two go do what you have to do, but I'm going to rescue my father and save my husband!"

"Nonsense," Lemuel said. "You'll never succeed on your own. It's too late for your dad, but maybe we can save your husband. We have to leave now, though."

Pamela knew Lemuel was right, and with frustration, she continued weeping against his chest.

Lemuel comforted her as best he could with sympathy. Silently he vowed to get Cain back for hurting her, and the other people Cain had hurt throughout the ages.

Clarence felt disappointment as they proceeded to a deserted warehouse in the desert. He wanted to torture Carlos personally, but Hernandez refused to allow him. He told Clarence he was a professional at such chores, and he knew how to torture better than Clarence ever could.

Clarence stood a short distance away as they tied Carlos firmly to an old metal chair covered with rust. They had found it in the abandoned warehouse.

He watched with a perverted sexual desire as Hernandez tortured Carlos with a sharp pocket knife.

Eventually Hernandez ended up cutting off Carlos's eyelids, lips, nose, ears, fingers, and toes. With the point of the knife, he also stabbed out his eyes, teeth, and left deep puncture wounds all over his body. Each slow cut sent Carlos into agonizing pain, punctuated with gut-wrenching screams.

Body parts lay scattered on the floor, and a pool of red blood glistened around Carlos's feet and under the chair.

Carlos became a pathetic, grotesque sight as his muscles jerked involuntarily, and his disfigured head rolled back and forth. All the while his swollen tongue extended out longer than average, hanging by his chin like a dead dog. Blood covered everything and everyone who stood near him. If Hernandez had not cauterized each wound with a blowtorch, Carlos would have bled to death.

During the torture, Carlos became filled with so much torment, he shrieked himself hoarse. He could now only work his toothless mouth with silent screams, begging in whispers for a swift death.

After a few hours of constant torture, Hernandez felt so much pity for him, he decided to give up. He decided to put Carlos out of his misery with a merciful stab to his heart. He slowly raised the knife above Carlos's chest.

When Clarence saw what was about to occur, he screamed at Hernandez with a perverted gleam in his eyes, with words that sent chills of disgust running down Hernandez's body, "Don't kill him, Hernandez! Let me cut off his dick first and stick it in his mouth!"

With reluctance, Hernandez agreed and handed Clarence the knife.

With perverted excitement, Clarence cut Carlos's pants off, causing Carlos to moan in terror.

With visible disgust showing on Hernandez's face, Clarence eagerly clutched Carlos's penis with one hand, and brought the knife down with perverted anticipation.

Carlos had endured Hernandez's excruciating torture bravely, but he felt unable to handle the humiliation of being castrated. He hoped his daughter and Lemuel were long gone. He had taught his daughter to never rat on anyone, but unfortunately, Clarence was about ready to make him into something he loathed even more than a rat, a man without a penis. He needed to die a man with his manhood intact. With that in mind he whispered, "Please—please, don't do that! The man you're looking for lives in a trailer park. He's located at..." He then proceeded giving them the correct address. Afterward, his head and shoulders slumped in defeat, and they knew he told the truth.

Clarence felt proud coercing the information from him so easily, yet somehow disappointed he did not get to castrate him. He really wanted to see his penis hanging from his mouth.

Hernandez reached over, wanting his knife back, but before Clarence gave it back, he told Carlos with a sarcastic whine, "It's too bad you broke down before I took your manhood. Oh, well, at least I can have the pleasure of taking your miserable life."

He immediately cut deeply across Carlos's throat with a quick slice. The knife sunk deep past his larynx, and blood spurted forth.

Clarence handed the knife back to Hernandez.

Turning back to Carlos, Clarence rubbed the spurting blood on his own face, shamelessly exhibiting a bloodthirsty lust Hernandez had never seen before. As the spurting blood continued spewing forth, Clarence kept rubbing it over his face, while licking and sucking on his own bloody fingers with expressions of perverted sexual ecstasy.

After the bleeding stopped, Hernandez felt relieved his job was almost finished. With a firm resolution, he silently vowed in his heart to never work with the psycho Clarence again. Clarence was a pervert who even scared him. With that in mind, Hernandez ordered with a firm voice, "Okay, back to work. Let's burn Carlos's body, these clothes, and go wash up. We need to apprehend Lemuel and James before dark. Our mission's about finished in this country."

Halfway across the world, Cain sat in a Jeep on the outskirts of Beirut, with a four-star American general.

It was dusk as they overlooked the military encampment. The American camp grew larger with every passing day. There would soon be enough troops to go on the offensive. Cain estimated that within a week Syria would belong to him.

The general exhibited macho characteristics. It radiated out from his personality like a shining beacon.

To Cain, he looked and acted a lot like the general who had become famous during the Second World War, and notorious during the Korean War. Cain still remembered MacArthur and the visions of his soldiers marching by in military formations. He thought of the general who stood by him, General Love. With contempt, he chuckled quietly to himself, "What kind of name is that for a big macho general?"

Looking over at Cain, General Love asked, "Mr. President, did you say something?" After no reply he continued, "You look a little amused, Mr. President, did I miss a joke somewhere?"

The question caught Cain by surprise. General Love did not usually engage in idle talk. Cain always initiated any conversation they participated in. Looking over at him casually, he said with a smile of reassurance on his face, "I'm fine, General. I was just thinking about your attack plan. Could you explain it again please?"

"There's really not much to explain," General Love said, while looking toward Syria with false modesty. "We simply bomb the hell out of them, then go in and pick up the pieces." Looking back at Cain, he said in a stern voice, "I don't know how the hell you talked me into leading this invasion, Mr. President, but I'll tell you one more time, this is a big mistake. This could get China and Russia in an uproar, and even cause a Third World War!"

Raising his voice, Cain retorted sarcastically, "I have some good news for you, General. It's not up to you." Speaking in a more threatening tone, he continued, "I suggest you watch your tongue, General, and follow my orders, or you may find yourself demoted to second lieutenant working at the Fort Leavenworth prison!"

The ominous tone in which Cain spoke the threat sent chills of fear rolling down the general's back. With reluctance, he swallowed his pride and said, "I'm sorry, Mr. President, I've just been under a lot of stress lately. I didn't mean to offend you, sir. I just fear for your safety. If anything should happen to you, the whole world would blame me."

Stretching his hand out toward the general, Cain said with a firm tone, "Let me see those fancy binoculars."

Without hesitation, General Love handed them over, relieved Cain had dropped the subject.

Cain felt amazed with modern-day technologies. He thought it marvelous he could look out of binoculars so advanced, he could see the night actually turn to day. By adjusting the lens, he could see up to twenty miles away with sharp clarity. He could even see small items like a multicolored leaf in all its glory so far away. He loved playing games with it.

Zooming the sights far and near, he suddenly saw a squad of Syrian scouts approaching surreptitiously. Looking at the binocular's adjustments, he saw the lenses were set at the ten-mile mark. At the speed they walked, he calculated it would take them around three hours to reach his position.

He found it difficult to believe the Syrians were embarking on an offensive maneuver, even if it was just for espionage. He assumed they would be digging trenches, preparing defensively for the American invasion he would soon send washing over them in waves.

A brilliant idea flashed in his mind like a streak of lightning. He would help the American military defeat Syria. He would demoralize their leadership by having their scouts destroyed in a natural disaster. He would do it in such a selective way they would have no other option but to believe God Himself fought against them. Perhaps they would then give up before a lot of blood was shed. They certainly would not be going on the offensive anymore.

With that in mind, he waved his arm with a magical flair and pointed his index finger toward the direction he stared in. With chanting incantations, he mumbled a bunch of alien words.

General Love stared at him as if he were an exhibit in a freak show. He knew six different languages, but he had never heard anything like what Cain mumbled.

"What has gotten into him?" he whispered with puzzled apprehension as Cain continued murmuring unceasingly.

Suddenly thunder rumbled in the distance and gusts of wind began blowing hard, rattling their clothes against their skin. Lightning flashed in the distance, with tendrils sending bright streaks across the sky, giving light to a dark night.

With trepidation, General Love whispered to himself, "Great, now I'm going to have to drag this lunatic out of this lightning storm before he gets struck dead."

Raising his voice above the storm, he screamed loudly, "Mr. President, we have to leave now! Can you hear me, Mr. Pres..."

Cain could not hear him. He felt too exalted to concentrate on anything but the limited power he possessed over nature. It made him feel invincible. Combined with the excitement of the hunt, he heard nothing as he watched through the binoculars all but one of the scouts being killed with selective bolts of lightning.

Many of the lightning bolts hit the ground, and they hit all the Syrian scouts but one. Because of the precision of the streaks, the scouts knew before their deaths the bolts were being directed to hit them.

The last scout turned, fleeing for his life back to Syria. Cain could imagine him screaming for mercy to his god, Allah, and the thought brought him a smug smile of satisfaction. He would allow the last scout to live. He needed to make sure he survived in order to be a witness on how Allah had destroyed his whole squad. He hoped the scout would give all the gory details.

As he thought about how the other scouts had flopped on the ground, their flesh sizzling under the electrical onslaught, he laughed with glee. He laughed so loudly, General Love gazed on him with worried concern, thinking perhaps the president had lost his mind.

(PAST)

Noah stood worried in a heavy downpour of rain, with deep, rumbling thunder echoing in the distance. Noah waited impatiently for his oldest son, Ham, and Lemuel. Lemuel was not his son, but a favorite hybrid nephew. Noah knew that Lemuel and the other human hybrids were mutated humans. He accepted Lemuel, and even decided to take him along. God commanded him to save something of every kind, and Lemuel certainly fell in that category.

A week before, Noah had turned six hundred years old. On his birthday it began raining nonstop. It had been raining for a week unceasingly, and God had commanded him earlier that morning to finish loading the ark, so they kept busy loading animals inside it.

With some room left, Noah hoped his grandfather, Methuselah, would join them. Noah's father, Lamech, had died five years earlier, but his grandfather still lived at nine hundred and sixty-nine years of age. Six days ago Noah had sent his eldest son to try to convince Methuselah one last time to join them, and to bring Lemuel along also.

Methuselah had become corrupted by the fallen angels. He became corrupted by their wealth, prestige, and power. The demons targeted him because of his status of being one of the most influential men on earth, so Methuselah eagerly gave them his most desirable daughters, and even his granddaughters.

Lemuel was one of his great-grandchildren by one of those unnatural unions.

As rain continued pouring down persistently, Noah searched with his eyes far off into the distance, looking for his son Ham. Sending his son now seemed to have been an impetuous folly, one done on impulse, not common sense. As he continued to look off into the distance, he wrung his hands together with agonizing worry. Methuselah's home took a couple of days to walk to, and Noah knew the floodwaters would overwhelm them all soon. He hoped with frustration Ham would not tarry much longer.

With disappointment he went back to work, but with worried concern he often stopped working in order to gaze off into the far horizon.

Finally, on one of his frequent stops, he saw Ham and another person in the far distance, leading a pack of mules. Methuselah apparently had given them parting gifts. "Just in time," Noah whispered with relief.

Soon Lemuel stood close to Noah, embracing him with tender love. Lemuel appeared young and in perfect health, with a radiant glow to his full cheeks.

Noah knew he was much older. Since Lemuel was a hybrid, he did not age past his perpetual youth.

"It's good to see you again, dear uncle," Lemuel said lovingly as he continued to embrace Noah.

Noah's heart swelled with a burst of love for Lemuel. Even though Lemuel was closer to his age, he felt fatherly love for him, and he cherished him as much as his other three sons. After the long embrace, he reluctantly pulled apart and gazed on Lemuel with a seriousness that belied the love he felt for him.

Lemuel agreed with a silent nod of his head. He knew tumultuous floodwaters could burst on them at any time. The continuous downpour had saturated the earth nonstop for a week, so without a word they finished the task of loading the ark.

After they finished, Lemuel watched curiously as Noah prayed. He prayed as the screeching of thunderous lightning punctuated his prayer; he prayed as lightning flared angrily across the sky like the bony fingers of a giant skeleton god; he prayed as thunder reverberated deeply far and near, vibrating the ark with its deep, ominous rumbles; he prayed as the heavy downpour continued beating hard, sounding like the applause of a million clapping hands; he prayed as the wind moaned mournfully, sounding as if God was weeping through it.

After Noah's long prayer ended, everyone went to their designated sleeping areas and immediately fell asleep. They were all exhausted.

Then the flood came.

They woke up the same time from the terrified screams of people begging to be let in. Desperate people cried, screamed, and pleaded in terror for their lives.

They jumped up quickly with fearful anxiety. Looking over at each other with an unspoken understanding, they rushed over to the latched wooden window and opened the heavy window shutter.

What Lemuel saw was imprinted on his mind forever.

The sky appeared melancholic with dark colors as hopelessness permeated the very air. Rain continued pouring down incessantly, as if it pattered in the last day of humanity. Deep waters covered the earth, leaving only one mountain to gaze upon.

The ark floated precariously while a vast multitude splashed around it in panic. Some floated on logs, limbs, or whatever other debris they found. Others beat against the ark with futile desperation, attempting to break in.

Through it all, the screams of panic echoed all around. Thousands of bodies of humans, human hybrids, and animals floated by, most hopelessly dead. The air became permeated with the vile stench of death.

Lemuel sadly raised his eyes to the last mountaintop he could see. Thousands of desperate people scurried up it. They became like a vast multitude of mindless lemmings trying to reach the top, relentlessly pushing the ones already there to their watery graves.

Screams throughout it all, hundreds of thousands of terrified voices were screaming hauntingly with absolute terror-stricken shrieks.

Lemuel watched with helpless futility as death, destruction, and impending doom claimed the hearts and minds of everyone outside the ark.

Lemuel's heart drowned in pity, sorrow, and frustration. He wanted to save them all, but he felt powerless to do so as tears slowly rolled down his cheeks. He could do nothing.

Noah closed the shutter in despair as a melancholic darkness saturated Lemuel's mind, clinging to it tenaciously for many centuries to come.

Chapter 7

Lemuel, James, and Pamela sat in the RV, which sat parked on a commercial ship. The ship was docked at a seaport on the Gulf of Mexico. They had escaped out of Mexico City before Clarence, Hernandez, and his last man found them. They immediately drove to the biggest seaport they knew of on the Gulf of Mexico.

They originally planned on sneaking into Washington, DC, in order to rescue Pamela's husband, then proceed to Rome in order to investigate the pope, to see if he was the beast with the horns of a lamb, as written about in the book of Revelation.

Because of the likelihood of capture if they traveled through America, Lemuel knew intuitively not to travel on American highways, so they decided to travel on a commercial ship. They would discreetly travel most of the journey over water.

At the seaport they met an American captain who transported factory products out of Mexico to New York City. The American captain finally capitulated after hours of intense negotiations. The deal consisted of two different stipulations: pay the captain one hundred thousand dollars, and in return he would transport their RV and allow them to live in it while at sea.

After sitting for hours on the commercial ship, they suddenly heard the loud grinding of metal on metal as the large anchor rose from the sea. Looking out the vehicle's window, they gazed upon a blue sky with puffy white clouds floating by.

White seagulls and other albatross flew above them with competitive dives and contentious screams. All the while the greenish-blue tide lapped gently against the hull of the ship, causing smells of the sea to fill their nostrils. They all breathed the refreshing air deeply with satisfaction.

James felt worried. Clearing his throat nervously, he said, "We shouldn't go to Washington from New York because it's too dangerous. We should go directly to Rome from New York."

Looking at Lemuel and Pamela's disapproving glares, he retracted his statement with a conciliatory tone. "Of course, Pamela's husband should be rescued first, but we should do it as quickly as possible, then we can go to Rome. I'd like to visit some museums while we are there."

Lemuel agreed as he stared at Pamela. He knew it was wrong because she was married, but he felt seduced by her. She appeared to be the most beautiful woman he had ever met. Her skin seemed flawless, with her small breasts bursting against her tight shirt, begging to be touched. The way her buttocks undulated when she walked drove him into a state of intense passion, filling his masculinity with erotic sensations. He felt past the point of no return. Ordinary infatuation he could handle, but he felt an overwhelming passion almost comparable to bewitchment. He knew better than to let his flesh become stronger than his mind, but it seemed like a losing battle. The struggle between flesh and mind tormented his heart every second, minute, and hour. He felt like a moth being drawn toward a flame named Pamela. No wonder Cain wanted her so intensely, he thought to himself with frustration.

Pamela also felt interested in Lemuel, which caused her feelings of guilt. She loved her husband with a faithful love, but Lemuel's persistent staring stirred passionate emotions in her heart. Combined with his kindness and impeccable manners, it caused her to crave his attention. No one had ever pampered her with such undivided attention before, and it captivated her like a drug mesmerizing an addict. She also found him handsome in a masculine way, with his strong, yet submissive nature pulling strings of sexuality in her feminine nature. The cravings she felt for him sent her hormones on a rampage throughout her body, especially when she watched him out of the corner of her eye staring at her.

Turning toward him, she said with a smile, "What do you think, Lemuel? Do you think we'll have time to stop at a few museums in Rome?"

Her unexpected question caught him by surprise as he stuttered nervously, "Of, of, of course we can. I'd be happy to accompany you anywhere, even if you're with your husband."

"I don't believe it!" James exclaimed jokingly.

Pamela giggled nervously as she said, "I think he's telling the truth, James. Lemuel knows I'm married, and I love my husband very much."

Looking back at Lemuel, she asked, while licking her lips seductively, "Isn't that right, Lemuel?"

Lemuel's face turned a light shade of red as he felt like burying his head in the sand like a shy ostrich. He opened his mouth to speak, but no words would come. He could only grunt in agreement with extreme embarrassment.

Both Pamela and James could not help but laugh at his apparent discomfort, turning him an even darker shade of red.

Clarence, Hernandez, and his last man stood at the boat dock where Lemuel and the others were last seen. They had heard from a man who watched an RV being loaded on the deck of a commercial ship. He had watched the ship slowly vanish out of the harbor a few days ago. He knew it was headed to New York, and it was a large commercial ship.

Hernandez said while feeling a sense of relief, "If we would've gotten here a couple of days ago, we would've captured them before they left."

Clarence felt determined not to let his prey escape. He did not want to face Cain's wrath again. He personally interviewed thirty people in order to keep on Lemuel's trail, so he felt determined in making sure his persistence was not in vain. He felt frustration build as he said, "It's not too late yet, Hernandez. We know where they're headed. We can still capture them, but we just need to steal a yacht to chase after them with." With frantic movements of his head, he looked around the dock, searching for a yacht to steal.

Hernandez did not like the path Clarence was taking. He wanted to go home. He had been gone for a while, and he knew his territory would soon be under attack from rival gangs, not to mention the disgust he felt while working with the psycho Clarence. He became weary of Clarence's unrestrained bloodlust and sexual perversions with death.

Clarence had ended up sadistically torturing three more people to death before they arrived at the dock. As far as Hernandez knew, the three victims possessed no real information, they were just poor peons whom Clarence wanted to torture to death for the sake of fiendish pleasures. With Clarence's perverse nature in mind, Hernandez said, "Clarence, we can't go around stealing yachts. Who knows, we may get life for that in Mexico. Let's go back and wait for them at New York. They'll turn up at one of the docks eventually, and we'll catch them then."

Clarence shook his head while saying stubbornly, "We can't do it that way, Hernandez. For one thing, we don't know what dock they'll arrive at. Another reason is we need to do this where it can't be traced back to us, and there would be witnesses at the New York docks. Our best option is to steal a yacht and chase after them. And we need to do it soon, before we lose any hope of catching them. We'll make sure to take the owner with us so he can't alert the police, then no one will call it in missing."

Focusing on a nearby yacht with a couple on it, he quickly pointed at them and said with excitement, "Look over there, Hernandez! Look, let's confiscate that one before they leave!"

Hernandez looked at the yacht. It appeared large, yet streamlined. He did not want Clarence torturing any more people, so he bravely attempted to dissuade him again by saying, "We can't! If we get caught kidnapping tourists in Mexico, we'll probably get the death penalty! Please, Clarence, let's just go back ho—"

Before Hernandez could finish, Clarence interrupted him with an angry admonishment, "Enough, Hernandez! I've never heard you whine before. I can't believe you're trying to convince me to give up, especially after all the shit we've been through." Lowering his voice, he said, "Listen, Hernandez, we almost have them. Please don't let the fear of the law stop us now." Gazing into the ocean, Clarence continued pathetically, "I can't go back without them. Cain would have my head on a platter." Looking back at Hernandez, he pleaded with a distressing tone, "Please, Hernandez, please don't give up, especially since we know where they're headed! Come on, let's go get those tourists and their beautiful yacht before they leave!"

Hernandez nodded with resignation as he said, "Okay, let's go, but no torture this time."

Walking fast, Clarence led them toward the yacht. Soon he stood beside it, gazing on it with admiration as he mumbled under his breath, "Yes, it's such a beautiful yacht."

Looking at him, the owner of the yacht asked with a southern American accent, "May I help you?" When no one answered, the tourist became confused when the three intruders climbed aboard without permission.

"Let's pull up anchor and get this show on the road," Clarence said happily.

The yacht owner stood frozen with fear, as he looked upon the immense size of Hernandez.

Clarence slapped him in the face with an open hand as he said with anger, "Snap out of it, man! Didn't you hear me? I said, let's get this show on the road! That means now!"

The victim stuttered with terror as he said, "Y-y-you can't do this! Th-Th-this is kidnapping!"

Clarence examined the man. He saw the gentleman possessed black hair, blue eyes, and deeply tanned skin. He appeared to be in his mid-twenties, around five foot four and 130 pounds. He licked his lips in anticipation as he gazed lewdly on the crotch area of the male victim's red trunks. The red reminded him of blood.

Hernandez gazed on the terrified woman with obscene stares up and down her body. She possessed blond hair and blue eyes. Her skin also had a dark tan. She appeared around twenty-one. "She's almost like a midget," he mumbled to himself with amusement. He knew she did not stand over four and a half feet tall, or weigh more than ninety pounds. Her petite body appeared beautiful to him with small yet firm breasts, shapely legs, and full-figured hips. She wore a red bikini. Hernandez also licked his lips with anticipation.

Clarence told the male victim with a threatening voice, "Listen, asshole, my large friend here's going to take your woman down to the cabin, and if you don't do exactly what I tell you, I'm going to have him kill her. Understand?"

The man's face became pale as he pleaded, with tears in his eyes, "Please don't hurt her! We're newlyweds, and she's still a virgin. Please don't—"

With callous impatience, Clarence interrupted, "Let's get this bucket of bolts moving now!"

The man jumped into action, moving fast with fearful urgency.

Clarence smiled smugly, motioning for Hernandez to take the woman below deck. He knew the woman would make a good reward for him. She would keep him pacified.

Hernandez grabbed the woman by the arm with eagerness and pulled her down the steps.

"Please don't! Please..." the woman kept saying in panic.

"I'm not going to hurt you if you do what I say," Hernandez said firmly in his deep voice.

After they went below, Hernandez observed what he expected while gazing on one large room. It consisted of a bedroom, living room, and kitchen, all overlapping together. The only room with a door was the bathroom. He knew it was a bathroom because the door stood ajar, and he could see inside. At the far wall of the room, he gazed on a large king-sized bed.

He quickly took off his clothes, letting them drop to the floor in a pile.

The woman's eyes opened wide in amazement as Hernandez's gigantic flesh sprung to life.

"Please don't make me do this," she pleaded with tears in her eyes. "I'm still a virgin, and I want to save myself for my husband."

"I don't care what you want," Hernandez said with indifference as he tore her red bikini off.

He then held her by the shoulders at arm's length and lewdly gazed on her beautiful nakedness. Her breasts were small but firm, with red nipples. Her abdominal area undulated with erratic breaths. As his eyes gazed down, he noticed with anticipation her blond bush trimmed neatly, showing the outer line of her intimate place.

She pleaded with fearful cries as Hernandez moved her relentlessly toward the bed, "Please don't do this! Please, no! You're too big! No..."

Hernandez felt carried away with waves of passion. He paid no attention to her futile pleadings.

She whimpered with shame, "Please stop! Please don't! Nooo...." Her aversion to what was happening excited him even more.

She closed her eyes tightly in terror, making whimpers of humiliation in the back of her throat. "Nooo...!"

He then laid her on the bed and moved his big body over her, spreading her legs wide apart.

After he finished ravaging the terrified woman, he collapsed on her, with her legs spread wide.

Shame and fear filled her as she begged, "Please get up. I can't breathe." When he withdrew, she felt as if a vital part of her went with him. She felt so empty.

She lay in shock with her legs still spread, her delicate assets opened achingly. She knew she would never be the same again.

President Cain lay in bed at the White House when he heard a knock on the door. Raising his upper body, he asked with irritation, "Who's there?"

A nervous voice answered, "Mr. President, it's me, your aide. You have an emergency call from the president of China. He demands you speak with him immediately. We have him on the video screen in your office now."

Many people believed China to be a new superpower as strong as America, if not more so. Cain refused to believe that, but he was not ready to find out. He wasted no time in getting up. Slipping on his robe, he quickly walked out of his bedroom into the Oval Office.

Sitting down in his chair, he looked into the screen at a very agitated Chinese dictator. Switching to a once popular Chinese dialect he had learned thousands of years ago, he said in their melodic language, "It is a pleasure and honor to have the great Chinese president speak with me. How may I assist the most honorable one of China?"

With anger flashing from his eyes, the Chinese president answered, "Enough with the flattery! I don't know who taught you one of our languages, but they taught you the archaic version. Our language has evolved beyond that, so speak in English. I'm sure I understand your language better than you understand ours."

Looking at Cain in a disgusted way, President Ting said with outrage, "I see you're attempting to conquer the Middle East. Apparently Afghanistan and Iraq wasn't enough. Now you also want to extend your sphere of influence over Syria, and probably every country left in the Middle East! I know what you're doing. You're trying to monopolize all the world oil reserves, and I'll not allow it. We need as much oil as your country does, and your aggressiveness is in blatant disregard of our world rights."

Cain thought about what Ting told him. He felt no surprise. He knew he would have to face America's number-one rival eventually, but he was not yet ready. Selecting his words carefully, he responded with all the diplomacy he could muster, "Great President Ting, most honorable one, I have no choice but to respond to Syria's aggressive tactics. Their blatant disregard for human rights has forced me to protect their own people from their murderous raids. I tried to negotiate, but—"

President Ting interrupted with rage as his bald head turned red. "Enough! You've no right! They are a sovereign government, and they have the right to rule their people as they see fit! If you don't pull out of their country soon, I will unleash our red armies into the Middle East, and then we'll see how you fight against someone your own size!"

The screen went blank.

Cain closed his eyes, racking his brain on how he could deal with China. He would not withdraw from Syria, but he still needed to pacify China. He felt certain he could defeat China, but he was not yet ready for a major war with them. It would be devastating, and would set his plans back.

"Somehow that worthless pope would have to buy me more time," he mumbled to himself.

(PAST)

After the flood, centuries passed with many years of good weather. Noah's sons were fruitful and begat many children, who in turn begat many children, who in turn begat many children...

Lemuel was amazed as he watched the earth become repopulated in a short amount of time. The rapid acceleration became a puzzling enigma he could not figure out, until he discovered how Cain had also escaped the flood with his own ark. Instead of saving animals, Cain had rescued part of his own government, which consisted of mostly young, fertile women, thereby helping to repopulate the Earth.

After the flood, Cain established the kingdom of Babel, and took the title Nimrod the Great. The city of the kingdom he named Babel also. Being the most renowned city, most people migrated to it for business opportunities. They came in droves, like moths to a flame, filling the city.

Since Lemuel and Cain were enemies, Lemuel rebelled against Cain, and righteous people all around joined forces with Lemuel. Lemuel's forces were always outnumbered by Cain's, so Lemuel never fought face-to-face; instead he engaged in guerrilla warfare.

Cain wanted to kill Lemuel in order to solidify his power, and Lemuel wanted to kill Cain because of Cain's debauched way of ruling, which caused people to become more corrupt with each passing century.

Since Lemuel and Cain were the last two immortal hybrids left in the world, Lucifer allowed them to war against each other under rigidly stringent conditions. They could not kill one another directly. They could not dispatch someone to kill one another intentionally. They could not devise conspicuous plots for killing one another. If they were to die by murder, it would have to be by happenstance; consequently, the stipulations made their animosity toward one another an even more difficult burden to bear, especially since Cain rarely engaged in battle personally, but instead sent his generals.

The chances of Cain meeting his demise in battle were extremely remote, but Lemuel's chances were high, especially since he led his rebels into skirmishes on every occasion.

One day Lemuel and his cavalry returned home from raiding a village in the kingdom of Babel, when they caught sight of their own village smoking with billows of black smoke.

Terror gripped Lemuel's heart tenaciously. He ordered his steed to run at maximum speed, with his rawhide crop lashing out quickly. His nine hundred men kept up the best they could with their own mounts.

On the outskirts of the burning city, Lemuel's counselor watched them sprint frantically toward him. He loved Lemuel with all his heart because Lemuel was full of love and goodness toward all righteous people. It broke his heart to have to tell Lemuel about the lives lost hours earlier.

Through the shimmering heat, a cloud of dust rose above the horizon. Lemuel frantically led his men with breathtaking speed on their sprinting mounts. After some agonizing moments, they arrived where Lemuel's counselor stood.

Stopping recklessly near him, they caused their angry horses to snort with loud neighs. After the sweat-lathered horses ceased their angry snorts and prancing, the counselor sadly lifted his hand up in greeting.

Lemuel stared down at him with worried concern etched on his face. Breathlessly he asked, "What happened here?"

The counselor could not find the words to speak of the tragedy that befell them, so he continued staring dumbly into Lemuel's face, not knowing what to say.

After no reply, Lemuel asked with dread seeping in his voice, "How many survivors are there?"

The counselor dropped his head sadly and breathed in the swirling dust that clogged his nostrils. He then said mournfully, with tears of sadness filling his eyes, "Lemuel, no one has survived but me. Everyone else has been killed."

Lemuel sat on his high-strung horse stunned, as his heart sunk into a deep state of depression. Reminiscent memories of his wife flooded his mind. Many times he jokingly told people he believed his wife would never die, but would aggravate him for eternity. Finally he breathed in a deep breath and moaned out a heart-wrenching cry, "All our people have died! Mourn o' stars, sun, and earth, because our people on earth have perished!"

In unison everyone ripped their garments with loud, tearing noises. In sorrow they jumped off their horses and prostrated themselves on the dusty ground. Grasping large handfuls of dry dust, they threw them on their heads while crying in sorrow. They cried over their vanquished loved ones.

Lemuel mourned incessantly with them for the rest of the day.

During the setting of the sun, Lemuel rose up on weak knees, wiped dry his puffy eyes, and brushed off with resignation the dust from his hair, skin, and robe. He then raised his arms while singing a woeful dirge, "In my dream I walked slowly home to you, and in my sweet dream you waited just for me. You waited there past dry grass, grass that crinkled loudly, leaving a redolent smell.

"With each step I came closer, closer to being home, back home to my wife. The blue sky welcomed me. Character-shaped white clouds waved with joy.

"Tears filled my eyes when I saw your face in one of them. It was filled with love, filled with smiles and joy. I then flew, flew fast to you, to my love."

Afterward, Lemuel said with angry determination, "I vow to honor our lost loved ones by destroying that wicked city of Babel!"

Everyone immediately rose up and cheered in agreement.

Chapter 8

James observed Lemuel and Pamela's relationship become more intimate. He found it impossible not to notice, since they all lived together in such close quarters. He often watched them sneak off to Lemuel's bedroom. He assumed they only talked, but with the way the erotic sparks flew when they were together, he felt more and more unsure about what they were doing with each passing day.

One night James worked in the kitchen preparing a surprise dinner for the couple. He considered himself a first-rate cook for an amateur. He had a talent of adding zest to food with just common spices. He felt more secure in the kitchen when worried. He decided to serve the couple a sumptuous seafood delicacy. The appetizer would consist of caviar and crackers, supplemented with clam soup. The main course would consist of lobster tails, crab legs, and shrimp scampi, with lots of spicy butter to dip everything in. Their side dish would consist of savory seaweed salad. They would wash it down with vintage wine.

As James prepared the meal, Lemuel sat on his bed with Pamela close. He felt lost in her eyes. "You have beautiful eyes," he said.

She smiled and lowered her eyes with modesty while saying in a serious tone, "Lemuel, I really like you a lot, but I'm married and I love my husband."

Taking her hand, he held it tenderly, which caused her to blush. He continued staring at her as he said with heartfelt sincerity, "I more than just like you. I'm deeply in love with you. It may be hard to believe, since we've only known each other for a few weeks, but it's true. I know I'm deeply in love with you, and I want you by my side for life."

Her emotions became conflicted. She did not know what to say. She felt confusion because she felt attracted to him. He caused her to feel more energized and alive. His presence caused her heart to beat fast with passion. Still, she was married, and she loved her husband. After giving the dilemma some deep thought, she said compassionately, "Lemuel, I know you have special feelings for me, just as I do for you, but I'm unsure if your feelings are actually love or just infatuation. Besides, I'm a married woman, and as I told you before, I love my husband, and I don't cheat. I take my marriage vows seriously."

Gazing at her with a lovesick expression, he gently squeezed her hand while saying with a hurt voice, "I know you're married. That's why this situation is so difficult for me. I've always respected the marriage vows, but in this case I feel powerless. I want you so badly I feel powerless in resisting. I've been infatuated many times, so I know what it feels like. The feelings I have for you go so much deeper than infatuation. I'm crazy over you, and I am deeply in love"

She then said, while slowly rising off the bed, "Lemuel, I'm sorry. I never realized how much you care for me. I think we should just end this now before it goes any further."

Before she rose off the bed, he leaned over and kissed her.

Her heart fluttered with desire as a small part of his hungry tongue flickered in and out of her mouth. In the back of her mind, she felt his hand move over her shirt and cover her breasts. She could feel his hand squeeze them gently, causing her nipples to protrude.

As she felt him unbutton the front of her shirt, her breath caught in the back of her throat with an emotion of frustration combined with anticipation. She wanted him so badly, and when she felt his hand cupping her firm, naked breast, passion ran through her body. She became lost in the moment.

Clarence followed them discreetly for a week. He did not want any National Coast Guards thwarting their kidnapping scheme. During the week, he and Hernandez raped the captives until they became virtual sex slaves. He felt sure they were so accustomed to it, they even enjoyed it. Because of the sexual games he played, he found the voyage quite pleasurable. He almost hated ending it, but Hernandez decided to finally capture their other prey. After they were captured and secured on the stolen yacht, Clarence would have to end his sexual games. He felt sure Cain would harm him if he harmed Lemuel.

The night sky appeared starless, with lots of dark clouds hanging heavy.

With lights off, they glided next to the ship unnoticed. Gliding to the stern of the lumbering ship, they drilled into the hull a large metal handle. They tied a rope to the handle, and then the other end to the yacht. They would keep the yacht in tow until they abducted Lemuel.

Clarence insisted on going also so as to make sure everything went smoothly.

They bound their sex slaves with rope. It would keep them restrained until they returned.

Hernandez looked forward to terrifying Clarence. With an eager heave, he tossed up the grappling hook he had attached to a light, sturdy rope. The grappling hook easily sailed up over the stern of the ship and hit the deck with a clang. He tested it with jerky movements. After he found it secure, he motioned for his last crew member to climb it.

Grabbing the rope with both hands, the man jumped against the hull of the moving ship. With both feet against the ship, he slowly walked his way up, pulling hand over hand on the rope. He climbed over the railing and disappeared from sight for a few seconds. Looking over the railing, he waved for Hernandez and Clarence to follow.

"Are you sure you'll be able to do this?" Hernandez asked Clarence with amusement in his voice.

Clarence waved Hernandez's pretended concern aside while saying with confidence, "Of course I can! Believe me, Hernandez, I can do this. I'm stronger than I look. I need to be there when you apprehend Lemuel and his friend, and the woman if she's with them."

After he finished talking, he grabbed the rope and scurried up it.

Hernandez felt amazed with how easily he climbed the rope. It reminded him of a nimble monkey climbing a tree. He watched Clarence look over the railing and wave for him to join them.

With his long legs, he made quick work of getting to where they stood.

Standing on the deck of the ship, they looked around cautiously. None of the crew appeared to be around on the spacious deck.

It was late, so Hernandez assumed they were in their personal quarters. Looking around, he saw a room built in the center of the ship. It reminded him of a little cottage, except it was made of metal with a glass window around it. He knew it was the navigation room because a bright light shone from the window, a sure sign someone occupied it. He raised his index finger to his lips as he whispered to the others, "You two stay here and be very quiet. I'm going to go take out the navigator."

Leaving them behind, Hernandez ran until he stood crouched under the navigation room window. Breathing hard, he kept his body bent under the window. Sweat beaded on his forehead, and his heart fluttered.

When his heart returned to its normal rhythm, he slowly raised his head up to the windowsill and peeked through the lower part of the window. He saw the navigator sitting down in a chair reading a magazine. He appeared bored.

Hernandez decided a quick entrance would catch the sailor by surprise, so he put his hand on the doorknob, opened the door quickly, and rushed in.

The sailor looked up casually, expecting to see the captain. What he saw caused his heart to skip a beat, and his eyes open wide. The shock of seeing a giant took away his words, as his mouth opened with amazement.

Before the man could regain his composure, Hernandez jumped forward and grabbed him by the head with his huge hands. He twisted it around with a quick, efficient jerk. He heard the sailor's neck crack loudly. He then let the dead body slump to the floor.

Turning with satisfaction, he walked out and back over to the others. Standing by Clarence, he told him proudly, "We should have no trouble now."

Clarence felt pleased as he said, "Great! By the way, Hernandez, your man found the hiding place of our prey. They're on the other side of the ship in their RV. You can see part of it from this angle."

Hernandez felt relieved as he said, "Good! Let's hurry and get them. We need to get off this godforsaken ship before we're caught."

Leading the way, Hernandez walked quickly to the other side of the ship.

Soon he found himself standing beside the front door of the RV. He knocked casually on the door.

James heard the knock and thought it was the captain visiting them. He quickly finished arranging the table by adding extra napkins, chinaware, and silverware for the captain.

Again he heard the knock, which sounded more persistent.

"I'm coming, I'm coming," he shouted gruffly as he walked toward the door while wiping his hands on his apron. "I hope the captain will eat with us," he mumbled as he opened the door, not knowing what awaited him.

Looking out the open door brought absolute surprise as he stared at the giant who had shredded his self-esteem.

Hernandez stood in front of him, smiling wickedly.

James opened his mouth to scream with terror, but no scream came as darkness filled his eyes. He never felt himself hit the floor as he fainted into a deep state of unconsciousness.

Hernandez felt proud James had fainted. It caused him to feel invincible. He then mumbled to the other two, "Good, it will make our job easier."

He walked into the RV with the other two following close behind. The smell of seafood caused his mouth to salivate. He stepped over the body of James, motioning for the others to do the same.

He led them through the RV, cautiously opening each door before entering. Coming to the last door, he took a deep breath and whispered for the others to prepare for trouble. He then opened the door quickly.

Lemuel and Pamela lay together on the bed, holding each other in an intimate embrace. Both still wore their pants, but their upper bodies were naked. Both breathed hard and sweated profusely with passion. The unexpected intrusion caused them to raise their heads in surprise. Their eyes opened wide with astonishment when they saw the immense size of Hernandez.

The memories of him at her father's home came rushing back to her. She opened her mouth and screamed a loud, piercing scream.

Hernandez lunged at them and slapped her senseless with a powerful swing of his hand.

Lemuel jumped out of bed while screaming a war cry that had curdled the blood of many a man, and he punched Hernandez in the eye with all his strength.

The punch caught Hernandez by surprise. He shook his head to clear away the bright dots blurring his vision, while punching blindly in the general area where Lemuel stood.

Lemuel easily ducked the blind punches and kicked Hernandez in the face, sending his body crashing against the wall, tearing it down with his weight.

He then rushed over to Hernandez and stomped on his head.

Hernandez's scream of rage reverberated past the walls of the RV.

Hernandez's collaborators were surprised. They found it difficult to believe anyone could take down Hernandez until after they saw it. After coming to their senses, they tackled Lemuel and fell on the bed with him, restraining his arms as best they could.

Hernandez stood up shaking with rage as he said, "You shouldn't have done that, Lemuel. That stunt's going to cost you your life."

He threw his collaborators off and grabbed Lemuel by the throat with his large hands.

Clarence screamed, grabbing Hernandez by the arms. "No,

Hernandez, you can't kill him! The president will have us all killed if you do!"

The captain heard the fighting and came rushing into the RV. Standing behind Hernandez's man, he shouted, "Everyone put their hands up!"

Hernandez's last crew member turned around quickly with surprise, as his hand grappled for the revolver that sat in his holster.

The captain saw the desperate move and shot the man in the arm with his gun. Blood trickled down, and he threw the man against Clarence.

The impact threw Clarence against Hernandez, which in turn brought him out of his rage.

He released Lemuel and swung around to face the threat.

They all watched as if in slow motion as Hernandez's last man used his other arm in an attempt to retrieve his revolver. He brought it out of his holster and pointed it at the captain, but before he could pull the trigger, the captain's weapon barked out, leaving a large hole in the man's chest as it threw him against a wall, tearing it down. Blood spurted out from the man's chest as he slowly sunk down into gangsters' hell, leaving behind a pool of blood around his dead body.

Hernandez and Clarence stared at the captain with surprise.

The frightened captain then asked, "Who are you people? How did you get on my ship? Put your hands up and answer me, damn it!"

Hernandez decided he would not go down so easily. He knew he would be lucky to get life in prison after all the laws he had broken. With a move based on mindless desperation, he threw Clarence behind him, bent down, and pulled the semiconscious Pamela up, holding her in front of him as he withdrew his weapon. Aiming it close to her head, he said desperately, "I'm leaving here with my partner, Lemuel, and this woman. If you don't stand aside, I'm going to kill her now! I mean it! Stand aside!"

Lemuel begged the captain, "Don't give him a reason to kill her. Please stand aside and let us pass. Tell James when he wakes up that we left with the kidnappers. He'll know what to do."

The captain submitted reluctantly as he backed up, keeping his weapon trained on Hernandez. After coming to the exit, he stepped out of the RV.

Hernandez shouted with an angry voice, "Okay, Lemuel, this is the way it's going to be. I'll kill her if you try anything foolish. As long as you don't try to escape, I'll not rape her."

Lemuel felt a nauseous wave course through his body as Hernandez continued, "We'll slowly walk toward the stern. Clarence will be walking behind you with a weapon aimed at your back. Don't run, or scream, or even talk. After we get to where our yacht is in tow, Clarence will climb down first, then you, then your woman. I'll climb down after Clarence incarcerates you both below deck. Understand how this is going down now?"

Lemuel nodded reluctantly as nausea left him feeling weak.

The Peking sun hung high in the sky like a fiery red orb, appearing to vibrate with the marching feet of millions of Chinese soldiers. The air felt balmy with redolent scents of humans intermingling with spicy Chinese food.

China's President Ting sat on the seat of honor in an outdoor stadium, surrounded by some of his advisors, political allies, and bodyguards. He felt like the greatest man on earth, who ruled the greatest nation.

Joseph sat next to him.

Since the Chinese nation had never embraced Christianity, Joseph found it difficult to gain any political leverage in China, but his plan of destroying President Cain appeared to be working. He had grown weary of Cain's disrespect, so he formulated a plan on how to turn the Chinese president against him. He convinced Ting that Cain desired to monopolize all the oil reserves in the world, and if Ting did not act soon, China would fall under Cain's aggression.

The Chinese were fiercely proud of their culture, heritage, and uniqueness. They were more patriotic than ever, and they would fight against any enemy who threatened their national security. Joseph convinced Ting that Cain wanted to conquer China and assimilate them into his new world order by destroying their languages, culture, and even genetic lineages with foreign intermarriages.

Talking with Joseph, President Ting said proudly, "As you can see, Pope, we've no problem in maintaining a large army. In fact, we have the largest army in the world. If Cain doesn't retreat out of Syria by next month, I'll unleash our millions upon America and destroy it completely."

Joseph spoke with concern as he said, "Most honorable one, please don't destroy America because of the foolishness of one man. Remember, that nation brings your country great wealth and worldly status. Instead, cut off the head, which is Cain, and America will be no threat."

The endless lines of soldiers continued passing them, their faces immobile. Their marching feet stepped with precision to the repetitive cadences.

Ting took a deep breath of resignation as he said reluctantly, "I guess you're right, Pope. No use destroying the goose who lays the golden eggs. Do you have any idea on how to eliminate Cain without causing a major war?"

Joseph smiled with relief as he said, "Yes, most honorable one, an American must assassinate him. I'm working on gaining the trust of one of his Secret Service agents even now. He'll be the perfect candidate for that."

(PAST)

The city of Babel bustled with life everywhere. Because of work and other benefits, people all around desired to live in Babel, so it grew larger with each passing year. The citizens spoke the same language and worked for one purpose: learning all the technologies Cain offered them. Cain promised them the gods would help them conquer death and travel to the stars.

General Sodom stood beside Cain on the palace roof. He said boldly while pointing to Babel's great tower, "Look, your highness, your icon almost touches the clouds. I hope we'll be able to walk in heaven soon and speak with the gods."

Cain agreed as excitement stroked his prideful ego. "Yes, thanks to my ingenious insights, the builders have learned the complicated techniques I've taught them."

Sodom then said with a nervous twitch of his eye, "Your highness, I don't know how much farther they can go. Workers are finding it hard to breathe at the upper part of the Tower. They're sure there's no air in heaven."

Cain said, unconcerned, "I've already devised a way to breathe with masks underwater. I'm positive it'll work in an airless heaven, too."

With concealed envy, Sodom watched Cain raise his head proudly.

Without warning, people at the building sites began scurrying about in all directions, like ants under attack from above.

Cain crunched together his eyebrows with puzzlement. "What's happening down there?" he asked with bewilderment.

Sodom became frantic with fear as he exclaimed, "Your highness, it appears we're under attack! Look, the invaders are setting fire to our Great Tower! We must alert our troops immediately!"

Cain ordered without hesitation, "Make it so, and bring me my pet serpent quickly! It'll help us find out what's going on down there."

Sodom hoped the serpent gave enough information to stop the carnage. Most of Sodom's power came from being the general of Babel, and he knew if they were under attack, it was either from the gods or from Lemuel. In either case, he knew they faced a serious crisis.

After alerting the troops, Sodom returned with the red-eyed serpent wrapped around his neck.

Walking over to it, Cain asked the serpent to speak to him and tell if they were under attack.

The serpent nodded its head as it extended its body until its head hovered inches from Cain's ear. Swaying, it hissed with a flickering tongue, "God'sss has'sss said'sss peoples'sss technologies'sss has'sss grown'sss too'sss fast'sss. He'sss has'sss gave'sss different'sss families'sss different'ssss languages'sss so'sss they'sss can't'sss work'sss together'sss. His'sss concern'sss is'sss people'sss will'sss become'sss like'sss Him'sss in'sss power'sss. He'sss will'sss not'sss allow'sss that'sss. His'sss decree'sss is'sss that'sss city'sss will'sss become'sss like'sss its'sss namesake'sss, city'sss will'sss become'sss babel'ssss of'sss different'sss languages'sss."

With a mischievous twinkle in its red eyes, the serpent added with a mirthful hiss, "Lemuel'sss and'sss his'sss men'sss are'sss also'sss attacking'sss your'sss city'sss."

Cain's dream of absolute power slipped away from his grasp, like the different tribes of people who ran out of his city. He screamed with rage as his voice reverberated throughout the palace, "Lemuel! Someday you'll pay for this treachery! I promise you! Someday you'll pay!"

Chapter 9

Hernandez and Clarence left them unmolested. They kept them locked below deck with the newlyweds.

Clarence fed them every day at specific times. The times never varied. When he opened the door to feed them, he always kept his weapon pointed at them. After leaving, he always made sure the door was locked securely.

Clarence and Hernandez slept in a tent on deck.

The newlyweds told Lemuel and Pamela horror stories on what befell them in a detached way, how they were abducted and raped. After the arrival of Lemuel and Pamela, Hernandez and Clarence had ceased raping them, and all the captives felt relieved it did not continue.

After a week of being incarcerated together, the prisoners knew something important was occurring. They could not hear the yacht motor operating, and they knew they floated near land somewhere. They heard seagulls screaming shrilly, and Hernandez saying good-bye to Clarence.

They worried about their future.

After hours of listening to the lapping waves wash against the shoreline, lulling them into a tranquil state of mind, they were not surprised when the cabin door opened with Cain and Clarence standing at the entrance.

"Your voyage is over!" Clarence exclaimed with a happy smile.

Lemuel noticed Clarence's hand held a pistol with a silencer on the nose of it. "Nooo!" Lemuel screamed out.

Before he finished yelling, the weapon sputtered twice, hurling death with ominous whispers.

It was too late. Before he'd finished his drawn-out "no," the weapon sputtered twice with a whispering death theme.

Clarence had shot the newlyweds.

The force of the bullets threw them back into a stagger. Red blood spread over the front of their shirts, blossoming like poisonous red flowers, saturating their shirts. They collapsed to the floor with eyes open in horror as they gazed on a murky death.

"Sorry," Clarence said, "but I can't leave any witnesses."

"How about us?" Lemuel asked with anguish filling his voice.

Shrugging his shoulders, Clarence smiled mischievously as his evil eyes looked in the direction of Cain.

Clearing his throat to divert their attention off of Clarence, Cain said with a fake tone, "Oh my, look what just happened. I'm so sorry. You know I detest murder, but Clarence is so bloodthirsty. He's really hard to control sometimes. Good help's hard to find nowadays." After smiling spitefully for a few seconds, he continued, "So, how has my immortal brother and best friend been doing today?"

Lemuel screamed with rage as he said, "I'm not your brother, and I never will be your best friend! How dare you have those two innocent people killed by your unscrupulous lackey, and Pam and I kidnapped! You were evil from the start, and I see you haven't changed a bit!"

Cain waved Lemuel's words aside while saying with irritation, "Don't be so melodramatic. They're both in a better place. You believe in heaven, don't you?"

Lemuel retorted back with hate radiating from his words, "I believe in heaven, but I also believe you'll never see that place. I believe you and your murdering stooge will be spending eternity roasting over the coals of hell!"

Cain chuckled as he said with sarcasm, "Speaking of roasting, I cordially invite you and your woman here to a private dinner with me at the White House. We'll be having roasted lamb. I know it's your favorite, at least it was during the era of Sodom and Gomorrah."

Lemuel shouted with determination flashing from his eyes, "You have to be joking! We're not going anywhere with you! Pamela and I are leaving now, so just get out of the way!"

Cain replied back threateningly, "You don't seem to understand. You both are prisoners now. I may not be allowed to kill you, but I can have Pam killed. Clarence here would love to kill someone else. He actually enjoys it. In fact, if you continue being troublesome, he may even shoot her by accident. As I said before, he's difficult to control. I'd advise you to cooperate for her sake."

Clarence nodded toward Cain like a lapdog with wagging tail, begging for table scraps. He hoped Cain would allow him to kill the woman. He wanted to feel another surge of power course through his bloodstream like an intoxicating shot of drugs. He felt so powerful when murdering people.

"Alright," Lemuel said reluctantly, "we'll go with you. Just don't hurt her."

After they arrived at the White House, Pamela received a beautiful purple dress made of velvet and silk.

Lemuel received an elegant black suit made of satin, with white silk shirt and black silk tie.

In Cain's personal dining room, they sat around a dining table. On the table sat a bountiful cornucopia of roasted lamb, beef, and turkey, surrounded by stuffing, gravy, mashed potatoes, green beans, leeks, carrots, and other vegetables. The mouthwatering scents caused their stomachs to growl with anticipation.

Cain looked at the food while saying with a hungry lick, "Let's dig in!"

Everyone ate fast, forgetting their table manners. Savory foods filled their mouths and excited their taste buds. Sounds of smacking lips and clanging silverware filled the air. After about a half an hour of continuous gorging, they sat back in their chairs while nursing their bloated bellies.

Cain broke the silence, saying with contentment, "Hmm, that was good, but I'm afraid we may have overdone it a tad. If everyone agrees, I think I'll call in the seltzer water. It may help with our digestion."

Everyone agreed.

With a loud command, Cain yelled for seltzer water.

Soon a beautiful waitress wearing a red skirt brought seltzer water in clear glass pitchers, setting one by Cain and Clarence, and one by Lemuel and Pamela.

They sipped with grimaces of pain. Their stomachs felt so bloated, they hoped the seltzer water would take away the uncomfortable stretching sensations their stomachs felt.

Cain said casually, "I can't believe you sold me out to that tabloid, Lemuel. I thought you were more loyal to our race than that. After all, we're the only two immortals left, brothers in a way. How could you betray your own race like that?"

Lemuel responded angrily, "Fleshly we may be alike, but spiritually we're as much related as God is to the devil."

Cain thought about Lemuel's statement for a moment, studying the turkey bone on his plate, as a multitude of different thoughts flashed through his mind. With an inquisitive stare he finally asked, "Do you believe God created all life?"

Lemuel squinted his eyes suspiciously as he said, "Of course He did, Cain. You already know He did. Why do you ask?"

Cain responded back with insight, "If God created life, it stands to reason He's the father of all living things. Do you agree with that?"

Lemuel felt perplexed while saying, "Yes, God's the Creator of all living beings, but—"

Cain interrupted rudely, not allowing Lemuel to finish. "Enough! I didn't ask for justifications, just the truth. If God created all life, aren't all of life His children?"

Lemuel appeared flustered as he said, "In a way, but—"

Cain interrupted impatiently. "Please, Lemuel, no more justifications. To sum it up, the fact is, we're all children of God. We're all related to Him, and not only that, but the angels and demons are brothers, too. After all, aren't the demons just fallen angels? We all share the same spiritual Father."

Lemuel screamed with indignation as he said, "God didn't make your father into a liar and murderer. He chose that path himself!"

Cain waved his objection aside, and said, "That's irrelevant. The point is, we're all children of God. There's not one human among us who hasn't sinned, so does that mean they're all children of the devil? Of course not! I've already established the fact that God created us all, therefore, we're all children of God and related!"

Lemuel kept his mouth closed. He did not know how to rebut Cain's blasphemous premise, especially since it was based on the truth. Finally he said with frustration, "May the Lord rebuke you!"

Cain wanted to bargain as he said, "I'm not here to debate religious doctrine with you. I know we've been enemies from the beginning, and I've grown weary with this conflict. I can't kill you, but I can hold you as a prisoner. I'd rather not do that, because I'm a reasonable man. I'm willing to negotiate. I could use you, so with that in mind, is there anything I could give you to get you on my side?"

Lemuel stared at Cain with a look of amazement in his eyes. He then said firmly, "You have to be joking! Me join forces with you? That's an absurd idea, to put it mildly, and it will be a cold day in hell."

After a moment of staring at Cain with an incredulous expression, his eyes became cold with hate. He then said with threatening undertones, "I strongly recommend you release Pam."

Lemuel's words outraged Cain. With an angry voice he yelled, "How dare you threaten me! You have a lot of nerve, threatening me in my own home. Remember, you're both my prisoners, not guests. I've tried to be hospitable, and threats are the thanks I get?" Taking a deep breath to calm his nerves, he continued, "I'm not going to let your irrational decision ruin my day. I'll give you a few more days to think over my proposal, and if you still refuse my gracious offer, she'll have to pay for you stubbornness." Looking over at Clarence, he said, "Take them to our hidden jail cells."

Clarence withdrew his weapon and pointed it at Pamela as he said, "You both walk in front of me, and I'll tell you which way to go. If you try anything, Lemuel, I'll shoot Pam first, and then you. I may just wound you, but I'll kill Pam."

Clarence told them which way to go.

They went to Cain's personal library, and Lemuel was ordered to remove a Bible from the shelf. The bookcase slowly opened like a door, revealing a long passageway.

They walked through the passage, and at the end was another door.

When Lemuel opened the door, he saw a line of jail cells, each sharing side metal bars, but each with their own front metal bars. Lemuel estimated there were at least ten of them, with each one being ten feet wide and ten feet long. Each cell was furnished with a metal bed frame and thin padded mattress. Each also had a sink and commode. There was a slot in each cell door through which the guard served trays of food. Lemuel also saw a guard sitting at a desk in the center of the cell block.

It was Cain's personal prison.

Clarence ordered the guard to open the two cells that were near Pamela's husband. The guard put Pamela in the cell next to her husband, and Lemuel in the one next to her.

Clarence left, disappointed, without saying a word.

When Pamela saw her husband, she felt overjoyed. She rushed to his side of the bars and held his hands through the opening. They professed their love for each other and talked for hours.

Lemuel sat dejected with his head down. He loved Pamela, and he felt jealous. He envied her husband, and he wished he were the one married to her. Depression set in as he sat in his cell alone.

Lucifer's brilliant body of fluctuating light glowed brightly with a surrounding aura as he stood proudly in the bedroom of Pope Joseph Lazarus, watching him sleep. He needed to speak with him in person because he had overheard him speaking with China's president, and he knew he planned on assassinating Cain. He knew his time was short, and he needed Cain more than ever. He needed to use him along with Joseph to implement his final plan of deceiving all of mankind. With that in mind, his voice bellowed out with authority, "Wake up, servant!"

Joseph's eyes opened wide when he saw Lucifer. He jumped out of bed terrified, and asked with a quivering voice, "Who are you? What are you?"

"That's not important," Lucifer said, "but I can tell you that I'm your boss."

Joseph became indignant as he said, "Do you know who I am? I'm the pope, with millions of followers! I have no boss! I—"

"Silence!" Lucifer interrupted with anger. "You can't do anything that's fun.

"You're forbidden to practice any kind of sin now that you're the leader of your religion. You know what that means? You're not allowed to have sex anymore. You're not allowed to do drugs unless prescribed by a doctor. You're not allowed to get drunk or high. There are a lot of fun things you're not allowed to practice unless it's done in secret, and if you practice it in secret, say good-bye to being a prestigious pope if you are caught."

Joseph thought about what Lucifer said, and he knew it to be the truth. He often craved to do the things forbidden, but unless it was necessary, he always chose to sacrifice his carnal desires on the altar of religion. He reluctantly accepted the losses because he felt so grateful for being pope, and for all the power that came along with it. Thinking about some of the sacrifices he had already made, he asked with curiosity, "Maybe you're right, but how can you help? Apparently you already know about the stringent rules of my office, and I doubt you could do anything to change them."

Lucifer gave a reassuring smile as he said, "I'm not going into a lot of details, but you'll see if you allow me to aid you in realizing your goal of gaining more power than you've ever dreamed of. If you obey me, you'll eventually be able to acquire whatever your heart desires."

Joseph stared at Lucifer suspiciously as he asked, "What do I have to do, or give up, for gaining such power?"

Lucifer chuckled as he said, "It doesn't work like that. I'm not here to take anything from you except loyalty. I've formed an elite cadre of loyal people to rebel against God, with me being the real god of this world. The only thing I want from you, and all mankind, is worship. I'm not forming this rebellion just for that, though. I'm mainly doing it for mankind's sake. I've loved humanity from the beginning. That's the original reason I rebelled against God.

"To sum it up, I've rebelled against God for every human who loves free will. For example, if you want to have sex with a thousand women, why not? You should be allowed to fulfill every desire you have without fear of punishment. People should have the right to live in any way that brings happiness, without fear of some kind of punishment. Is that so wrong?"

Joseph stuttered with fear as he said, "You're—you're—you're Lucifer!"

Lucifer's body brightened more with pride as he said, "The one and only."

Lucifer's humorous attitude put Joseph at ease, and he liked him. Of course he would rather have the free will of living in any way his heart desired. He decided then he would join Lucifer's organization, but he wanted to be the leader. He rubbed his chin with his hand as he asked, "All of this sounds good, but how will I rank in your elite organization? Will I be leader over all the humans?"

Lucifer chuckled with confidence as he said, "At this time you'll be third in command with only two commanding you, Cain and myself. If you follow our orders with complete obedience, you'll eventually become the human leader of this world. Cain's heart is not as loyal as I'd like, so I'd be more than happy to replace him if you show me you can be more obedient."

Joseph gritted his teeth. He hated Cain more than any man, and it seemed intolerable to have him as a boss. He would be a fool to refuse Lucifer's offer, though, knowing he would not succeed with Lucifer against him. He breathed a deep sigh of disappointment, then said with resignation, "Okay, I'll do it. What should I do first?"

Lucifer smiled as he said, "Great! I'm happy you made the right decision. Right now I need you to continue discouraging the Chinese president from attacking America, even if they don't withdraw from Syria. Cain must also not be assassinated. He's my servant, and for now he must be obeyed as if his orders were coming directly from me."

Joseph felt confused as he said, "I have no control over the president of China. The vast majority of his people aren't even Christian. How am I to stop him from attacking America if I can't get rid of Cain?"

Lucifer casually waved his objections aside while saying, "Don't worry about that. Just obey me and I'll help you and make you the most powerful man on earth."

Joseph felt exhilaration flood through his body as thoughts of being the most powerful man on earth filled his mind. He then remembered the aliens he communicated with on his Ham radio. They had promised him the very same thing.

Curiously he asked, "Are you one of the aliens I've been keeping in touch with all these years?"

Lucifer laughed loudly. After the laughter subsided, he said with a smile on his face, "I was wondering when you were going to figure it out."

Joseph had many questions, but did not know where to start. He decided to ask the question Lucifer had never answered over the radio. The few times he asked, Lucifer always ceased communicating for a while, so Joseph had stopped asking. Now that Lucifer was speaking to him in person, perhaps he would finally answer the question. With a deep breath, he mustered up the courage to ask him that unanswered question one more time: "You know I was born on 9-9-1962. Is that birthday significant in some way? Especially after taking into consideration that you communicated with me through a secret code based on nines?"

Lucifer sighed as he said with reluctance, "I didn't want to tell you, but I guess you're ready for the truth. You were born on 1962 C.E., which is the 666th set in a series of nines. For example, 1953 C.E. is the 665th set in the series of nines. 1944 C.E. is the 664th set in the series of nines.1935 C.E. is the 663rd set in the series of nines, and so on, all the way back to the year Eve gave birth to her firstborn.

"The sets are easy to understand, you just have to subtract nine years from each last set. Each set always adds and/or divides up to one nine, or two nines, or even three nines, with no remainders. For example, 1962 has two nines in it, you have the one noticeable nine, and then the one, plus six, plus two, which, when added together, also equals nine.

"Throughout history, loyal servants of mine who have been born on a set of nines have made a big difference in one way or another. For example: Elvis Presley, Marilyn Monroe, Ernest Hemingway, David Eisenhower, Rasputin, Charles Darwin, Edgar Allen Poe, John Brown, Abraham Lincoln, John Hancock, Ivan the Terrible, William Shakespeare, Hernandez Cortez, Kublai Khan, Attila the Hun, Augustus Caesar, and so on. I could go on, but I think you'd grow weary if I told you how I used each of those people for the good of mankind.

"Needless to say, 0 C.E., which is set 448, is the only set in the series of nines that doesn't add up to a nine, and/or nines. The next set after 0 C.E. is the 449th set, which is 9 C.E. It's like that set tells you in English that it's 'for for nine!'

"I hope that answered your question sufficiently. I must go now. You'll not see me in person again for a while, but I'll keep in contact with you through your radio, just as I've been doing for years. Until then, keep your head up, and feel secure with the knowledge that you'll someday be the most powerful man on earth, if you continue obeying me."

In his fantasy, Joseph then saw the world of mankind serving him like slaves, as a deceitful Lucifer slowly faded away.

(PAST)

Centuries passed rather quickly for the immortal Cain. He continued reigning over the city of Babel, even though the population decreased significantly. He eventually modified its name to Babylon. He gradually constructed a fortified wall around it beside the river Euphrates in order to provide it with even more protection. He discontinued building the enormous Tower of Babel in order to devote his energies into constructing enormous temples, hanging gardens, and other prominent monuments. His colossal structures bestowed on the city prestige, which in turn added to his own. Through the centuries, he rebuilt the city into a large metropolitan area again.

New cities sprouted up, and Cain's attention became riveted on one in particular, Sodom. It was a city one of his generals had founded soon after the exodus of most of the citizenry of Babel.

The people of that region became exceedingly depraved with their perverted sexual practices. Cain desired to corrupt all of mankind in order to gain more political power, which would establish him as leader of the world. Cain knew Sodom would be the place for recruiting people. He would then spread them like seeds throughout the civilized world.

Since they were so debauched, he often traveled there to recruit wicked Sodomites and have them transferred to different cities in order to spread their deviant sexual practices.

The citizens he chose felt honored to spread their wicked culture to other cities, but they were also motivated by yearly stipends from Cain, under the condition they teach their wicked sexual practices to the peoples they were sent to.

Lemuel also observed the great wickedness of Sodom, and through espionage he knew what Cain was doing. He lost his cavalry long ago, so he posed no military threat to Cain.

Since he posed no threat, or so Cain reasoned, he would leave Lemuel alone. He did not know Lemuel led an extensive network of spies and was secretly killing many of Cain's wicked recruits.

Lemuel did not want mankind to practice wickedness, but he wanted all men to practice righteousness. He worked hard at accomplishing that goal, even if it meant killing wicked men to do it. Still, even with all his undercover agents and resources, Cain recruited so many Sodomites that many slipped through Lemuel's espionage net.

Lemuel finally came to the conclusion that in order to foil Cain's devious plot, he would have to reside in the city of Sodom to discover everyone whom Cain recruited. Lemuel implemented his plan by finding the only righteous man in Sodom and residing with him. It would be the perfect safe-house.

The man's name was Lot, the nephew of the great patriarch, Abraham.

From Lot's home, Lemuel worked undercover with his other agents in finding everyone whom Cain recruited, and then had the recruits killed as quickly as possible. Since crimes ran rampant in Sodom, their deaths went unnoticed.

Lot eagerly hired Lemuel as his counselor and steward in charge of all of his household. He recognized in Lemuel honorable traits, with intelligence unsurpassed. He never realized Lemuel's true purpose for being there. He never knew how old or powerful Lemuel was. By Lot's time, no one realized there were still human hybrids around who were immortal.

Lemuel loved the beauty around the region of Sodom. The country thrived with fertile vegetation. It possessed a beautiful lake, river, and creeks. It appeared like the Garden of Eden with the city of Sodom situated in the midst of it. He knew it was the most beautiful place on Earth.

One day Lemuel and Lot stood by Sodom's gate, trading and accumulating material goods. With a clarity only immortals possessed, Lemuel heard every sound, smelled every scent, and saw every color. Suddenly Lemuel's mouth fell open with astonishment. Standing before him he saw two of his father's people in fleshly bodies, with ambiguous gray robes on.

They brought back to Lemuel reminiscent memories of the way things had been before the Great Flood. The bright aura illuminating around their heads, which only he could see, brought back memories of the aura his own demonic father possessed when in human flesh. Because of it he knew they were not from Earth.

After he regained his composure, he pointed them out to Lot with excitement. "Sir, look there! Those men are new to this city, and I think wealthy. Invite them to your home, and show them your hospitality. Perhaps you could trade with them."

Lot deliberated upon Lemuel's request with uncertainty. With the way immorality ran rampant in Sodom, he needed to be very cautious with whom he invited into his home.

Lemuel persisted with unyielding pressure. He finally convinced Lot with how beautiful and vulnerable they appeared, they would probably be raped by the unscrupulous homosexual population of Sodom. After he pointed out the homosexual population's promiscuous behavior, Lot reluctantly agreed and decided to take them under his protection.

Walking over to them, Lot welcomed them to Sodom by bowing low and bestowing on them his best heartwarming smile. "Welcome to Sodom, honorable ones. My name is Lot, and this is my loyal servant, Lemuel."

"Get lost, Lot, we were talking to them first!" the jealous homosexual ringleader exclaimed.

Lot became aggressive by jumping in their midst and pulling out the disguised angels with assertiveness. He told the angels as kindly as he could, "I'm sorry, most honorable ones, but I felt obligated to warn you about people such as those. It's not safe in this city to talk with just anyone. That's a bunch you shouldn't be associating with. Please come with me. I'll take you home and make your stay here a pleasant one, at no cost."

"No thanks, we'll stay in the streets all night," one of the angels said with determination.

"God forbid you do that!" Lot exclaimed. "I'll take you home, feed you, care for you, and respect you with all of the honor you both deserve. Please come home with me because...."

Lot persisted until they submitted reluctantly to his obstinate request.

After they arrived at Lot's home, Lot ordered Lemuel to entertain the guests while he directed preparations for a major feast. Lot decided to bestow on his guests all his hospitality, which included cooking the feast himself since he excelled in the fine culinary arts.

Lemuel bowed low to them, then pointed over to a large pile of luxurious cushions while saying eagerly, "Please make yourselves comfortable while I get some refreshments."

Lemuel arrived back soon, handing each a goblet of wine while saying with a smile, "The finest wine in Sodom."

They both thanked Lemuel with humble nods.

Lemuel then heard a knock on the door. He opened it and with consternation saw Cain standing before him. Hate filled his heart as he asked contemptuously, "What do you want, Cain?"

Cain pretentiously feigned a hurt expression as he said, "Lemuel, after all we've been through, I'd think you'd be a little kinder to me."

"Get out!" Lemuel screamed with animosity.

"No," Cain said with a smile as he walked in. "The king of Sodom sent me here to find out about these two strangers, and besides, I'm a little curious myself since they're the talk of the town with how beautiful they are." With a smirk he added, "I've spoken with your boss, Lot, and he agreed."

Lemuel gritted his teeth with frustration as he said while walking out of the room, "I'm going to go talk with Lot. If you're lying, I'm going to toss you out on your ass. Unlike Lot, I'm not afraid of you or the king of Sodom!"

After the door shut loudly, Cain chuckled. He then riveted his attention to the two angelic guests who resided in human bodies. He gazed at them curiously, giving them a moment of respectful silence.

Impatience overcame his self-control as he blurted out, "I thought God wouldn't allow your kind to create human bodies to live in anymore?"

They glanced up from their goblets, then stared at each other with surprise.

One of them stared back at Cain while saying, "We've heard about you. You must be one of the last remaining sons of our fallen peers who were demoted. Most of their powers were stripped away because they misused it when they came to Earth. They knew it was wrong to copulate with an inferior species, yet they did it anyway. You're the result of that unnatural union. You shouldn't even be alive. What they did was an abomination. You're an abomination."

Cain listened calmly at first, but when they called him an abomination, he became angry. His mind became cluttered with an assorted variety of justifications. He was not an evil man. Lucifer, his father, was not evil. He felt the Creator was the evil one for condemning mankind to death for just wanting to be wise. His father tried to help humans regain what they lost.

After his silent justifications, Cain asked bitterly, "Why are you here?"

God's delegate answered disdainfully, "We'll not continue communicating with you. We detest abominations, and don't associate with them."

They then became resolved in excluding Cain, as they stared silently into their wine goblets.

Cain turned away with rage building in his heart.

After he left Lot's home, he intuitively knew what needed to be done. Looking straight ahead, he walked to a homosexual crime lord's home. Cain came to depend on the crime lord to strong-arm and intimidate for him. Because of his pent-up rage he walked fast. In a short amount of time he found himself at the door, knocking impatiently.

The door opened quickly with a fawning crime lord looking at him.

"Cain! Good to see you. We were just talking about you and those beautiful men you visited at Lot's home. Ummm, what I'd give to screw those—"

Cain interrupted while grinning with a smile, "Enough! I actually want you to gather your gang together and screw them to death."

His smile created an illusion of a joke, but Heth never knew of Cain joking in that manner before, so he asked with eyebrows raised quizzically, "Are you serious, Cain? Surely you can't be serious. It seems like a waste of beautiful male flesh to me. Allow me to make them my sex slaves instead. You know I deplore raping people to death unless it's business, especially beautiful men."

With a grim tone that could not be mistaken, Cain said earnestly, "I'm dead serious, Heth, and this is business. No sex slaves! Those men are a danger to me, and to this city. Rape them in the vilest way possible. Rape them until they die!"

Heth then said with resignation, "Alright. Are they still at Lot's home?"

Cain nodded. "Yes. I'm sure they'll be staying the night. I'm sure you'll be able to fulfill my request easily. I'll need to get some sleep while you gather your gang. Wake me up when you're ready to leave for

Lot's home."

Chapter 10

As Lemuel sat in the cell at the White House, he wondered how long he had been incarcerated since there was no way of telling time. He could not see outside, but he assumed he had been locked up for approximately a week.

Pamela had pleaded with him to lie to Cain by saying he would join him after all. She reasoned that after they were released he could renege on his word.

Lemuel had never told a deliberate lie in his life. He would not start now. He felt heartbroken with Pamela being with her husband again, and he was too depressed to lie for anyone, even if it meant they would all lose their lives. While he still pondered on what day it was, Cain entered into the detention area and walked over to Lemuel's cell.

Cain smiled down at Lemuel, who lay on his bunk. Cain then said, "I see you've enjoyed your stay here. We all need a little rest and relaxation every once in a while. Well, I'll not take up too much of your time. I'm just visiting to see if you've reached a decision yet on joining me. I've gave you ten days to think about it, so you should have decided by now."

Lemuel hated the way Cain acted. His smug attitude infuriated him. He answered Cain with stubbornness seeping out, "I wouldn't join you if you were the last man on earth! I wouldn't join you if—"

"Enough!" Cain interrupted loudly with anger, not allowing him to finish. With a mischievous expression, he then said, "I was hoping you'd refuse to join me. I want to hurt you as badly as you've hurt me. I know you really like Pam, and I warned you she would have to pay if you refused to join me. Guess what? Time's up. It's time for her to pay for your stubborn decision."

Lemuel jumped up and lunged at the bars, grabbing them so tightly his knuckles turned white. He then said with fiery emotions lashing out from his voice, "I swear, if you hurt her, I'll kill you! I know it's against our law, and I'll lose my life, but I don't care! Lay one hand on her, and you're a dead man!"

Cain chuckled with sarcasm as he said mockingly, "I'm scared!

Please don't hurt me. I'm not going to hurt her, sir, I'm just going to bring her lots of pleasure, and I'll do it right in her cell so you and her husband can watch to make sure I don't hurt her. After all, I'm a man of my word."

Cain walked over to Pamela's cell with excitement flowing through his veins. He then gazed lustfully at her.

As he stared, her husband in the adjoining cell screamed at him, trying to explain they had been wrongfully arrested.

Cain ignored him as he continued staring at Pam, who calmly ignored him. She looked away from him, hoping he would vanish from her life forever. Taking his key, Cain unlocked her cell and walked in. He sat down beside her on the bunk and said, "Hello, Pam, it's been awhile since we've talked."

She remained silent, ignoring him. She refused to acknowledge his presence by staring away.

Cain became frustrated with her silence, so he said with a balking frown, "Oh, the silent treatment, huh? That may have worked with Lemuel, but it only encourages me more."

She continued looking away from him as if he did not exist.

Cain laughed hideously as he said, "I know you haven't forgotten about that little escapade that happened in the woods. You hurt my feelings. Now I'm going to have sweet revenge."

George screamed angrily at him from the adjoining cell, "Now you plan on raping my wife?"

Lemuel also screamed from the other adjoining cell with a warning, "Leave her alone, Cain, if you know what's good for you."

Cain answered them with a smirk of delight on his face, "Gentlemen, please. I give my word of honor I'm not going to rape her or hurt her. Everything I do she'll enjoy. I want you both to watch while I make her squeal with delight."

"You're sicker than I thought," George said with disgust, "but if you release us now, I'll not tell anyone you kidnapped us."

Cain laughed hilariously, as if he had just been told the best joke ever. After his laughter subsided, he said, "I don't believe you. I'm sure one of you would tell, and then I'd be in trouble. No, I'm going to keep you both locked up for the rest of your lives. I do have some compassion, though. I'll keep your cells next to hers so you all can be together. It'll also make it sweeter having you both watch whenever I decide to do what I'm going to do now."

Worried lines creased George's forehead as he begged, "Please,

Mr. President, don't do it. Turn her loose and torture me to death if you want, just don't hurt her."

Lemuel could say nothing. Tears filled his eyes, and his throat became constricted with what felt like a knot.

Cain ignored them. His attention focused on Pamela. He secretly withdrew a little sharp needle and pricked the skin on her hand with it.

"Owww!" she yelled with surprise as she jerked her hand back.

Cain smiled with a mischievous gleam in his eyes. Leaning over, he whispered, "I've injected you with a fast-acting drug. It causes feelings of excitement and sexual desires, sort of like the drug Viagra, except it's made for women, and it works on the emotions more."

Her emotion changed from fear to lust. She wished her husband sat next to her instead of Cain, because she wanted to feel him deep inside of her. Her intimate parts unfolded like a blooming flower, and she could feel the wetness trickle down. Sexual feelings spread around her body, causing her nipples to become perky.

Cain smiled with anticipation as he whispered, "Mmm, I see everything's going as planned. Your lips are fuller, and your face is flushed."

She became so sexually aroused she felt wanton. She felt like ripping Cain's clothes off and pulling his hardness into her intimate place. She used all the self-control she had in keeping her mouth shut and staring away.

"Mmm, I'm looking forward to loving on you," he said while caressing her trembling leg.

"What are you doing?" George asked with jealousy. "Leave her alone! She's my wife! She doesn't want you! She only wants me!"

"Shut up, George!" Cain exclaimed angrily. "Don't worry. I'll not force her to do anything. If she fights back I'll be sure to stop."

George kept his mouth shut. If all she had to do was fight back, he felt sure she would. He knew his wife was high-spirited, so he waited for her to struggle.

Lemuel could say nothing. Hurt filled him, as tears fell from his eyes. He wanted to kill Cain more than ever.

She did not struggle. When Cain bent over and kissed her passionately, lust filled every cell of her body, causing her to tingle with sexual pleasure. In her mind she wanted to pull away, to slap him, to struggle against him, but her body felt as if it was being blissfully scorched with blazing lust. She needed to extinguish the burning fires.

Lemuel and George watched speechlessly as Cain continued

kissing her. They heard her whimper with passion.

They watched in shock as Cain peeled off her dress, allowing her firm breasts to bulge forth, with red nipples extending out unhindered.

They watched with frustration as she continued staring away, while her abdomen moved quickly back and forth.

They watched with jealousy as Cain sucked on her protruding nipples, smacking his lips loudly.

She kept her eyes closed but moaned with passion. They watched with hurt as Cain took off his clothes.

He gently pushed her back on the bunk without resistance.

She did not resist because her self-control lay shredded deep in her consciousness. With a deep, inner strength she used what little self-control she could find, and pleaded with a whisper, "Please, I can't do this. I can't do...."

Cain smiled as he said huskily, "Sure, you can, and you'll like it, too." She whined passionately as intense jolts of lust ran through her.

Lemuel and George were at a loss for words, as feelings of betrayal filled their hearts. They watched with jealousy as Cain positioned himself between her legs.

She gasped with wonder and moaned a deep wail of feminine carnality.

Lemuel turned his head away with a deep hurt.

George watched with extreme frustration and continued watching as Cain violated his wife...

He heard her cries of ecstasy become even more intense...

n going to have a lot of great times together."

He chuckled while looking at her broken husband with a cruel smile, as she withered under him, still in the throes of continuous climaxes.

After Lemuel and Pamela were kidnapped, Professor James White woke up in the infirmary on the ship.

The captain explained everything that happened, finishing up with Lemuel's last words. Lemuel said James would know what to do.

At the time, James did not know what to do, but he devised an elaborate plan. As he stood in front of a mirror in a hotel room in Washington, D.C., he felt his new nose and lips with fascination. His cryogenic mask looked real, portraying him as the vice president of the United States of America. It was the perfect disguise for the operation they were embarked on.

They would be leaving soon for the White House.

James convinced a formal student to join him in his mission of rescuing them.

Harold Nelson became an agent for the CIA. He specialized in changing appearances and forging government documents, but he had reservations for what they were doing, and he did not feel comfortable sneaking into the White House. He knew James well, and he knew James spoke the truth, so he felt it was his civic duty to rescue the president's captives and expose him to the public. With reluctance, he asked James again with nagging doubts filling his mind, "Are you sure we have to do this, James? Maybe you're wrong. Perhaps the president isn't involved. Even if he is, couldn't you obtain a search warrant to search the White House instead? It would be legal anyway."

James turned around from the mirror while saying with exasperation, "You know I don't lie. I'm positive we can't get a search warrant. You know I don't have enough evidence for it. The main question is, are you absolutely certain Cain has a secret cell block?"

Harold nodded with certainty. "Yes, we've reliable information he does from a guard who worked there. He even told us how to find it."

James nodded with satisfaction. "Great! I guess we're ready to go, then. Are you ready?"

Harold nodded nervously.

Everything went smoothly with all the security checks, and they soon found themselves walking down the secret passageway.

As soon as they walked into the cell block, the guard at the desk stood up and recognized who he thought was the vice president.

Harold walked over to him and said with a friendly smile on his face, "I'm the vice president's aide, and I'm here to have Lemuel and Pamela released."

The guard became confused as he said with hesitation, "What? There must be some kind of mistake, because I can't release them. President Cain gave me direct orders in person. No one's allowed to be released."

Harold frowned as he drew out his revolver, pointing it directly at the guard. He then ordered the surprised guard with an angry voice, "Turn around and face the wall!"

The terrified guard turned around as he pleaded, "Please don't kill me! I have a wife and—"

Harold did not allow him to finish as he hit the guard in the back of the head with the butt of his revolver. The hard blow knocked the guard unconscious, dropping him to the floor.

James and Harold walked over to the cells where the three captives were held.

James told Harold with unbridled enthusiasm, "It's them, alright! Now how do we get them out?"

Lemuel spoke up with relief as he said, "I would have never believed the vice president could ever rescue anyone, let alone me. I'm not complaining, just surprised. The keys you need are over there behind the desk. There's a secret compartment in the wall right behind the chair."

James told Lemuel with excitement, "It's me, Lemuel, James! I'm just wearing a mask!"

Lemuel looked at James with a surprised expression on his face. He said with amazement, "You sure had me fooled."

James smiled with pride as he said, "I do look like the vice president." Turning to Harold, he ordered, "Go get those keys so we can get out of here."

As Harold retrieved the keys, George said with bitter sarcasm, "Don't worry about my wife. I'm pretty sure she wants to stay here, since she enjoys having sex with the president. She showed us a couple of hours ago how much she enjoys having sex with him, so just leave her here."

Lemuel shouted at George with a threatening tone, "Shut up and leave her alone, George, or maybe we'll leave *you* down here!"

Pamela rose lethargically off the bunk. Standing up, she faced George. With hurt in her eyes, she said, "If he would've given you the drug he gave me, you would've enjoyed sex with him, too. How dare you talk about me in such a disrespectful way?"

George glared back with disgust as he said, "No drug would have made me respond to him in such an uninhibited way. Apparently you never loved me. If you loved me, you would've never reacted in such a shameless way. When this is over, I want a divorce. I never knew you were such a dirty slut!"

Lemuel shouted at George with anger, "If you don't shut up, George, I swear I'll leave you here! Then you can see if you'll respond to Cain."

As hurt filled her heart, tears rolled down her face.

After Harold opened the jail cells, James said, "Quick, everyone, we need to get out now! We've got a hotel room already. We'll go there until we can get out of this country."

"I'm not going to any hotel," George said stubbornly. "As soon as I get out of here, I'm going to the nearest police station to press charges against Cain."

Lemuel shrugged his shoulders with indifference as he said, "Your funeral."

Harold spoke up, saying, "I'll help you press charges, George, but I'll have to keep you hidden for a while until this is over."

As he finished speaking, the cell block door opened, with Cain and Clarence stepping in.

Clarence pointed his revolver at them while screaming, "Everyone put your hands in the air now!'

Everyone reluctantly raised their hands in the air.

Smiling triumphantly, Cain walked over to Lemuel, saying in a mocking way, "The great hero thought he got away. You must think I'm a fool. I know everything that goes on here. Did you really believe for a minute I'd let your friend steal my sex slave? I may have to kill everyone but you to teach you who the real boss is!"

"I don't care what Lucifer may do to me, but I swear I'm going to kill you for hurting Pam!" Lemuel exclaimed vehemently.

Cain raised his eyebrows up as he said with boastful arrogance, "I don't think you're in the position to threaten anyone. In fact, just for threatening me, I'm going to make you watch every time I pleasure her now. I assure you, she'll enjoy it every time, too. Of course, I really don't need James, Harry, or George, though." Glancing quickly at Clarence, Cain nodded.

Clarence knew what to do. He walked closer to them with his revolver still drawn. It was an old, well-oiled German Luger. "Germans always made the best weapons," he said with a proud smile.

Without warning, he hardheartedly shot Harold and George without blinking an eye or losing a smile.

The force of the bullets propelled them a couple of feet before they hit the floor.

With outstretched arms and legs, they lay lifeless as blood bubbled out from the holes in their chests.

Pamela screamed in panic as she rushed over to her deceased husband. She dropped to the floor and cradled his head near her bosom while rocking slowly back and forth.

"You're not dead. You're not dead," she moaned over and over in denial, with tears streaming down her face.

Clarence continued smiling as he gazed on the two dead men. "See how good this old Luger still works," he said proudly.

He then looked at James and shrugged his shoulders with mocking resignation. "Well, I guess you're next." He turned his gun and pointed it at James.

Before he could pull the trigger, Lemuel screamed at the top of his lungs and lunged at Clarence with lightning speed, punching him hard in the face, which caused Clarence's weapon to drop out of his hand and onto the floor.

Lemuel punched him again, knocking him over to the desk.

Lemuel then ran over to him. Grabbing Clarence by the hair, he began banging his head against the desk.

Somehow Clarence jerked his head away from the firm clutch, leaving a handful of hair in Lemuel's hand.

He quickly looked around for his dropped weapon, but as soon as he saw it, Lemuel kicked him as hard as he could in the face, hitting him in the nose.

The hard kick broke his nose like a twig, spewing blood all around, knocking him unconscious. His inert body fell backward in an awkward position, with his lower legs lying under him.

Everything happened so fast that Cain stood frozen in surprise.

After he observed Lemuel dispatching Clarence so easily, he knew he needed to make a hasty retreat. He felt he could win in a fight against Lemuel, but if he accidentally killed him, there would be hell to pay with Lemuel's demonic father seeking revenge. He could then kiss his elaborate plan of ruling the world good-bye. He felt he went too far after thousands of years of intense plots and strategies to just throw it away over a stupid fight. He turned and fled out of the cell block toward his personal quarters.

While running, he notified a few of his other Secret Service agents on his cell phone to capture the intruders.

Breathing hard, Lemuel screamed impatiently, "We have to leave now!" Running over to Pamela, he dragged her off George while screaming frantically, "He's dead! We have to leave now!"

(PAST)

Cain watched the sun sink past the horizon, with a reddish tint glaring out its last rays.

The homosexual gang arrived at Lot's house, as Cain slipped out of view beside a neighboring home in an alley. He kept discreetly hidden from the loud homosexual mob that assembled in front of Lot's place.

Heth began shouting boisterously, "Lot! Lot! Where are those beautiful men you brought to your home this morning? Bring them out so we can get to know them, and make passionate love to them! We'll bring them so much pleasure they'll never want to leave!" He continued shouting with grandiose taunts.

Lot came out, trembling with fear. Shutting the door firmly, he told them in a conciliatory tone, "Brothers, go home. I hope you're not that wicked."

Heth bellowed out angrily, "How dare you judge us for being wicked! You don't know us! Now send out your guests or we'll go get them!"

Lot then pleaded frantically with tears in his eyes, "Please, brothers, don't do this great evil. Listen, I'll make a deal with you. You can have my two virgin daughters to do with whatever you want, just please don't hurt my guests since they're under my protection."

Heth then rushed over to Lot, lasciviously pressing against him as he said with a husky voice, "Are you trying to insult us? You know we're homosexuals. Your bitch daughters don't interest us. As far as your being our brother goes, you're not even our people, let alone our brother. You're a foreigner. Since you're in such a determined state of opposition, we'll do you first, and do you worse than what we'll do to them!"

The crowd began pressing toward Lot.

With terror Lot felt many hands groping over his robe. He felt squeezing hands over his covered buttocks and genitals, bringing him embarrassment and pain. He felt powerless as their hands tore riotously at his robe, ripping it from his body.

Before they actually defiled him with their perverted sexual desires, one of Lot's angelic guests opened the door and blinded the perverted homosexuals with a flash of light from his finger. The angel then pulled Lot back inside and shut the door securely, leaving behind the lingering smell of roasted sheep and spicy lentil soup.

While in the alley, Cain realized the angel's magical powers had blinded the perverted gang, and it had terrified them. Everyone by Lot's door groped around with panic. For so many people to become blinded so fast, amazed him. He watched with curious fascination as all the sightless people moaned and groaned with fearful confusion. They became completely lost. They groped along the sides of the street, feeling on houses, attempting to ascertain where they were....

Cain waited patiently outside in the alley all night, until early the next morning. As the sun began peeking its yellow head over the horizon, Cain observed two angels escort Lemuel, Lot, his wife, and two daughters out with a hurried walk.

Cain followed them from a discreet distance. He watched as they quickly passed the blind people who begged for help. He followed them out of the city gate and miles afterward.

Suddenly Cain heard loud roaring sounds. He watched Lot's wife turn around to investigate the noise and immediately transform into a statue of salt. Not being able to resist, he turned around out of curiosity to see what happened. What he saw became imprinted in his memory for many years.

He watched as large boulders of fire and brimstone rained from the sky. The smoky smell of sulfur filled the air as they hit the city like a bombarding hailstorm, shaking the earth with loud explosions. With his perfect eyesight he could see some of the citizens of Sodom disintegrate, leaving behind dark puffs of smoke and putrid smells of burnt flesh. He watched all the lush vegetation around the city turn to ash in an instant. It appeared as if it became exposed to a giant furnace, as a fiery wind kicked up great clouds of dust and smoke. He knew the plain of Jordan would never be the same. He knew it would just be an arid, salty desert from then on.

After the horrendous scourge, Cain continued following them from a distance. He took note of the angels vanishing without a trace.

The family eventually arrived at a city called Zoar.

Realizing it was deserted, Lot decided to leave with his daughters.

Lemuel knew his need to stay with Lot had ended, so he decided to stay in the deserted city of Zoar. Since Sodom was destroyed, his clandestine mission had ended.

Lot and his daughters continued trekking over the mountains, with Cain following at a discreet distance, keeping hidden from their eyes.

Lot found a large cave in a mountain and made a primitive home out of it. Cain continued observing them secretly from a distance.

After a few days, Lot and his two daughters became comfortably settled in the cave, so Cain decided the time had arrived to deceive Lot's daughters. He would show God a true abomination.

The next day, as the two daughters were out gathering firewood,

Cain surprised them with his presence. "Hello, ladies!"

They dropped their firewood and turned quickly to see who spoke to them. Recognizing Cain as a human male, they squealed in delight, running to his outstretched arms.

Cuddling close to his chest, they exclaimed excitedly, "Thank God more people than us survived! Except for Lemuel, we thought everyone had perished!"

Cain soothed them with reassuring words. "Now, now, little ones, be calm. Everything will work out in the end."

They exclaimed excitedly, "You can stay with us and be our husband!"

After living in the decadent city of Sodom, he knew their thoughts could be influenced with perverted images, thus deviant plans of having sex with their father would plant a seed of wickedness in their minds. With that in mind, Cain replied back with deceiving sadness, "I'm afraid I can't. Lemuel can't, either. Other than your father, I'm sure Lemuel and I are the only men left alive in the world, and we're homosexuals. In order to ensure the survival of mankind, you'll both have to become pregnant by your father."

Lot's daughters felt disappointed.

Cain then helped them come up with different plans on how to have sex with their father, since their father would probably not do it willingly.

The women became flush with perversion as they discussed the different plans among themselves.

Cain noted the redness of their faces, and he knew his villainous seed of deception had taken root in their hearts. Cain then smiled with satisfaction. He knew his villainous plot would be successful in corrupting mankind even more in the future, thus making him even more powerful.

With his vile act accomplished, he said his good-byes and eagerly headed back down the mountain.

Chapter 11

Cain sat in his chair. Leaning back, he closed his eyes. A nagging headache tortured him. He wished someone would invent a cure for migraines. He had never had migraines until the nineteenth century. He knew it was caused when humanity began polluting the atmosphere with their burgeoning industrial smokestacks. As he continued rubbing his temples, Lucifer materialized behind him, illuminating the room with his yellow aura.

Cain's eyes opened with curiosity, wondering why the room had become so bright. Lucifer reached over, grabbing Cain by the shoulder, dislocating it.

Cain jerked around quickly with an agonizing scream, ready to hurt whoever had the nerve to assault him. With surprise he saw Lucifer. "Father, why have you hurt me?" he asked with a grimace of pain on his face.

Lucifer smiled as he shrugged his shoulders and said with sarcasm, "Did I hurt my little baby boy? Sorry. Sometimes I forget how strong I am in comparison to fleshly bodies."

"Why are you here?" Cain asked with a perplexing raise of his eyebrows.

Lucifer said with excitement, "I came to give you good news. The time has drawn near for you to rule the world, and for me to receive the worship of humanity. I now know how to keep the human cells reproducing forever by mutating the nucleus within them."

"You're joking," Cain said with astonishment. "I've been dreaming about this day for thousands of years. I want that secret now!"

Lucifer laughed at Cain's eagerness. "Slow down. I already gave it to your chief scientist. He should have a radioactive serum synthesized within a week.

"You can use it as proof that you're the Messiah. Most Jews still believe the Messiah hasn't arrived yet, so with this miracle drug, you can prove you're the Messiah, and then you can direct humans to worship your father, which is me.

"Jerusalem will be the perfect place to let the world know they can have eternal life, and you can use the power you receive from giving them everlasting life to rule the world. All I ask in return is for you to convince mankind to worship me as their god."

"With that serum, I can!" Cain exclaimed with excitement.

"Good," Lucifer said with satisfaction. "I must go now. Please arrange for a grand speech at Jerusalem soon."

As Lucifer vanished, Cain felt overwhelmed. There was so much to do. Could he rule the whole world in just a few months? With the eternal life serum, he would attempt it.

Reaching over, he turned the webcam on with excitement and called the leader of the United Nations.

Graham's image appeared on screen. He was a white-haired Caucasian who possessed brown eyes and a bulbous nose. He reminded Cain of his secret agent Clarence. The resemblance was eerie.

"How may I help you?" Graham asked nervously, with an anxious grimace twitching his eyelid.

Cain exerted his power by ordering with a robust voice, "It's imperative you get all the world and financial leaders to show up for my speech. I'll be arranging one in Jerusalem soon. I have something extremely important I must share with them. Convince the United Nation's council members to have their main political leaders there. It's important they all be there when I make my speech. I know it's a lot to do in such a short time, but I know you can do it if you set your mind to it. I know you have a lot of worldly influence."

Graham shook his head doubtfully as he said, "Mr. President, I don't think I'll be able to get Russia, Iran, North Korea, or China to go along with it. Perhaps I can get the rest, maybe even some I just mentioned, but never China. You know the Chinese leader hates you for invading Syria. He's still contemplating whether he should start a war with you. I may not be able to get some of the other nations, either. You know how leaders can be if they feel like they're going to be asked to give up power, even if it's just a little power. Besides, a lot of leaders don't trust you, Mr. President."

Cain shouted with frustration, "I'm not asking them to give up any power! I just want them there when I make my speech in Jerusalem. I'll give you a couple of weeks to have them convince their leaders. If they refuse, I'm through with them. The leaders who don't show up will pay the ultimate price, so you can just pass that message to them! Understand?"

Graham became flustered as he said, "Yes, Mr. President, I

understand, and you have my word. I'll try to convince them all to be there."

Cain flicked the screen off with irritation. His spot on the world's center stage would arrive soon, and he had little patience for those who stood in his way. With a deep breath to calm his nerves, he dialed Clarence's number.

Clarence answered, "Hello, Mr. President. How may I help you?"

Cain screamed with rage as he said, "You know how you can help me! Have you located Lemuel, James, and Pamela yet?"

Clarence spoke with a self-assurance he did not really feel, "I haven't found them yet, but I have info they're in Rome somewhere. I'm in touch with an agent there who's sure he'll find them soon."

Clarence's voice did not reassure Cain. With a threatening tone he said, "You had better find them. I'll be going to Jerusalem in a couple of weeks to make a major speech, and they could ruin it. If you find them, make sure James and Pamela are killed, and Lemuel incarcerated. I don't need any witnesses tarnishing my image, especially at this stage in the game."

Before Clarence could respond, he quickly disconnected. He did not have time for socializing.

With suspicion he called Joseph.

Joseph appeared on screen. "What a surprise. How may I help you, Mr. President?"

Cain frowned as he stared at him for a few moments. He then said with a harsh voice, "I've heard Lemuel and his accomplices are in Rome somewhere. Rome's your back yard, so it shouldn't be difficult to find them. I'm sending you pictures of all three of them so you'll know what they look like. Use your agents to track them down now." Clenching his teeth angrily, he added with an evil expression, "By the way, Pope Lame Duck, if I ever find out you've double-crossed me, you'll be a dead duck! That's not a threat, it's a promise."

Joseph replied back sarcastically, "I'd never double-cross you, Mr. President. After all, you're my hero."

Cain hung up with disgust contorting his face into an ugly grimace.

Joseph stood behind a bulletproof shield that sat on a podium at the Vatican auditorium. In front of him sat an audience of imposter cardinals and other counterfeit religious leaders he had installed after murdering the real ones with hired ninjas. With the aid of plastic surgery, they looked like the ones he replaced, and even sounded like them. Joseph smiled proudly as he said, "Gentlemen, I called you here today to enlighten you on my plans of gaining control over the world's economy."

The fraudulent religious leaders mumbled in surprise. They knew the pope was powerful, but they had never realized how powerful.

With false modesty Joseph continued, "You're probably wondering how I, a lowly pope, plan on gaining control of the world's economy.

"To answer your unspoken question, it's through a technological marvel called the nano chip. To explain more in depth, my scientists, along with help from my spiritual friend, have invented a small chip the size of a mustard seed. It can painlessly be implanted under the human skin.

"These nano chips emit detectable thought waves directly to the victim's mind in order to influence them. It doesn't control them completely, because they can go against the thoughts, but if they do, it also causes them to feel bad physically. It's enough nausea to cause most of them to buy certain brands of food, clothes, and other consumer goods I want them to buy.

"Because of this power, I'll know where to invest the Catholic funds at in the world's stock markets. I'll eventually gain control of all the world's governments, because money buys power. Are there any questions?"

After no questions, Joseph smiled as he said, "Very well then, I'll start my operation on you all. The difference between these chips and the ones that will be implanted in the general public are significant, because these will be programed to self-destruct if necessary, thereby killing you instantly.

"After you return back to the countries I've assigned you to, I want the chips I supply implanted in all your followers. Be creative, I'm sure most will follow your directions if you scare them with tales of a worldwide contagion, or something of that nature."

A frightened crescendo of voices rose as the fake religious leaders stood up from their seats.

Joseph smiled as he said, "Please calm down. Those who remain loyal will reap vast economic rewards, and even share in some of my power. Those who do not will die."

The doors opened and armed guards marched in, stationing themselves around the auditorium, standing at attention with weapons drawn.

A squad of doctors in white frocks carrying black leather bags followed close behind.

After everyone entered, two formidable-looking guards closed the doors and stationed themselves by it with arms folded.

As the phony religious leaders reluctantly relented to the transplant whenever their names were called, Joseph decided to go to his office in order to tie up some loose ends. He felt confident his job in the auditorium was finished, so he walked boldly to the exit.

Joseph was surprised to find Lemuel, James, and Pamela sitting tied securely to chairs in his office.

The pope's personal bodyguard cleared his throat, then said, "We found them trying to sneak into your bedroom window, your holiness. Apparently they used ropes to climb the wall."

Joseph recognized Lemuel as the one who had made slanderous accusations against President Cain. He did not know Lemuel personally, but since Cain had sent pictures of Lemuel and his two cohorts, he recognized them. Joseph felt elated as he wondered if Cain would reward him. With pretentious anger rising in his voice, he asked Lemuel, while staring into his eyes, "What's the meaning of this? Why have you tried to sneak into my personal quarters?"

Lemuel spoke honestly, "We've escaped from Cain. We're investigating to see if you're the false prophet foretold in the Bible. If you are, and we kill you, we'll save billions of human lives. We'll then avoid the catastrophes God has planned for humanity."

Joseph thought about it, then burst out laughing. He liked Lemuel's courage. After his laughter subsided, he said, "You're mistaken, my friend. I'm not the false prophet, but even if I were, it wouldn't change God's plans. You should be killing Cain if you want to avoid God's catastrophes. Allow me to explain why.

"Don't misunderstand me, because I'm as much of an American as you are, but America is the Beast spoken of in Revelation's chapter thirteen. For example, it says he saw a beast rise up out of the sea. Most biblical scholars recognize the sea as the sea of humanity. What other nation has more immigrants from other nations than America?

"It continues saying that the beast had a mouth of a lion. When we speak of a mouth, isn't the mouth where language comes from? America's main language is English, which is mostly derived from Great

Britain. What's Great Britain's icon? It's the lion!

"It goes on to say the beast had the feet of a bear. Well, didn't Alaska used to belong to Russia? What's Russia's icon? Isn't it the bear? There are also a lot of bears in Alaska, and depending in what direction you're looking, Alaska could be classified as a foot of America. California can also be classified as one. Isn't a bear on the California flag? If the original thirteen colonies were the head of the body, then California could be classified as a foot. Most creatures have at least two feet, so Alaska and California are each a foot.

"It was like a leopard. What nation has as many racial spots? The Old Testament also refers to Africans as having spots like leopards. America certainly has a lot of minorities, and a lot of them are African Americans. With the way integrated relationships and marriages have been occurring the last fifty years, probably a lot more African Americans than most people even realize.

"Lastly, it asks in the book of Revelation, who is able to make war with him? As the only superpower, most people would agree America's the most powerful nation on earth. Who could defeat America in any kind of major war? In an all-out war, no country could defeat America because of its nuclear weapons, if for nothing else.

"As you can see, it's not I whom you need to kill, but Cain, the leader of the beast. If you chop off the head, the symbolic beast will die. Then you can avoid all the calamities God has planned for the world, and save billions of lives."

Lemuel refused to believe that America was the beast. In all his thousands of years, he never knew a nation as great. It was more prosperous and free than any other country he had ever lived in. He did agree with the pope on one thing: Cain must die in order for humanity to avoid the calamities God had in store for them. Cain must die, even if it meant Lemuel must sacrifice his own life. Over the millenniums he had grown to love mankind. If he had to, he would lay his own life down for them. The false prophet would be powerless if Cain died. With that in mind, he said to Joseph, "I still believe you may be the false prophet, but I'll not argue with you. We agree on one thing: Cain must die. Have you any ideas how to kill him?"

Joseph patted Lemuel on the shoulder with affection as he said, "I can understand why you'd think I was the false prophet, but I'm really not. I'm just a humble pope trying to do the right thing for God's followers.

"I do know the best place to kill Cain, though. Through

information I've recently received, I've learned Cain plans on giving a speech about something of major importance in Jerusalem soon. Many high-ranking people from around the world will be there to listen. It would be the perfect place to kill Cain. I'll even aid you in this endeavor with a secret agent, a high-powered weapon, a hiding place, and a plan for escape. I'll pay all the expenses for you, and your friends, if they wish to accompany you."

Lemuel replied stubbornly, "Absolutely not! I'll kill Cain, but I don't want James or Pamela in—"

James interrupted indignantly, "Lemuel, you can't leave me behind after all I've done for you, and after all we've been through btogether! That just wouldn't be right, Lemuel."

Pamela added with her own indignation, "James is right, especially after all I've been through. After what that bastard did to me, I want to see him die with my own eyes!"

Lemuel knew they would not be dissuaded, so with reluctance he agreed. "Okay, you can both go with me, but it's me who actually kills Cain. When the time arrives for me to kill Cain, you two stay out of the way. Until then the pope can rent us a three-bedroom suite at one of the best lodgings in Jerusalem. I'm sure he knows where the best are."

Joseph agreed. "Yes, my friend, I'll get the finest suite. As I said before, all the expenses will be on me. Food, clothes, whatever. My agent there will make contact with you to keep you updated on current events and obtain everything you may need for the assassination. Please do me the honor of staying here in my personal quarters for a few days while I arrange everything."

Everyone agreed with nervous compliance.

(PAST)

Cain scrutinized the Hebrews from afar with the aid of spies. Since they claimed to be the people of the only true God, he had decided long ago to work against them and thwart their plans. He wanted to bring reproach on their God, because their Deity was his father's enemy, which made their God his enemy, too.

Cain still ruled the city of Babylon and its surrounding provinces with absolute power. He also influenced a lot of other nations. Because of his influence, he easily swayed nations surrounding Israel not to allow them to travel through their lands, or even sell them food. Cain hoped the nation of Israel would starve to death in the wilderness, but his plan failed miserably when their benevolent God sustained them with food from the heavens called Manna.

After that strategy failed, Cain devised another, more devious plot—a plot designed to slowly assimilate the nation of Israel until they lost their identity. In order to implement his new strategy, he traveled with his entourage to the mountainous kingdom of Moab.

The smell of cedar filled the room as Cain lay on purple pelt cushions at a comfortable distance from the large fireplace. The fire flickered brightly with reddish flames, tinged with blue and yellow, casting dancing shadows around the semi-lit chambers.

Cain gazed at the Moabite king with wonder. He then mumbled softly to himself with contempt, "So this is the incestuous offspring of Lot and one of his daughters. No wonder he looks so stupid. It should be easy enough to use them to assimilate the Israelites into their incestuous race. The Hebrews deserve no better than to be assimilated by a bunch of inbred idiots."

King Jehu gazed curiously at the king of Babylon, wondering what he mumbled about. He did not like Cain. In fact, he hated him with every fiber of his body. He felt envious of him because Cain ruled a powerful city. Because of Cain's power, King Jehu pretended to like him, even love him.

When Cain arrived, Jehu bowed to him three times, and kissed his hand with submissive compliance. He did not bow to anyone, so his pride hurt secretly, but he knew he needed to show respect to one of the most powerful men on earth.

Since it was the Moabite custom not to speak before a superior one in status did, Jehu refused to speak until after Cain spoke. As he kept staring at Cain with puzzlement, Jehu thought with contempt that Cain must be touched mentally, so much so he could not begin a normal conversation.

As they continued staring at each other with odd expressions, it brought muffled sniggers from the Moabite palace guards.

With an aristocratic sniff, displaying a sense of superiority, Cain said boldly with disdain, "I want to speak to you alone. Please dismiss your guards so we may do so. Do it now!"

King Jehu bowed humbly while saying with a rasping voice, "Your wish is my command, sire." He then dismissed the guards with a flourishing wave of his arm.

Cain chuckled as he said with a smirk on his face, "Good! I'm glad we understand each other, and where we stand in this worldly political arena."

Jehu gritted his teeth while saying with forced submissiveness, "Everyone knows Babylon is one of the most powerful cities in the world."

Cain nodded with amusement as he said, "That's right, so let's cut out all this bullshit. I know you don't like me, but personal feelings aside, I've a proposition you may find quite agreeable. I want you to send your Moabite women out to the Israelite encampment in order to seduce them, marry them, and lead them astray into worshiping all your gods."

King Jehu became so indignant he could no longer restrain himself as he said angrily, "Sire, you insult me and all the Moabite people! Our women are not whores to just give to anyone, especially to that barbaric race who lives in tents in the wilderness!"

Cain chuckled with relief. Finally he saw the true man behind the submissive mask. He then said with candidness, "That barbaric race is distant kin to your race. You know your patriarch, Lot, was the nephew of Abraham."

"That's where the similarity ends!" Jehu exclaimed fervently with an embarrassed blush to his face. "The Israelites have become a mongrel race with Egyptians, Syrians, and no telling who else interbreeding with them over the centuries! My people are a pure race. We keep to our own kind!"

Cain smiled politely, but inside felt contempt as he mumbled to himself, "The Moabites certainly do keep to their own kind, especially fathers with daughters, and sons with mothers."

"What did you just say?" Jehu asked with curiosity.

Cain stopped his mumbling, and said with a persuasive tone, "Oh, nothing really. Just talking to myself. I do that a lot when things aren't going my way. I know how you feel, Jehu, and I sympathize with you, but I desperately need your help. The Moabites must be the people to assimilate the Israelites. They'd probably not trust the other nations as much as they would Moab, since your people are distant relatives to them.

"Do this for me, Jehu, and I'll make sure I'll be your ally against any nation who may attack you. Not only that, but I'll give you one-tenth of a talent of bronze for every Israelite man who marries a Moabite woman. We both know my money could enrich your kingdom

significantly."

King Jehu hated intermarrying his people with any race, especially with the mongrel Israelite race, but Cain's offer appeared irresistible. Not only would he have one of the most powerful cities on earth protecting him, but his kingdom could also become one of the richest in the world, and Jehu knew more money spelled more power. "Perhaps," he said softly to himself with hope glittering from his bloodshot eyes, "Moab could also become a powerful nation someday." After a few moments of dreaming about immense riches and power, he smiled while saying with eagerness, "Agreed!"

Cain smiled with satisfaction as his contempt for the Moabite people grew even more. "These people are so foolish. Must be all the inbreeding," he mumbled with disgust.

One day, when the Israelites were residing as nomads in a barren land called the wilderness, Lemuel sat with Moses in his tent. Lemuel deplored living in the wilderness, but Moses felt resolved in not invading the prosperous Canaanite lands until after God told him to do so.

After much conflict among the Israelites, the day finally arrived when Lemuel decided he must convince Moses to begin the invasion for the sake of Israel. With determination, Lemuel stared at Moses while saying candidly, "Moses, we've been in this wilderness for many years. The people have grown restless. We need to invade the Canaanites now so the people can have good land to live on and good homes to live in."

Moses felt sad as he agreed, "I know. I wish we could invade, but God has forbidden it. He told me personally we'd be defeated without His help, so we have to wait until He decides—"

"But, Moses," Lemuel interrupted impatiently, "we'll not make it in this wilderness much longer! What have we done to elicit such cruel punishment?"

Moses then remembered, and said with disappointment, "Soon after we left Egypt, God ordered us to invade the Canaanites, but because of Israel's lack of faith, the people disobeyed, and did not invade. Because of that, God will not help us if we invade now. We have to wait until He gives us permission."

"Please reconsider, Moses," Lemuel begged. "Because some of the Israelites have left for Moab, and some of them are bringing Moabite women into our camp, marrying them, and worshiping their gods. If you

don't invade soon, I fear the nation of Israel will cease to exist."

Moses sighed with discouragement, then said, "I know, Lemuel, but there's nothing I can do. All I can do is pray that God will keep us together until it's time to invade."

Lemuel felt frustrated. Moses was the meekest, yet most stubborn man on earth.

Chapter 12

Lemuel, James, and Pamela sat enjoying a cup of tea in the dining room at the luxurious suite in Jerusalem. They arrived earlier that morning, and after a long conversation at the dining room table, became sleepy since it was getting late into the night.

They had talked a lot about the pope, and they still felt nervous concerning him.

James finally said with a yawn, "I don't know about you two, but it's time for me to go to bed. I'll take the first bedroom by the door so as to give a warning if anyone should happen to sneak in," he added with a light, halfhearted chuckle. "I think I'm a lighter sleeper than both of you lovebirds." Rising off the chair, he walked into a bedroom.

Lemuel smiled lovingly at Pamela, which caused her to blush as he said, "I think James has the right idea, since I'm also tired. I'll take the bedroom next to James, and you can have the last one. If anyone does sneak in, they'll have to go past James's and mine first. Hopefully we'll hear them before they get to yours."

Pamela agreed with a silent nod of her head as she stood up to go to her room.

Lemuel stood up and said politely, "Please allow me to escort you to your room." Smiling, he added, "I want to make sure it's safe and secure. I wouldn't want anyone to be hiding under the bed or in the closet."

Pamela soon sat on her bed with Lemuel sitting close.

Lemuel asked with concern etched on his face, "So what do you think, Pam? Do you think I should trust the pope? Do you think he'll help me kill Cain?"

She felt concern while saying, "If he's the false prophet, I wouldn't trust him, but it's apparent he doesn't like Cain. I think he feels he's in some kind of competition with him. I do believe he'll help you kill him, and I think you should kill Cain. Even if he's not the devil's son, he's certainly a monster. You saw what he did to me." Tears then filled her eyes as hurt filled her heart.

Lemuel gently drew her close and held her head against his chest as the sobs burst out, shaking her body with small tremors. He felt so much empathy for her he felt like crying himself, but he needed to be strong. He held her tight as tears filled his own eyes, and sadness filled his heart.

After a few moments of heart-wrenching sobs, she regained control of herself and dried her eyes with a tissue from a box sitting on the nightstand. After blowing her nose, she tossed it in the waste basket by the bed and said with determination, "I'm sorry, Lemuel. It's just that we've been through so much in the last month. I guess it's been kind of overwhelming, to say the least."

Lemuel caressed her cheek while saying, "I understand, Pam, and I hate that you've been dragged into this. We'll get through this together, somehow, then everything will be alright."

He felt an urge to kiss her and leaned over, but she pushed him away.

Looking at him with a hurtful glare, she said, "I'm not ready for that yet. After being raped by that monster, and having my husband killed, I'm not ready for any kind of relationship right now. I'm sorry, Lemuel. I do care for you a lot, and maybe someday we can have an intimate relationship, just not right now. I'm hurting too much."

Surprised, he nervously said, "Of course, Pam. I understand and apologize for my lack of control. Especially since you're so vulnerable right now. I'm sorry."

Standing up, he looked down at her while saying with concern, "Before I go, I want you to remember to keep your door locked. Please don't hesitate to scream if you find yourself in any danger."

She agreed with a tired nod.

He walked out reluctantly with concern still clinging to his face.

After he left, she stood up, walked over to the door, and locked it securely. She then walked over to the closet and looked in. To her surprise she saw a vast array of female clothes, all her size and all beautiful. "They must have decided this was going to be my room earlier," she mumbled absentmindedly.

Browsing through them, she searched for a nightgown. She soon grew weary of the search, so she walked over to the dresser. As soon as she opened the first drawer, she saw a beautiful pair of silk panties and matching bras. They were white and translucent.

She did not like the translucent part, but she knew no one would be seeing her in them. The design looked gorgeous, and the silk felt so soft she could not resist wearing them to bed.

She quickly stripped off her dress and slipped the panties up her shapely legs. They felt comfortable, even though her black pubic hair could be seen clearly through the material.

She slipped the bra over her small, yet firm breasts, showing her dark-red nipples just as clearly.

She continued to feel uncomfortable with the transparency of her attire, but she felt pleased with the comfort. She knew she would have no trouble sleeping in it, so walking over to the bed, she slipped under the white sheets.

Reaching over, she turned out the lamp that sat on the nightstand, leaving the room pitch-dark.

Closing her eyes, memories of traumatic events filled her mind in a terrifying array of blood and gore: memories of her husband killed, memories of the innocent couple killed, and memories of being raped by Cain.

Eventually her mind wandered to Lemuel, and her heart filled with love when she thought of him. She gradually drifted off to sleep with Lemuel on her mind, locked in an intimate embrace.

In her erotic dream, Lemuel caressed her breasts. It felt sexually soul-stirring, causing her nipples to become swollen with passion. Warmth flowed through her in waves of pleasure.

He kissed her with a tantalizing kiss, sending more currents of stimulating heat through her. It was the best kiss she had ever received, a kiss that gradually woke her with the realization it was actually happening.

She opened her eyes in a state of drowsy wonderment, only to look into the eyes of a being made of thick, yellow light!

She felt confused. How could she feel him since his body appeared to consist of pure light? How could light feel so solid? His touch felt so mesmerizing that she felt helpless against it.

The beauty of his body lit up the room with a smooth, yellowish light. It emanated off his naked body in shiny waves of glory. She felt paralyzed by the magnetic light.

"Who are you?" she asked with a quivering voice and trembling limbs. He raised his body off of her and stood, touching the ceiling with the top of his head.

Looking down at her, he said in a resounding voice, "My name's Lucifer, the most beautiful and powerful being ever created." He laughed with a mischievous twinkle in his eyes as he continued with pride, "You must really enjoy this meeting since you've not moved a muscle. You haven't even told me to stop."

Deep inside her mind, she became alarmed with fear. She knew he was the devil, but her body wanted to meld with his. It became an intense struggle, mind against body. Somehow her willpower overcame the obsession long enough to ask, "What do you want with me?"

Looking at her with amusement, he said, "I want you to convince Lemuel not to kill Cain. I'm not asking for anything immoral or wrong. You know murder's wrong, so I am asking you to do the right thing. Okay?"

She hated Cain with a fervor almost as strong as the sexual passion she felt for Lucifer, so with determination she said, "No! Cain raped me in front of my husband, and he doesn't deserve to live! I'll not do it."

Lucifer smiled, and with what sounded like empathy, he said, "I know what happened, and I'm truly sorry, but you'll do it because I know you want me with every fiber of your being, and I know you want to please me."

Pamela's eyes grew wide with wonder as they transfixed on Lucifer's growing torch. It bobbed in front of him like an excited bloodhound, running toward a wounded pussycat. With extreme willpower she overcame her intense longing and said stubbornly, "I don't care how much I may want you, I'll still not do it! That monster deserves to die!"

Lucifer purred with reverberations punctuating each word, "No one deserves to die. Everyone makes mistakes. Do the right thing and forgive him. Spare his life. You can do it. All you have to do is convince Lemuel not to kill him. Agree to do this, and I'll give you what you crave."

He then ran his large hand up and down her body while saying with echoes of seduction, "You're one sexy lady. I want to fill you up so you can become one with me in sexual heights you've never experienced. All you have to do is agree to convince Lemuel not to kill Cain."

Her body felt starved for him, like a drug addict hungering for drugs. She wanted him more than anyone or anything in her life, but in the back of her mind she prayed for Lucifer to stop. She begged for mercy, to be released from his sexual hypnosis.

She maintained high moral standards, and she knew she loved

Lemuel. She did not want to hurt him. Clutching to every ounce of willpower, she said defiantly, "No! I'll not convince Lemuel. Cain deserves to die, and I want to see him die with my own eyes!"

With an erotic need never felt before, she craved him intensely. She could bear no more, so she pleaded passionately, "Okay, I'll do it! Just please make love to me now! I need you now!"

She trembled ecstatically as his spear of fluctuating light penetrated her, sending jolts of thrilling lust throughout her body, causing her to scream with wonder...

Lucifer moved faster, sending stimulating light to every cell of her body, causing her to tingle with spasms...

A sheen of sweat covered her body as his light explored her inner depths, leaving her gasping for breath and quivering with endless climaxes...

She wanted to remain in a state of continuous sexual bliss forever...

After what seemed like hundreds of continuous climaxes by Pamela, Lucifer became concerned.

Her abdomen undulated fast, as her mind became obsessed on one thing, to scratch the irresistible itch tingling deep inside...

She needed every bit of his flaming spear, as she grasped onto his thrusting buttocks of light...

Lucifer said with concern as he continued stoking her inner inferno, "Pamela, I must stop now or it'll kill you."

She begged in between whimpers of ecstatic delight, "No! Please don't stop! Please don't stop..."

Lucifer decided to give her the ultimate treatment as he said, "This will knock you unconscious, but it will save your life. Don't forget to convince Lemuel what we agreed on. You've gave me your word."

He raised her legs up and placed her feet beside her ears, leaving her more vulnerable. He submerged his quivering light deep inside, swirling around and around, exploring her intimate fleshly crevice...

His erotic motions caused her to feel like quivering gelatin inside. With each swirl, the intimate connection caused her to cry out with a feminine whimper and shake intensely with ecstasy.

With a deep grunt, he spurted out glittering light, coating her sorely stretched passage, causing her to grip unto him with intense spasms, sending her over the edge of overwhelming rapture into a state of unconsciousness.

In Washington, President Cain sat in his office at the White House. Casually glancing at his watch, he saw it would soon be evening, "About dinnertime," he mumbled to himself hungrily.

He raised his gazing eyes on one of the most beautiful woman in the world, the year before she won the Miss Universe pageant. She still appeared around eighteen years old with a youthful vitality sparkling from her chocolate brown eyes. Her eyes glistened brightly with life.

Her physical attributes were on the threshold of perfection. At six feet tall, she only weighed one hundred twenty pounds. Her muscles appeared firm and well developed with aesthetic lines at just the right places, her voluptuous breasts and sensuous thighs attesting to it. Her coal black hair shimmered in the light, accenting her delicious brown skin and full red lips.

The former beauty queen gazed back at Cain with hurt as she said with a trembling voice, "Cain, I can't believe you're asking me to do that. I thought we had an intimate bond, or at least something special together." Her upper lip quivered as a lone tear crept down her cheek. "I thought you loved me. How could you use me in such a disgusting way?"

Cain responded with pretended concern while saying, "Rosa, you know if there were any way out of this problem, I'd take it. There isn't. I trust you more than any other woman, and you're the only one who would stand a chance in seducing the pope. I know he'll not succumb to the charms of just any woman."

After giving her a few moments to think about it, he gave her his most flattering smile while saying, "Only an extraordinary woman such as yourself has the ability to seduce him. If you do, as soon as you complete your mission, I'll—"

Rosa interrupted with an angry cry, "But why do I have to sleep with him? Why can't I just get information from him? Why? You know I've only slept with you, so why are you sacrificing our love on the altar of politics? I thought I meant more to you than that!"

She wept profusely. Hurt racked her body with sobs, as she mumbled, "Why? Why? Why..."

Cain rose from his chair and walked over to her. He bent over and held her while saying soothingly, "It's okay, sweetie, hush now, it's okay. I love you, and I'll always love you. No one will ever destroy the special bond we share."

Kissing her tenderly on the cheek, he whispered in her ear in a conspiratorial way, "You know I don't trust the pope. I have information that he may be trying to have me assassinated. You don't want me killed, do you?"

"No," she moaned in between her sobs.

He cuddled her tenderly while saying, "Of course you don't, darling. I know you love me, and sleeping with him doesn't mean you're going to lose me. What you do with him will just be physical, but what we share goes a lot deeper than just physical boundaries."

Rosa continued weeping, with Cain cuddling her tenderly through it all.

When she stopped, Cain dried her beautiful eyes with his handkerchief while saying with pretentious empathy, "You'll not have to do it very long, darling, just long enough to find out if he's involved in a plan of getting me assassinated. After you sleep with him, we can use that to blackmail him. Popes aren't allowed to have sex, so we can get him impeached. Even if he isn't trying to have me killed, I'd rather have another pope, anyway. I don't like him, and as I told you earlier, I don't trust him. I have complete faith in you, sweetie. I know you can do this if you put your mind to it. So, will you help me get rid of the pope, and possibly even save my life in the process?"

She sighed with resignation, and then said, "All right, I'll do it, but you'll owe me big-time."

(PAST)

Months passed with Lemuel observing more and more Israelite men becoming seduced by Moabite women, becoming their husbands, and worshiping their gods.

One day Lemuel sat concerned in Moses' scantily clad tent. "Please tell me why you're so worried?" Moses asked meekly.

Lemuel replied with frustration, "I'm worried because I've been watching the Moabites infiltrate Israel's society with their women and gods. Every day there appears to be some of those pagan marriages, and I've even noticed a lot of tents turned into foreign temples to worship the Moabite gods. Because of these frequent occurrences, I've an ominous feeling Hebrews will soon cease to exist as a nation."

Moses nodded his head with agreement while saying, "I know, Lemuel. I've also watched some of them become seduced by the pagan women and their gods, but I feel completely helpless. How can I force them not to marry someone they want to? How can I force them to serve a God their hearts aren't into serving? I don't know what to do."

"There's only one thing you can do," Lemuel said with a sad resolution. "Give the death penalty to any Hebrew who has married a pagan woman, along with their pagan wives. Also burn to the ground all the foreign temples that flourish among us, and kill all their priests and followers. If you do this, it will send a clear message to the rest of the population that pagan marriages and idolatry will not be tolerated. You'll save the nation of Israel in the process."

"But that would mean killing thousands of people!" Moses exclaimed with anguish.

"There's no other way," Lemuel said adamantly. "We must halt this devious assimilation before it's too late!"

Moses rubbed his beard, contemplating what was said. Finally he agreed with a reluctant nod as he asked, "You're right, but where do we start?"

Lemuel had already formulated a plan before he spoke with Moses, so he knew the answer. With confidence he replied, "Phinehas is a zealous servant of God. He's also against pagan marriages. We'll have him take some loyal Hebrews who are renowned for their fierce fighting abilities and have them kill everyone who has become part of this treacherous sedition. I beg your permission to act immediately. Their pagan temples must also be destroyed."

After a few moments of intense inner conflict, Moses gave a reluctant order with a sad nod of his head. "Very well, do as you've proposed, only spare the lives of the men who have gotten their pagan wives to serve the True God. All the Hebrews are very precious to God since we're His chosen people."

Lemuel agreed with empathy as he rose up and walked out of the tent. "There will be a lot of killing soon," he said to himself with dread.

The late afternoon sky appeared cloudy with dark billows of smoke filling it with a gloomy overcast, hiding the desert sun, giving the day an ominous feeling.

Phinehas chose two hundred men and split them into ten groups of twenty. With twenty men behind him, he came upon the next tent of an idolatrous Hebrew and his pagan wife. He had already destroyed hundreds of tents since mid-morning.

Screams of terror had reverberated throughout the Israelite encampment most of the day. All ten squads of Phinehas's men had worked meticulously at destroying all forms of paganism out of their encampment.

"Come out! Come out, traitor of the True God and the Israelite nation!" Phinehas bellowed out with authority.

After no answer, he gave the order, and torches were thrown on the tent.

After the tent became ignited, reddish-blue flames licked greedily along the sides. Soon the terrified occupants came running out with screams of terror.

Phinehas's men apprehended the struggling occupants, a Hebrew with two Moabite wives.

Phinehas walked over to them and screamed fanatically for all to hear, "These people are an abomination to God, and to the whole nation of Israel! They are all worthy of death! This is what I do to such people!"

With a quick slash of his blood-soaked sword, he decapitated each one without mercy. Red blood spurted out from their headless necks, sending showers of red droplets down on those who stood close by.

"On to the next idolatrous tent!" Phinehas screamed with bloodcurdling enthusiasm, sending shivers running through the spines of his men, though they followed without hesitation, leaving the headless victims lying in their blood.

Cain watched with frustration from a nearby mountain as Phinehas and his men wreaked havoc on the Israelite encampment. With his perfect vision, he could see thousands of dead Israelites and Moabites lying out in the open beside their smoldering tents. He stood beside Jehu, the Moabite king.

"Some of the Hebrews are killing your people who reside among them. Can't you raise your army and attack them?" Cain asked with frustration.

Jehu shook his head dejectedly in a negative way, while sadness filled his eyes. He could not raise his army on such short notice. Even if he could, he knew they would not stand a chance against such formidable odds. He knew all the Israelite men of fighting age were well equipped with superior weapons and military accouterments.

Cain sighed with disappointment. He would have attacked the Hebrews with his own powerful army and won, but he knew intuitively such an action would weaken him, and leave him vulnerable to his enemies, and he knew he could not stand against them all in a weakened state. The only thing keeping him secure from his many enemies was his powerful army. He would not sacrifice his security just to overrun a nation of nomadic peoples, even if they were the chosen people of a God he despised.

Cain watched with anguish as his dreams of corrupting the Israelites became dreams of disillusionment. His devious plot dissolved away like ice under a fiery sun, as thousands of tents were consumed with flames. He watched with repugnance as Phinehas and his men killed the people he had counted on to corrupt the Hebrew men. He then vowed in his heart to destroy the nation of Israel, even if it took thousands of years to do it. The Hebrews became his enemy as much as God was his enemy.

"There's no point in watching the rest of this massacre," Cain uttered with disgust. "It's apparent your people aren't strong enough to assimilate them."

Jehu did not say a word, but with an indignant, haughty stare, he held himself erect with all the royal poise he could muster.

Cain spat on the ground with disgust as he walked away from his well-plotted plan. "Someday I'll destroy all the Israelite," he said with determination as rage seethed through his perfect veins.

Chapter 13

Before Pamela awoke from her unconscious state, she found herself standing in a vast empty place. She looked around and saw nothing but a bright red void. With shock, she wondered if she had died. She then heard a deep voice bellowing from above.

Looking up, her heart felt caught in her throat as she gazed on a bright red throne. It appeared radiant, as if made from a giant burning coal, with a being sitting on it who appeared to be made of thick light.

"Who do you think I am, Pamela?" the deep voice bellowed out the question again, shaking Pamela out of her mindless shock.

She said with trembling awe, "You are God."

Lucifer laughed hilariously. After the laughter subsided, he replied, "No, but someday I will be. Look closer, maybe you'll recognize me. I'm more glorified in my domain. My servants surround you. You just can't see them because of my bright glory and holiness. I'll back up some so you can see your surroundings more clearly."

She watched with astonishment as Lucifer zoomed back to a reasonable distance. He still sat on his throne, casting out red light like a large, twinkling red star in all its glory. She recognized Lucifer as the one sitting on the throne.

As she looked around with wonder, the fiery redness faded, only to be replaced with creatures materializing around her, so many they appeared to go on forever. For the ones she could see close, she noticed they all resembled Lucifer, though not quite as bright. They also featured another aspect, each creature consisted of their own unique color of different tints of yellow light. There were millions of different shades of yellow. She had no idea there were so many different hues of yellow.

All the fallen angels began singing a song about Lucifer's glory. The song sounded like the most beautiful heavy-metal music she had ever heard. She did not recognize the words, but it caused her to feel a deviant emotion of lustful pride.

The demons sang shrieking praises to Lucifer.

Throughout the song, her heart soared with egotistical gratification.

After the song ended, Lucifer bellowed out in pride, "What a wonderful song of praise to me."

She then said with conceit in her heart, "It was the most beautiful song I've ever heard."

Lucifer smiled with pleasure while saying, "Enough. We have more important things to focus on. I'm giving you this vision before you awake to remind you to keep your promise by convincing Lemuel not to kill Cain. I alerted Cain about a possible assassination attempt on his life the very day the pope recruited Lemuel, but I never told Cain who was involved. I don't want Cain or the pope killed.

"I want you to meet Cain tomorrow night at nine. He'll be at a Jerusalem hotel. I want you to discuss your secret alliance with him. I've ordered him not to harm you, so you'll be safe. Make sure no one knows of the secret alliance you'll have with him. As long as you keep it secret, he'll never harm you again.

"He'll also not harm Lemuel or the pope, though I know he'll attempt to ruin the pope's reputation if given the opportunity. Don't give him the opportunity. The pope's also an important part of my plan in obtaining the world's worship."

After he gave her the name, address, and room number of the Jerusalem hotel where Cain would be, everyone and everything vanished, only to be replaced with a black void all around.

She felt an awesome power hurl her upward until the void disappeared, only to be replaced with Earth's atmosphere. She appeared to float between the clouds and Earth. With curiosity she examined the Earth while she flew at high speed toward Jerusalem...

She awoke suddenly in bed at the suite the pope had rented for them. It was early morning, and with clarity she remembered every part of the vision and every detail she had shared sexually with Lucifer.

She felt love for Lemuel, and she did not want to betray him, but whenever she thought of the swaggering song sung by the fallen angels, and about the sexual pleasures Lucifer gave, her heart filled with vanity, and her loins trembled with an anticipation bordering on corruptness.

The day passed uneventfully for Pamela as she sat in the living room at the suite, with Lemuel and James sitting beside her. She had been trying to convince Lemuel not to kill Cain all day with little success, though she could tell her persistent arguments seemed to be wearing down his resolve. Her persistence became like a flooding river, slowly eroding away his determination to kill Cain.

When James decided to fix dinner, she continued with stubborn attrition to wear away Lemuel's resolve. Looking at him, she said convincingly, "You have to admit, Cain was considerate in not having us killed when he held us as prisoners."

Lemuel sighed with frustration. He could not understand why Pamela had reversed her decision in having Cain killed. The day before, she had wanted him killed more than anyone. Her daylong arguments caused him to become weary as he said, "Believe me, Pam, he has a devious reason for any kind act he may do. Cain's more evil than you could ever realize."

She squinted her eyes with pretended doubt while saying, "Maybe, or maybe he really wants to bridge the rift between you two. Maybe he really wants to be friends. Maybe he really doesn't have any other ulterior motives. Maybe he's not as evil as you think. I'm sure he's not the devil's son. Maybe he's really not evil, just stressed out a lot with all his presidential duties."

Lemuel felt flustered while saying, "Do you believe that, Pam? Remember the innocent couple who was killed? Remember him raping you? What's wrong with you? You've been a different person all day. Yesterday you wanted him killed."

She knew Lemuel was right, but she needed to maintain her deception if she were to convince Lemuel not to kill Cain. She controlled her hatred for Cain as she said with a large measure of truth, "Yes, I remember the innocent couple, and I remember the horrible way he raped me, and I'm still upset about it. I'm sorry. I didn't mean to upset you. I just want you to get out of this mess safely. I now feel a special bond for you. I've fallen in love with you, and I don't want to lose you. I know if you kill Cain, they'll find you somehow and kill you."

Lemuel's heart leaped with joy. It was the first time she had ever confessed her love, and her openness caused his love to grow even stronger for her. He replied back with hope in his heart, "I didn't know if you loved me, or if you just liked me. Now I understand why you've been acting so strangely today. Now that I know you love me, what do you propose I do? If I don't kill Cain, he'll continue searching for us, and someday he'll catch us."

She looked at him while whispering in a conspiratorial tone, "You could get in touch with him and tell him you've decided to be his ally."

Lemuel felt indignant as he said with determination, "You know

I can't do that, Pam. He's the devil's son! To join forces with him would be like joining forces with Lucifer! I'll not do that."

She pleaded with desperation, "Please, I'm afraid he'll kill us both if you don't. We're eyewitnesses to his horrendous crimes of murder, rape, and kidnapping." Her desperation combined with fear as she continued, "Please, Lemuel, lie to him and act like you'll be his ally. We can then work at getting him in trouble with planted evidence."

With resignation, he thought about her plan. He did not want to implement it because he could never remember telling an outright lie, though he had practiced subterfuge during different periods in his life. Maybe somehow he could formulate a plan where he could pretend to join Cain without telling an outright lie. He could not think of any at the moment, so he said candidly, "If there's a way where I can keep my integrity, yet still deceive Cain into believing I'm on his side, I'll do it. I'm sure I've never told an outright lie, and I don't think I know how. Give me time to think up something, and then we can proceed from there."

Pamela sighed with relief. She then said with gratefulness, "Thank God you finally see the logic of all my arguments."

Looking at her watch nervously, she saw the time drawing near to meet Cain. She then said urgently, "Oops, I forgot to tell you. I want to buy you a special gift. It's my way of reaffirming the love I have. Today's been special since it's the day I fell in love with you. I want to commemorate it with a special gift for you."

Lemuel felt surprised, so he said, "It's getting late, and James almost has dinner ready. Can't you wait until tomorrow? I know James will be disappointed if you don't eat his meal. You know he takes pride in cooking."

She stood up and said with determination, "No, tonight must be the night. Tomorrow's a day late. Tell James to save some leftovers. I'm sure it will still be good with how good he cooks. I'll be back in a few hours, so please try not to worry."

Lemuel said, "I'll be worried. You know Cain's searching for us, so you shouldn't be going out by yourself. Let me go with you."

She replied back with determination, "No. I don't want you to know what kind of gift I'm getting you! Just stay here, and I promise to wear a shawl over my face so no one will recognize me. I'll blend in since it's the custom for women in this part of the world to keep their faces covered in public."

Lemuel agreed with a reluctant nod of his head. Pamela reached in her purse and withdrew a shawl. She put it on while walking bravely toward the door. She felt very sore from the night before with Lucifer, and each step caused her to wince with pain, but she hid her pain with remarkable inner strength.

She opened the door and blew a kiss at Lemuel, while saying with affection, "I love you, and I'll be back soon, my love."

Lemuel looked anxiously at his watch as she walked out. He felt bad letting her go by herself, but he reluctantly conceded the facial shawl would keep her face hidden. He would give her a few hours. If she was not back by then, he would go looking for her whether she wanted him to or not.

Pamela became lucky and flagged down a taxi right away. The taxi driver recognized the address because he knew the streets of Jerusalem like he knew the back of his hand, so it did not take him long to get her there.

She soon stood by the door Lucifer had told her about in the vision. Taking a deep breath of courage, she knocked on the hotel door with fearful anxiety.

The door opened quickly, as if Cain had waited beside it. With a big smile he said, "Oh, what a pleasant surprise. I wasn't expecting you this early. I figured you wouldn't show up until the last minute."

She kept her hatred hidden while saying breathlessly, "I got lucky in getting a taxi fast, and the driver knew where to go. Let's finish this quickly. I've other things to do, and not much time to do them."

"Of course, please come in and we'll discuss our alliance. There's no use wasting time with a bunch of small talk," he said while opening the door wide.

She hobbled in on weak knees and internal soreness, though she hid the pain with a deceptive smile.

The small room disgusted her. It looked as if it had never been cleaned. The filthy floor and walls were overrun with disgusting roaches, and the mattress looked as if it were a hundred years old with repulsive yellow stains on it. It possessed no headboard, footboard, sheets, blankets, or pillows. The small room possessed no bathroom and reeked with smells of feces, urine, liquor, and unclean sex combined, culminating into a vulgar stench. She felt her stomach flip-flop as nausea overcame her, causing her to almost vomit.

After she walked in, he shut the door softly and turned around with an expression of regret on his face while saying, "I'm sorry I couldn't offer you a more hospitable surrounding, but Lucifer picked this place. I guess he wants to make sure our alliance is kept secret. After all, who would believe the president of the United States would frequent such a disgusting place? No one knows I'm here, and that's the way I want to keep it. Besides, we'll both leave this disgusting dump after our meeting's over."

He motioned toward the lice-contaminated bed while saying, "Would you like to sit? I'm afraid the bed's the only thing we can sit on, unless of course you'd rather sit on the floor."

Pamela looked at Cain with an incredulous expression while saying, "You have to be kidding. No thank you, I think I'd prefer to stand."

Cain said with a chuckle, "I was kidding. You couldn't get me to sit on this bed, or floor either, so let's get down to business. Have you convinced Lemuel to join me yet?"

The question caught her off guard, but she quickly regained her composure. She then said, "Not yet, but it shouldn't be much longer. He decided to join you, but he hasn't figured out how to tell you. He has little trust in you."

"Ah, I see," Cain said with self-assurance. "He's basically afraid to see me in person to tell me he wants to join me. His pride is standing in his way. We've been archrivals for more years than you could ever imagine. Well, I do have a certain amount of patience. I can wait a little while longer, but not much longer. Time is running out. You have one week. If you can't get him to change his mind by then, I'm coming to get him—and you. Understand?"

She nodded her head nervously.

He handed her a paper with his cell phone number, and said briskly, "This is my private number. Only a few people have it. Keep me updated every day on what you're doing, even if you feel like it's not important."

She took the paper and put it in her purse. She then said impatiently, "Okay, will do. I guess this meeting's over. I'll call you tomorrow as soon as I find a private place to do it in. Bye." Turning around, she proceeded to leave.

With a quick movement, he grabbed her by the shoulders and pinned her firmly against the filthy wall.

Pressing his body against hers, he whispered lustfully in her ear, "I loved getting in your tight pussycat! It felt so tight and stretched so snugly! I'm getting a huge erection just thinking about it."

His hands raised her black dress to her waist, then one had dropped down, rubbing over her panties with excitement.

She whimpered with a pain mixed with unwanted obscene excitement. She then pleaded, "Please, don't! Stop now! No!"

"Come on, darling, I'll go fast. We'll be done in five minutes!" he said while continuing to rub over her soreness, causing her to become inflamed as wetness seeped through her panties. Her wetness encouraged him as he said huskily, "Ummm, your pussycat's ready for me now."

She screamed words with a combination of hate and anger intermingling, "No! Stop now! I mean it, or I'll tell Lucifer you've hurt me, then we'll see what he'll do to you. I mean it, just continue and you'll see."

Cain knew the truth when he heard it, and though he wanted her badly, he knew the wrath he would face from Lucifer if he continued, so he reluctantly stopped. He let his arms drop limply, and with disappointment he said, "Okay, if you insist. I thought maybe you'd enjoy a quick one. After all, you enjoyed it a lot when we did it the last time."

She stared at him with flaring hatred while saying, "Don't flatter yourself! You injected me with some kind of sexual drug. I never want you to touch me again. I'll go along with you and be your spy for the sake of Lucifer, not for you. If you ever try to take advantage of me again, I swear I'll kill you! Even if I have to go against Lucifer."

He shook his head with a pretended sadness while saying, "You've hurt my feelings. I thought you liked it. Very well, we'll do it your way, but I warn you, if you betray me I'll make you my sex slave. I'll keep your pussycat filled good every day then. I'll pet it so often, I'll be the only thing on your mind!"

After gritting her teeth with anger, she said, "Even though I'm now on your side, don't think I'll ever forget what you did to me. Someday I'll make sure you pay for that. Until then, I'll stay your loyal spy."

He replied back with a tired sigh, "Fair enough. You may go now." She left with throbbing pain causing her to wince with each step.

(PAST)

"Your majesty, you have to listen to me! Now that you've become powerful, you must attack the kingdom of Babylon and destroy

it! If you don't, Cain's sure to destroy Israel eventually. Please, you have to listen..."

King David trusted his counselor's advice, but what Lemuel proposed was impossible. The God of his people only allowed them to possess a certain territory, and Babylon was not included. To become filled with greedy aspirations by encroaching on territory not ordained by God would mean certain disaster for Israel. David felt sure God would not allow him to do it, though he contemplated on it while Lemuel tried to convince him.

After giving it a lot of thought, David said with frustration, "I'm sorry, but I can't take that advice even though I want to. It's against God's wishes for us to have other lands beyond what has been promised. We would only be allowed to attack Babylon if they attacked us."

"By then it will be too late!" Lemuel exclaimed with frustration. "You don't know how Cain is, but I do. He may not conquer your kingdom in your lifetime, but he will someday. It's just a matter of time. Cain has been Israel's enemy for more years than you could possibly imagine."

"Are you saying that Cain will take away God's promise to me?" David asked with amusement in his eyes. "God has promised me rulership of Israel through my descendants forever, so who should I believe, you or God?"

"I also believe in your God," Lemuel asserted with desperation, "but as surely as I'm alive before you today, Cain will eventually destroy Israel if you don't destroy his kingdom first."

David said bravely, "Let him attack me first, then I'll destroy his kingdom with the help of my God."

David then shrugged his shoulders helplessly while saying, "I'm sure it would go against God's wishes if I attacked without provocation. It would mean certain defeat if I attacked then, and I refuse to go against His wishes." Breathing a sigh of relief, David finished the conversation, "Besides, I've enough faith to know God will continue with my genetic line forever as rulers of Israel. He told me that through His prophets, so I don't have to worry about Babylon or any other nation. I sure don't have to worry about any individual. Relax, Lemuel, everything will turn out okay. You worry too much."

He then patted Lemuel on the back while laughing with relief. The more he thought about it, the more certain he became that God would not sacrifice His people to Babylon, Cain, or any other entity.

"My lord, how could you ask me to do such a dastardly deed as that? I'm already sinning more than I should be by sleeping with you. My husband, Uriah, would have me killed if he knew I was," Bathsheba said with fear.

Cain held Bathsheba while uttering seductively, "I need you to do this for me. I love you so much, and you mean everything to me.

"You know I'll pay you a fortune if you succeed. Besides, your husband will know nothing about it. He'll never find out. He's at the city of Rabbah with General Joab right now. You have to do this for me because I fear King David will cause a major war with my nation if I don't have something to blackmail him with, and I know I'll have something with your help."

Bathsheba felt distressed while asking breathlessly, "Why? Why would he want to attack Babylon?" After no answer, she said indignantly, "I thought you loved me. I'd never have made love with you if I knew you were only using me."

Cain appeared lovesick while gazing into her eyes. After a moment of silence, he said deceitfully, "I do love you. I love you more than you'll ever know. If there were any other option, I'd take it. I have to do it this way for the sake of my nation. My informants have assured me King David plans on attacking my kingdom soon. Please, Bathsheba, please help me. If not for myself, at least for the sake of my kingdom."

She consented sadly with a nod, "Okay, I'll do it. Let me make sure I understand what you want again. You want me to take a nude bath on my roof tonight in order to seduce King David?"

"Yes!" Cain exclaimed excitedly. "King David is troubled with insomnia. Every night he complains of restlessly tossing back and forth on his bed because of the hot temperature. He usually cools off by walking on his roof. Since your home is right next to his, though a little lower, he'll be able to see you clearly if you surround yourself with lit candles."

She said with reluctance, "Okay, if he becomes tempted, I'll have sex with him, but you'll owe me big-time for this one, Cain."

Cain breathed a sigh of relief as he bent over and kissed her lustfully.

It was dark when King David strolled leisurely on his roof, cooling off so he could get some sleep. As he walked around, his peripheral vision caught sight of a falling star, so he gazed up into the sky and marveled upon God's handiwork. He gazed with marvel on the vast multitude of stars. Some were small, some were big, and some twinkled brightly. He decided he would write a psalm later about all the beauty he saw in the sky.

He then decided to walk over to the edge of his wall in order to gaze on his capital city. He loved observing the different sights in it, especially at night. It helped rid him of the stress he accumulated throughout the day. Since his palace was the highest building in the city, he possessed the best view of it.

As he proudly gazed down on the great city, he saw it bustling with a vast multitude of people going to and fro. Even at night his city stayed awake and active as he saw most of the houses and apartments well-lit with their oil lamps and candles. The large full moon cast a pale glow over the surroundings, adding to the artificial lights. As he continued gazing with curiosity on the citizens who scurried through the streets and alleys, like working ants on important missions, he looked toward his neighbor, falling right into Cain's trap.

David's heart fluttered with passion when his eyes fell on Bathsheba.

The nude woman bathed on her rooftop, surrounded by high brass candlesticks, with each candle burning brightly. Each candle appeared to flicker out a bright seductive flame of yellowish red and cast out erotic shadows around, showing her with red rose petals floating with enticing buoyancy around her nakedness. She appeared like the most enchanting woman he had ever laid eyes on.

Her voluptuous nakedness stirred a passion in David's loins more intensely than he had ever experienced before. He keenly felt the unhindered passion flow through his bloodstream; through his mind, heart, and loins. His body felt as if it ached all over with intense sexual desire. His face felt flushed as the sexual cravings filled the pit of his stomach.

Crying out with a loud voice, he ordered his bodyguard to fetch the beautiful naked woman he was gazing on.

Cain watched secretly from a distant rooftop with his perfect vision. He felt satisfaction when he watched Bathsheba being led into David's palace. He knew David had fallen into his trap, and he felt confident his plan would succeed.

Chapter 14

Joseph sat curious in his office.

Rosa, the former Miss Universe, sat quietly in front of him in the guest chair.

Some of his fingers tapped thoughtfully on a large desk, as he stared with wonder at her beauty. She appeared to shine with a rare beauty, which maximized his curiosity. It made no sense to him why she wanted to be his personal maid. He knew she could easily obtain a better position, especially with her credentials. Suspicion filled his mind as he continued staring at her boldly.

He finally asked her with a disarming smile, hiding his suspicious thoughts, "Why do you want to be a maid after winning the Miss Universe title? Don't you think you could do better than that?"

She smiled back with a charming smile and, licking her lips suggestively, said with a seductive purr, "Yes, being a maid is a common occupation, but you're the greatest man on Earth, so it would be an honor to become your maid."

Joseph smiled happily. He felt satisfied with her answer. With sexual desire piquing his interest, he replied back with deceptive modesty, "I'm really nothing important. May God have all the glory. You honor me more than I deserve, especially since you just want to be my personal maid when it's obvious you deserve a more prestigious position. If you really want to humble yourself to such a lowly position, I'm sure my personal butler can fit you in somewhere."

She agreed, nodding her head with excitement while saying, "Please allow me to be your humble servant, your holiness."

Joseph nodded back with approval, and with eagerness said, "You're hired. Go see my personal butler and tell him you're my new personal maid. He'll explain to you the rules, duties, hours, and everything else your job entails. He'll also show you to your quarters. You'll be living in the Vatican now. I look forward to having you work with me."

He then stood up and offered her his hand.

She stood up, bowed her head to kiss the large ring on his finger, while saying, "Thank you, your holiness."

After the kiss, she swished out of the room, causing her buttocks to oscillate sexually with each step, hoping he noticed her suggestive departure.

As he watched her leave, he became erect. He smiled with a blush as thoughts of sex filled his mind. He wanted to become an intimate part of her.

He finally regained control of his senses. Thinking with cold logic, he decided not to have sex with her until after her credentials were investigated meticulously. He did not get to where he was by being a foolish man. He would not sacrifice his future for sex, even if it was with a formal Miss Universe. He quickly erased her from his mind and concentrated on a more important issue.

Lemuel had been in Israel for over a week and was becoming a problem. He refused to cooperate with Joseph's secret service, even though the agent gave Lemuel a high-powered rifle, and a well-thought-out plan on how to kill Cain. Lemuel told the agent he would not implement the plan because he was formulating a better one.

Joseph worried Lemuel would not kill Cain, or even worse, would betray him.

Joseph had ordered his agent to kill Lemuel the day Cain was assassinated. He felt determined to keep his reputation clean. He would not become incriminated with assassinating anyone, especially someone as powerful as Cain. It would ruin his nano chip plot, which was already set in motion, and if Lucifer found out, perhaps his own life even. He knew Lucifer was not omnipresent, so he figured it was a chance worth taking.

The nano chips were being implanted in most people, and more quickly than he imagined. Soon he would program most people of the world to purchase what he commanded them to. Because of that power, he would become the richest man on earth, and afterward the most powerful one. He knew worldly wealth meant power. He would then arrange events catapulting him as the leader of the world. Then everything and everyone would belong to him. He licked his lips and trembled with anticipation as he thought of gaining absolute power.

The morning sunrays filtered through the motel room window, casting streams of bright light throughout the room, exposing miniature dust specks floating serenely by in the filtered rays of light.

Lemuel, still half-asleep, gazed over and saw the others still asleep in their own beds.

After he told the pope on the phone he felt unsure about killing Cain, Joseph went into a rage and promised not to send any more money until Lemuel assured him he would follow his plan in assassinating the president.

After the pope's outburst, Lemuel decided they would go into hiding. He still had not come up with a plan on how to deceive Cain into thinking he would be his ally, and he knew the pope would have them all killed if he refused to kill Cain, so he decided their best option was to go into hiding from everyone.

They had checked into their dilapidated hotel room soon after.

He wondered if they could remain hidden as he looked over at the window, at the dirty, moth-eaten white curtains. He dreaded getting up and stepping onto the darkly stained, flea-infested carpet. His body itched all over. He imagined thousands of fleas feasting hungrily on his itchy skin, causing him to grimace with distress from the prickly sensations. He did not know if he could take another night of it.

Looking over at Pamela, he observed that her eyes were open. "Hello, darling," he said romantically. "How's my woman this morning?"

"Itchy," she said with a grimace while scratching different parts of her body frantically, "and tired of this. When are we going to leave this flea trap? I don't think I can take another day."

"Hopefully today. I'm sure I'll figure out how to get my money wired without being traced back," he said encouragingly.

Watching her frantically scratch all over, he admonished her, "Please, Pam, stop. It only encourages them, and it'll draw blood at the rate you're scratching."

"I can't help it! It itches so badly!" After biting her lower lip with anguish, she asked, "How long will we have to stay hidden? Why can't you at least pretend to join Cain? He'll keep us safe."

He felt determined to refuse her request, so he said stubbornly, "I can't lie, and I don't know how to join him without lying. We'll have to stay hidden until we can figure it out."

By then James had woken up, scratching as frantically as Pamela. He said with his own frustration, "I don't mind staying hidden, but I'll not be able to take another night here. I'd rather sleep outside."

Suddenly they heard a quick rap on the door, causing them to gasp with fearful surprise.

Lemuel put his finger to his lips, signaling for them to be quiet. He stood up and walked to the door, ready to attack any intruder.

The knocking continued, becoming louder with each rap.

Finally a voice outside said, "I know you're there, Lemuel. It's very important you let me in if you want to escape the pope and the president."

"Who are you?" Lemuel asked with puzzlement.

"I'm on your side. You'll find out who I am when you open the door."

Lemuel opened the door and gasped with surprise. He stuttered as he said, "Y-Y-You're..."

The visitor interrupted Lemuel with a humble bow of his head. "Yes, I'm Kim Foo, the most notorious Chinese insurgent alive."

Lemuel recognized him from some pictures in the world news, and he knew he told the truth.

"How did you find me, or even know who I was?" he asked, bewildered.

Kim Foo smiled reassuringly as he said, "I have an extensive network of spies. I try to keep updated on most of the world leaders and what they're doing."

"Wow!" Pamela exclaimed with a surprised smile on her face.

"Yeah, wow," Lemuel stated with obvious worry. He then asked Kim Foo, "What do you want with us anyway?"

Kim Foo answered happily, "I'm here to rescue you all. I've found out Jesus wants you to help usher in His heavenly kingdom."

"I thought the Chinese were mostly Buddhist," Lemuel said with surprise.

"Do you really believe I'm Buddhist?" Kim Foo asked with hurt showing from his eyes. "Believe it or not, I'm a Christian. I don't advertise it to the press because it would hurt my political cause. Since most Chinese are Buddhist, if I want to win their hearts I must keep my religion out of it."

"Thank God you're a Christian," James said with a relieved smile on his face.

Lemuel asked Kim Foo hesitantly, "How-how do you plan on rescuing us?"

Kim Foo replied diplomatically, "Since I found you so easily, you know the pope will also find you. It's imperative I hide you all immediately. I've a safe house in Jerusalem where I can keep you all until we bring down these worldly governments. You'll help me usher in

Jesus' kingdom from there. It's actually a mansion. It's big, and it has plenty room for everyone. Please allow me to hide you all there. It will be a lot better and safer than this flea trap you're staying at now."

By then Pamela and James had walked up beside Lemuel, one on each side.

Pamela grasped Lemuel's hand and squeezed it with excitement, while James nodded with consent.

Lemuel could not refuse. All three were tired of the fleas, and they felt sure they could trust Kim Foo.

After glancing over at Pamela and James, Lemuel nodded with consent while saying, "Thank you. We accept your offer."

Kim Foo smiled with excitement. "Great! It will be wonderful to have guests, but we must leave now! The pope's spies could be here anytime! I have a vehicle we can leave in from here."

After loading up in Kim Foo's humble solar-powered vehicle, Kim Foo weaved gracefully through Jerusalem's treacherous traffic. "Driving is like a martial art," he explained humbly. "One must allow the inner force to take control and not one's own reflexes."

The estate where Kim Foo took them appeared glamorous. It stood with prestige in the upper-class district of Jerusalem. At the entrance a black iron security gate stood, with a twelve-foot redbrick wall surrounding the whole estate. Kim Foo opened the large double gate with an electronic gadget.

The grounds were patrolled by Chinese security men with sleek German police dogs. The grounds were decorated with a well-manicured lawn and exotic flower beds. It also possessed a built-in sprinkler system that kept the vegetation vibrant and fresh smelling.

The brick driveway stretched a considerable distance to a brick parking lot, which appeared large enough to hold twenty cars easily, with a large brick garage sitting behind it.

The two-story mansion was made from red bricks, including the porch and overhanging balcony. It boasted a post-Israeli architecture style, placing special emphasis on security.

The security inside the mansion consisted of electronic sensors placed on the doors and windows, all controlled by the same remote gadget Kim Foo possessed.

Since Lemuel and Pamela were not married, Kim Foo insisted they have their own bedrooms.

So began their new life in hiding.

In the Pacific Ocean, close to the coast of Oregon, a large oil freighter floated serenely upon pristine waters. A large killer whale nearby blew a spray of water from its waterspout. Sunrays beat down unmercifully on the waters, sending sparkles of light bouncing everywhere, causing the crew members to keep their eyelids squinted with protective grimaces.

Suddenly, a dark shadow crept its way across the surface of the ocean.

A crew member looked up into the sky and screamed with excitement, "Look! An eclipse!"

A shadow slowly covered the sun until only a thin bright line around it remained, leaving a bright yellow ring of light around a black ball of darkness.

"The sun has turned black!" a crew member exclaimed. Everyone gazed upon it in amazement.

Around that time, in the eastern part of America, darkness ruled.

In New York City, the moon shined full, sending its yellow pristine aura over the metropolitan area. Merchant ships continued coming to and fro, and thousands of colorful vehicles continued clogging up the municipality's roads. People continued walking the city sidewalks, using the city subways; shopping, eating, drinking, and other common activities they did every night. Commercial airlines continued flying unhindered over the millions of lights that lit up the city, looking like an endless nest of glowworms.

Soon the moon changed color to bloodred, changing the color of the city's landscape. Because of everyone's attention being diverted up to the luminous red moon, cars screeched their tires while crashing loudly with tearing sounds of metal, causing pandemonium to burst forth.

Still, everyone continued gazing up in amazement at the wonder of a brilliant red moon. Their mouths dropped open as the city crashed around them.

Around the world, the earth began shaking and increased in intensity until it shook violently, experiencing the most powerful earthquake the planet had ever experienced. People worldwide screamed in terror as the catastrophic upheaval shook down buildings small and large, and opened up many parts of the earth.

Large boulder-sized meteorites fell worldwide, demolishing ships and everything they hit. It became a worldwide hailstorm of large meteorites.

Giant tornadoes formed and ran rampant, as if they were conspiring with the other destructive parts of nature to destroy every living thing on earth.

Giant waves from the oceans crashed unmercifully against land, submerging all the coastal cities and islands.

Hundreds of millions of people worldwide embraced death in the first hour.

Even after the meteorites, earthquakes, tornadoes, and floods ceased, people continued dying because of the fires erupting. They burned with a consuming rage. Because of them, the death toll continued to rise long after the other calamities ended.

After the calamities hit, worldwide economies lay in shambles. Money became worthless. The earthly regimes managed to keep a mediocre amount of power in comparison to before the cataclysmic events, but most power was for appearance's sake only.

The local governments collapsed worldwide, and crime ran rampant. In the first month after the devastation, most people fought viciously against desperados and roving bands of scavengers, not even having time to bury their dead. Bodies lay everywhere, and decomposing stench filled the Earth.

Murder, rape, and looting were everyday occurrences.

The third month brought religious compounds sprouting up for protection. By then all the bodies left in the open had become bleached bones. The malodorous smell had dissipated along with the rotting flesh.

By the fifth month, the worldly governments had established a makeshift economy with their rebuilding projects and had regained some power.

(PAST)

Surreptitiously disguised as a common Babylonian soldier, Lemuel scrutinized the tragedy as he watched a long line of Jewish captives pass by. The deep sorrow in the inner depths of his heart could not be expressed with mere words. Disillusionment marred his countenance. His dream of caring for the last remnant of Israel appeared to stream away with the captives who passed him.

As Lemuel glared at Cain, who stood with ostentatious pride a short distance away, he knew Cain had gained a major victory. He had finally succeeded in bringing reproach on Israel and their God.

Lemuel gazed unblinkingly at the ground and shook his head with sad disappointment. "If only King David would've taken my advice, he could have defeated Cain, and all this could have been avoided."

Grim determination suddenly filled Lemuel's heart. Somehow, someway, he felt determined to rise up a nation against Babylon, thus Cain, and rescue the remaining remnant of the Israelite nation, even if it took him centuries of cunning plots to do it.

Cain stood proudly looking at Jerusalem, as a gentle breeze tousled his white hair. He felt proud in conquering Jerusalem, but he wished they would have given up without a fight since sieges were expensive. The obstinate city would not yield to his entreaties.

The reasons he had conquered Jerusalem were not just political. Even though Egypt had recently become his rival, thus making the Israelite territory more important to him strategically, the main reason he had conquered Jerusalem was because of the age-old grudge he nursed against the Hebrews.

Memories of an earlier Israel filled his mind as he continued observing the defeated Jews pass him by into captivity.

He mumbled to himself with disappointment, "If only King David would have listened to reason, perhaps all this wasted money could have been avoided. I could have destroyed Israel long ago with his help, at a lot cheaper cost."

Memories of King David permeated his mind in a flood. At the time Cain felt he could trust David to join him since David's grandmother had been a Moabite. Because of that he felt he could easily influence David into convincing most of the Israelites to marry the Moabites, thus becoming assimilated by them.

David had rejected Cain's proposal for the sake of Israel, and his God.

Since David refused to cooperate, Cain decided to cause adversity in David's royal household by corrupting it beyond repair. That was when he convinced Bathsheba to tempt David into committing adultery.

His plan took centuries to fully bear fruit and corrupt the whole nation of Israel, but since he was an immortal, he had plenty of time on his hands.

As he watched the last Jew proceed into captivity, he chuckled with satisfaction. The devious plan he implemented on King David, and thus the nation of Israel, finally bore the ultimate, tragic fruit for the ruined nation.

Suddenly one of Cain's Babylonian generals walked over to him and bowed while saying, "Your highness, all the Jews have been apprehended and are being forced to Babylon. What shall we do to this Great City of Jerusalem? Shall we fill it with inhabitants from another one of our conquered regions?"

Cain shook his head robustly while saying, "No. These Jews have caused nothing but trouble. Pull down their walls and burn their city. I'd kill all the Jewish scum and be rid of them if not for the money I'd lose. Instead, sell them all into perpetual slavery. I want them, and all their descendants, to be slaves forever, to ensure their tragedy will bring reproach on them and their God."

The general opened his mouth with astonishment. What Cain proposed was unheard of. Yes, they could destroy the city, and even enslave the whole Jewish nation, but not forever. The children of slaves were always free.

After coming to his senses, the general said with a fearful tone, "Your highness, we can destroy the city, and even enslave all the Jews, but we can't enslave their descendants! Even the Egyptians have stopped that antiquated practice. We can't—"

"Enough!" Cain interrupted with anger. "I rule Babylon, and because of me Babylon has become a superpower. If I wish to pass a law to enslave the Jewish nation forever, so be it! Who's powerful enough to stop me?"

The general agreed submissively as he said, "You're right, your highness. No one is as powerful as you. I'll have the legal scribes draw up the scroll for you to sign as soon as we return home."

Cain smiled smugly. At last his longstanding grudge against the Hebrews was being fulfilled, with the last tribe being carried away into perpetual slavery.

Chapter 15

Nine months after the climatic and social catastrophes, President Cain stood on stage at a stadium in Jerusalem, with television cameras set up all around to broadcast his speech worldwide.

Beside him stood Joseph, who appeared thirty years younger, and he felt it, too. The eternal youth serum Cain had given him worked quickly, and he felt young and vibrant again.

President Cain spoke to the enormous crowd while looking at Joseph, motioning toward him with open arms, "Ladies and gentlemen, behold the pope!"

The audience gasped loudly with surprise as Cain continued, "As you can see, he looks younger than he did nine months ago. Nine months ago he appeared at least upper middle age. His skin was losing its youthful elasticity, wrinkles were forming along his eyes and mouth, and his gray hair was turning white. Look at him now! His skin's supple like a young man's, with no wrinkles, and his hair's all black. He has grown young in a short amount of time!"

Before the crowd became too loud, Cain interrupted them with excitement in his tone. "Do you want to know how he became young? He became young because I gave him an eternal youth serum. I want to do the very same for all of you because I love humanity! I'll bring everyone who accepts it eternal youth, and I'll bring everyone eternal youth with security.

"In case you haven't been listening to the world news, I'll tell you what I've been doing in the last nine months after those horrific calamities killed millions of people, and left millions more homeless, I've been giving trillions of dollars to countries around the world in order to build homes for the homeless, provide food for the starving, and give medicine for the sick. I've been eradicating poverty, sickness, and death worldwide! I'm doing this because I love every single one of you. You're all a part of my family, the family of humanity!"

A loud cheer from the audience reverberated throughout the stadium, bringing tears of joy to most of the participants.

After the cheering subsided, Cain shouted with even more zeal,

"All I want in return is love! If you don't believe me, believe the pope!"

He then stepped back, motioning for Joseph to take center stage.

Joseph felt dazed. He still hated Cain, but he felt stupefied with all of the recent past events. He found it difficult to believe he was young again, but the evidence was irrefutable. Because of it, he would vouch for Cain until he figured out how to be rid of him. Until then, he would tell the people what Cain demanded him to tell.

He had made a wager with Cain before he administered the serum to him that if it worked he would tell the world anything Cain wanted him to tell. He made that wager with skepticism, not believing it would actually work. Cain would have to recognize him as the world leader if it did not work. Since it worked, Joseph felt no other option but to keep his end of the bargain.

With a deep breath of reluctance, he gathered up all the courage he could muster, and said loudly with a deceitful smile on his lips, "Ladies and gentlemen, as you can see, I really have grown younger. I'm living proof that President Cain is telling the truth! I also have more glorious news to tell you. It will send the world into a fervent state of worship. Last night I had a vision from God. He assured me that President Cain is the Messiah!"

The audience stood, quietly stunned. After they regained their senses, a loud cheer went up. It became so loud the stadium felt like it was shaking.

Joseph became caught up in the excitement of the audience as he screamed above them on the small microphone pinned to his robe, "Join me as we honor our Messiah with songs of praise."

He began singing songs of praises to Cain.

The audience followed his example, singing praises along with Joseph. Cain puffed out his chest with pride. Their songs made him feel invincible.

They felt like an electrical currents infusing him with robust power.

After an hour of devout songs of praises, he reluctantly raised his hands in the air and said, "Please stop, my children, for there's one greater than I. He deserves your worship even more. Someday I'll introduce you all to him. Until then, please continue to love me and one another, for that's the greatest act you could ever do. For everyone who has accepted me as the Messiah, I offer you eternal life in youthful bodies. All you have to do is to go to any Catholic priest, admit I'm the Messiah, and he'll administer the serum to you. Please don't postpone it for long because my invitation is only extended for a few more months. After the time limit is up, you'll lose your opportunity for gaining eternal life."

The audience rushed for the exits, wanting to obtain the serum quickly.

As Cain watched them leave, his cell phone rang. He wondered who was calling since only a few people knew his personal number. He removed the miniature microphone from his lapel, and with curiosity answered, "Hello?"

"Hello, Mr. President. This is Clarence, your Secret Service agent."

With frustration Cain said, "I know, Clarence. I can recognize your voice. For Christ's sake, I hired you. What do you want? I'm extremely busy, so make it fast."

Clarence replied back nervously, "I'm sorry to interrupt you, but I felt it extremely important that you know about this as soon as possible. I've information from the CIA. They know exactly where Lemuel and his two cohorts are. They're living in Jerusalem with a Chinese insurgent."

"Do you have their address?" Cain asked with excitement.

"Of course, Mr. President," Clarence said with certainty, giving Cain the address without hesitation.

After Clarence had finished giving him the address, Cain ordered with enthusiasm, "Keep me updated. If anything should change before I apprehend them, be sure to tell me immediately. Thank you for the information, Clarence. You were right in getting in touch with me."

After hanging up, Cain contemplated silently the actions he would take. He would apprehend Lemuel and Pamela, while winning mankind to his side by eliminating poverty, sickness, and death. He smiled with satisfaction as he thought about all the power he would soon possess. Of course he deserved it, or so he reasoned, since he would transform the whole world into a paradise, with peace, security, prosperity, and immortality for all who accepted him as their Savior.

Pamela sat with Lemuel, James, and Kim Foo, near the Weeping Wall in Jerusalem. They ate a delicious lunch in the bright afternoon sun, and washed it down with a refreshing bottle of Israeli wine.

The calamities did not hit Israel as hard as they did the other nations. Kim Foo did not lose his mansion.

Everything had worked out as planned, though their routine had become mundane.

They rose early every morning, disguised their appearances, then went to the Weeping Wall of Jerusalem to preach on the book of Revelation in the Bible. Through it they always implicated Joseph and Cain as being the False Prophet and the Antichrist. Since they rarely spoke to large crowds, but instead to families, friends, and small tour groups, they hardly ever attracted a lot of attention.

Pamela continued falling deeper in love with Lemuel with each passing day. Lucifer never made contact with her again after their last meeting, and she regretted the night she allowed him to have sex with her. She wished she would have said no, but she could not change the past. If anything good came out of it, it was the fact that she knew how hypnotically tempting Lucifer could be. She felt determination to never fall into his seductive trap again.

As she glanced over at Lemuel, she hoped the day passed fast because Lemuel had promised to take her out for a romantic dinner. Suddenly her cell phone rang piercingly, interrupting her romantic emotions.

She looked down at it and saw on her caller ID that Cain was calling her. After they went into hiding from the pope, she had ceased answering it whenever Cain called. This time the phone rang incessantly, causing her aggravation.

She looked down at it again and saw a text message streaming across the miniature screen: "I KNOW WHERE YOU'RE AT. IF YOU DON'T ANSWER, I'LL APPREHEND YOU ALL SOON."

The message ran across the screen over and over, causing her to feel feelings of panic and confusion. She did not know what to do.

Lemuel finally said with impatience, "Pam, I think you may want to answer that. It could be something important."

She knew she needed to take the call in private, so she said hurriedly, "I hope no one minds, but I'd like to take this in private."

Lemuel said with a chuckle, "I'm sure we understand, since everyone needs a little privacy occasionally. We need to get back to our prophetic teachings anyway."

She thanked him while standing up.

Walking a little distance away, she asked reluctantly, "Hello?"

"Hello, darling, your stud here!" Cain exclaimed with sarcasm.

She cringed while saying, "Believe me, I'm not your darling, and you're not my stud. In fact, I can't stand you!"

After her blunt statement, he asked angrily, "Why haven't you been answering my calls? Why haven't you convinced Lemuel to join me yet?"

Pamela felt dumbfounded. She did not know what to say.

"Answer me, damn you!" Cain screamed out in rage.

Pamela took a deep breath and lied as best she could. "Listen, Cain, I've been trying to get him to join you, but he's very proud. Just give me a little more time and I'll convince him."

"How much time have I given you already?" he asked with anger punctuating each word. "Let me remind you, over nine months! Guess what, your time just ran out! I now know where you're at, and I'm coming to apprehend you all. Then Lemuel can watch you get screwed again, though this time you may not enjoy it as much."

Pamela pleaded, "No! No, please don't! I love Lemuel more than you realize, and I don't want him hurt. I'll convince him, please give me—"

Cain interrupted with an unsympathetic tone, "I could care less if he gets hurt or not, but I could use him on my side. He could be an asset to me. Because of that, I'll give you three more days. Don't try to run, because I already have your hiding place under surveillance. You'll be followed no matter where you go. If you haven't changed his mind within three days, you can kiss your relationship with him good-bye. You'll be my woman then, and I'll make sure he watches whenever I ravish you!" He then laughed cruelly before hanging up.

She hung her head down with worry. Desperation tugged relentlessly at her heart, as despairing thoughts ran through her mind. Somehow she needed to convince Lemuel to give up his foolish aspiration of being God's prophet, and convince him to join Cain. She wanted him to leave with her, go back to America, and live a good life with a house, a white picket fence, and a dog. She wanted to live the American dream with him.

As she walked back over to the wall, Kim Foo was explaining to a family why the catastrophic events nine months earlier had happened.

Lemuel stood listening intently, while James took notes in a writing tablet. The family appeared mesmerized as Kim Foo explained it with zeal.

She walked directly over to Lemuel. Standing up on her tiptoes, she leaned toward him and whispered lovingly into his ear, "You're my man, and I'll always love you."

He looked down at her with a tender smile while asking, "Is

everything okay? Did you receive any information about your father?"

"No," she said tersely with disappointment, "it was just a friend."

"I'm sorry," he said with concern.

"It's okay," she said with a shrug. "At least I still have you."

He looked away with worry. It was a bad time for a romantic relationship. He still loved her, but he did not want to see her suffer, and he knew the days of suffering would soon be on them, perhaps even worse than in the days of Noah.

"Lemuel, are you okay?" she asked worriedly.

He looked back and said, "I'm sorry. I just have a lot on my mind."

"I understand," she said with empathy. "I've been under a lot of stress lately, too. Let's just think about something positive, like that fancy restaurant you'll be taking me to tonight."

"Sure, sure," he said with a smile, "but don't make too big a deal over it. We still have to wear our disguises since we'll be out in public. It's really not going to be that special since we have to keep such a low profile. We go in, quickly eat, and get out, okay?"

"No! It's not okay! Dates are a big deal!" she exclaimed with mocking indignation as she puckered out her lips with stubbornness.

He laughed, then bent over and kissed her puckered lips, bringing a smile of joy to their connected lips.

(PAST)

After Cain took the Jews into Babylonian captivity, Lemuel desperately befriended the Mede and Persian monarchs. Through cunning manipulations, he managed to make them allies by intermarrying their son and daughter. The royal marriage bore fruit with Cyrus the Great becoming their son.

Lemuel counseled Cyrus the Great from childhood, and after he became a man, he incited him to turn against his Babylonian overlord.

After over seventy years of the Jewish nation being in captivity, Lemuel was ready to make his move with Cyrus the Great. As Cyrus's counselor, Lemuel advised him to gather his large army at the city of Babylon.

Lemuel and Cyrus sat on their personal white Persian steeds. Their high-spirited horses neighed with irritation and swiped their heads contiguously close to each other, jockeying for control and dominance over the other. All the while the two men continued sitting calmly on their mounts, contemplating military plans on the banks of the river Euphrates, watching the great city of Babylon.

Cyrus the Great gazed over at Lemuel and said with concern, "Lemuel, are you sure my engineers will succeed in damming up the Euphrates River today?"

Lemuel spoke with confidence as he said, "Don't worry, your highness. If your engineers follow my instructions, the river's current will slow until it's just a little trickling stream. Of course, the river may not dry up completely, but it shouldn't be more than ankle-high by late nightfall, so your army should be able to cross easily enough by then."

With every passing hour, the river appeared to grow a little more shallow, with more and more dry land appearing around its banks. By night the river had shrunk with hardly any current left to carry it along.

"It's working! It's working!" Cyrus exclaimed excitedly.

"Yes," Lemuel said with a self-assured smile, "it's working, and soon we'll be able to walk right inside Babylon. They'll think we can't cross the river, so it'll be a complete surprise to them when we do. We'll be able to sneak into the city before they know we're there."

By late night, when most of the Babylonians were in bed, the river had slowed to a trickle and shrunk to the size of a small creek.

"Attack!" Cyrus ordered.

His large army moved forward, running on the depleted riverbed that ran through the city. Since there were no walls or gates there, they ran right into the unsuspecting city. With stealth, tens of thousands of Persians and Medes slipped into the sleeping city.

Lemuel and Cyrus rode in front of the large army.

The Babylonian guards were caught off guard. Some were on the parapet walls, unprepared for an improbable attack, while others were home since their shift was over.

Some of the captains of the Babylonian guards managed to muster together a force of five thousand troops and ordered them to attack the large invading army.

Lemuel and Cyrus watched their army surround the Babylonian guards and systematically kill them with arrows, swords, and spears. Soon all five thousand lay in a bloody heap.

"On to the palace!" Cyrus screamed out with anticipation...

Cain sat on his throne as he watched a troop of naked dancing women twirl around erotically.

Suddenly his chamber door flew open, and a messenger ran in screaming shrilly, "Your highness! The Persians and Medes have taken the city! At this moment they're marching toward the palace to apprehend you!"

Cain felt his heart drop to the pit of his stomach. His mouth opened wide with astonishment. After a moment of stunned silence, he asked angrily, "How did they get across the river and over the double parapet walls? No army could cross that river and knock the walls down, so how did they do it?"

Shivering with terror, the messenger said, "Your highness, they didn't cross the river, or knock the walls down, they dammed up the river and walked across on practically dry land, in part of the river that runs through the city."

"Lemuel!" Cain screamed with frustration. He knew only Lemuel could accomplish such an ingenious feat as that.

"Your highness, you must leave now!" the messenger exclaimed with anxious worry, "they'll soon be here to apprehend you."

Cain forced himself to control his anger as he ordered, "Have my personal bodyguards defend the palace entrance. It'll give me enough time to escape. Have all my treasures loaded on mules, then lead them through my secret tunnel. Do this quickly with help from my staff."

As everyone rushed around frantically, Cain ran to his personal chambers and retrieved his pet serpent. Without delay, he asked, "The enemy will soon be here. Where do I escape to?"

The serpent hissed with concern in its voice, "You'sss must'sss go'sss to'sss Macedonia'sss. You'sss must'sss befriend'sss the'sss monarch'sss there'sss, and'sss be'sss his'sss counselor'sss. With'sss your'sss wisdom'sss his'sss kingdom'sss will'sss become'sss the'sss most'sss powerful'sss one'sss in'sss the'sss world'sss, then'sss you'sss can'sss reclaim'sss what'sss you'sss lost'sss."

"How long will that take?" Cain asked with concern etched on his face. The serpent just flickered its tongue at him in a mocking way.

Cain gave up trying to get more information and tossed the serpent back in the cage. Carrying the cage, he ran toward the tunnel with vengeance engraved on his heart. He felt determined to pay Lemuel back, even if it took thousands of years...

Lemuel stood beside Cyrus, who sat on his throne in Babylon. Cyrus preserved Babylon because of its great defensive walls and rich economy. He decided to make it the capital of his own kingdom because everyone knew Babylon was the greatest city in the world. He would also reside in the city.

"Your highness," Lemuel pleaded, "Cain mistreated the Jews horribly. Please allow them to return to their homeland to rebuild their city of Jerusalem."

Cyrus smiled with benevolence emanating from his facial features. "How can I refuse you, Lemuel? If it wasn't for you, I never would have conquered Babylon in the first place."

Lemuel breathed a sigh of relief but felt worried as he said, "Have your spies found out where Cain has fled to?"

Cyrus's eyes brightened as he said with certainty, "As a matter of fact, they have. Cain has run like a little scared rabbit to an insignificant country called Macedonia. He has befriended the king there, and has become his counselor."

Cyrus chuckled while saying, "I almost feel sorry for him. Counselor's a big drop from being the leader of a superpower."

Nervousness filled Lemuel's voice as he said, "You mustn't feel sorry for a snake such as him. If you do, he'll bite you. In fact, I insist you invade Macedonia now and destroy it. If you don't, Cain will come back and destroy your kingdom with the aid of the Macedonians."

Cyrus stared at Lemuel with an incredulous look on his face. He then said, "Lemuel, you're getting a little carried away. The Greeks are an uncivilized people, and I've no desire to rule such savages. Let Cain die a bitter old man there with defeat always on his mind. That would be the best punishment."

"But you don't understand," Lemuel pleaded with frustration, "Cain will never die unless someone kills him."

Cyrus burst out laughing. After his laughter subsided, he said with mirth in his voice, "Lemuel, I think the sun has gotten to your head today. Everyone dies, it's as natural as being born."

Lemuel sagged his shoulders in defeat. He could not tell Cyrus about the immortals who lived before the flood, with Cain and him being the last to survive. It was a secret he feared to tell anyone. He knew Cain would someday be back if he did not destroy him first. His only hope was time. He would also be counselor to Cyrus's descendants, and perhaps he could get one of them to invade Greece before it was too late.

Chapter 16

Cain sat in his office at the White House with Clarence. Ever since Lemuel and his cohorts had been found, Cain stayed in a perpetual good mood.

Because of Cain's continuous good mood, Clarence felt comfortable enough to address him on a first-name basis. "Cain, people are becoming suspicious. They're wondering what happened to the senators. They've seemed to have vanished off the face of the Earth."

Cain appeared slightly amused as he asked, "What do *you* think happened?"

Clarence laughed as he said, "I think you killed the stuffy old bastards."

Cain grinned proudly as he exclaimed, "You'll never know!" With a chilling undertone he added, "No one will ever know."

Clarence shrugged his shoulders as he said, "I really don't care, but what do I tell the investigators who do care? They'll eventually question me, too."

Cain gazed at him with puzzlement while saying, "You have to be kidding. I don't know what you should tell them, since you don't know what happened." He then added jokingly, "I know, you can tell them God took them in the Rapture."

After a short pause, he continued in a more serious tone, "I'll keep you away from the investigators by sending you to Jerusalem. You can keep an eye on Lemuel and his cohorts since we know where they're at. If they don't join me, make sure everything goes smoothly when we apprehend them."

Clarence objected strenuously by saying, "We already have some Jerusalem operatives following them everywhere. Why can't they just do it? Besides, I can protect you better if I'm near you."

Cain stared sternly at him while saying, "Are you trying to disobey me? Believe me, I know what I'm doing. I'd feel more secure if you also watched them. You do really well in the subversive arts, and so you are the perfect candidate. If they do join me, you can help them elevate my status even more."

Clarence nodded reluctantly as he said, "Okay, if you insist. I'll go but I want you to know I'm not going to enjoy it."

Cain replied back angrily, "I never asked you to enjoy it. Just do it."

Suddenly the phone rang.

As usual, Cain let it ring for a minute in order to exert his power. Clarence could never understand why he did that, and it agitated him.

Cain finally picked it up casually and said, "Hello?"

The voice on the other end sounded excited. "Mr. President, this is Red Dragon, your operative in China. I just wanted to alert you that something major is about to happen. It appears that a major Chinese force is mobilizing on the Chinese border. Rumor has it they're afraid America is trying to take over the Middle East in order to gain control over the vast oil reserves."

"So what if we are? I'm not bothering them."

Red Dragon tried to explain with insight as he said, "China's a major industrialized nation, and they need a lot of oil for their industries. Rumor has it they're determined to gain control of the Middle East before you do. They're mobilizing forces of over one hundred million in order to completely overrun the Middle East with their superior numbers. The only way to destroy such large forces is with nuclear weapons. Of course, China has a lot of nuclear weapons also. A nuclear war with them would mean the end of this world."

"We can't allow nuclear weapons to be used," Cain said with determination, "since it would destroy the Earth."

"I agree, Mr. President, but how can we stop them if they invade?" Red Dragon asked with exasperation spilling from his voice.

"You let me worry about that," Cain said with a calm, reassuring voice. "You just keep your eyes and ears open. Let me know when they attack."

"Yes, Mr. President, I'll do that. You can rely on me," Red Dragon said encouragingly.

Cain hung up as he looked at Clarence. "It looks like we'll both be going to Jerusalem, Clarence."

Clarence looked at him with a puzzled expression. What could have brought that on? It must have been a rather unpleasant call, he thought with hidden glee. He felt delighted he would not have to go to Jerusalem alone. Maybe he could get Cain to do some partying like they used to do.

"You'll have to leave now, Clarence. I need to talk to the pope in private," Cain said with a worried expression on his face.

Since Cain was going with him to Jerusalem, Clarence felt eager to leave soon. With that in mind, he said, "Okay, Cain. I'll go pack my bags since we'll be leaving for Jerusalem tonight, right?"

Cain agreed with a nod and a thoughtful expression on his face.

After Clarence left, Cain reached over and turned his video-cam on, then pressed in the private number of the pope. After a few moments of static, the screen came into focus with the image of Joseph looking at him with a curious expression on his face.

"How may I help you, Mr. President?" Joseph asked with curiosity.

Cain hid his hatred with a pleasant smile. "Joseph, I know you tried to turn the Senate against me, but I forgive you. Just don't do it again."

"I have no idea what you're talking about, but I do agree we should continue working together and not against each other," Joseph said.

Cain continued to smile deceitfully as he said, "To show my trust, I've decided to share with you a top secret. I found out today it appears China is amassing major forces at its borders in order to invade the Middle East."

Joseph's face became deathly pale, which brought an even bigger smile to Cain's face.

"How do you know?" Joseph asked.

"I have my sources," Cain said with pride. "The main thing for you is to influence the world against this invasion if it does happen. I know you have a lot of influence with the other religious leaders, and they could get the people of the world to stand up against this invasion."

Joseph nodded with agreement as he said, "Of course, you're right. I'll get right on it. I'll call you back soon. Good-bye, Mr. President."

His image was quickly replaced with irritating pixel static.

Cain chuckled with malice. He hoped Joseph would literally worry to death.

He leaned back in his chair and held his hands on his head to think. He needed to recollect his thoughts. China had become a powder keg on a short fuse, and he needed to come up with a plan to avert the possible catastrophe. He hoped the Chinese president would not carry out an invasion of the Middle East, but he did not want to underestimate him. While thinking about it, the answer soon became obvious. He would have to dissuade the Chinese leader over his video-cam.

After dialing the number, he knew Ting would take his time in answering, so he ignored the static on the screen while thinking of the different approaches he could take concerning him.

After an hour, President Ting's solemn image appeared on screen. "What do you want, Cain?" he asked with impatience.

"Good question," Cain said with a serious expression, "but before I answer your question, I want you to answer mine. What are you doing?"

"I've no idea what you're talking about," Ting said with a shrug.

"Oh, but I know what I'm talking about," Cain said angrily. "I know you're amassing large military forces on your border."

Ting smirked at Cain in a sinister way as he said, "I gave you many months to withdraw your troops from Syria. You never did it, so time's up!"

"Please don't do this," Cain pleaded. "Let's work this out like rational human beings. I don't think our world can handle a major war."

Ting stared at him with an accusing glare as he said, "Too bad! You should have thought about that when I told you to withdraw from Syria. There's nothing more to talk about. If your forces aren't out of Syria by the time I get there, I'll have them all killed."

Cain decided it was time for his other dissuasive argument. "I warn you, President Ting, you'll never beat America in a war. Yes, you have superior numbers, but our technology surpasses yours. We'll decimate your armies like a terminator killing hordes of yellow ants."

Ting laughed at his caricature, bringing an angry flush to Cain's face.

After Ting's laughter subsided, he said threateningly, "We've our own exterminators who specialize in killing red, white, and blue maggots!"

Cain's screen immediately lost Ting's image, replaced by static.

"Damn!" Cain swore in frustration as he slapped his hand against the desk. He would have no other option but to destroy China. He hoped his father would help him, otherwise there was a possibility China would conquer the Middle East.

Joseph sat at his desk, stunned at what Cain told him concerning China. It put a major chink in his plan of gaining control of the world. He looked at his video-cam, then tapped in Clarence's number.

"What took you so long?" a worried Clarence asked.

"I've been trying to figure out how to get out of this China mess. Did you know about China's plans to invade the Middle East?" Joseph asked suspiciously.

Clarence exclaimed with a horrified expression, "You have to be joking! How would I've known? I'm just the president's Secret Service agent."

"I wish it was a big joke," Joseph said seriously, "but it's not. Since it's not a joke, I'm going to need your help more than ever."

Clarence nodded his head with understanding as he said, "Of course, your holiness. I understand, and I'll help you as much as I can. After all, I'm an American, too."

Joseph breathed a sigh of relief. "I'm glad to hear that, Clarence. It's good knowing you're on my side. By the way, did the president ever confess to killing those missing senators yet?"

Clarence replied back with disappointment, "No, he hasn't. He did insinuate he might have had them killed, but he made it clear he'll never admit it."

"That's too bad. I was hoping we could have him implicated," Joseph said with his own disappointment.

Clarence then said with dread, "Cain and I are traveling to Israel tonight, and I don't know how long we're going to be there. He wants me to spy on Lemuel and his cohorts, and if Lemuel joins us to train him in the art of subversion, but now that I know China's invading the Middle East, that's the last place I want to be."

"I understand," Joseph said sympathetically, "but that may be the best place for you now. You can keep me updated on the president's moves there. Maybe a stray bullet will solve both our problems and kill the bastard. You do know if some unfortunate mishap overtakes Cain, I'll use all the power I have in making you the next president."

Clarence said wistfully, "I've never given it much thought. I don't think it'll ever happen, but I think it would be a great honor to be the next president of the United States."

Joseph replied back with encouragement, "I hope it happens, but enough of that. So Cain is still trying to get Lemuel on his side?"

Clarence nodded with a dubious grunt before saying, "Yeah. I don't think he'll succeed. Since he's still on the run, he has no idea Cain knows where he lives at now. Pam knows, but she hasn't told him yet."

"Interesting," Joseph said with fascination.

"Maybe we'll still be able to get Lemuel on our side."

"Oh, it's possible," Clarence said with hope, "and probably his girlfriend, too! I know both of them hate Cain."

"I want you to keep me updated on Lemuel's activities also," Joseph said with a tired yawn. "Enough intrigue for one day, Clarence. I'm tired, and I need to get some rest. I'll go for now. Keep in touch."

"I'll keep you updated on everything, your holiness. I'll let you get some rest now," Clarence said, smiling before disconnecting.

Joseph left his video-cam on. After the image of Clarence vanished, he tapped in the number of his head steward.

His head steward's image immediately came into view. "How may I help you, your holiness?" he asked respectfully.

"Please send up Rosa. I need my quarters cleaned again," Joseph said.

"Right away, your holiness," the steward said with obedience.

Joseph had checked her background thoroughly, and he could find nothing that would hurt him. After the investigation, he engaged in oral sex with her, so the only thing she kept clean was his manhood. Because of their intimate relationship, Joseph trusted her implicitly, even trusting her with top secret information concerning his future plans of ruling the world.

Lemuel and Pamela sat together in a Jerusalem restaurant. They often went out together in their disguise. It helped kill the boredom of the lonely mansion they stayed at.

The sunshine was bright, with puffy white clouds moving peacefully over their outdoor dining area.

"It's such a beautiful day!" Pamela exclaimed with happiness.

Lemuel blushed with embarrassment as he said, "Please, Pam, not so loud. Remember, even though we're in disguise, we still don't need to draw attention."

"Oh, Lemuel, there's hardly anyone here," she said while looking around the area, and only seeing one table with a couple of men sitting at it.

"I'm sorry, Pam," he said nervously while looking at the only occupied table, "it's just not my day. I think we're being followed. I'm almost certain I saw Cain's man following me. You remember him, I think his name was Clarence. He's the one who helped kidnap us. I'm sure I saw his face briefly several times today in the crowd."

"Oh, honey, please don't ruin our dinner. Don't worry anymore.

Just enjoy the day because I've a special treat for you soon," she said shyly.

He perked up his eyebrows while saying huskily, "Hmm, sounds good. I can hardly wait."

She licked her lips, and with a seductive smile she said, "I love you, and I want to make you the happiest man on earth."

He looked at her with contentment while saying, "You have all my love." A lone tear of happiness slowly rolled down his cheek.

A baker stepped out into the outdoor dining area and gazed around, searching. He caught sight of them and pushed the cart next to their table.

Lemuel secretly waved him away.

With a curt bow, the baker left them to their privacy.

"Why's he leaving?" Pam asked with confusion. "I told him before we even sat down I wanted him to sing us a romantic song along with the cake."

"Don't worry about it, Pam, he's probably really busy. You can sing me a romantic song tonight when we cuddle," he said with twinkling eyes.

Their faces flushed red, and both laughed with embarrassment.

After the laughter subsided, they dug into the German chocolate cake.

After they became full, they stuck their fingers in the brown icing and smeared it over each other's faces, laughing with hilarious outbursts.

As their faces became covered with chocolate icing, their shrieks of joy filled the dining establishment.

The manager then appeared by their sides.

"I'm sorry to disturb your jubilation, but I must ask you to stop laughing so loud since it's disturbing our other customers. Your laughter has become so loud it has carried all the way into our kitchen area."

They stopped laughing, though they could not hold back their uncontrollable giggles. They found it hilarious that their faces were covered with chocolate.

After gaining control, Lemuel said sincerely, "Please accept my apology for any trouble we may have caused, and we'll leave now. I'll make sure to leave an extra tip for you. Before we go, we'll use your restroom to wash our faces. Okay?"

The manager nodded with reluctance, then left angrily, causing them to giggle like two adolescents.

After a few moments of giggles, Lemuel said happily, "Let's go wash our faces off before he calls the police on us. We can go home so I can give you a sensuous massage."

She nodded while saying with a giggle, "Sounds good, sweet face!"

(PAST)

In the palace at Babylon, Alexander the Great sat with his generals and other staff members behind a large wooden table made for at least fifty people.

Alexander raised his goblet of fine Babylonian wine and exclaimed boastfully, "Cheers!"

As all his generals raised their goblets, Aristotle, one of his counselors, asked with reserved caution, "Cheers to what, Alexander?"

Alexander looked at Aristotle with a surprised glare as he said, "Cheers to what? Have you lost your mind? We've just defeated the Persian Empire. We're free of all Persian influence now. I have absolute power."

He then hit his goblet aggressively against Aristotle's with a loud clang.

Aristotle just wanted to go back to Macedonia. He did not like foreigners or their barbaric ways. The only reason he had come was because Alexander pleaded with him to, so he reluctantly decided to go, neglecting his school of philosophy in the process.

Alexander said with a twinkling gleam in his eyes, "I have a special treat for you today."

Aristotle raised his eyebrows while uttering with surprise, "Oh?"

Alexander answered back boastfully, "Yes, oh! My counselor, Cain, wanted me to kill the Persian monarch, so I did. He also wanted me to kill all the Persian government officials. I killed them all save one, a man called Lemuel. I found that man fascinating with all the wisdom he has. He may be as wise as you. Anyway, I spared his life. I may even hire him as my own personal counselor, if for nothing else, just to show Cain I can have a lot of good counselors. Cain thinks he's too smart for his own robe sometimes."

Alexander then clapped his hands once while screaming, "Bring them in."

The banquet hall door opened immediately. Lemuel and the late emperor's beautiful daughter walked in with two Greek guards on each side of them, guarding them diligently.

Cain walked behind them with an evil gleam in his eyes, as he stared at Lemuel with pure hatred.

Alexander ordered the men who sat close to find other places to sit, then patted a chair with his hand, motioning for the woman to sit beside him.

Lemuel sat on the other side of Alexander, with Cain sitting beside Lemuel. Two guards stood at attention behind each prisoner.

Alexander gazed over at Lemuel as he said, "I've heard you're a very wise counselor, so I've decided to offer you a proposition. I think you're smart enough to see who's the boss now, so I don't think you'd betray me. I'm willing to make you my own personal counselor. Do you accept?"

Before Lemuel could answer, Cain interrupted with jealousy, "He'd betray you! He's more treacherous than you know!"

"Shut up, Cain," Alexander ordered, "because if I'd been your enemy, I'd have been treacherous, too." He then laughed, causing most of his staff to laugh along.

After Alexander stopped abruptly, he said with a serious expression, "I don't judge any man on just hearsay."

Looking back at Lemuel, he asked, "I'm waiting. Do you want to be my personal counselor or not?"

Lemuel mumbled with uncertainty, "I'm not sure right now. I'll have to think about it."

Alexander raised his voice. "What? I didn't hear you. Speak up so everyone can hear."

Lemuel swallowed his pride and repeated what he had said in a louder voice. Alexander felt disappointed, but he respected Lemuel's honesty.

"At least you're honest and obedient. I like those traits in my hired help."

Cain cruelly stomped on Lemuel's foot while staring straight ahead, pretending he did nothing.

With extreme pain, Lemuel jerked his foot away, as he kept his mouth shut with self-control.

Alexander looked at Lemuel curiously as he said, "Are you okay? I've noticed you jerked for some reason."

"I'm fine, Alexander. I think a dirty rat just ran across my foot is all," Lemuel said with anger as he stared at Cain, who looked back with

a smirk.

Alexander took a deep breath of air as he regained his composure. He hated secrets, and he knew Lemuel and Cain shared secrets he knew nothing about.

Alexander then said with a quirky smile, "I hate rats, too. In order to get the rats out of our mind, I propose we eat dinner. My finest chef has it prepared." He then clapped his hands together loudly three times while shouting, "Bring the feast in immediately!"

The banquet door opened with a line of chefs carrying covered silver platters. They walked in and placed the platters on the long table, lifting off the silver covers and letting the aromatic steam escape, filling the whole room with delicious scents as the colorful food was displayed to everyone.

They left with waiters carrying in plates, bowls, silverware, and other eating accessories. They gave everyone everything they needed to eat with. They then filled all their goblets with fine wine.

Afterward, they stood back at attention, prepared to serve whenever needed. The aroma of the food permeated the whole room with sumptuous aromas, causing everyone's mouths to salivate with hunger.

Alexander smiled with contentment while saying proudly, "I told you I had my best chef prepare this feast. Okay, everyone, let's eat!"

Lemuel sat in his locked room at the Babylonian palace. Alexander had decided to keep him prisoner until he joined him.

The room held only a bed, a dresser, a desk, a chair, and a toilet. It appeared to be an ordinary room, but the walls were made of stone, so there was no escaping.

Two guards suddenly opened the door, surprising Lemuel with their quick intrusion.

One guard ordered uncompromisingly, "Follow me."

Lemuel followed him down a multitude of stone corridors, as the other guard followed behind.

Eventually they came to a personal suite. It had a guard standing by the door.

That guard opened the door and led him past other rooms until they came to the bedroom door of the suite.

The guard knocked on that door with quick raps.

Cain laughed happily inside the bedroom while saying, "Send him in."

The guard opened the door and motioned Lemuel in. He followed Lemuel in and stood at attention behind him.

Lemuel stood frozen in shock at the scene he looked upon.

Cain lay without covers on sheets of silk in between the princess's legs. Her ankles were chained to the two lower corner posts of the bed, causing her legs to spread widely. Her wrists were chained to the two upper corner posts of the bed.

Looking at Lemuel lewdly, he said as sweat streaked down his body, "I've just started. Alexander has already taken her virginity, so he said it was alright if I pleasure her some, too. I got her nice and hot, so you can enjoy watching me ravish her. I've chained her up just to make sure she doesn't resist, though she may not enjoy you watching since you two were such good friends. Enjoy."

Lemuel wanted to kill Cain so much he could taste the hatred he held for him. He gritted his teeth together and closed his eyes with anguish as Cain captivated his confused friend with seducing repetitions, stoking her blaze even higher...

"You'll pay for this someday, bastard!" Lemuel mumbled to himself as rage seethed in his heart.

Chapter 17

Cain and Clarence sat disguised in a Jerusalem restaurant so no one could recognize them.

Clarence was watching the television when he opened his mouth in surprise. "China has just invaded Afghanistan!" he exclaimed with excited terror.

Cain yawned with disinterest, as if Clarence had just told him mundane news. "Don't worry about it, Clarence. It's really none of your concern."

"None of my concern?" Clarence asked shrilly.

"That's right, none of your concern," Cain said with anger rising in his voice. "Your concern should be watching Lemuel. Now tell me, did he preach against me today?"

Clarence sighed with frustration as he said, "Yes, he did. He does so every day. He stopped before noon today, though."

"I guess I'll have to let him know his girlfriend's my ally now," Cain mumbled to himself.

He had recorded his secret meeting with Pamela, as well as all the calls they'd shared. Perhaps those secret calls would convince Lemuel to join him.

With authority he said, "Fine, Clarence. I guess it's time to give Lemuel the gift of facts. I have a package I want you to deliver to him today. Make sure the bastard receives it."

Clarence accepted the package with concern. Looking at Cain, he asked with curiosity, "What are you going to do about the China problem?"

Cain stared back at Clarence with anger radiating from his expression. "Don't worry about that. Just make sure Lemuel gets that package, understand?"

"Of course, Mr. President," Clarence said nervously.

"Okay, go now," Cain said with an impatient wave of his hand. He then bent over to closely examine an important Chinese document.

Clarence walked out the door onto a busy Jerusalem street. He did not know why Cain had acted so secretive toward him. He wondered if he had found out about him being a spy for Joseph. If Cain had found out, he was a walking dead man. With worry, he jerked his cell phone out and dialed the number of the pope.

"Yes?" Joseph answered with curiosity.

"Hello, your holiness," Clarence said with a sigh of relief. "It's me, Clarence. I just wanted to tell you, China has invaded Afghanistan and Cain doesn't even seem to care."

"I know, Clarence. I've just seen it on television," Joseph said with worry.

With a hopeful expectation, Joseph asked, "Is there anything else important you can share with me besides Cain's apathy?"

Clarence blurted out with fear, "No, your holiness, but I think Cain knows I'm spying on him. He's become very secretive. He refuses to tell me anything of importance. I'm afraid he's going to have me killed! I'm afraid he's—"

Joseph interrupted, "Calm down, Clarence. I'll protect you if that's true. I have men watching you and the president. They'll protect you if they see you're in any kind of danger, so just calm down and don't panic. I'll ask you one more time, is there any other kind of information you can give me?"

"That's the problem," Clarence said with frustration. "He hasn't been telling me any more of his secrets."

"Where are you going now?" Joseph asked.

"Oh, he just ordered me to deliver a package in person to that idiot Lemuel," Clarence said with irritation.

"Oh?" Joseph said thoughtfully. After a few seconds of thinking deeply, he said, "Make sure you let my agent in Jerusalem make copies of it before you deliver it. He'll get in touch with you in an hour or so. Good-bye for now."

He then disconnected, and after making a quick call to his agent in Jerusalem, he lay back in bed. He assumed Clarence did not have long to live. He did not like him, but he still wanted him alive long enough to bring about the downfall of Cain.

He felt worried over the China problem. Distributing millions of religious propaganda fliers to them with cargo planes did not pacify them; it only kept them warm since they had made gigantic bonfires with them.

Sending hundreds of Chinese protestors did not pacify them, either, for the Chinese government just incarcerated them.

China was becoming a thorn to his future plans, and it had to be dealt with soon.

After an afternoon of shopping, Lemuel sighed with satisfaction as he drove home. "I hope you enjoyed yourself today," he said.

With a smile, Pamela said, "I enjoyed it, but it's not over yet. We have one more thing to do at home."

Naively he said, "Oh, I wonder what that could be."

"You'll find out soon enough, big boy," she promised with a seductive lick to her lips.

They then came in sight of the estate where they lived. At the gate stood Clarence. They did not recognize him because he was in disguise, and the day had become dusky with the coming evening.

Pamela did not like surprises. She felt leery of strangers. "Shouldn't we turn around?" she asked with a worried tone.

"No, Pam, no one can harm us now," Lemuel said with confidence. "After all, we have God on our side. God will make sure we complete our mission, so I'll just drive up and see what he wants."

Soon they were beside Clarence.

Lemuel rolled down his window and asked with an inquisitive expression, "How may I help you?"

"I'm just an errand boy delivering a special package from Cain," he said with an unfriendly smirk.

"I don't want it!" Lemuel exclaimed adamantly. Cain had finally found him, and the knowledge brought fear to his heart. He did not fear for his own safety, but for the safety of Pamela. He knew he loved her more than any of his past lovers, and he knew how treacherous Cain could be with women.

"I'm afraid I have to give it to you, anyway. Otherwise Cain will have my head. I really don't care what you do with it, but I'd advise you to look at it. Perhaps you can get some useful information from it."

Lemuel's curiosity became aroused. Perhaps the stranger was right. Perhaps he could glean some useful information from it. He needed to make sure it wasn't a bomb before opening it, but that would be no problem since Kim Foo had the necessary equipment to determine whether it was an explosive. With nervousness, he said, "Okay, give the package to me."

Clarence handed it over with relief. It was a big load off his shoulders. He waved good-bye and walked away.

Lemuel looked over at Pamela, who appeared fidgety and

nervous. "What's wrong, honey? Are you okay?" he asked with concern.

She replied back with disgust, "I'm fine. You know I just can't stand Cain. Accepting anything from him makes my stomach turn." She then added with a pleading tone, "Please, honey, let's just throw that package away."

Lemuel felt empathy because he knew the trauma she had undergone at the hands of Cain, but he needed to be as sly as a snake with him. Cain now knew where they were staying, and he probably had them watched around the clock. He could take no chances. Every bit of information from Cain could be useful. With regret he said, "I'm sorry, darling, but I can't throw this away. Maybe there's something here we can use against Cain. If there's some incriminating evidence in it, we could distribute it to the media and have it sent worldwide."

He noticed her look at him with a mortified expression on her face. "Are you sure you're okay?" he asked with concern.

With a paleness tinting her complexion, she said with a weak smile, "I'm okay. Let's just get home so you can open my gift to you."

He smiled eagerly, then said in a joking manner, "Hmm, honey, I hope it's something sweet."

She knew she needed to retrieve the package from him before it was too late. She knew how treacherous Cain could be, and she knew he had probably recorded their secret phone calls together. She knew if Lemuel heard the recordings, it would destroy his trust in her, thus their relationship. She loved him with all her heart, and she felt determined to not let that happen.

In his bedroom, Lemuel checked the package for explosives. After he found it safe, he said with anticipation, "Let's see what Cain has sent us."

"Wait," Pamela said. "Don't you want a piece of cake or a bowl of ice cream first? It may help us feel better."

"No, honey. I feel like I've been eating continuously all day," he said while ripping open the package.

Her eyes opened wide with horror as he withdrew a disk from the package. "Have a seat on the bed while I play this," he said with anticipation. "I'm curious to know what Cain has to say. Perhaps we can use it against him."

"Wait!" she exclaimed anxiously, while running over to him.

"Don't you want to open your other package from me first?" she said while pressing her breasts firmly against him.

He looked down at her. "Hmm, I do want to open my gift from you first. After all, you're much more valuable than anything Cain could ever give me."

Reaching down, he gently tilted her head and kissed her wetly on the lips. She responded with her lips harmonizing with his.

After a few moments of passionate kisses, he moved her toward the bed. Standing by the bed, he kissed her lips, cheeks, and neck. Nibbling passionately on her ear, he sent chills down her spine.

While he nibbled, he unbuttoned the back of her dress, letting it slide off her shoulders and quietly to the floor. He unhooked the back of her bra, allowing it to fall unhindered to the floor. He slide her panties enticingly over her buttocks, letting it slide down the contours of her legs.

He unbuttoned his shirt and pants, letting them fall to the floor haphazardly. He did not wear any underwear except for socks, and he kept those on.

He held her arms with his hands and gently pushed her back on the bed. Her nipples perked up, extending out with hot blood. Her abdomen undulated with quick breaths. She felt wet with lust.

She felt him against her. She felt his lips travel down her neck, collarbone, on down to her full breasts. She gasped with rapture as he sucked. She moaned with pleasure as his hands squeezed her firm buttocks, causing her to spread her legs more. She whimpered with wanton desire when his twirling finger found her intimate place.

"Hmm, sweetie, you taste so sweet," he said with a husky voice.

She moaned with desire as he continued suckling. She whimpered with sensuous tones as he continued twirling his finger. Unable to restrain the uncontrollable desires, she cried out with delirious fervor, "Please make love to me! Please make love to me now!"

He felt more than willing to accommodate. Without saying a word, he lightly moved over her body and in between her spread legs.

After they climaxed a multitude of times, he lay exhausted beside her while cuddling her tenderly and whispering in her ear how much he loved her...

She felt so secure and loved that her heart overflowed with pure joy...

After an hour of tender cuddling, he said with a contented sigh, "Honey, let's listen to what Cain has to say."

Fear rushed to her heart as she exclaimed, "No! Please, throw it away!"

Lemuel caressed her tenderly, attempting to calm her as he said, "Relax, sweetie, it's just a recording. If we don't like it, we can throw it away."

He then rose off the bed and walked over to the recording. "Please, Lemuel, no," she pleaded with fear.

"It's okay, honey. We'll throw it away if we can't use it against him," he said with reassurance while slipping the recording in the device.

Suddenly an unfamiliar voice came from the recorder with a man saying, "We've traded disks with the president. He has no idea, so don't tell him. Lemuel, Pamela, James, and Kim Foo, the pope would like to talk to you all in exactly three days to discuss plans on how to get rid of Cain. We'll meet you all at the estate you're residing in now. Don't worry, we know where you live. Thank you for your time."

The recording then went blank.

Pamela breathed a sigh of relief while asking, "What are we going to do?"

Lemuel felt backed into a corner. He disliked both the pope and Cain, but he knew Cain was more treacherous than the pope. If he had to choose sides it would be to side with the pope. With that in mind, he said reluctantly, "Apparently the pope and the president both know where we're staying now, and they're probably having us watched. Either one could apprehend us at any time, so there must be a reason they haven't.

"Perhaps they're giving us an opportunity to see which side we'll choose. Maybe we can change the course the pope is on, since he's just human. We can show him all of the research we've done on Cain in order to strengthen his resolve in getting rid of Cain, and then we can figure out how to get rid of the pope if he hasn't changed his evil ways."

General Su Woo sat in his pavilion in Afghanistan, surrounded by his staff.

"General Woo, sir," a subordinate general said respectfully, "our armies will soon have complete control over Afghanistan. We're encountering little resistance. The Americans retreated before we arrived. Our source has told us they're pulling back all their forces to the borders of Israel, so except for Israel, the Middle East is ripe for the plucking. We should have every country in the Middle East, except for Israel, under our control very soon."

General Woo smiled with an evil smirk as he said, "Very good,

General Wing. I'm sure our Great Leader will be pleased with our progress. Keep to my strategy, and we'll back the Americans into the sea, then they can surrender or die."

Suddenly the mobile phone rang, and one of the staff members answered it. Fear transformed the face of the man into an apprehensive grimace. He shouted out urgently, "General Woo, sir, it's imperative you answer this now!"

General Woo snatched the phone from the alarmed man. "What!" he snarled with impatience.

On the other end of the phone, he could hear screams and terrified shrieks of dying men in the background.

With absolute terror, a Chinese colonel blurted out, "We're being attacked by unknown entities who can't be harmed! The entities are humanoid, but their heads have goat-like horns and their mouths have canine-like teeth. They're all naked and sexless. Their bodies look like black holes with no light escaping. They appear to be invulnerable. They're taking everything we give them, all manner of bullets, mines, hand grenades, even missiles. General Woo, they're killing us all! We can't stop them! Please help us! Please help—"

General Woo interrupted him and ordered firmly, "Shut up, Colonel, and gain control of yourself." He then asked in a milder tone, "How many of those entities are there?"

The colonel took a deep breath to calm his nerves, then said with self-control, "We think six of them, but we can't be sure. Please hurry before they destroy us all. They've already killed thousands of us!"

General Woo said with a reassuring tone, hoping to calm his terrified colonel, "We'll be there soon. I'm sending a squad of helicopters to observe and destroy those anomalies. Now where are you located?"

General Woo and his squad of twelve helicopters flew over the carnage. Thousands of dead Chinese soldiers littered the parched Afghanistan ground. Red blood soaked into the thirsty ground and covered their bodies.

Thousands of Chinese ran, panic-stricken, in all directions, screaming with panic as the black hole creatures quickly jumped from one man to the next, ripping out throats in split seconds. The dead bodies continued to accumulate on the blood-soaked ground.

"Fire your missiles into those ungodly monsters!" General Woo screamed over his radio. He had never observed such a grisly sight before, and he felt sick.

"General Woo, we'll kill our own men if we do that!" a sergeant screamed.

"If we don't, they're all dead men! Do it or face court martial!" General Woo screamed with anger.

All the aircraft flew with rotating blades over the black hole entities, two for each entity.

They all watched with horror as the entities ran amok throughout the scattered ranks of the Chinese army.

"Fire!" General Woo screamed shrilly over his radio.

Large missiles shot forth, whistling from the sides of the helicopters, leading a white stream of smoke down to their targets. The fiery explosions sent human bodies flying in all directions. Great flashes of smoke and fire spewed from the earth where the missiles exploded, kicking up great chunks of earth.

Even before the smoke dissipated and the dust settled, they observed the black hole creatures continue to run like cheetahs out of the ground zero craters and pounce on the backs of more fleeing Chinese.

"How did they survive?" General Woo screamed with frustrated puzzlement. An aide who had read one of the propaganda fliers the pope had dropped on the Chinese forces asked respectfully, "May I speak, General Woo, sir?"

"Yes!" General Woo exclaimed desperately.

"Those entities appear to be made of black holes, and they are untouchable. It caused me to think about the Christian New Testament. What is the opposite of darkness?"

"Light!" General Woo exclaimed excitedly.

"Of course," the aide said with a humble nod. "You're right, sir. Therefore, I propose we use the floodlights we've attached to our helicopters. If we turn them on full power and fly above the monsters with the full force of the lights shining on their black hole bodies, wouldn't the light destroy them, since their bodies consist of absolute darkness?"

"Of course!" General Woo exclaimed with even more excitement. "You're a genius, young man. Make it so!"

Everyone aimed their floodlight mechanisms while hovering above the black hole creatures.

General Woo then ordered with excitement, "Open the floodlights!"

All the lights blinked on, showering the creatures with shimmering light. Suddenly the coal-black shadows screamed, shrieking with spine-chilling screeches that sounded like thousands of tormenting whistles. A vast array of sparks flew from their black physiques, as tendrils of black smoke whirled up off them. After a minute of shrill shrieking, they exploded in flashes of light.

General Woo then said to his aide, "You're promoted up three ranks for that ingenious idea." Breathing a sigh of relief, he continued, "Now that we know how to kill these ungodly creatures, make sure every company has its own personal floodlights, just in case those monsters attack again."

Everyone agreed.

(PAST)

Lemuel fled west after his escape from Babylon. He fled to Rome since it was far northwest, and at the time it was a place of little worldly significance.

Through the years he helped the Romans become free from the Eurasians, and he helped in building a more civilized society with fairer laws, and better engineering, which led to bigger and better building projects, like stone roads, bridges, and buildings. All the extra work led to a stronger, more robust economy, with the roads especially helping with transportation of goods and services. This helped hurtle the Roman economy to the top of the world, which in turn led Rome to superpower status.

Lemuel felt amazement at how fast Rome grew from a small city to one even larger than Babylon. With his guidance, it had become large and prosperous...

As Lemuel walked down a street, markets lined both sides of it, with people scurrying back and forth, conducting their individual businesses. A large variety of commerce items, such as colorful clothing, trinkets, and other goods, filled the streets with exotic sights.

Men on horses and on horse-drawn carts crowded the roads, as different languages intermingled with creaking wagons, rickety carts, neighing horses, braying donkeys, clucking chickens, and other sounds of animal life, mixing into a medley of indistinguishable sounds and languages, adding to the clamor of the bustling city of Rome.

Scents of animals, fishes, and fresh produce sent delicious aromas rising like tempting vapors of seduction, causing Lemuel's stomach to growl with hunger.

After what seemed like a long journey through Rome, past the marketplace, stores, taverns, temples, bath houses, apartments, monuments, and government buildings, he arrived at the palace of Emperor Augustus, who ruled the Roman Empire with a firm but fair hand. Since Lemuel was his wisest advisor, the Roman Empire continued to thrive under his advice.

The guards allowed him to pass by with respectful Roman salutes.

Augustus's personal bodyguard escorted him, and he soon found himself standing beside the door of Augustus's personal chambers.

The bodyguard knocked on the door politely.

"Who is it?" the voice of Augustus, the majestic Roman emperor, cried out.

"It is I, your majesty, Lemuel," he replied with reverence.

Augustus yelled with pleasure, "Enter, wise counselor."

Lemuel found himself standing before the emperor at full attention.

"At ease," Augustus said with a smile of pleasure on his face. He then chided Lemuel by saying, "How many times have I told you, you're not military, so you don't have to stand at attention whenever we meet?"

Lemuel smiled back with modesty. He liked Augustus immensely, and he knew that showing Augustus the ultimate respect by standing at attention brought pride to the emperor, so he continued doing it regardless of Augustus's mild objections. With frankness he answered back with his usual response, "I'm sorry, sir, but your majestic status of being the most powerful man in the world prompts me to stand at attention whenever we meet."

Augustus waved aside Lemuel's flattery with his hand as he said, "I'm just an ordinary human being who was born lucky." He then added with a chuckle, "Though I've considered becoming a god. I do have the power to arrange that."

Lemuel did not laugh, but instead smiled at Augustus's proud remark. He did not want Augustus to think he was making fun of him. He knew Augustus could actually arrange it among some of his priests to make him a god, and even have his citizens worship him at some of the temples that flourished throughout Rome.

Augustus then became serious as he said, "Lemuel, I've called you here today because I've been having a problem with Herod, the king in Judea. He believes a child is to be born in Bethlehem who's supposed to cause a rebellion and replace him as ruler of Judea.

"His main counselor has advised him to kill all the children in Bethlehem, just to make sure the child who is to replace him is killed, but he wants my permission to do so first. He realizes he's under Roman law, and he fears punishment if he doesn't obtain permission from me. What should I do, Lemuel? You know I detest killing little babies or children."

Lemuel knew Herod, and he hated him. He hated his counselor even more because he knew his counselor was Cain. Lemuel had pleaded with Augustus a multitude of times in the past to replace Herod with a more righteous ruler, but he refused to do so. Augustus liked the loyalty Herod gave to the Roman Empire, even at the expense of his own Jewish population.

After giving the dilemma a few moments of careful contemplation, Lemuel said with resignation, "Sir, you know I don't like Herod. Personally, I think you should have him killed and replaced with a more righteous ruler, but that's my personal opinion. Since I know you'll not, you should tell Herod to find the child, then hold him as prisoner. He shouldn't be allowed to kill anyone innocent."

Augustus chuckled at Lemuel's sulking response as he said, "I know how you feel, Lemuel, and if Herod wasn't such a loyal subject to Rome, I'd take your advice on that matter, but he's a loyal subject. He makes Jews pay the Roman taxes, and he obeys me faithfully. I can't have him killed just because you don't like him. However, your advice is right on target concerning the innocent children, so I'll tell him to attempt to find the child first, and if he does find it, to hold it prisoner instead of killing it."

Augustus then changed the subject as he smiled broadly. "I'm having a big party tonight, and it would be an honor if you joined in."

Lemuel smiled back as he said, "Thank you, sir. It would be my pleasure to come to your party. They're always so much fun."

Though his expression showed happiness, deep inside Lemuel felt troubled. Cain was going to hurt some more innocent people, this time little babies. It caused Lemuel deep sadness whenever anyone innocent was hurt, but the sadness went even deeper when babies were hurt. That man needs to die, *Lemuel thought bleakly to himself.*

Centuries before Cain arrived at Judea to counsel Herod, Cain had secretly assassinated Alexander the Great with a poisonous concoction in his wine, and he convinced Alexander's generals to split up his empire so each would have their own territory to rule. Of course, since it was Cain's idea to begin with, he decided who got what. Because of that, he held influence over all the generals, though complete power over none. At the time Cain thought that would be sufficient until he established his own kingdom again.

The problem was, as the passing decades turned into centuries, the generals' offspring ceased taking Cain's advice, and became rivals to one another instead of allies. Because of his loss of influence over the generals' offspring, Cain never had an opportunity to forge out a kingdom for himself. Instead, he settled for being counselor to one king at a time...

As counselor to Herod the Great of Judea, Cain disliked him as much as he had disliked Alexander the Great. The world's power had shifted from East to West, and Herod was just a puppet king to the Roman Empire. Cain knew he would someday need to someday travel west if he was to regain any major political power.

As Cain roamed the deserted streets of Bethlehem with his band of soldiers, searching for the child who was supposed to be the Jewish Messiah, the one who was prophesied as the next king of Israel, rage filled his heart. It insulted his pride that Herod had ordered him to lead a common band of soldiers, searching for an unknown child who might not even exist. He had once been the most powerful man in the world. It infuriated him that he was performing such a lowly assignment.

The night felt infected with an ominous evil. It seemed to permeate every fiber of the town, as the black clouds hid the full moon, adding to the melancholic feelings that roosted in everyone's heart.

They were heading to a Jewish priest's home. They had information the Jewish priest knew who the child was and where he lived. Cain and his squad of soldiers eventually made it to the priest's house.

Cain and three of his chosen soldiers walked up the steps and onto the porch with loud, bold steps.

Walking over to the door, Cain knocked loudly. "The king's guard is here!" he then yelled with authority. "Let us in immediately!"

No one answered. The house appeared deserted, but Cain knew better. He twisted the door handle hard, but it held firmly. He then stepped aside and motioned for his soldier with an ax to break in the door.

The soldier chopped at the door with zeal. The blade on the ax ate at the door hungrily, sending splintered wood flying in every direction. When there was a big hole in the door, the soldier put the ax down and reached through the hole. He unlocked the door from the inside. He then stepped aside so Cain could open it.

Cain opened the door with a shove of his hand. The door swung open, leaving a clear view of a deserted hall and stairway.

"Find the priest and everyone else in this house, and bring them to me," Cain ordered.

After ten minutes they returned with the home's occupants.

The residents stared at Cain with fear, while he looked at them with contempt.

There was one old man, one old woman, two young men, and one young woman. Cain assumed the old man was the priest, and the old woman his wife. The two young men and one young woman had to be their offspring.

The young woman began pleading with panic, "Please don't hurt my family! I'll go anywhere with you, just please don't hurt my family!"

"Shut up!" Cain said angrily while looking at everyone. He then said in a negotiable tone, "I'll not hurt anyone if I get the information I've come for."

After he got no response, he stared at the old man who appeared to be the priest, and demanded with authority, "Tell me where the Messiah baby is, and I'll let you and your family live!"

The old man raised his white-haired head and said with brave defiance, "There's no way I'll tell you. I'm sure I'm speaking for all those who live here. We'll not betray our Messiah. We're certain he'll be our king someday, so do what you have to do."

Cain's complexion became livid with rage as he walked over to the old man. Looking down at him with unblinking eyes, he screamed incoherently as he slapped him with the back of his hand.

His slap sent the old man reeling against the wall, causing his daughter to scream with a high shriek.

The humiliated old man felt his cheek with a trembling hand. He could not feel any blood, but anger rose in his heart. He had been humiliated in front of his family, so he screamed out with his own rage, "I'm not afraid of you! I'll never tell you! Do you understand? I'll never—"

Before he could finish, Cain jerked out a knife and plunged it into the heart of the old man as hard as he could.

The old man's daughter screamed in absolute terror as blood gushed out from her father's chest.

The old man stared down at the spurting geyser that consisted of his lifeblood. With his mouth open in shock, he slid down the wall, leaving a bloody trail.

Cain walked over to the old woman and the two younger men, then quickly stabbed each of them in a cold, methodical way, splattering blood against walls, as they fell to the floor, dead.

He turned to the young woman, who continued to scream insanely, as if she were in a nightmare.

Cain screamed with his own insane rage, "Shut up, bitch! Do you hear me? Shut up!"

The furious way in which he ordered her helped her regain enough sanity to cease screaming mindlessly.

He then told her in a normal-toned voice, "I'm not usually this nice, but I like you. Tell me where the Messiah baby is, and I'll spare your life."

"No!" she shrieked with a cry of agony as tears ran down her face. With defiant rage building in her heart, she cried out with a wail, "I'll never tell you, so you can kill me, too!"

Cain took a deep breath to control his anger.

"No, I don't think I'll kill you, not right away, anyway," he said while reaching over and viciously tearing her robe from her body, leaving her naked.

"No, please, no, don't do that! Please, just kill me," she pleaded. He refused to listen as he reached over and squeezed a nipple. She screamed with humiliation and agony.

Chapter 18

Joseph sat in secret with Lemuel, James, Kim Foo, and Pamela at the mansion in Jerusalem. He came disguised as an Orthodox Jewish rabbi with black beard, black robe, and other Jewish rabbi accoutrements.

They sat together in the mansion's library around a decorative cherry-wood table, polished to perfection. It consisted of enough space to sit all comfortably.

After all were seated, Joseph cleared his throat and said with a cordial voice, "I'm pleased to be here. I hope this alliance succeeds and bears fruitful works. Our main goal should be to get rid of Cain in any way we can. We should—"

Lemuel interrupted politely as he said, "Pardon me, your holiness, but I think you should know who Cain really is before you continue."

"Is this really necessary?" Joseph asked with resignation. "We all know that Cain's a bad apple who needs to be thrown away before he spoils the American barrel."

"Oh, it's absolutely necessary," Lemuel said while nodding his head, "because you have no idea who Cain really is."

"Very well," Joseph said submissively. "Proceed."

Lemuel set a black leather briefcase on the table and opened the metal locks. He raised the top of the briefcase and pulled from it a ream of research papers. He passed most of the papers around until everyone received copies.

He then said with excitement, "As you can see by the scientific data, when God created our solar system, He placed a special significance on the number nine. For example, our sun contains over ninety-nine percent of the mass in our solar system, most of the rest distributed among the nine planets. At least it was nine, until Pluto was given dwarf status in the year two thousand and six of the Common Era. Personally I still consider it a planet, though.

"He also placed special significance on the number nine with His heavenly creatures. For example, there are nine different life forms in heaven that are recognized by these names: seraphim, cherubim, thrones, dominations, virtues, powers, principalities, archangels, and angels.

"Also, famous people born in certain astrological years who influenced our world were born on the series of nines. For example, Elvis Presley was born in nineteen thirty-five. Abraham Lincoln was born in eighteen o'nine. King James was born in fifteen sixty-six. Nostradamus was born in fifteen o'three. Attila the Hun was born in four o'five, and Augustus Caesar was born in sixty-three BCE."

Taking a deep breath, Lemuel looked around the table as he continued, "I'm sorry for going into so much detail, but it's the only way I know how to explain to you about the series of nines. There are a lot of famous people born on the series of nines who have influenced mankind's history in one way or another, such as President Kennedy, Marilyn Monroe, Ernest Hemingway, President Eisenhower, Rasputin, Charles Darwin, Edgar Allen Poe, John Brown, Nathan Hale, John Hancock, Ivan the Terrible, William Shakespeare, Alexander the Sixth, Hernandez Cortez, Kublai Khan, Herod Agrippa the Second, Marcus Agrippa, Cato the Elder, Amenhotep the Third, and Amenhotep the Fourth. I could go on and on, but I'm sure you get the general idea.

"As you can see, those born on the series of nines represent both good people and bad people. It really depends on the individual. For example, your holiness, you were born on nine, nine, nineteen sixty-two of the Common Era, so not only were you born on the series of nines, the month and day you were born on are also nines. That's why we think you'll be playing a significant role in the coming last days of this world. Hopefully it'll be for the good, but it could be for the bad. You have free will, and we hope you join the side of good, but your actions haven't been encouraging.

"As you can see by the research papers, there are six hundred sixty-six sets of nines starting at nineteen sixty-two of the Common Era, the year Joseph was born. It subtracts its way back six hundred and sixty-six times with each set equaling nine years."

Everyone looked at their research papers and saw what Lemuel had told them. They saw each set was numbered with parentheses: (SET 666) 1962 CE (SET 665) 1953 CE (SET 664) 1944 CE (SET 663) 1935 CE (SET 662) 1926 CE (SET 661) 1917 CE (SET 660) 1908 CE (SET 659) 1899 CE...

They saw the sets of nines going all the way back to (SET 0) 4032 BCE. Everyone found it disturbing that 9 CE was numbered as (SET 449) 9 CE, as if the numbers were trying to tell them in English that the first nine in the beginning of the Common Era was FOR FOR NINE.

After a half hour of looking at the series of nines, Lemuel looked at Joseph while saying with conviction, "I declare, Adam and Eve began counting their years after they were expelled from the Garden of Eden, and bore Cain as their firstborn. Even the Jewish calendar puts it around that time with their chronologies, and it only makes sense. After eating from the Tree of Knowledge, they gained enough knowledge to count their years."

Everyone looked at the ages of some of the people who were recorded in the Bible, and saw that what Lemuel said was true.

Lemuel continued while staring at Joseph, "Cain's the seed of Lucifer. Not only that, but since he's the seed of the devil, he's also immortal, and he has been around for thousands of years. America's not the beast like you thought, your holiness, but it's Cain who's the beast.

"If you don't change your wicked ways, I'm pretty sure you're the beast with the horns of a lamb. All the numbers and religious power you possess point to you as being the one."

"That's preposterous!" Joseph said with anger. "I'm not a beast! Perhaps Cain is, but you've got me wrong. I'm not on Cain's side. I despise him, and I want him destroyed."

Lemuel looked sad while saying, "I hope you're right, but even if you're not, and you are destined to be one of the prophetic beasts, we've all been created with a free will. You can change and be a righteous man fighting for good instead of evil."

Joseph felt frustration as he said sarcastically, "Your belief is unacceptable." He then stood up and walked stiffly toward the library door. Before opening the door, he turned around and looked at them with piercing eyes while saying, "We'll keep in touch. If I come up with something to destroy Cain, I'll let you know so we can implement the plan together. If any of you come up with a good plan, feel free to let me know. You all have my personal number now."

Everyone nodded with agreement.

He then beckoned toward Pamela while saying, "Please come here for a moment, young lady. I need to tell you something confidentially."

She stood up and walked nervously to him on weakened knees.

He bent his head to her ear and whispered, "I've heard the secret discussions you've had with Cain. I'm sure Lemuel would love to hear it, too. I don't know if you really are Cain's spy or not, and I really don't care. You're unofficially my spy now. Keep me updated, and that includes information from Cain, too. Understand?"

Pamela agreed with a small nod of her head as her mouth opened with surprise. It appeared it was the pope's turn to blackmail her. She felt relieved that Cain had not blackmailed her anymore, but fear still flowed through her heart. She knew the pope's willingness to join them was too good to be true. The thought of his treachery made the hair on the back of her neck stand up.

Joseph waved a friendly good-bye to everyone and walked out of the room. His two rabbis disguised as bodyguards waited for him patiently in the foyer. After he walked back to them, they all left together without a word.

Clarence sat with Cain, both in disguise, at a restaurant in Jerusalem.

Cain continued staring at Clarence suspiciously as he said, "Are you sure you gave Lemuel that package I ordered you to give him a week ago?"

Clarence began to sweat as he said nervously, "I swear, Mr. President, I gave it to him. Now whether he opened it or not, I don't know. I didn't stick around to find out."

Cain then probed curiously, attempting to catch Clarence in a lie. "Have you been keeping a close eye on them?"

"Yes, of course I have," Clarence said defensively, "and they're still preaching against you near the Weeping Wall, though they've stopped preaching against the pope for some reason."

Cain sat for a moment in silence as he thought about the ramifications of that information. They must have joined sides with the pope. He asked Clarence with eyebrows raised in curiosity, "Is Pam still with Lemuel? She must have thrown her phone away because no one answers."

"Yeah, the bitch is still with him, and they're more affectionate with each other than ever. You'd think they were newlyweds or something," Clarence said with a disgusting expression.

Cain mumbled with disappointment to himself, "Lemuel must have not heard the recordings of me plotting with Pamela. I guess I'll have to invite him over for tea, so we can listen to the recordings together. Luckily I did make copies, and—"

Clarence interrupted Cain's private mutterings by saying, "If I heard you right, I can assure you that Lemuel will never visit you for tea, or anything else for that matter. You'll have to abduct him, and that will be difficult now since he's never alone."

"Where there's a will, there's a way," Cain said with a positive smile. "Just keep your eyes open. I'm sure an opportunity to apprehend Lemuel will arise."

Clarence responded with a dutiful nod.

Cain took a deep breath while saying anxiously, "Enough of that. I've recently received word that three rabbi priests visited Lemuel and his cohorts at their mansion recently. Is that true?"

Clarence fidgeted in his chair while saying, "Yes, that's true, Mr. President. I never told you about it because I didn't want you to worry. It was just a few rabbi priests visiting. It wasn't like it was anyone important."

Cain then stared coldly at Clarence as he said between clenched teeth, "Oh, but I do worry about it, especially since I'm getting so close to becoming ruler of this world. Don't you dare keep any more information from me, no matter how insignificant it may seem to you! Understand?"

Clarence gulped with fear as he nodded yes.

Cain then said with authority, "Find out who those rabbi priests were and what they were talking about with my enemies."

"Okay," Clarence said meekly, not wanting to get Cain upset again. Changing the subject, he asked, "How's it going on the Chinese front?"

Cain replied back with curiosity, "Why would you ask such a question? It's really none of your business how it's going."

Clarence shook his head with pretended sadness as he said, "It's just a tragedy that millions of people will die if China continues on its destructive path."

Cain spoke back angrily with harsh words, "Just shut up, Clarence! You're not fooling anyone, especially me. The only person you're concerned about is yourself. If you had a heart, you'd be dangerous." He finished while looking away in disgust, "Just get out of my sight."

After Clarence left, Cain reclined in his chair. Thoughts of ultimate power flashed through his mind. Soon the whole world would be under his power, and then he would eliminate all of his enemies, starting with Lemuel.

Joseph sat in an Israeli government complex in Jerusalem. He sat by himself behind a large desk with a video-cam on it. He looked with frustration on a smiling President Ting, who appeared full of glee.

"Please, President Ting, please stop this bloodshed," he pleaded desperately. "I'm sure I can convince Cain to pull out of the Middle East completely, including Israel."

Ting laughed with a guttural laugh that seemed to originate deep. "It's too late now, Pope. You should have done that before I started my invasion. I gave you plenty of time to do it. By the end of the week, my troops will occupy Jerusalem, and thus all the Middle East. I think it's a little late for peace now. Here's the deal you can give Cain: unconditional surrender. If he surrenders now, I'll show mercy to his troops. If he doesn't, tell him to prepare for an extremely bloody defeat."

"President Ting," Joseph begged with a pleading tone, "please listen to me. I'm begging you to listen to reason. Cain will not accept those conditions. You know I'm a very godly man, and it upsets me to think about all the millions, perhaps even tens of millions of people who'll lose their lives over this fiasco."

Ting laughed even more before saying, "Pope, my nation has about five hundred million more people than it actually needs or wants, so what you're telling me is a favorable proposition, not detrimental. I hope America kills at least five hundred million of my countrymen, so we can become a more efficient country. Your fears do not dissuade me. On the contrary, they encourage me to conquer the entire world after we finish with the Middle East. For the sake of finances, since wars are so expensive, I'll give Cain the opportunity to surrender if he does it soon. Do you think you can convince him?"

With a helpless shrug, Joseph shook his head.

"Very well then," Ting said with a smile, "I'll see his country defeated then." The screen went blank, leaving pixel static in place of President Ting's face.

Joseph reached over and turned the screen off. Leaning back in his chair with shoulders slumped and head down, he felt depressed. He knew if China ruled the world, his dream of becoming the sole world leader would be destroyed. Suddenly his office door opened, and Cain walked up to his desk.

Joseph opened his eyes wide with surprise. "How d-d-did you get past my body guards?" he asked with astonishment.

"I have my ways," Cain said with a pleasant smile on his face. "The real questions are, what are you doing in Jerusalem, and why are you plotting against me with Lemuel and his cohorts?"

Joseph pretended he did not know what Cain spoke of, so he said, "I've no idea what you're talking about. I'm here to strengthen the Jewish Christians who face the invasion of a mighty Chinese horde who are now right across the Jordan River. There's no way your army can stand against their numbers. I've been told by the Chinese president that he'd accept your unconditional surrender if you did it soon. I beg you, for the sake of millions of human lives, to surrender."

Cain replied back obsessively, "I can't prove it now, but I'm sure you're plotting with Lemuel and his bunch. I have an inside informant watching you closely, and you have no idea who it is. This person knows you recruited Lemuel awhile back, and somehow the alliance ended. Make sure it stays ended. On the day I find out it hasn't, it will be the last day of your life, regardless of what Lucifer has told me.

"As far as surrendering to China, that's ludicrous. I've talked with Lucifer about China, and he assures me his forces in the air will overcome the Chinese, so you have nothing to worry about."

Joseph replied back with desperation, "The Chinese have devised a way of killing the black hole creatures Lucifer sent."

Cain chuckled at Joseph's ignorance as he said, "You really don't know much about the spiritual realm, do you? You think those creatures were Lucifer's soldiers? Allow me to let you in on a little secret. Those were just his spiritual war dogs. His true soldiers can't be killed by light. They thrive on it. Stick around for the fireworks, Pope, as Lucifer's air force takes care of the Chinese."

"I hope you're right," Joseph said with a sparkle of hope in his eyes. "I've grown weary of all this bloodshed."

"Oh, I'm right because I'm always right," Cain said as he walked casually toward the door.

Before he left, he turned around and threatened with confidence, "Just make sure you know the right side to be on. We'll have a lot of cleaning up to do afterward, and then we'll make plans for my final push as world master. That's if you're still on my side."

Joseph nodded with submissive agreement as Cain walked out, rudely closing the door loudly.

With hurt pride, Joseph decided he would have Cain killed within a week or so. He did not believe Lemuel when he said Cain was Lucifer's son. That was an absurd belief. He had a good relationship with Lucifer, and he had been cultivating one with him for many years. He felt sure if Lucifer became angry with him for killing Cain, he could deal with Lucifer's anger easy enough. After all, he knew Lucifer needed him to convert all of humanity to his side. What better man than him, the foremost religious leader in the world? Even if Lucifer stayed angry at him, at least he would be rid of Cain, his only rival. After Cain was dead, Lucifer would forgive him after he saw all the new worshipers Joseph could bring him. Then Joseph could concentrate on being the absolute ruler of humanity, and Lucifer could be their god. A fair trade.

Reaching over to his intercom, he ordered the captain of his bodyguards, "Freddy, get in touch with Clarence, and tell him I want to see him as soon as possible. Also, see who let Cain in my office and have that bodyguard killed."

He then leaned back in his chair, exhausted.

He dozed off for about an hour, when the knocking on his door woke him from his slumber.

"Yes, who is it?" he asked while still half-asleep.

Opening the door halfway, the captain of his bodyguards bowed his head low while saying subserviently, "It's me, your holiness, Freddy. Clarence has just arrived. Would you like to speak with him now?"

Joseph cleared his throat and cantankerously growled, "Yes, send him in."

Rising from his slouch, he stretched his tight arm muscles out as Clarence walked in and over to the desk.

"Did you want to see me, your holiness?" Clarence asked with concern.

Joseph stared at Clarence suspiciously as he said, "I've received news that someone I trust is betraying me. I hope it's not you, Clarence, because if I find out you've betrayed me, you'll be praying for death by the time I finish with you."

Clarence stood aghast with surprise. He said with all the honesty he could muster, "The only one I'm betraying is Cain, your holiness. I'd never betray you."

Clarence appeared so sincere with his answer that Joseph had no option but to believe him. It must be someone else, then, he thought with puzzlement to himself.

Looking at Clarence again, he said with determination, "I've decided to have Cain assassinated soon. He's becoming a loose cannonball, and the sooner we're rid of him, the better."

Clarence's eyes opened with horror. "Impossible on such short notice. He possesses powers you know nothing about."

"Precisely why we have to have him assassinated as soon as

possible," Joseph said with a firm resolve. "The man's insane, and we can't allow him to live after this conflict is over. If we don't assassinate him soon, he'll lead us all down the path of total annihilation."

"How do you purpose we do him in?" Clarence asked with curious concern.

With a thoughtful stare, Joseph answered slowly, "Of course, we'll have to have him assassinated at a time and place he would never suspect. A place while he's still in the White House if possible, probably while he's sleeping. If he's as powerful as you assert, we certainly wouldn't dare attempt it while he's awake."

"Who would you have do it?" Clarence asked with dread growing in his heart.

"You can't be that stupid, Clarence!" Joseph exclaimed with an incredulous look on his face. "You know since you're the president's personal Secret Service agent, you'd have the easiest access to him. You could sneak in his bedroom while he's sleeping and kill him quickly."

"What if I fail?" Clarence asked with trembling fear.

"Not possible," Joseph said with confidence. "But just in case you do, we'll have a contingency plan. We'll use one of my agents to accompany you just in case. I'll make sure no harm comes to you, Clarence."

With uncertainty filling his heart, Clarence said with puzzlement, "It sounds like a good plan, but where does that leave me after the president's dead?"

Joseph rubbed Clarence on the back reassuringly as he said, "I'll take care of you, Clarence. I'll make sure you become the next president of the United States, and the second most powerful man on earth."

Covetous desires sprouted in Clarence's heart as he said, "Sounds like a good plan, your holiness, and I assure you I'd make a much better president than Cain."

"I know you will, Clarence, and that's why I'll help make you one, but I'll need your help, too," Joseph said with his most flattering tone.

Clarence gazed off into his own make-believe world, daydreaming of becoming the next president of America.

Joseph interrupted his daydream with a coarse rattle of his throat. "Clarence? Earth to Clarence?"

Clarence awoke from his daydream and said apologetically, "Sorry, I was just thinking."

Joseph chuckled. He knew exactly what Clarence was thinking

about. "Yes, we both have a lot to think about," he said with understanding, "so you should go now while I perfect our assassination plan. I'll get in touch with you as soon as I'm ready to implement it."

Clarence nodded as he made a curt bow. He turned around and walked out of the room with dreams of power still fresh in his mind.

Joseph breathed a sigh of relief. It would soon be over. He would have Cain killed with the cooperation of Cain's own personal Secret Service agent. He would rather torture Cain first, but he would be relieved to just be rid of him. He leaned back in his chair with hope in his heart and daydreams in his mind. He thought of all the fun he would have after he became the absolute world leader.

The day felt hot with a few puffy white clouds floating in the sky, pushed by a cool northeastern breeze.

General Woo stood beside what appeared to be an endless line of Chinese infantrymen, tanks, and other armaments. General Woo had decided to send his whole force against the armies that protected Israel. He felt certain the enemy forces would be swept aside like leaves blown away with a blustery wind. His antiaircraft stood behind his main force, ready to knock down any enemy jet that might appear. Everything and everyone appeared ready. General Woo only needed to say the word, and tens of millions of his soldiers would run with berserk abandonment toward the border of Israel—and absolute victory.

"Are you ready, General?" one of his aides asked with subdued impatience.

General Woo wanted to savor the last moment before complete victory over the last country in the Middle East. The other Middle Eastern countries had fallen easily under his blitz of superior numbers, and he expected the successful invasion of the Middle East to climax in a successful invasion of Israel.

With anticipation, he slowly raised his sword high in the air, then with a quick downward slice, screamed with excitement, "Attack!"

The earth trembled with millions of Chinese feet pounding against it in a double-time march. Tens of millions of Chinese voices drowned out the rumble of the earth with a battle cry that filled the air.

Suddenly, cylinder-shaped spaceships the approximate size of large automobiles zoomed above the Chinese. The ships appeared transparent, with only the outer lines visible. Within each ship was one alien creature piloting it. The aliens appeared humanoid in shape, with each body looking as if it were made of their own distinct color of a solid yellow light.

There were so many of them, General Woo could not count their numbers. He knew they were not from Earth, and he knew they posed a danger to his forces.

Without hesitation, he screamed, "Activate our antiaircraft batteries! Fire on the unidentified aircraft at will!"

The antiaircraft batteries fired thousands of missiles at the UFOs.

To the general's consternation, the missiles exploded harmlessly against unseen shields that surrounded each aircraft.

Tens of thousands of exploding missiles slammed harmlessly against the invisible shields, like birds slamming against the windshields of speeding cars.

The UFOs spewed forth beams of bright light. The laser beams swirled back and forth through the Chinese ranks.

To General Woo's horror, the lasers were lethal to anyone they shone on. Whoever they touched, that person would burst into a bright red flame before disappearing into oblivion.

Panic broke out among the troops. Most turned around and fled in the opposite direction. Screams of terror reverberated on the whole field, as millions of soldiers became vaporized.

General Woo felt confused. The aliens killed them like they had killed the black hole aliens with their own floodlights. He felt completely defenseless and did not know how to strike back. He remained frozen in place, unsure and indecisive as men ran past him, screaming in absolute terror.

Finally a panicked man ran into him, knocking him down and out of his lethargic shock. He quickly stood up and ran to his radio. Turning it on, he screamed with as much authority he could, "Have the men dig in and cover themselves with the soil to escape the lasers! Quickly! Quickly!"

To his horror, a voice answered back on his radio. It was a voice with the most perfect Chinese inflection he had ever heard. "It's too late, General Woo. Our species, our ships, our technologies are vastly superior to anything you have ever encountered. We'll kill all of you as easily as you could kill an infestation of roaches. Throw down your weapons and accept death. It'll come quicker and more merciful that way."

General Woo looked around in horror as his people screamed with terror. Bright red flames appeared all around him, leaving behind thousands of swirls of black smoke that used to be human. Smells of burnt flesh filled the air and clogged his nostrils, causing him to sneeze with disgust.

Jumping in his Jeep, he drove as fast as he could, screeching tires against the barren ground, casting up Jordanian soil. He hoped if he could make it past the carnage, he would be able to escape. Men continued screaming all around him, bursting into flames and floating away on wisps of black smoke. Still he drove at top speed, not bothering to stop for anyone. He ran over everyone in his path, regardless of their pleas for mercy. Blood splattered his Jeep as he ran over more men than he bothered counting.

Suddenly he saw a ship hover above him, and in a split second he saw a death laser rush for him. He screamed with horror while raising his arms around his face. It hit him instantaneously, and he screamed in torturous pain as his body became a flaming red torch. Since he possessed no communist god, he died with a scream of hopeless terror on his disintegrating lips. Afterward, he floated away in a wisp of smoke on the light breeze.

Without mercy, the demons destroyed every Chinese man they could find. Tens of millions lost their lives. Only a few million escaped by hiding under vehicles and under the Jordanian soil. The battlefield appeared completely deserted with Chinese military equipment scattered around everywhere like a junkyard.

The demon pilots continued flying around the battlefield, hoping to catch the remaining soldiers they knew were hiding. After a few sporadic laser shots and subsequent screams, the remaining Chinese soldiers learned to stay hidden under the shadows and in the ground. After a few more passes around the deserted battlefield, the alien aircraft gathered together in a tight formation, then collectively vanished.

(PAST)

The sun felt hot as Cain sat on his sturdy speckled pony beside the famous Attila the Hun and his red pony. They gazed on what appeared to be an endless line of men and ponies. Cain estimated it to be at least one hundred and fifty thousand cavalry troops, and he was not even counting the reserves.

King Attila looked on his cavalry with pride while saying boastfully, "Soon, Cain, soon we shall conquer Rome, and afterward the whole world!"

Cain felt pleased with King Attila. The king followed his instructions explicitly. Soon they would rule the world together.

After the whole world came under their control, Cain planned on unifying all of mankind under one language and one purpose, to serve him and his father faithfully. After they found the secret to eternal life for mankind, they would thwart the Jewish God's plan of having all of mankind taste death, and in the process turn mankind against that Entity and drive the Jewish God far from the hearts of them all. He looked forward to obtaining that ultimate prize of complete power over the whole earth. He would also be like a god.

He said in agreement while looking at Attila with delight, "Yes, my lord, soon you shall rule the whole earth, and you shall become a god to all of mankind, worshiped by all."

Both laughed with exaltation.

After the laughter subsided, Attila said with a friendly smile, "I'm having a big party tonight. Please join me in my celebration of almost conquering Europe. I've captured a Germanic princess whom I want you to meet." Winking at him with a lewd smile, he bent over close to his ear and whispered, "She has to be the sexiest woman in all my kingdom. Last night we..."

While Attila shared his sexual conquest, Cain smiled even more and nodded eagerly with each new sexual deviant act Attila boasted about. Sparkles of lust beamed out of Cain's eyes as Attila continued boasting about his sexual power over the helpless Germanic princess.

After he finished with the erotic details, Cain winked back and said with a conspiring whisper, "Yes, I'd be more than happy to meet your sex slave..."

It was late night when Cain walked into Attila's grand pavilion.

The king's personal bodyguard let him in and escorted him toward the king's personal quarters. As Attila's bodyguard led him past immense troves of treasure, Cain was impressed with all the priceless treasures that cluttered Attila's home. He passed large wooden chests filled with golden, jewel-encrusted goblets, chests filled with precious golden necklaces and rings of all sizes, some encrusted with sparkling gems, chests filled with a variety of different-colored gems, reds, purples, and greenish gems that glistened against the light of the flickering candles and oil lamps.

After the impressive tour of riches, the bodyguard led him into the personal quarters of Attila.

The king lay on large silk cushions, while his naked Germanic captive lay in front of him. One of his hands cupped part of her large breast, while his other hand held a golden goblet filled with wine.

The captive appeared every bit as sexy as the king had said. She possessed straight blond hair that cascaded over her shoulders and large breasts. Her blue eyes and thin lips corresponded well with her thin, long nose. Her naked abdomen appeared flat and muscular, with lots of bushy, blond pubic hair underneath, hiding the line of her womanhood. Her waist curved sensuously, with sexy legs adding to her sensuality.

"What do you think, Cain? Isn't she as hot as I said?" Attila said with pride.

"Yes, you're right, my lord. She's a sex-goddess! A vision from heaven!" Cain exclaimed, with his own excitement causing him to become aroused.

Pointing to another pile of luxurious cushions, Attila said, "Go over there and relax. The food will be coming soon, along with more wine. Until then, you can watch me show you how a real man is supposed to ravage a woman!" He chuckled with pleasure while saying, "Then you can show me if you learned anything by ravaging her yourself!"

Cain blushed with anger. He was ravaging women long before Attila was even thought of. His blushing caused Attila to think Cain was embarrassed, which caused Attila to laugh with heckles at what he thought was Cain's obvious shame. He made practical jokes at the innocence of Cain's supposed embarrassment.

After Attila grew weary of the practical jokes, he began roughly squeezing the Germanic woman's breasts, as he took another long swig from his goblet.

The Germanic woman lay still and passive, with pure hatred radiating out from her eyes. It became clear by looking into her blue eyes that she hated Attila.

Attila said with an instructional tone as his hand slid off her breast down to her heavily bushed private area, "See, Cain, a woman such as this has to get warmed up before she can enjoy it. As you can see, I've begun to—to—uuugg!"

Attila began to choke and gurgle as he dropped his goblet and reached his hands to his throat. He forced out one word in between his gurgles, "Poison!" He gasped with surprise as saliva trickled down the corner of his mouth.

Attila knew he was dying, and Cain knew it, too. All he could do was watch in stunned silence.

The Germanic captive smiled with satisfaction, while licking her lips at Lemuel in a mocking way. She then slowly stood up from the cushions.

Cain knew she had poisoned Attila, so he quickly jumped up to snatch a golden bell. He proceeded to shake it frantically, hoping the constant ringing would bring the bodyguard in as soon as possible. The ringing reverberated in the great room. "What's taking him so long?" he mumbled impatiently to himself.

"They'll never get here in time," the Germanic woman said tauntingly, knowing she had Cain scared. "An old ally named Lemuel gave me this poison for Attila if I was ever captured. He said I would not be able to kill you with poison, so he also gave me this for you."

Suddenly the woman jumped at him with the glint of a dagger flashing against the light of the oil lamps, with an expression of savage ecstasy on her face.

Cain gasped and held his breath with terror as the Germanic captive flew at him in a lunge with the dagger pointed straight at his heart.

At exactly that second, everything appeared to become slow motion.

Cain slowly opened his mouth to scream in terror as the dagger came slowly plunging toward his terrified heart.

Before the knife reached its target, the woman appeared to stop in midair, surprise in her eyes.

The king's bodyguard made it just in time to save Cain with a throwing spear. The head of the spear pierced the woman's heart, sticking out from her breast as her blood showered Cain.

She fell on him, knocking him down and soaking his body with warm blood. After a moment of lying there immobilized with shock, Cain became infuriated with rage. He then screamed loudly, "Lemuel, someday you'll pay for this! Somehow, I swear, you'll pay for this!"

Chapter 19

Lucifer stood by a throne in heaven, in front of the Entity known as God of the Universe. Different-colored lights sparkled throughout the holy chamber, like a swarm of celestial lightning bugs.

Sitting on His enormous throne of light, God said with righteous indignation, "Lucifer, I called you here because I found out some of your spiritual followers attacked a large Chinese force and destroyed it."

"That's correct," Lucifer said nervously.

The Majestic Voice boomed out like thunder, shaking the heavenly room with His righteous anger. "You know My policy concerning humanity! No spiritual entity may interfere or meddle in mankind's policies without My permission. Who do you think you are? What gave you the right to break My policy? Answer Me now!"

Lucifer trembled with fear as he said, "Most Holy One of Israel, that Chinese force would've destroyed Israel and Your chosen people without my intervention. They would've massacred all the Jews."

God's righteous anger overflowed as He said, "Do you think I am a fool, Lucifer? Believe it or not, I see every emotion in your heart and every thought in your mind. I know you even better than you know yourself. I know how you feel, and what you are going to say even before you say it. I know what you will do even before you do it. Not only can I see the present, but I can see the future also, and all the different scenarios in it."

After a moment of silence, God said with an ominous tone, "Because you did rescue My chosen people, I will not punish you at this time, but this will be your final warning. You must not meddle in human affairs without My permission. If you do so again, I will confine you and your misled followers not only to the Earth, but inside the Earth for a thousand years. It will be a prison for you all. There will be no more roaming throughout the Earth until the sentence is completed. Do you understand, Lucifer? Do you understand the penalty?"

Lucifer became full of suppressed anger as he said sarcastically, "Yes, Most Holy One, I understand perfectly. I must allow the flawed humans to make their own decisions so they may see a society without

You is a society based on vanity and dust in the wind."

God overlooked Lucifer's sarcastic anger as He said, "Yes, Lucifer, that's the main reason, but I have other reasons I do not wish to share at this time. Just remember to not intervene in human affairs again. That includes giving supernatural powers to Cain. That must end now. Do you understand?"

With frustration, Lucifer asked, "Most Holy One, may I be open and honest?"

"I would not want it any other way," God said.

"Thank You, Most Holy One. Your policy is unfair if I can't give Cain any of my supernatural powers, because Cain's not fully human. After all, he's a hybrid as You know. Besides, I don't tell him how to use the powers I've given. If Cain uses them for his own purposes, how am I then meddling in human affairs?"

God became righteously irritated as He answered, "Because the powers you have given him are not free. He feels indebted to you for them, thus easily influenced. Accordingly, since you have been intervening in human affairs through him, I forbid you to—"

Lucifer interrupted God with frustration, cutting Him off before He could finish His sentence. "God! That's unfair. You're being un—"

Before he could finish, God shut him up with a bellowing, righteous rage, sending Lucifer hurtling across the chamber. "How dare you interrupt Me, and say I am unfair! I should destroy you immediately, and I would if not for the sake of My Holy Name! If you think that unfair, I also forbid any of your other spiritual followers to help the humans in any of their human endeavors. You and your spiritual followers may communicate with them, but nothing more. No more supernatural powers bestowed on humans, even if they are hybrid humans. Do you understand, Lucifer?"

Lucifer trembled with fear, but with defiance he said bravely, "What about the temptations? You've allowed us to tempt humans since the beginning, because You can't tempt humans with evil. Are You saying You don't need us any longer for that?"

With righteous anger still resonating off His Holy Body of Light, God said with immense self-control, "The humans have sunk so low in their hereditary sins, they no longer need temptations from you or your spiritual followers. Their hearts and minds will tempt them more than you ever could, so from now on, you and your spiritual followers must cease tempting them."

With suppressed rage changing Lucifer's complexion to a dark yellow light, he said in between clenched teeth, "Yes, Most Holy One, I understand. I understand everything but one thing. I don't understand why You allow humanity to continue to exist since they've become so sinful and disgusting. You've already admitted that none of them are perfect, that every one of them is a disgusting sinner. Why not just destroy them all and start over again?"

"Because it still would not answer the question, namely, can they live a better life without Me?" God said with righteous disgust while looking away. "Now stop taunting Me and leave."

The order was spoken in a low, ominous Voice that vocalized an underlying threat. It sent sparks of fear racing through Lucifer's mind.

Bowing low, Lucifer said meekly, "I shall go now, Holy One." He immediately walked out of the Great Palace as fast as possible.

After he made it outside, he jumped in his transparent ship with bubbling rage churning in his heart. He flew past the colorful atmosphere of heaven, then accelerated as fast as his ship could fly. He released his pent-up rage on his celestial ship as it zoomed past stars and galaxies faster than the speed of light.

Lucifer found himself in a black hole that hid all the stars and galaxies of the universe. It consisted of just an empty blackness everywhere. It was his favorite place, a place where he loved to meditate after speaking with God. A place where he made devious plans before returning to Earth.

After his rage subsided and a plan formulated in his wicked mind, he decided to collect together all his spiritual followers. He would order them to implement his plan immediately. Gathering together all his supernatural powers, he sent telepathic messages to all his spiritual followers to meet him at a certain secluded place on Earth.

He soon arrived at the place he ordered them to be. They all awaited his arrival with anxiety. He stepped out of his celestial ship and levitated in the secluded area that was lit by the living lights of his followers.

Spreading his arms of light wide apart, he said with a deep, charismatic voice that could easily be heard by the great multitude. "Brothers, I called you here to share with you the news our Creator has given me. Our Creator has forbidden us to intervene in any human affairs again. We're now not even allowed to tempt them anymore!"

A murmur of disapproval rose throughout the spiritual crowd.

Lucifer frowned as he nodded his head sadly with agreement. "That's what I thought also, brothers, it's not fair. His unfairness is one of the main reasons we rebelled against Him before. He continues to love humans more than us. We also know that's not right, because we were created first, and we are more superior to any physical flesh. They are so inferior, they should even worship us!

"I tempted Eve into rebelling to show our Creator how unfaithful, unreliable, and inferior humans really are. Now He's ordering us to stop in our goal of showing Him just how disgusting they are."

A loud murmur of disapproval rose from the spiritual crowd.

After the noise abated, Lucifer continued fervently, "We can't allow that, brothers. We must start a war that will not only include heaven this time, but also the Earth. We must enlist the aid of as many disgusting humans we can recruit to help fight with us. Even if we lose, we'll make sure God loses also. Since He loves humans more than us, perhaps the pain of losing so many humans to our side will disillusion Him so much He'll start over again with another universe and leave this one for us to rule!"

Raising his demonic arms high over his head, he screamed fanatically, "We will fight to show our superiority!"

All the demons cheered in agreement with exultation.

Lemuel, James, Kim Foo, and Pamela sat near the Weeping Wall while eating their lunch. To their surprise, Cain walked up to them in casual clothes. The general public did not recognize him, but they did.

"Hello, everyone," Cain said with a mischievous expression on his face.

"Wha—wha—what are you doing here?" Lemuel asked with stuttering surprise.

"Oh," Cain said casually, "I've just come over to invite you and Pamela to lunch at the place I'm staying at in Jerusalem."

"We're not interested," Lemuel said curtly. "Besides, we've already eaten lunch, so I respectfully decline your offer."

Cain chuckled with a sneering expression on his face, which caused them to feel nervous. He then said with a sarcastic jeer on his lips, "I don't think you understand, Lemuel. That wasn't a request. It was an order."

"Don't go, Lemuel, it's a trap!" James exclaimed fearfully.

"He's right," Pamela pleaded with fear-stricken eyes. "Let's not go. Cain probably has something devious planned for us, especially since we've been preaching against him. Please, Lemuel, let's not go. He can't abduct us here. There are too many witnesses around."

"She's right, Lemuel," Kim Foo said with his wise expression. "Something doesn't sound right. Stay here and we'll protect you. He doesn't dare draw attention to himself with such a large crowd around."

Lemuel did not need their advice. He did not plan on going anywhere. Their good advice only strengthened his resolve as he told Cain with determination, "You have to be kidding. First off, I know you're a cold-blooded killer and a rapist, and because of that Pamela and I would be fools to go anywhere with you. Second, I know you'd love to at least torture me since I've refused to join you, so if you don't mind, Pamela and I will just stay here with our friends."

Pamela then snuggled up close to Lemuel with relief, and he reciprocated by wrapping his arm around her.

"I'm afraid I do mind, and it's not up to you," Cain said angrily. "I've made up my mind, and you two are going to come along, whether you want to or not." He immediately snapped his fingers twice.

Lemuel and Pamela found themselves restrained by an unseen power and forced to stand up.

"Lemuel, what has he done?" Pamela asked with panic.

"I don't know, Pam, but it appears he's using some sort of supernatural power to force us to go with him," he answered, astonished.

James and Kim Foo jumped to their feet with alarm, and they moved toward the frozen couple, but before they could reach them, Cain snapped his fingers twice again, and they also felt an unseen force restrain them, causing them to freeze in place like frozen snowmen.

James shouted out to them, "Everyone scream. Maybe we'll draw attention from the crowd to this supernatural atrocity."

Before they could scream, Cain snapped his fingers four times, and they felt their mouths shut so firmly they could not scream.

"I'm afraid I can't allow that to happen," Cain said with a gleeful look. "We don't need a lot of attention." Looking at Lemuel and Pamela sternly, he said with a threatening undertone, "You both can either walk on your own, or you will be drug standing up, which I'm sure will be uncomfortable. Hopefully you both will make the right decision since resistance is futile, but personally I could care less." With a smile, he turned around and walked away without a word.

They felt the invisible force pull them in the direction Cain walked. At first they stumbled, but the invisible force would not let them fall. They soon learned to keep pace with the relentless force that pulled them with unyielding power right behind Cain.

At the American Embassy, Cain shut the office door, then turned around, gazing at them both silently. He then said mockingly, "Thanks for joining me. I didn't know if I'd ever get the pleasure of seeing you two again, especially after all the negative things I've been hearing."

He then walked over to Pamela. Standing with his nose close to hers, he exclaimed with an outburst of anger, "I thought we had a deal! I thought you were supposed to be on my side! Why are you determined to destroy my reputation? Come on, tell me. I've released your mouth restraint."

Pamela stood mute, not knowing how to respond.

Cain sighed with exasperation before saying, "I see you've left me with no other option but to let Lemuel hear the secret dialogues we had together."

Lemuel looked at Pam as he asked with alarm, "What's he talking about, honey? You never told me you were in secret contact with Cain."

She glared hatefully at Cain while saying, "He made me do it, Lemuel. He knew where we were, and I feared he'd capture us if I didn't cooperate. I didn't want him to hurt us again."

"Stop lying, dear," Cain said with a snide tone. "You know you wanted to because my father convinced you by giving you lots of hot spiritual love, and I'm sure you loved it when he was showering your insides with spiritual light!"

Lemuel struggled violently against his invisible restraints, as he screamed with a jealous rage, sputtering spittle with each word, "Bastard! I swear I'll kill you with my bare hands as soon as I break free from these invisible restraints!"

Cain stepped back with mock fear as he said with a cruel smile on his lips, "Oh, please don't hurt me." He then gleefully said with contempt, "I didn't know you had it in you. I guess you're high-spirited after all. Still, you're struggling in vain. You'll never break free until I release you, so save your strength." He then walked over to his desk and put in a recording. "Now it's time for you to hear what Pam and I had to say in private," he said with anticipation.

After the recording was over, Lemuel felt hurt and betrayed. In the back of his mind, he could still hear her conspiring with Cain in secret.

Pamela interrupted his hurtful thoughts with her own

justification. "You have to believe me, Lemuel, he knew where we were, and I had no other option but to pretend to go along with it. I did it so he wouldn't use me again. You have to—"

Lemuel interrupted her with a voice that seemed far away even from his own ears. "You could have told me about it, Pam. You could have trusted me enough to tell me he was blackmailing you."

He lowered his head with a disheartened shake of his head.

Cain walked over to Lemuel and put his arm around his shoulders. He said with a pretended sympathetic voice, "I understand how you feel, Lemuel. It took me awhile to figure out how treacherous women can be, too. Join me now, and I'll release you. Okay?"

Lemuel spit in Cain's eyes, then said with angry disgust, "I'd never join you, even if you were the last person on earth!"

Cain took out his handkerchief and wiped the saliva away from his eyes while speaking calmly with self-control, "Very well then. I have some comfortable cells at the White House where I'll keep you two. You've been there before, so you know where they're at. I'll have you and Pamela ride with me in my personal jet tonight.

"We'll be back to America in no time at all. I'm disappointed you still refuse to join me, but I'm sure she'll enjoy the attention I'll be giving her. I look forward to having you watch me ravish her again, especially now that she's your woman. It will make it all the sweeter."

James and Kim Foo waited for several hours for Lemuel and Pamela to return. When they realized they were not returning, they decided to alert the public that Cain had abducted their friends.

Kim Foo first called his wife to join them, in order to bring Lemuel's papers, the ones showing Cain as the son of the devil.

Mrs. Foo wasted no time in gathering up the papers and quickly bringing them. She watched them gather together a large crowd and teach them by showing them the important papers, proving Cain was the son of the devil and strengthening their argument that their friends had been abducted by Cain. She wondered if the crowd believed them, but she was mainly concerned over the abduction of Lemuel and Pamela. She liked them both a lot.

Suddenly James stopped his teachings in midsentence as he watched a man with bodyguards push his way toward them through the crowd.

"Move aside! Move aside!" a disguised Cain ordered, forcefully parting the large crowd with shoves. Soon he stood in front of James.

"Hello there," he said with a friendly smile that helped mask his shrewd eyes. "How's life treating you?"

"Good until I saw you," James said sarcastically. "You've disguised your looks, but I know who you are. When are you going to release Lemuel and Pam?"

With a deceitful smile, Cain pretended ignorance as he said, "I don't know what you're talking about."

He then said in a lower voice that only James, Kim Foo, and his wife could hear, "I don't know why I'm doing this because I could care less about your miserable life, or Kim Foo's, but my father has told me if you two don't cease and desist in slandering my name, he'll come over this very day and kill you both, so I recommend you both go home and leave me alone."

"I'm ready to die now," Kim Foo said as he looked over at his wife with sadness, "because I know God has a better place waiting for me in heaven. I just hope He'll take care of my wife until she can join me."

She heard him, and hurt filled her heart. Even though she had been taught since childhood that a man's wife always remained subservient no matter what, she still wanted him to leave. She loved him so much, and she did not want to lose him, but regardless of her desires, she remained subservient.

James became inspired with Kim Foo's defiance, and he said courageously, "If Kim Foo's willing to give up his life, and even his wife, whom he loves more than anything in this world, giving my life as a sacrifice for the people of this world is a small price to pay, so I'll not be leaving, either."

"I don't have time for this soap opera," Cain said sarcastically. "I've just returned to try to save you idiots. If you refuse to leave, that's your problem. Make sure you give it some more careful thought before you continue on this destructive course. Whatever you decide, I've done my good deed for the day. I've at least given you two idiots a warning. I've nothing more to say." He then turned around indignantly and walked off with his bodyguards.

Kim Foo continued preaching against Cain, with James verifying what Kim Foo said with Lemuel's research papers. They continued accusing Cain of abducting their friends and begging the crowd to help have them released. After teaching and begging incessantly for help most of the day, James and Kim Foo's mouths opened with amazement.

Everyone looked to where they stared.

Behind the crowd stood a giant humanoid-shaped being who appeared to be made of a bright, fluctuating light, with a yellow aura surrounding him. At ten feet tall, his thick body of solid light appeared to be in constant motion, like a humanoid-shaped transparent cup, filled with thick, yellow honey.

Everyone dropped to their knees and worshiped the creature. They thought he was God.

James recognized the creature immediately. It was the same creature he had seen in his vision. Lucifer had finally showed himself in person.

"He's not God," James screamed frantically above the worshiping voices. "He's the devil! Don't worship him! Flee! Run for your lives!"

The crowd would not listen. To them the creature appeared so glorious, it could be no one but God himself, so they continued worshiping the creature with their foreheads to the ground.

Lucifer walked past their prostrated bodies over to James. With a deep, echoing voice, he said, "Let them worship me. I'm more superior than any fleshly creation. Leave them alone because it brings them joy to worship me." Lucifer looked at Kim Foo as he said, "I've been watching you and James preach against my son, and it brings me great sorrow. You both are ruining his reputation. I want you to stop now."

Both James and Kim Foo bravely said at the same time, "No."

Lucifer's complexion changed to a dark yellow as he said angrily, "I originally came here to just ask you both to stop preaching against my son, but since you both have refused, my requirements have gone up. Now you both must fall down and worship me. Otherwise you'll both die this day. Worship me and live, disobey and die."

"We'll never worship you!" both exclaimed bravely.

Lucifer smiled. "I thought you'd say that. Too bad." With that said, he turned around and walked away. After he walked past a multitude of worshipers, he turned back around and pointed one bright index finger at James, and the other at Kim Foo. "You'll both die, then you'll leave my son alone."

Vibrant lasers of light shot from his pointing fingers. One hit James, the other Kim Foo. They both dropped to the ground, screaming in agonizing pain. They died a fast, excruciatingly painful death, as they screamed with torment through the last few seconds of their lives.

Mrs. Kim Foo ran with panic over to her husband, screaming

with a shrill voice. She held his head close to her bosom and rocked back and forth, trying to comfort him as best she could with whispering endearments. "It's okay. You'll survive. You'll survive! Hang in there. Please hold on until medical help arrives. It'll be okay then. They'll help you."

Kim Foo made no movements because death had claimed him.

She finally looked into his unseeing eyes and came to the realization that he was dead. She buried her face into his neck while weeping with a deep sense of loss. "No! Please, no! Please don't die! I love you, Kim Foo! You're my man, and I love you! Please don't leave me! I need you! Just hold on a little longer, help will be here soon. Kim Foo, don't die. Please don't..."

Lucifer walked away with a smile, slowly vanishing with each step.

A sympathetic stranger in the crowd attempted to pull her off Kim Foo's body while saying, "Ma'am, please get off him. That yellow glow clinging to his body could be radioactive, and it could kill you, too."

"I don't care!" she screamed with a heart-wrenching cry. "My world has ended anyway!" She dropped her head to his chest and wept even harder. Hurt, pain, and misery became her only companions.

(PAST)

Kublai Khan, the grandson of Genghis Khan, lay on his deathbed with only a few precious hours left. As he lay dying, incense drifted up in smoky spirals from the golden holders throughout the room, filling the room with pleasant odors of cinnamon and myrrh. Colorful Chinese vases and furniture, inlaid with gold, filled the room.

Mongol bodyguards dressed in ceremonial uniforms stood at rigid attention side by side against the walls throughout the room. Being the emperor's Honor Guard, they would follow Kublai to his final resting place. They would guard his body until they succumbed to starvation. They would give the emperor their highest honor by sacrificing their lives for him.

Kublai Khan felt he deserved their ultimate sacrifice. He became the founder and first emperor of the Mongol Yuan dynasty in China, and the most honored man in China.

Lemuel sat beside him and mourned silently over his dying leader, as tears trickled down his cheeks. He knew the last day of Kublai

Khan's life had arrived.

After an hour, the emperor regained consciousness again. Looking at Lemuel, he asked in his Mongol language, "How long was I out this time?"

Lemuel smiled with relief as he said, "Only an hour or so this time, your greatness." With sadness he continued, "Your doctors have said you'll eventually sink into a comatose state, one you'll never be able to wake from."

Chuckling lightheartedly, Kublai said merrily, "No more sleep for me."

"If only it were that easy," Lemuel said with grief written all over his face.

"So are you going to stay by my side to the end, my most trusted counselor?" Kublai asked with concern on his face.

He smiled at Kublai with a sad, yet tender smile as he said, "You didn't think I'd leave you alone to begin your most exciting journey, did you?"

Kublai watched tears slowly glide down Lemuel's face, so he said with a comforting tone, "Don't cry, Lemuel. I go the way of all mankind." Opening his eyes quizzically, he continued, "Which causes me to wonder about you. I still remember when we first met. I was as young as you then. Now I'm an old, broken-down man of seventy-nine years, yet you appear as young as you did the day I met you. How did you manage to stay so young? What's your secret? Tell me before I die. I promise you it'll be a secret I'll take to my Imperial Sepulcher."

Lemuel always managed to steer the emperor's curiosity elsewhere whenever Kublai delved into the riddle of his eternal youth, but he decided to grant the emperor's last wish. Since the emperor lay dying, he saw no harm in telling him his secret. He told him about his immortal father, and about his father's brethren who came from a different part of the universe. He told him about his own immortality, even though his mother was just a human. He told him about some of the experiences he underwent during his thousands of years of life. He stopped talking after about an hour when the emperor began wheezing laboriously.

After a few moments of forced breathing, Kublai regained his breath and said with admiration shining from his eyes, "That's why you're my wisest counselor. You've had thousands of years of experiences to draw on. With your help, I've subdued the most populated nation on earth. The Chinese warlords don't dare oppose me anymore, and the Chinese peasants don't dare revolt against me either.

"With the implementations of your advice, this great nation is at peace, and rich. With your help, I've become the richest, most powerful leader in the world. Only one riddle puzzles me now, Lemuel. Why did you decide to counsel me?"

Lemuel did not want to hurt Kublai's feelings, but after all the years he had devoted to him, he owed him the truth. "Out of all the men, you'd have been the one I would've chosen, but I didn't choose you because of your benevolence. I chose you because of the year in which you were born. You were born in a year that's in the series of nines. For some reason, and I don't know why, some people who are born in a year that falls in the series of nines seem to influence the world in some significant way. Since you were already born into great power, I knew you were one of those people. Anyway, I decided I had to become your counselor before an evil man named Cain did. He would've influenced you in an evil way, and he would've hurt this world through you."

Kublai gently patted Lemuel's hand with understanding as he said, "Yes, Lemuel, no counselor could have counseled me as well as you have. I only wish I could continue living so we could be a benefit to the whole world, not just China and the Middle East. Before I go, promise me you'll stay long enough to help my successor gain firm control over my vast Chinese Empire. You know how the Chinese people are. After they find out I have died, they'll try to regain control of their nation once again. The only thing they understand is brute force, so you must act decisively after I die."

Kublai then began wheezing worse than ever, and Lemuel knew the time had arrived. Lemuel's heart filled with desperation as he screamed loudly, "Doctor! Doctor!"

Chapter 20

For three days James and Kim Foo's bodies lay dead by the Weeping Wall.

No one dared move their bodies since the yellow glow clung to them tenaciously. The Israeli government guarded their bodies with soldiers from a safe distance, just to make sure no one retrieved them. Because of the shimmering light that radiated off their bodies, the government considered them a public health hazard. Crowds of curiosity seekers observed them from behind the line of soldiers. The only one who dared stay close was Kim Foo's wife.

She lay with her husband, clinging to him as if he were a life raft in a secluded ocean. Her eyelids were puffy from all the tears she shed. For three days she refused to eat or drink anything, so she slowly perished from dehydration. She did not care because she wanted to die. Since her man had died, she did not want to go on. She possessed no will to live, so she made up her mind to die in her man's arms. She nuzzled against his chest and mourned her loss with subdued moans.

Suddenly, she felt a hand on the side of her head. She turned quickly and saw no one. She looked back to the face of her husband and watched in wonder as his eyes opened with a gentle smile on his face.

"I love you," he said tenderly.

Tears of joy burst from her eyes as she said, "I thought you were dead!"

"I was," he said, while slowly rising into a sitting position with her still clinging to him, "but I've been resurrected."

"I'm so happy!" she exclaimed hoarsely in between parched lips. "Now we can go home and leave this godforsaken place."

"I'm afraid not, my love," he said sadly as he looked over at James, "because God will soon call James and me into the air. You'll have to stay here for now." Looking at her with pity, he added with hope, "Maybe I'll be allowed to come back and get you someday."

"No," she moaned with a heartbreaking plea. "We belong together because we're a team!"

He caressed her face with his hand as he said sadly, "Before I go,

I just want to tell you, I love you so much, and I have from the day I met you. You've been the best wife any man could ever hope to have, and if I could take you with me, I would, but it's not possible right now."

She became fearful of losing her man again as she pulled him closer while saying, "No, Kim, please don't say such ridiculous things! You're my man, and I'll follow you wherever you go."

He held her tenderly while saying in a soothing tone, "No, my love, you'll not be able to follow me where I'll be going."

Suddenly, two giant beams of kaleidoscopic light fell from the sky like a colorful rainbow. One covered James and the other covered Kim Foo.

They both floated up in the colorful beams.

Kim Foo's wife grabbed desperately on to her husband's leg as she pleaded, "No, Kim! You must not leave me! You must take me with you!"

He looked sadly down and said, "I can't take you with me. I'm sorry."

"No, Kim, don't leave me!" she screamed in desperation, holding on to his feet and fighting against the inexorable force that pulled him into the sky.

"Good-bye, my love," he said as the colorful beam of light jerked him from her clutching fingers.

"No, Kim! Please take me with you!" she begged with gut-wrenching sobs as she stretched her arms high in the air, hoping to follow him in the beam.

With her vision blurred with tears, she watched him ascend higher and higher, until he appeared to become as small as the head of a needle, disappearing soon afterward. The ray of light disappeared with him.

She fell to the ground grief-stricken, and wept against the dry earth. Suddenly, she felt the earth shake. The noise of it sounded like a continuous explosion. She rose up in a sitting position as she heard distant buildings falling with loud crashes. She heard people screaming with terror and watched them scurrying around like terrified rats. She heard car horns blaring and crashes all around. Pandemonium ensued, and confusion encompassed the whole city as certain parts of the earth opened up to claim properties and victims.

She stood up on wobbly legs. While the earth continued to shake, she staggered off toward the nearest building. She hoped it would fall on her if she could get close enough. She wanted to be with her man so much, she hoped the earthquake would be her ticket to where he was going.

James felt himself rise in the beam of vibrant light. His speed increased as he flew past the clouds, leaving them far behind. Suddenly, he felt his flesh painlessly disintegrate from his skeletal frame. As he reached the outer limits of the atmosphere, his physical body vaporized, leaving just his spiritual body.

The higher he went, the faster he flew. He zoomed past the yellow moon, colorful planets, sun, stars, the Milky Way galaxy, and innumerable other galaxies. He felt himself fly so fast, the galaxies appeared to be long streaks of colorful lights. He flew so fast, individual stars were not even visible, but instead they blended together into colorful streaks of light. He traveled many times faster than the speed of light. He felt as if he were falling with miraculous speed into a spiraling pit of streaks of light. Down and around he flew, around and around into an abyss made of endless streaks of colorful lights.

Gradually he slowed down in part of the universe no human telescope had ever found. The place appeared to be saturated with a glorious array of individual lights, all a different color, sparkling throughout like zillions of specks of glitter.

Looking around with wide-eyed astonishment, he found himself in a celestial city. Everything appeared to be made of a light so thick it portrayed all objects as being made of physical matter. The walls around the city appeared to be made of a giant red jasper stone. The gates appeared to be made of giant diamonds. The streets appeared to be made of pure, yellow gold.

The billions of mansions in the sprawled city appeared to be made of giant, hollowed-out gems of different colors: sapphire mansions, emerald ones, topaz ones, amethyst ones, jade ones, and ruby ones.

Colorful fruit bearing trees of light lined each side of the streets, two in front of each mansion. Each bore delicious-looking fruits of many colors, which appeared to vibrate with life.

The bustle of the city amazed him. Translucent vehicles, with colorful skeletal frames of light, zoomed quickly by like working bees. Spiritual beings, whose bodies were composed of different-colored lights, piloted the vehicles.

There were beings who walked past him on the streets of gold: Spiritual human beings, angels, seraphim, cherubim, and other spiritual aliens who appeared really bizarre: Spiritual aliens who were as small as ants, and those as large as dinosaurs; aliens who had no eyes, but traveled by sound; aliens who had hundreds of eyes, but could not hear. The odd-looking creatures appeared to be endless, with one thing in common: every one possessed a happy, blissful expression on their faces.

James knew he had arrived in heaven.

Suddenly a large humanoid creature stopped in front of him. It stood ten feet tall with a body made of a thick sapphire light, with large wings on its back. It said to James, "My name is Michael, and I'm an archangel. I've been directed to take you to our Ruler, the Most Holiest Person who has ever existed, and who will ever exist."

James stood frozen in stunned bewilderment. Joy filled his heart in waves of unrelenting surges, while puzzlement filled his spiritual mind. Why would the Creator want to speak with him, out of all the myriad of spiritual beings who walked, crawled, flew, and zoomed past him? He asked with wonderment, "Why would God want to speak with me? How can He even find the time?"

"Because He speaks in person to all the new arrivals, and since time is irrelevant here, He has plenty of time to talk with everyone every once in a while, after all, eternity is forever," Michael said with a pleasant smile.

James feasted his eyes on the most beautiful city any creature could ever conceive. He wanted to pour out his heart and sing of God's glory at the top of his spiritual lungs. He wanted to do God's will. "Of course," he said with a joyful smile, "I'll get a purpose like everyone else has. I'll be able to serve my God and bring Him pleasure. He deserves all the pleasure I can give."

Michael bent over and hugged him close to his bosom. His wings flapped gently, raising them in the air. After they were high in the air, he flew James over the huge spiritual city. Eventually they floated above the center of the spiritual metropolitan area.

In the center of the city stood an enormous palace. Like everything else in the city, the palace appeared to be made of a thick light so solid-looking, it could be mistaken for solid material. It appeared to be made of a vast assortment of gems of different colors. Each thick stone of light appeared to be made of a different gem. Each stone was as large as Michael, and there were thousands built into it. The palace's aura radiated out from each stone of light, casting colorful light rays for miles around.

Michael flew James past the open gates and into the palace. They passed a thousand rooms, each one filled with spiritual creatures who walked to and fro, busy with activities.

Finally he flew him into a huge, majestic room. Sitting in the middle of the room was a gigantic throne that appeared to be made of a million different-colored lights that vibrated with such intensity it appeared to be a major power source.

Sitting upon the throne was the Most Holiest Person in the universe. He appeared to be made of a light so bright and powerful that the glory of His spiritual body was practically blinding. Everyone needed to squint their eyes to look on Him directly.

When He saw Michael and James, He stretched forth His colossal hand, and Michael flew over to it, gently placing James in the palm of it.

James immediately felt the essence of absolute love fill every cell of his spiritual body, so much so that it seemed to wash over him in waves. He felt like fainting with pure joy. Every cell in his body felt more alive than it had ever felt in his life. He then realized what pure, unadulterated love felt like. He recalled what his physical body had felt like, and in comparison it was like living in a loveless machine. There was no comparison.

As the most beautiful creature in the universe, God's inner beauty was even more beautiful than His outward appearance. James did not know why that was so, but he could feel His inner beauty surging over him in waves. The beautiful, perfect love that surged out from His palm filled every cell in James's spiritual body with pure love. He became so full of God's love, it gushed out of him like a spring of spiritual water, refreshing him in every conceivable way. It was as if every part of his spiritual body was soaked in complete love. He felt paralyzed from the pure love that washed over him in unrelenting waves. He squirmed in His palm in a continuous orgasm of perfect love.

"Hello, my son. Welcome home," a benevolent Voice said with absolute love.

James could not speak. He continued to quiver violently from the waves of pure love that washed over him.

"I know you cannot speak. My Holy Love has overwhelmed you. Eventually you will grow accustomed to it and be able to function doing what makes Me happy, and therefore yourself, for bringing Me happiness is your purpose in life, and the more happiness you bring Me, the more happiness you bring yourself."

James wanted to do whatever God told him to do without

question. He loved God with a love so complete, he would gladly spend eternity in hell if he knew it would bring God happiness. His driving passion and meaning in life was to bring ultimate happiness to God, and do whatever it took to accomplish that.

God then whispered deeply with pure love, "Be strong, my son, and do not be afraid ever again. My love will be with you wherever you go. I will love you and care for you for all eternity. Sleep now, my son. Sleep, sleep, sleep..."

James felt his consciousness slip away in a contented sleep, as the soothing Voice continued to saturate his mind like a spiritual ointment, sending tingling waves of pleasure throughout his body.

On Earth, at the White House, Lemuel and Pamela sat in the same jail cells they had been forced to sit in when first abducted. Cain treated them harsher than before by having them both stripped naked and one of their legs attached to a metal chain that connected to the jail cells' stone walls.

Cain and Clarence stood outside Lemuel's cell.

Cain looked at Lemuel with disgust as he said with a sarcastic smirk, "Did you know my father told me I'm allowed to kill you now? Apparently there's a full-scale revolt against God, and he has more important things to be concerned about than saving your puny life, so it appears you're in serious shit now. I've decided to keep you alive for a while, so I can torture you for all the bad things you've done to me through the ages.

"To give you a few examples of what I plan on doing, I'm going to start by pulling out all your fingernails and toenails, one for each day. Then I'll pull out all your teeth, one for each day. Then I'll cut off little bits and pieces of you. An eye here, an ear there, and so on, one piece for each day. I'll keep you alive for as long as possible. I'll have my personal doctor keep you alive.

"Eventually I'll skin you alive. Skin off your head first, then your shoulders, then your back, and so on, one segment of skin for each day. After all your skin is gone, I'll start cutting of sections of your exposed muscles. A bicep here, a neck muscle there, and so on, one segment for each day.

"Eventually you'll just be a disgusting mass of blood vessels, life-sustaining organs, and bones, intermixed with continuous, excruciating pain. I'll stop torturing you then. My doctor will have orders to keep you alive at all cost.

"Of course you'll have to be placed on a life-sustaining machine. You'll have to be hooked up to a machine to keep your remaining organs functioning properly, receive sustenance, get rid of your waste, give you medicines, drugs, and so on."

Cain then walked over to Pamela's cell, which was next to Lemuel's. He squatted down on his legs as he looked on her naked beauty. "You I'll not torture," he said with a seductive lick of his lips. "Instead, you'll become my sex slave. While here I'll screw you in the mornings, afternoons, and evenings. I'll hump on you so much, you'll even stay open when I'm not inside. I'll fill you so often, your mind will become obsessed with me. You'll crave my attentions every day. So, what do you think about my erotic plans for us?"

Pamela spit in his face with bitter hatred.

"You shouldn't have done that," Cain said as her spittle rolled down his face. He unlocked her cell door and walked in.

Standing beside her, he said with anticipation, "I was going to be gentle until you became used to me, but now you've forced me to teach you a lesson. Now I've decided to ravish you hard and fast, and it'll hurt. Maybe you'll show me a little respect afterward."

He reached over and squeezed her breast hard, causing her to whimper in pain. Moving his hand down over her abdomen into the nest of her black pubic hair, he felt her as she whimpered with fear. "I'm looking forward to stretching you out real good again," he said as his index finger flickered in and out of her, "but it'll have to wait for now."

He then stood up abruptly. Looking at both of them, he said with disappointment, "Unfortunately, I've a meeting in Rome tonight. I'll have to set things in motion to gain control of this godforsaken world. I should be back within a few days, and then the fun can begin." Without another word, he turned and walked out of the cell, locked it again, and headed for the cell block exit.

Clarence followed closely behind, as if fearful of being left behind.

The cell block felt so frigid, it caused the naked prisoners to shudder from the coldness. They hoped the cold would kill them before Cain returned.

She asked in between chattering teeth, "What are we going to do?"

Lemuel felt helpless as he mumbled, "I don't know. It appears we're doomed. It seems our only hope's the pope, and I wouldn't trust my life to him. This would be a good time to do some major praying."

The lights went out, leaving the cell block dark with a blackness that felt like death itself.

Joseph and a few of his bodyguards stood in the Israeli prime minister's office with the prime minister sitting back in his chair comfortably.

The prime minister felt secure with his squad of professional bodyguards spread throughout the Israeli complex. He felt as safe as a turtle in a shell. Looking at Joseph, he asked with a touch of arrogance, "How may I help you?"

Joseph responded with a sly smile as he said, "Oh, you feel comfortable enough to not even address me by my title now, Mr. Prime Minister? Good, it will make my job a lot easier."

"What may that be?" the prime minister asked with an impatient sigh.

"You'll find out soon enough," Joseph said with darting, secretive eyes. "But for now I just want to catch you up on the recent events. As you well know, the Chinese army has been annihilated with the help of my God, so I don't think we'll have any more Chinese problems."

"That's good," the prime minister said with relief. "One less major power I have to worry about."

Looking at Joseph suspiciously, he added, "I think you're up to something. I don't think you're here to reminisce about past events."

"He's so intuitive, isn't he?" Joseph said sarcastically while looking at his bodyguard.

His bodyguard smiled weakly and nodded with agreement.

Joseph looked back at the prime minister. Smiling with malice, he said, "I've actually come to invite you to the Vatican. I'll be leaving tonight on my personal jet. Shouldn't take us more than a couple of hours to get there from here."

Fear spread through the prime minister's heart as he looked into the pope's evil-looking eyes. "I'm afraid I'll not be able to make it tonight, but maybe another day," he said nervously.

"I'm afraid this isn't negotiable, Mr. Jackass," Joseph said with as much sarcasm as he could muster. "You'll be coming with us whether you want to or not. You're in this predicament because you wouldn't allow my priests to implant your public with my nano chips."

"Let me get this straight," the prime minister said with an incredulous look on his face, "you plan on kidnapping me now?"

Joseph nodded with seriousness.

The prime minister laughed with unbelief. "Your holiness, I hate to burst your bubble, but you'll never be powerful enough to get away with that. For one thing, this building is crawling with my elite bodyguards. The most important thing is, even if you did get past my bodyguards, you'd have the whole world looking for me. You'd become the most wanted man on earth. Your pope status would not save you then."

Joseph agreed as he said, "You're certainly right, Mr. Prime Minister, if I were to kidnap you. However, we're going to leave you right here."

The prime minister then scratched his head in a puzzled way, which caused Joseph to laugh. He then motioned to one of his bodyguards, who left the room, and then returned quickly with a body double of the prime minister.

Joseph then said proudly to the body double, "How are you doing today, Mr. Prime Minister?"

The body double replied back in a voice sounding just like the prime minister's, "I'm doing fine, Most Holy Master."

Chills of terror tingled through the real prime minister. The body double looked and sounded exactly like him. The uncanny resemblance caused him to go into shock.

Joseph said with a triumphant voice, "It's amazing what a little plastic surgery and voice therapy can do. He's respectful and obedient. If you would have been like him, I wouldn't have to be doing this."

Joseph then said in an uncompromising tone, "We're going to put a cryogenic mask on you so you'll look like someone else. Your double will escort us out of the building, so none of your bodyguards become suspicious. Of course, he'll come back in after we leave the building. After all, he's you.

"If you say anything, or bring your hands up to your mask, we'll inject you with a drug. It'll instantly render you unconscious. We'll just say you fainted. Since your double will be in full sight, and all right, I'm sure no one will be concerned over a stranger, so don't do anything stupid. Okay?"

The real prime minister could only nod his head in shock. He felt like a mute man. He stood up obediently when Joseph raised him off the chair. He stood meekly while they slipped the cryogenic mask over his head and led him out of the office like a helpless calf to slaughter.

(PAST)

Cain sat next to Nostradamus's bedside in France, as Nostradamus lay dying. Cain held his hand tightly with desperation, wishing he could help him survive another day. He felt sure Nostradamus could see the future, and that meant more power for Cain.

"Cain," Nostradamus said with a laborious breath, "I know who you are. The visions have told me who you are."

"Who am I, then?" Cain asked.

"You're one of the last seeds of the sons of God who mated with human women thousands of years ago," Nostradamus said solemnly.

"I don't consider myself a grandson of God, or even a great-grandson," Cain said with a facetious smirk, "so what's your ridiculous opinion based on?"

Nostradamus felt nauseated as he said, "I grew suspicious of you when you never grew old. You've stayed perpetually young. Eternal youth's a blessing worth investigating, so I researched it from three different angles, biblical, astrological, and most importantly, through my heavenly sent visions. I've found you're the progeny of a fallen angel, which one I don't know. You're one of the offspring of the sons of God who came down to earth to mate with human women."

Cain felt speechless. He'd found someone who knew about his hidden roots. He knew then that Nostradamus was more of a seer than he ever thought.

He'd become interested in Nostradamus soon after he became famous for being a seer who could see the future, so he researched Nostradamus's roots. He found Nostradamus was born on 1503 CE, and he knew those numbers added up to nine, a prerequisite for most people who were to influence the world in some major way.

He knew Nostradamus would die soon, and since it was 1566 CE, he knew it to be a significant year to die in, since it added up to two nines with no remainders.

Even more significant, he knew Nostradamus would die at sixty-three years of age, which added up to a nine with no remainders. Because of all the nines in Nostradamus's life, Cain knew him to be a true seer.

With burning curiosity, Cain asked, "If I'm the offspring of a fallen angel, who are you, then?"

Nostradamus turned his head aside with modesty as he mumbled, "I'm just a lowly prophet who often speaks in riddles, but who can see the future with heavenly sent visions. I have even seen visions of the last days of this world."

Cain asked with frustration, "Are you saying this earth will be destroyed?"

Nostradamus shook his head sadly as he said, "Not the earth, just the human civilization as we know it. God's kingdom will put an end to all worldly governments, and rule in their place."

Cain felt concern as he said, "You mean, God's going to invade the earth?"

Nostradamus nodded in agreement as he said, "That's exactly what I mean, and you'll see it happen with your own eyes."

Cain asked with wonder, "How will I know when I'm in the Last Days?"

Nostradamus looked past him as if he were staring into the future. After a moment of silence he said, "You'll know you're living in the Last Days when China invades the Middle East with hundreds of millions of men. The fallen sons of God will then defeat the Chinese force. It'll be the prelude to Armageddon."

Burning curiosity blazed in Cain's heart as he asked, "Is there any way to stop God from conquering mankind?"

Nostradamus breathed raggedly with deep gasps. He finally managed to say with all his strength, "Yes, one way."

Cain demanded, "Tell me how."

Nostradamus did not answer. He would never answer anyone again on earth, as his sightless eyes stared heavenward. He died instantly, as if struck down by an unseen force.

Cain refused to accept his death. He needed Nostradamus's answer so he could defeat God when the time came. Grabbing hold of his lifeless shoulders, he kept shaking him violently over and over while screaming, "You're not going to die on me now, damn you! Wake up! Wake up! Tell me how to stop God! Wake up, damn it, and tell me how to stop God! Tell me..."

Chapter 21

Clarence walked with nervousness to the cell block in the White House. Joseph had ordered him to rescue the couple before Cain returned from Rome.

After Lemuel, James, and Pamela had escaped before, Cain decided against using guards. He had grown suspicious of everyone. Because of that, Clarence felt a little relieved since there would be no witnesses, though nervous anxiety still nagged at him as he walked to the cell block. He knew Cain was to return from Rome that day.

After Clarence arrived at the cell block, he walked into the cold dampness. He quickly turned the lights on and saw a pitiful sight. Pamela lay curled like a ball in her bunk, and Lemuel lay curled in his bunk. They were naked and motionless. They were pale and appeared dead.

Clarence's heart leaped for joy. It appeared his plan of neglect had worked. Just to make sure, he walked into Pamela's cell and touched her on the neck with his hand, searching for a pulse. Her skin felt frozen, but with disappointment he detected a faint pulse.

She woke up when she felt the warm fingertips touch her. Rising to a sitting position, she asked between chattering teeth, "What do you want?"

Clarence felt surprised. He thought she was at least unconscious. He said reluctantly, "The pope's ordered me to rescue you two. Of course, if Lemuel's dead, I'll just leave him here. I'm sure Cain will give him a proper burial."

"I'm sure he'll give you one, too," Lemuel said with sarcasm as he rose to a sitting position on his bunk. "As soon as I tell him you're a traitor."

Clarence gazed on an angry Lemuel. With surprise he said, "I thought you were dead."

Lemuel felt disgusted while replying, "No thanks to you. I'm sure Cain will be interested in hearing about how you joined sides with the pope. I'm sure he'll torture you like he planned to torture me, unless of course you keep your bargain with the pope and help us escape. If you're having second thoughts and don't help us, you're as good as dead as soon as I tell Cain about your treachery."

Clarence pretended not to be alarmed as he said, "That's why I came, to help you escape. As soon as we leave here, I'll get us some plane tickets for Rome. The pope wants to talk to both of you."

Lemuel refused with a negative tone. "No thank you. We're not jumping out of the skillet into the fire. No, you can get us some plane tickets to Israel. I'm sure the Israeli prime minister would like to know how dangerous Cain is."

Clarence, Lemuel, and Pamela sat in a commercial jet on their way to Israel. Lemuel and Pamela felt relieved to be free again, and they spoke words of love to each other. Hope and love flowed through them.

Clarence sat silent, thinking of different scenarios on how to extricate himself from the dangerous situation he found himself in. He only saw two options. He could continue going along with the pope's plan in helping them escape, hoping Joseph would prevail in the end, or he could kill Lemuel and Pamela, thus leaving no witnesses. He could tell Cain the two had somehow managed to escape, then kidnapped him, forcing him to go along with them.

He decided to keep with the pope's plan of helping them escape. After he arrived in Jerusalem, he would tell the pope where they were. If things went badly, he would revert back to his second plan and kill them. He would portray himself to Cain as a victim.

Eventually everyone became lost in their own thoughts as the purr of the jet's turbo engines caused them to feel a lethargic drowsiness.

Cain watched the computer-enhanced recording of Clarence, Lemuel, and Pamela in the cell block. Unknown to anyone else, he had a camera hidden in the cell block. Everything they did and said had been recorded. The more he watched, the more infuriated he became with Clarence.

He knew the pope was his enemy through his Miss Universe spy, but he never knew Clarence was working for the pope. He not only felt betrayed by Clarence, he was also hurt. He had thought Clarence was his friend. He decided then to kill Clarence in the most cruel way possible.

He used extreme self-control by not apprehending them right away. In a shrewd way, he decided to leave them alone for the time being in order to see who else might be involved. He wanted to eliminate all his enemies in one stroke. He would see if he needed to add the leader of Israel to his list of enemies.

Suddenly his phone rang, interrupting his devious thoughts on how to exterminate his enemies. He looked at the phone with a curious expression on his face. Allowing it to ring for a moment to exert his control, he turned the video-cam on and looked into the face of his chief scientist.

"Mr. Feinstein, how are you today?" he asked with a pleasant voice.

"Not good, Mr. President. I called to tell you of a disturbing event that's happening worldwide," Feinstein said with a grave expression.

"I'm listening," Cain said as a nervous knot began tightening up his abdomen.

With fear, Feinstein spoke quickly, "Mr. President, I know you're busy, but I felt it imperative you know about this immediately. Red tides have covered the oceans worldwide. There's an untold number of dead sea life washing up on all the beaches. What's even more disturbing, it's seeping into the lakes, rivers, and even creeks of the world, so it's killing a lot of the indigenous life forms in them, too."

Cain thought about it for a moment while worried concern creased his forehead. He finally asked, "Is there any way of getting rid of this red tide?"

Feinstein breathed a sigh of relief before saying, "Of course, Mr. President, we have the chemical compounds to destroy it, but it'll cost billions of dollars, and it won't save the creatures already infected."

"How's this going to hurt us?" Cain asked.

"It could start another inflation. The fishing industry will be hit the hardest, and edible fish will be priced outrageously high," Feinstein said with concern.

Cain thought about the ramifications of the red tide before asking, "Will the sea life recover?"

Feinstein raised his eyebrows with puzzlement as he said, "I have no idea, Mr. President. Personally I believe everyone should stop eating water creatures in order to give them time to replenish. Otherwise, I fear we may eat them to extinction, which in turn will have a major negative effect on the ecosystem of the whole earth, and in the long run, may cause the extinction of all life. That's the reason I called you. You need to convince the worldly governments to pass temporary laws to prohibit people from catching any kind of water creatures."

Cain breathed a deep sigh of frustration. He then said, "I can do that, but it might not be enough to save them from extinction. Keep in mind there will be a lot of fishermen who'll continue catching and selling their catches on the black market, and that's not even counting the common citizen who'll continue fishing. I guess I'll have to contact the only person I know who can influence the common man more than governments. Keep me updated on this scourge, Dr. Feinstein."

Cain then switched the video-cam off.

He leaned back in his chair and thought about what had to be done. Through his spy, Rosa, he knew the pope had technology that influenced people with nano chips. Since he had seen no immediate danger to himself, he had allowed the pope to believe he knew nothing about his technological scheme, but the time had come to let Joseph know that he knew, and not only that, but he would insist on having control over that technology.

Cain turned his video-cam back on and dialed the pope's private number. Soon Joseph appeared on the screen. He smiled while saying cordially, "Mr. President, what a pleasant surprise. How may I help you?"

Cain wasted no time with chitchat. In a businesslike manner, he barked out his order efficiently, "I want you to contact the worldwide media and declare a state of emergency. Tell the world about the red tide that's permeating the world's waters."

"Red tide, Mr. President?" Joseph asked with curiosity.

With impatience, Cain said, "Yes! Red tide. I've found out today. Make sure everyone knows not to eat any more water creatures until this scourge is over. The water creatures need to replenish back to acceptable levels."

"I can do that," Joseph said with amusement.

Cain then said, as if as an afterthought, "You can also give me all the technology you have concerning that nano chip you've been implanting in people. I know it doesn't control them completely, but it does influence them enough to buy, or not buy, what you tell them to."

Joseph became shocked with surprise. How did the president find out? Only his most loyal associates knew about it. With hesitation, he said as deceitfully as he could, "I…I have no idea what you're talking about, Mr. President."

Cain burst into a rage while yelling, "Do you think I'm a fool? I know exactly what I'm talking about! I'm having you watched at all times. There's nothing you do I don't know about! I want that technology, and I want it now! Meanwhile, I want you to influence all the people you control not to buy or catch any more water creatures. Understand?"

Joseph knew he was caught. With resignation he said, "Yes, Mr. President."

With frustration Cain said, "It's imperative you do it as quickly as possible before all water life becomes extinct, which will then make *us* extinct.

"I'll help convince the other worldly governments to have their remaining citizens injected with the nano chips. I'll give them the excuse that it's for some kind of killer virus that's running rampant in the world. You shouldn't have any trouble getting their cooperation then. Just make sure you send me that nano-chip technology immediately. I want to control what people purchase and don't purchase also."

Joseph bowed his head in disappointment. "Yes, Mr. President." Cain hung up without a word.

After Joseph sent some of the nano-chip technology, he breathed a sigh of relief. Yes, the president had found out about the nano chip, but he did not know everything about it, so he did as Cain ordered, but he did not send all the technology. He only sent the part Cain knew about.

The technology had advanced even further than what Cain knew about. Now he could control people completely, as if they were robots doing whatever he programmed them to do.

Everything was on track. Clasping his hands on the top of his head, he leaned back in his chair with confidence. Soon everyone implanted with the chip would be under his complete control by a few strokes on his key board. It felt as if pure power surged through him, causing him to feel like a god.

He heard a knock on his door.

He stood up, brushing away the wrinkles from his white robe. Licking his lips with anticipation, he walked to the door. He opened it in a relaxed manner, wanting to give a casual appearance.

Standing before him was a twenty-one-year-old nun who was a devout Catholic, a true servant of God. She was a virgin, and she planned on staying one for life. She had blond hair, with a baby face consisting of thick lips, small nose, chubby cheeks, and innocent-looking blue eyes. They appeared to sparkle with excitement. She weighed one hundred and ten pounds, and she was well proportioned at five feet, two inches in height. Her firm breasts were well shaped and stretched tantalizing against her black habit.

"You must be the nun who won a visit with me in the raffle," Joseph said with an eager smile.

She giggled shyly with a red face while nodding yes.

"Welcome to my humble office, young lady," he said with a mirthful undercurrent. "We're going to have a lot of fun today."

As she walked in, he watched the outline of her full buttocks move temptingly under her black habit.

"Yes, we're going to have a ball," he purred deeply to himself with sexual arousal while shutting the door.

She turned around with a puzzled look on her face.

He regained his composure and said, "Don't mind me. I like to pretend I'm a wildcat sometimes."

She giggled once more with a face portraying embarrassment. He walked over to the desk and sat down.

"First off, let's see exactly who you are," he said while turning the computer on. "What's your name, young lady?"

"Maria Costello," she said modestly with downcast eyes.

After he typed in her name, her picture and everything about her appeared on the screen. She had been implanted with the new, improved nano chip, and he was going to use her to test the effectiveness of the newer technology.

He began typing orders in quickly.

As if in a trance, she reached back and slowly unbuttoned her habit. She unclasped her white bra. She allowed both to fall to the floor unhindered. She pulled down white panties, leaving them on the floor, over her socks and shoes.

Joseph looked lewdly at her firm, well-proportioned breasts. He gazed down her beautiful body, and saw her blond pubic hair was well trimmed, exposing her slit. He licked his lips in anticipation as he became hard with lust.

As he typed in more instructions, she slowly walked over to him, as if sleepwalking.

She felt as if she were in a nightmare, one where escape was impossible. As the unrelenting commands kept bombarding her mind, she felt compelled to continue forward without compromise.

He smiled lewdly while saying, "You'll forget about this after I'm finished."

Her rational mind struggled against the program, screaming

silently for her to flee out of the office, but her physiological responses were the opposite. Her nipples became swollen, and her unexplored intimate parts became wet.

He stood up and undressed while saying with anticipation, "Mmm, my program's working. I look forward to bursting your hymen. I love virgins."

She did not resist. She wanted to scream in frustration, to plead for her virginity, but sexual feelings tingled in her private areas, and she felt powerless.

Clearing the top of his desk with a wide swipe of his hand, everything fell to the floor. He then gently laid her across the desk, with her lower legs dangling over the side.

She moaned in fear as he spread her legs.

In her mind she begged him to stop, but her body wanted him...

Lemuel waited nervously to talk with the prime minister of Israel.

Pamela and Clarence had accompanied him, and they had been waiting since departing from the Jerusalem airport. That had been hours ago. They all felt tired, and Lemuel could not understand why it was taking so long since he had helped the prime minister become elected years ago. Lemuel knew the prime minister could not have forgotten since he had been a major contributor to his campaign.

Finally an official-looking lady walked over to him. She was the aide.

She stopped in front of him and said cordially, "I apologize that you had to wait so long, but the prime minister's very busy and is unable to see you at this time. His schedule is always full, and he wants you to make an appointment."

Lemuel lost all patience, so he said with anger, "I've been here for over three hours. Tell him it's imperative he see me now because I'm sure the president of America wants to bring down his government and rule in his place."

She looked at him with an incredible expression of surprise intermingled with pity, as if he were an escaped psychiatric patient.

"I'm sorry but—"

Lemuel would not let her finish as he exclaimed, "You have to believe me! Go tell the prime minister what I just told you, and I'm sure he'll see me. Please, just try one more time. I've brought a witness to back up my story. His name's Clarence Sexton, and he's a Secret Service agent to the president. Please, just try one more time, and I'll not bother you again."

She sighed with resignation before saying with pity, "Okay, this bizarre theory you've formulated sounds outrageous, but I'll try one more time with what you've told me. If he still doesn't want to see you, promise me you'll leave and give up trying to see him. Deal?"

He breathed a sigh of relief. "Deal."

She left, wanting to rid herself of Lemuel as soon as possible.

Twenty minutes later, she returned with a friendly, yet puzzled expression on her face. She became surprised when the prime minister told her he would see him after all.

With her most professional voice, she told Lemuel, "I don't know how you did it, but the prime minister will see you, with one stipulation. He just wants to see you, so you'll have to leave your two friends here. If you would just follow me, I'd be more than happy to escort you."

Lemuel followed her.

After they arrived, the aide introduced him to the fraudulent prime minister.

Standing up with an outstretched arm, he walked over to Lemuel and took his hand in his own. He said with a firm handshake, "Good to see you again, Lemuel. It has been awhile since we last talked." Looking over at his aide, he said with a curt smile, "You may go now. My friend and I have a lot to talk about in private."

The aide nodded with compliance and left without a word.

The imposter motioned for Lemuel to sit down in a guest chair.

After sitting in a chair next to Lemuel, he asked, "What's this all about? Are you sure the president of the United States is trying to take over my government?"

Lemuel sighed with exasperation as he said, "As I told your aide, I have proof, and a witness that President Cain plans on conquering Israel, and the whole world for that matter. It's just a matter of time. I've came here to warn you so you can prepare for that day."

The imposter looked serious as he said, "Those are rather grave accusations you're making, and they could get you in major trouble if they are untrue."

Lemuel became indignant as he said, "I don't lie, Mr. Prime Minister. What I said is true, and you'd be wise to heed my warning."

The impersonator knew by Lemuel's reaction that he spoke the truth, though he did not want Lemuel to know, so with a deep sigh of resignation he said, "Of course, I'll have to investigate what you're saying. I want you and your friends to stay at a safe house until after the investigation is over. I may need you all as witnesses. You may go now. My aide will take you to the safe house."

After Lemuel left, the fraudulent prime minister dialed the pope's personal number on his video-cam.

After a few moments the pope's image appeared on screen. "Hello, Mr. Prime Minister," he said mockingly. "How may I help you?"

The imposter answered nervously, "Bad news, your holiness. Lemuel just visited me with news that Cain plans on conquering the whole world. I've sent him and his friends to live at a government safe house until we get to the bottom of this."

Joseph laughed. After he regained control of himself, he took a deep breath and said with a happy smile, "What you've told me is old news. I've known about Cain and his lofty goals for a long time now.

"You did wisely in putting Lemuel and his friends in a safe house, though. Make sure you station extra guards around it. I don't want them escaping. I may be able to use them someday in bringing down Cain."

"Yes, your holiness, your wish is my command," the body double said, attempting to curry as much approval from him as possible.

(PAST)

King James lay in his chambers, breathing with gasps while dying.

Lemuel sat by his bedside looking at his Royal Master, wishing he could help, but feeling powerless to do so. All he could do was try to make his king's last day as comfortable as possible. While thinking of other famous men, he remembered King James as being born in the same year Nostradamus had died in fifteen sixty-six CE.

Lemuel had never cared much for Nostradamus. He found him to be egocentric. He assumed it was because Cain had been the one to counsel him. He knew there was some kind of numerical connection between King James and Nostradamus, though, because of the years they were born in. Again the number nine kept arising.

He had been counseling King James for many years. He still remembered when they first met on the Thames River. As the currents rushed by, they would watch the seagulls scream shrilly for more bread.

James loved feeding the seagulls, and he often fed them many pounds a day. It usually bloated them so much they would be unable to fly for several hours. He still remembered James throwing pieces of bread high in the air, while laughing at the screaming seagulls that swooped down greedily to catch them in midair. It was like a game for James. Instead of using dogs to play fetching games, he used seagulls.

Since then Lemuel had counseled King James on how to live and rule righteously. He advised him to sponsor a new translation of the Bible into an English version, so his people could also read it and become more righteous. He also wanted to end the strife that existed between the different religious sects in the kingdom.

"Are you still here, Lemuel?" James asked with fear, for he dreaded death. "Of course, your highness, you'll not get rid of me that easily," Lemuel said with a comforting smile and a gentle pat on James's shoulder.

"Promise me, Lemuel," he said with a laborious wheeze, "promise me you'll keep my people from killing each other. You know I'm half-English and half-Scottish, both mortal enemies to one another."

Lemuel agreed with a sad shake of his head as he said reassuringly, "Yes, I know your mother was Queen of the Scots. You have my word I'll keep peace between the citizens. You deserve at least that much."

James said with excitement, "I think we should make a hundred thousand more copies of my version of the Bible and distribute it to the Scottish peoples. You know yourself they're a proud, high-spirited race. We must keep them pacified and lovers of peace. My version of the Bible will help."

"You're right, your highness," Lemuel said with encouragement, "because I've found religious propaganda is often the best propaganda to have."

"I feel so cold," King James said while trembling.

Lemuel picked up a heavy blanket lying on the end of the bed and gently covered James. Leaning over, he tucked the king in with it. Afterward he walked over to the giant fireplace and threw more miniature logs into the reddish-blue flames, kicking up ashes and a multitude of red sparks, causing odors of burnt wood to drift throughout the room.

"You've been a faithful servant and a wise counselor, Lemuel. I've not known once when you gave me bad advice or been unfaithful. How can I reward you?" King James asked weakly.

"I expect nothing from you, my lord," Lemuel said.

James persisted with determination, "Tell me what you want, Lemuel, and I'll decide if I can give it."

Lemuel replied back jokingly, "Okay, I want you to get well. I want you to reverse the aging process for humanity so they all may have immortality. I want you to take away all diseases and famines."

King James gazed at Lemuel with a smile of happiness on his face. He knew Lemuel was joking. The happiness in his eyes suddenly changed to fear as his body shook convulsively. Foamy froth bubbled from his mouth, streaking down his chin. His eyes rolled back, showing only the whites. Gurgling noises came from the back of his throat, as if he were drowning.

Lemuel became alarmed. He jumped forward and shook the debilitated king, "Your highness, snap out of it!"

James stopped and looked into Lemuel's eyes, as his face filled with disgust and loathing. Then a deep, alien voice came from the king's mouth, "I almost forgot how disgusting imperfect human bodies can be, so I'll make this fast. I just wanted to tell you, I, not King James, will fulfill your requests. All I ask from you is to try to get along with Cain. You don't have to like him, but at least try to work with him for the good of humanity.

"Don't make more Bibles of the King James Version. We don't want to unite humanity in serving God. After all, it was God who took away human immortality. Instead encourage science, for science is the real truth. After we give immortality back to mankind through science, we'll show God we can live without Him."

Lemuel stood frozen in place with astonishment. He did not know how to answer the alien voice.

Suddenly King James opened his mouth wide, trying to catch his breath as his heart stopped beating.

As James clutched at his chest, Lemuel watched his terror-filled eyes lose their glint as life slipped away.

Lemuel knew Lucifer had just spoken to him through King James. He felt devastated that King James had died, but relieved Lucifer had left his body.

Chapter 22

The day was dark with ominous clouds hanging over the city of Jerusalem. Lemuel, Pamela, and Clarence lived in the safe house the impersonating leader of Israel allowed them to live in. They had been residing in the house for over a week, with nervousness causing them to become irritated easily.

When they first arrived, the fraudulent prime minister had told them he would make their stay as comfortable as possible. The government employees would cater to their every need. His only requirement was that they could not leave until he got to the bottom of Lemuel's claim.

They became nervous when Israeli guards were stationed around the guest house to make sure they did not leave. The guest house had become their prison.

Clarence felt more than just nervous; he also felt frantic with worry. The pope had ceased all communication with him, and he felt it was taking an abnormal amount of time for the investigation. He unknowingly made the others more nervous with darting eyes, fidgety movements, and irrational outbursts.

He eventually became so worried, he secretly made plans to kill Lemuel and Pamela himself before Cain found him. He knew Cain would kill him in the most hideous way possible if he was found with them. With no witnesses, he hoped his lie of being abducted by them would work. He knew it was his only hope.

Pamela felt confused over the entire situation. She did not trust Clarence or the prime minister. She knew they were running out of time, and Clarence's unpredictable outbursts caused her to be even more emotionally unstable. She would often sit in private with Lemuel in his bedroom, sharing her fears with him.

Their secretive meetings made Clarence even more worried. He often lurked covertly near the bedroom door in hopes of overhearing their conversations. He felt sure they plotted against him, so he kept his ear near the closed door whenever they were together in the bedroom.

As Pamela sat beside Lemuel on his bed, purple pillows lay

scattered around on the silk bedspread, giving it a sloppy appearance.

Pamela kept asking what to do. She had become trapped in a maze of confusing thoughts, not knowing which plan to choose. They were in a desperate bind, and she knew they needed to find a way out.

After discussing their problems and attempting to come up with different plans on solving them, she decided to take a break. Gazing at Lemuel, he appeared surrounded by a sexual aura that seemed to seep from his pores in waves, causing her to sense sexual essences radiating out. With romantic fantasies running through her mind, she said with a dreamy gaze, "You're so sexy. I'm very lucky you're my man."

Her statement caused him to stop thinking of plans on how to escape from the house they had become incarcerated in. With a smile of sincerity, he said, "No, Pam, I'm the lucky one. I love you, and no one will be able to replace you."

His words sent a flush of sexual heat rushing through her, so she stood up and said, "You're making me hot, so I'd better get something to drink to cool down. Would you like anything?"

Lemuel felt hot also, so he said with a smile, "A glass of ice water will be fine." She stood up, walked over to the door, opened it, and left.

Several seconds later Lemuel heard a gagging noise. Jumping up quickly with concern, he rushed out of the bedroom to investigate.

Pamela lay near the bedroom door with Clarence crouched over her. He was choking her with both hands on her throat. While trying to pry his hands off, she choked with foamy saliva streaming down the corners of her mouth.

Lemuel ran toward Clarence, and with a flying tackle, he knocked him off of Pamela and onto the floor.

While lying on top of him, Lemuel restrained his arms against the floor, then exclaimed with confusion, "Have you gone mad, Clarence! Why are you trying to kill Pam? Answer me, damn you!"

Clarence's face held a terrified look as he shouted, "We're doomed! The prime minister's not going to help us, and Cain's going to find us! He's going to torture us all to death!" Looking around quickly, he pleaded with panic, "Please get off of me! I have to escape. Get off of me!"

"Shut up and listen," Lemuel said with a menacing hiss. "That still doesn't explain why you just tried to kill Pam."

"She...she called me a bas-bastard!" Clarence sputtered out fearfully.

"That's not true," Pamela said indignantly. "He attacked me for no reason."

Clarence tried to squirm loose with all his strength.

Lemuel said intuitively, "I've figured it out. You were going to kill Pam, and later me, in order to eliminate witnesses. You'd then tell Cain you were abducted by us."

Pamela agreed with nods.

"Don't you understand?" Clarence said with a delirious grin. "I would've been doing you both a favor. The prime minister's not going to help us. Instead he's going to hold us as prisoners until he hands us over to Cain, then Cain's going to torture us all to death!"

With those ominous words clinging in their minds, Lemuel and Pamela felt a cold chill run down their spines.

Cain sat in the Israeli prime minister's office. He felt determined to retrieve the three fugitives as he continued, "As I've told you earlier, Mr. Prime Minister, the three Americans you're keeping hidden are fugitives from the law. Turn them over to me, and I'll keep them safe in protective custody. I do have a lot of powerful friends who'll have them killed if possible.

"I'm a reasonable man, forgiving even. Though they're trying to destroy my reputation, I don't want them killed. There's no other government in the world but yours who dares give them sanctuary. If you continue keeping them hidden, you'll be causing hard feelings between your government and mine." He then added with a warning, "If you continue keeping them hidden, you'll also be increasing their chances of becoming assassinated by CIA operatives. I'm sure you don't want them killed, so give me custody of them, and I'll protect them."

Everything the president said made sense, but he still felt ill at ease. Word was out in the community that Cain was not as benevolent as he appeared to be in the public eye. He did not trust Cain, and he could not give up the three fugitives anyway without the pope's permission first.

Looking at the president suspiciously, he said with pretended regret, "I'm sorry, Mr. President, but I can't turn them over to you until I get to the bottom of this mess. I appreciate your offer to help, but at this time I can protect them. I'll keep your offer in mind, though."

Cain's expression remained impassive, though he felt rage rise to his face. He also felt frustration that the prime minister was the only world leader whom he did not have some control over.

He thought to himself with bitterness, *Why does the prime minister have to be so stubborn?* Instead he said, "I was afraid you were going to say that. That's why I did some investigating into your life, Mr. Prime Minister."

Cain stood up, then walked over to the desk and rested a black leather briefcase on it. He clicked open the briefcase and began laying large, glossy pictures on the table. They were naked pictures of the prime minister engaging in sexual intercourse with a young Arab man.

Cain smiled a mischievous grin while saying, "I don't think your wife will understand. I don't think your political supporters will understand, either. If you don't hand them over to me today, you'll leave me little option but to release these pictures to every news network in the world. I'm sure you'll be impeached and die a humiliated man."

The impersonator clenched his facial muscles angrily. He found it hard to believe that Cain had him under constant surveillance, and now was blackmailing him.

He could care less about his supposed wife, or even the supposed title of being the prime minister since the wife and job were not really his anyway.

He did care about the young Arab man. He was his first cousin, and his cousin knew he was not really an Israeli prime minister. If word got around he was an imposter, it would bring him down, as well as the pope. He needed to negotiate to save the pope.

After a moment of desperate thoughts, he said reluctantly, "Okay, I'll tell you where they are—under three conditions. First, no one must ever know who told you where they were. Second, I want all the pictures, negatives and all. Third, you must never blackmail me again. Understand?"

"Of course," Cain said with a smile as he patted the briefcase with tenderness. "My lips are sealed, and I have everything in here. Don't worry about me blackmailing you again. You have my word of honor, and you'll never meet a more honorable man than I."

Cain handed the briefcase to him while saying politely, "In order to make my job less dangerous, please alert your guards at the safe house that I'll be arriving soon. Also, have them restrain the prisoners with handcuffs. I don't want the fugitives attacking me after I arrive."

The fraudulent minister reluctantly picked up the phone to arrange everything. He hoped the pope would never find out about his treachery, but if he did, he hoped he would forgive him. He was, after all, doing it to protect the pope.

Clarence sat bound with ropes to a living room chair.

Lemuel and Pamela had lost what little trust they had in him. They felt certain he would kill them both if given the opportunity.

"What will we do if a guard notices him restrained?" Pamela asked worriedly.

"We'll explain to him that Clarence lost his mind," Lemuel said.

"I think we should kill the perverted animal anyway," Pamela replied bitterly as she remembered the couple on the yacht whom Clarence had murdered.

Clarence rocked back and forth in the chair, mumbling incoherently.

Lemuel understood Pamela's hatred for Clarence. He also remembered the coldblooded murder of the innocent couple. Instead of complying with her wishes, however, he chided her gently. "Pam, we can't do that. We would be sinking to his level, and we're better persons than he'll ever be." With a musing expression, he continued, "We'll leave him here instead. I've decided Clarence is right. The prime minister has probably betrayed us because we've been here too long. I've decided we must escape, and escape now."

"But how are we going to escape, Lemuel?" Pamela asked fearfully.

Lemuel smiled reassuringly as he gazed toward the kitchen. "I've given what we discussed earlier a lot of thought, and I've decided we'll have to create a diversion. We'll start a fire in the kitchen. After it starts burning good, you'll scream 'fire' at the top of your lungs. As soon as the guards run into the kitchen to investigate, I'll knock them unconscious while the fire diverts their attention. I'll use an iron skillet on their heads, which should do the trick." Looking back at Pamela, he continued, "Of course, you'll be the one directing them to the kitchen. I'll be hiding by the doorway, so when they come in I'll be able to hit them without being seen."

Feeling pleased with his ingenious idea, he continued with confidence, "After they're knocked out, we'll retrieve their weapons and leave. After we're outside, we'll shoot any guard who tries to stop us. We'll have the element of surprise on our side. We'll then run to the garage. After we're in the garage, I'll hotwire a car and ram through the gate with it."

"Where will we go after we escape?" Pamela asked with worry creasing her forehead.

"Let's just worry about escaping first," Lemuel said. With excitement filling his voice, he asked, "Okay, you know what to do, right?"

She nodded nervously in agreement.

"Okay, then," Lemuel said with his own nervousness. "Let's get this show on the road."

He then headed toward the kitchen with Pamela following close behind. Soon they stood beside the kitchen table.

Without hesitation, he took a cigarette lighter and quickly set ablaze the red checkered tablecloth that covered the wooden table. The flames quickly consumed the tablecloth, while eating their way into the wooden table. Acrid smoke began filling the kitchen, bringing tears to their stinging eyes and a burnt wood smell to their nostrils.

Lemuel went to the kitchen cabinets and rummaged through them, causing a loud, clanging noise as metal pots hit hard against one another. He soon found what he was looking for, and he walked over to the kitchen doorway. He stood beside it with a large iron skillet held high in each of his hands.

He then ordered urgently, "Okay, Pam, go out and direct the guards in here. Scream to them at the top of your lungs that the kitchen's on fire."

Pamela nodded her head with excitement, then ran out of the kitchen and to the front door of the safe house. Opening it quickly, she screamed with a shrieking cry, "Help! Help! The kitchen's on fire! Help us, please!"

Two guards ran past her toward the direction she pointed in. They ran unsuspectingly into the kitchen. Their eyes opened wide in astonishment as they saw the wooden table burning in a hungry blaze of yellowish-red flames.

Lemuel's metal skillets clanged out loudly, and the guards saw darkness as they dropped to the floor, unconscious.

Lemuel retrieved two automatic rifles from them, and then walked toward the front door with rifle barrels pointing alertly in front, prepared for any surprises.

Pamela stood frozen by the front door.

"I saw a guard by the gate, and one patrolling the grounds," she said with a trembling voice.

Lemuel handed her a rifle while saying, "The safety's off. All you have to do is point and pull the trigger. The rifle will do everything else. Follow me!"

He then jumped out of the house and ran bravely toward the garage. The patrol guard saw them and aimed his rifle while screaming, "Halt!" Lemuel sent a barrage of bullets at the guard.

The bullets slammed the guard down with an unmerciful force, splattering blood on the green lawn.

Lemuel ran even faster toward the garage with Pamela falling behind.

A guard from the gate ran toward the fleeing pair with rifle drawn. He yelled threateningly with an Israeli accent, "Halt! Halt or I'll shoot!"

Lemuel was so close to the garage and so full of anticipation, he made a mistake by not stopping or looking back. He continued to run as fast as he could.

The guard let loose a short burst from his automatic rifle, punching holes in the metal door of the garage.

Pamela screamed as Lemuel abruptly swung around and dived toward the ground, landing on his front torso in one fluid motion. In a prone position, he shot a hail of bullets toward the guard.

The bullets picked up the guard and threw him on the ground with a loud thud. Red blood gathered around his dead body.

Pamela stopped screaming. Somehow Lemuel had averted certain death and had gotten the jump on the unfortunate guard instead. In the distance, she observed another guard jump out of the guard shack, running toward them. She knew he would be next to them within a minute. She ran even faster to Lemuel as he raised himself up from off the ground.

She ran up to him as he continued looking sadly at the young guard he had just killed.

She shook him roughly while saying with urgency, "We have to go now! Another guard will soon be here."

The mention of another guard snapped him out of his empathy, so he quickly picked his rifle up and grabbed Pamela by the arm, pulling her into the garage with him.

Out of the three vehicles available, he chose the one that appeared to be protected the most with discreet armor. He chose a black limousine. He could tell it was reinforced with heavy metal to protect against bullets and bombs. The front door was unlocked, so he jumped in the driver's seat.

As she lunged in the front passenger side, he took a screwdriver he found on the dash, and in record time he broke apart the ignition box. He wired the wires together quickly and started the car up.

Since time was of the utmost importance by then, he did not bother opening the large garage doors. Instead he stomped down on the accelerator, leaving behind black tire marks and the smell of burnt rubber. As the tires screeched, the large vehicle crashed through the garage doors with explosive force, sending shards of metal from off the demolished doors everywhere, and almost hitting the guard who had made it to the garage.

The limousine raced down the long driveway toward the metal gates. The fortified car crashed through the iron gates as if they were made of cardboard, barely slowing it down. Its tires made a loud screeching sound as Lemuel quickly turned onto the main road.

With eyes wide open, Pamela lowered her tensed-up arms that had clutched tightly to the dash. She said while in a state of shock, "Where are we going, Lemuel?"

He appeared frazzled with stress as he said, "I really don't know. We'll have to go to a hotel somewhere until we can figure out what to do."

Pamela nodded reluctantly, still in shock. It was not a good plan.

President Cain pulled up to the safe house. He immediately knew something was wrong, since the large iron gates lay strewn on the ground at the entrance. He drove over the mess, causing his car to bounce uncomfortably.

When he saw dead bodies lying on the lawn, he said to himself, "I'm too late."

Parking near the front of the house, he climbed out of his car with his two bodyguards by his side. They walked up the steps and into the burning house.

Smoke came out of the house in thick billows, so they put handkerchiefs to their noses to breathe easier. They walked in and came to the living room.

In the living room they saw Clarence covered with black soot. He was squirming in a chair, trying desperately to free himself. Looking up, his eyes opened wide in terror as he stared at an amused Cain.

"I didn't do it, Cain! They escaped and held me captive! See, they left me like this to burn to death. Release me so we can get them together. We'll take care of our enemies together, just like we used to do," he said with pleading eyes.

Cain's face became unmerciful as he said, "I know what happened, Clarence. I know you betrayed me. I know you've been the pope's spy for a while now."

With tears of desperation rolling down his face, he cried out, "No, Cain, you have to believe me. I'm a loyal follower of you! Please, Cain, don't torture me. Please Cain—"

Cain interrupted him with an angry shout, "Just shut up, Clarence. I don't want to hear it! You've betrayed me, and I'll not forgive you for that. For the years of loyalty you've given me before your treason, I'll not kill you or torture you. Their fire will do that for me."

He then turned around and walked away, with bodyguards following close behind. Clarence screamed unceasingly in an insane manner as terror filled his mind.

(PAST)

Lemuel stood on the Union side at Gettysburg. It had been months since he had talked with Abraham Lincoln, warning him about General Lee's impending offensive invasion.

The day appeared dreary with gun smoke so thick it clogged up the noses and eyes of everyone. The gun smoke became so thick in some places that one could not see more than a couple of feet. It was like walking through clouds of man-made fog.

Lemuel admired the courage of the Confederate army. The Union artillery had been mowing down their beachnut-colored ranks like a farmer's sickle cutting down waves of barley.

Still, the Confederates moved forward through all the explosions, gunshots, and screams of death. They moved forward as cannonballs ripped large holes through their bodies, splashing red blood, yellow intestines, and other colorful organs all over the ground. Disgusting human waste and pus bubbled among the thousands of splattered Confederate bodies that were spread out on the ground like a bloody sandwich.

It seemed like a great waste of human lives to Lemuel, so he hoped the blood would help cleanse the nation of the great evil of perpetual slavery.

Finally, a small number of Confederates broke through one part of the impenetrable Union lines and tried to hold it as their force grew larger with each minute. They made a determined push farther into the Union line, threatening to split it, then route it.

Lemuel quickly pointed out the breach, and the Union generals rallied their reinforcements, quickly recapturing the lost territory. The reinforcements sent the surviving Confederates hurling back.

After the gun smoke dissipated, Lemuel gazed with horror on the bloody carnage. Streams of blood flowed everywhere around dead and wounded Confederates. Body parts, including arms, legs, heads, organs, intestines, and other parts, lay splattered on the battlefield ground like a disgusting giant omelet. Swarms of flies and flocks of carnivorous birds feasted on the ghastly morsels of human flesh.

Lemuel bent over and puked, as the putrid smell of death filled his nose and mouth. He retched until there was nothing more, then he dry heaved with retches because nothing more would come out. Still his stomach heaved, trying to expel all the death, decay, and stench that permeated the very air, contaminating every breath he took. After a few more dry heaves, he held a handkerchief over his nose and mouth, trying to keep out the unnatural smells of death.

He hoped President Lincoln would keep his word and carry out the Proclamation of Emancipation. He had told Lemuel he would if the Union army in Pennsylvania stopped the Confederate invasion. They had stopped them, and now it was time for the president to do his part.

Lemuel felt sure Gettysburg would be the turning point for the North's misfortunes in battle, and he hoped President Lincoln would take advantage of the Union victory. Lemuel wanted to save mankind, and perpetual slavery did not fit in to that equation.

A grisly-looking, bloated chartreuse fly landed on Lemuel's nose, turning his stomach once again, causing burning stomach acid to rise up to his throat.

Chapter 23

Cain stood in the pope's office at the Vatican in front of Joseph. He felt frustrated while saying, "So you're telling me that out of over three hundred million people in America, you've only implanted the nano chip in approximately two hundred million of them?"

Joseph felt nervous as he said, "Yes, Mr. President, that's exactly what I'm telling you."

"Why couldn't you implant them in the others?" Cain asked angrily.

Joseph sighed with frustration. It felt like he was trying to teach a little child, but he was determined not to lose his temper, so he replied back patiently, "Because, Mr. President, many of them are illegal immigrants who are afraid to come forward because of getting sent back to their home countries. Others are homeless people who either have a mental disorder, or are fugitives from the government. They even raise their own food."

Cain mumbled to himself, "This is what I'm going to do. First, I'll have a law passed that grants American citizenship to all illegal immigrants who come forward voluntarily. I'll then have them implanted with the nano chip. I'll have a law passed outlawing homelessness, arrest all the homeless, then implant the nano chip in them, along with the rest of the criminals who are arrested."

Joseph nodded with approval. "That should work, Mr. President. It may take a few years, but eventually you should have most of the people who have slipped through the cracks. Just out of curiosity, what are you going to do about the religious fanatics? You never said anything about having them implanted."

Cain barked out angrily, as if offended that Joseph was overhearing his private conversation, "Mind your own business, and don't worry about it!"

"Yes, Mr. President, your wish is my command," Joseph said sarcastically. With defiance filling his heart, he added as if it were just an afterthought, "I guess you'll catch the religious fanatics like you plan on catching Lemuel."

Cain's face turned an angry red as he said, "First off, it's really none of your business. Remember, Mr. Asshole, curiosity killed the cat."

With immense self-control, Joseph kept his mouth shut to pacify Cain.

It worked, and Cain became calm and reasonable. He then said, "To answer one of your indirect questions, I'm sure I'll find Lemuel and Pamela soon enough. They can't hide forever. After I've found them, I'll have them both killed just to be on the safe side."

Joseph secretly hoped he found them first. He wanted to use them in bringing down Cain, but instead he deceitfully said, "Yes, Mr. President, I agree. You should have them eliminated as soon as possible for your own security."

Agitation crept into Cain's voice as he said, "Don't worry about me. I've got everything under control. I'll keep you as my ally as long as you continue being obedient. Just keep in mind that I can easily have you replaced, so don't cross me. No more plots of getting rid of me. I'm still having you watched closely."

"Yes, Mr. President," Joseph said nervously.

"Enough of that," Cain said with boredom as he changed the subject. "Has the typical consumer been slowing down on the consumption of water life?"

Joseph smiled with relief as he said, "Yes, Mr. President, and the red tide's been killed off."

"Great! The nano chip appears to be working just great," Cain said.

"I knew it would," Joseph said with pride.

"Just shut up," Cain said disdainfully. "I was just talking to myself. On the one hand, I really like your humble obedience. You're more obedient than you used to be. On the other hand, you've become such a big pussy you disgust me."

Joseph kept his head down and his mouth shut with poignant self-control, as rage boiled with churning hatred in his heart.

Lemuel decided to take Pamela to the town of Megiddo in Israel because he had heard there was a large cult residing there that was against human governments and that eagerly awaited the kingdom of God with fervent devotion.

Soon after they arrived, Lemuel saw they were on the world news—and every news station in the world. Because of that, he decided to change their appearances by wearing wigs. He wasted no time in purchasing them. Soon afterward, he infiltrated the cult he had heard about and arranged a meeting with their leader.

When the day of the meeting arrived, Pamela stood in the hotel bathroom, slowly putting her wig and makeup on. She felt conflicting emotions in getting involved with a cult, and earlier she had pleaded with Lemuel to just hide away from everyone so they could have a happy life together. She saw no good in joining a cult of religious fanatics.

Lemuel understood how she felt, but he knew her way was doomed to failure. He knew that Cain would not give up looking for them, so Lemuel insisted they do it his way to survive.

With urgency he told her while standing by the bathroom door, "Pam, we need to leave soon. We don't want to be late for our appointment. I'm sure Samson will not wait for us if we're late."

As Lemuel and Pamela sat nervously at a dining room table in one of Meggido's finest restaurants, Samson came over and sat beside Pamela, while a woman who accompanied him sat beside Lemuel.

Samson stood tall at six foot, nine inches, and he appeared as if he were in his mid-thirties. He looked like a typical cult leader with long black hair and beard.

With an Israeli accent, he said, "I want to make this fast. If you're Lemuel, I want to make sure we're not assassinated before we leave here. Before I go on, I want to introduce you to my aide." Looking over at the woman with pride, he continued, "This is my aide, Esther. Isn't she a beauty?"

Lemuel nodded with agreement while looking at her. She possessed shiny brown hair, beautiful brown eyes, a delicate soft face, and full, voluptuous breasts.

Pamela watched Lemuel stare at Esther, and she felt a sharp stab of jealousy. Lemuel looked back at Samson, and with a cool appraisal of the situation, he said, "She must be your wife, or your girlfriend anyway."

Samson laughed while saying, "That's very perceptive of you, Lemuel, if that's who you really are. Unfortunately, it's a wrong deduction on both counts. She's just my personal aide and bodyguard. She's an expert on the firing range, and a third-degree black belt in karate. I've brought her along because I may need her expertise tonight. Especially if you're not who you say you are.

"Until I find out, I'm warning you not to make any sudden moves. She already has her weapon out, and it's aimed at you under the table. She'll not hesitate in using it if you make any threatening moves."

Looking at Pamela with curiosity, he added, "Let me guess, the woman with you is your wife?"

Lemuel shook his head in a negative way while saying, "No, she's just a girlfriend."

Pamela felt hurt by Lemuel's pallid response. She had thought she was much more than that to him.

Getting down to business, Samson said with a serious tone, "I hope you can prove who you say you are, because if you can't, you'll leave me little option but to have you both killed before we leave this restaurant tonight."

Lemuel nodded compliantly as he said, "I understand, Samson, and I'd do the same thing if I were in your position."

With a slow movement of his hands, he proceeded in taking his wig off.

Samson's eyes opened wide with wonder as he said, "Yes, you match the photo on the news. I now believe you're Lemuel, the most notorious man on earth."

Lemuel sighed with resignation as he said, "Yes, I'm really Lemuel."

Suddenly patrons at other tables stood up and stared at Lemuel with alarm in their eyes, while whispering frantically among themselves.

Lemuel jerked his head around in all directions, briefly looking at all the other staring patrons. He then asked with concern, "Samson, did you tell very many people about our meeting?"

Samson said with worry seeping from his voice, "All my followers know about it since we keep no secrets, but I'm sure they can be trusted. Apparently the crowd has also recognized you since you've removed your wig."

"You're probably right," Lemuel said with dread, "but we have to leave now before the crowd alerts the authorities. I have a huge reward on my head."

All four stood up from the table while staring at the other customers.

Esther waved her 357 Magnum around, pointing toward the crowd as she stood in front of Samson in a protective stance.

The four slowly began walking toward the exit. By the time they were halfway there, some of the brash patrons began stalking them with slow steps.

Lemuel pulled out his illegal handgun and aimed it at those who slowly gathered around them.

They would not stop their slow yet steady progress.

After what seemed like an eternity, the four made it to the exit door. They ran quickly out onto the street with Samson leading the way.

"Follow me!" Samson cried as he ran over to his car and jumped in the driver's seat.

Lemuel and Pamela jumped in the backseat, with Samson's aide jumping in the front passenger seat.

As soon as the car started, the crowd was on them.

"Lock the doors!" Samson ordered with alarm as the crowd began beating on the car and shaking it back and forth.

Samson put the car into gear as his foot pressed down on the accelerator. The car jerked forward with a lurch, squealing its back tires with a screechy scream. Noxious smoke left an odorous smell of burnt rubber hanging in the air as the car surged forward. Loud thuds reverberated under the car as it ran over three of the people who were in front of it.

After they sped away from the crowd, Samson quickly drove down different roads, making sure to lose anyone who might have followed. He ran through red lights and veered recklessly with screeching tires down side streets, barely missing other cars and pedestrians.

When Samson felt sure they were finally alone, he slowed down to a reasonable speed, causing everyone to breathe a deep sigh of relief.

Lemuel then asked, "Where are we headed, Samson?"

Samson appeared worried while saying, "I'm taking you to my compound. You'll be safe there. My compound's self-sufficient. We raise our own food, have our own water well, and generate our own electricity with solar panels and windmills. Our main purpose is to usher in God's kingdom by standing against all human governments."

The compound they arrived at sat in the countryside not far from Megiddo. It sat on one square mile, with a ten-foot-high metal fence surrounding it and strands of barbed-wire strewn on top, giving it extra security. Every quarter mile a twelve-foot-high wooden guard tower was placed near the fence.

On it three thousand converts lived in peace and security. The one square mile consisted of enough space to grow their own crops and raise livestock, spices, and herbs. Samson had imported thousands of tons of rich Midwestern topsoil and spread it over the whole compound evenly, so it had excellent soil for grazing and farming. Since it had an extensive irrigation network attached to the deep well, there was abundant water.

Everyone was assigned a job. Since there were people living there who were once doctors, nurses, teachers, mechanics, farmers, and other occupations, Samson used them on the compound with jobs matching their abilities. He even had a small military force, well trained and equipped.

Samson's military force consisted of three hundred men, with twelve tanks, twelve antiaircraft guns, and twelve military helicopters. Samson had secretly confiscated the military equipment at bases across America after the disastrous earthquakes, meteorites, and tornadoes had occurred. Since most of the world was in chaos during the early part of those catastrophes, no one had stayed around to stop them. Shipping them on a freighter to Israel was done quickly after he had accumulated all the military equipment he wanted.

The day Lemuel and Pamela arrived was bleak, with dark clouds and lightning flashes. Thunder rumbled far and near.

Lemuel, Pamela, and most of the converts sat in a large auditorium, with Samson standing on stage.

Opening his arms wide, Samson began his sermon by bowing his head and bellowing out zealously, "O Lord, hear us. Thank You for aiding us against all the spiritual forces in high places. Thank You for protecting us from all the ungodly governments of this world. Please continue blessing us with food, water, and everything else we may need. Help us grow stronger with every passing day. Help us win all battles, spiritual ones and physical ones. Thank You for all the good things You bless us with every day. Amen."

Everyone in the congregation agreed with fervent voices.

Samson gazed at the whole congregation. It appeared he looked into the eyes of every single person, looking deep into their intimate souls. After a few moments of intimate stares, he said happily, "Brothers and sisters, as you know, we have among us the notorious Lemuel, whom the world hates. He also brought along his girlfriend, Pamela. I'm sure they'll help us become victorious over any spiritual and physical battles we'll encounter. Lemuel has assured me he's prepared to help usher in God's kingdom, with the Messiah ruling as king. Until then, let's work at turning the whole world to the kingdom of God!"

Everyone in the congregation cheered wildly.

Kim Foo, James, and others lay in front of a gigantic, golden throne.

Compared to the size of the throne, Kim Foo felt like a tiny ant that looked up at a gigantic person with the shape of a human, but who glowed like a sun.

The light that emitted from God's body was like a rainbow of different colors, fluctuating all around. Waves of pure love radiated out from every inch of God, like invisible, yet tangible heat waves.

God gazed down at Kim Foo, James, and other holy men who lay at His feet. They were all looking up at God when they begged together with one voice, "O Great God, Holy and True, how long are You going to refrain from judging Lucifer and his followers, and avenge our blood on them?"

Suddenly, spiritual robes made from thick, white light materialized upon them. The robes appeared white, like unblemished snowfall, and each sparkled with celestial luminosity.

God's compassionate voice bellowed out with holy empathy, "Rest a little longer until your numbers are complete. Wait for your brothers who are also ready to be killed."

God's love then cuddled them like a mother cuddling her newborn baby. It rocked them back and forth, as if they were little babies in a giant cradle. They felt as if they were floating in a cradle of love, as His perfect love sank into their spiritual bodies to the very core and carried them away on sweet dreams.

No dream ever experienced was as wonderful as the one God gave. The dream bore all the fruits of perfect love. They did not want to wake up from their dream, as God's love permeated their bodies with pure holiness, causing them to writhe with continuous, righteous ecstasy.

(PAST)

"When are you going to shave off that horrendous beard, Rasputin?" Cain asked with disgust.

"Don't worry about my beard," Rasputin said with indignation. "I'll grow it as long as I want. It should be no concern of yours. Remember, you're just one counselor among many whom the czar has.

Nothing more."

"Don't get puffed up with pride, Rasputin, just because you live in the czar's palace, and act like a powerful priest. You're still nothing more than a Russian peasant at heart. Always remember that if it wasn't for me, you would still be a lowly priest digging up potatoes somewhere," Cain said with his own indignation.

Rasputin rasped out threateningly, "I'm more than just a priest. I'm also the personal advisor to the czar's wife. Their child has hemophilia, and I'm the only one who can keep him alive. I also influence her to direct the czar on how to deal with the rebellious peasants and powerful nobles. His empire would have fallen if it wasn't for me! You need to remember who's really ruling here, because I'm the true ruler in everything but title! Don't you ever insult me again! You should be on your knees kissing my feet right now."

Swallowing his anger, Cain said with restraint, "You know as well as I do I should be the one getting credit for your miraculous powers. I'm the one who taught you the ancient arts on how to alleviate the boy's hemophilia under the condition that you would obey me. The queen only keeps you around because she thinks you're the only one who can keep her son alive. The czar only listens to you because of his wife.

"Unfortunately the advice you're now giving the czar's wife is not the advice I've told you to give. Because of your foolish advice, the rebellious factions are growing stronger, and the czar's power is growing weaker. Because of your foolish advice, I can soon see the czar being overthrown and replaced by sleazy nobles, or even worse, communist fanatics.

"If this nation falls under the rulership of communists, there's no telling how far that political cancer will spread. Listen to me, Rasputin, and listen closely. You have to—"

"Just shut up! Do you hear me, Cain? Shut up!" Rasputin interrupted angrily, not allowing Cain to finish. With an ugly face, he continued spitefully, "For your information, I'll be the new czar someday. I already screw the czar's wife whenever I want, and that idiot czar doesn't even know. As I've told you before, Cain, I'm the real ruler here. I'm basically already ruler of this nation in all ways but title, and someday I'll have that, too.

"When I become the new czar, I'm going to have you killed. Then I'll conquer all of Europe and Asia, turning everyone into peasants. Their primary goal in life will be to serve me in every way. I'll then..."

Cain felt rage course through his body as Rasputin boasted about taking the power Cain felt was rightfully his. As Rasputin continued boasting, rage caused Cain's body to tremble with loathsome hatred for him. He decided then with blind rage that Rasputin was a competitor and he had to die. He grabbed the dagger in his vest and screamed in an insane frenzy.

Rasputin opened his eyes in surprise, as the dagger came down forcefully, piercing through his black orthodox robe and into his cold heart.

Red blood spurted all around as Cain kept plunging the dagger deep into the mangled heart of Rasputin. "Die! Die! Die, you son of a goat!" he screamed with rage as red blood spurted onto his face and over his clothes.

It happened so quickly, Rasputin died even before he hit the floor. By the time he hit the floor, Cain had already stabbed him nine times in the heart.

As Rasputin lay on the floor in a pool of his own blood, his unblinking eyes still held the look of surprise.

Cain watched the lifeblood swirl around as Rasputin continued to twitch unrestrained with death throes. With loathsome disgust, Cain mumbled, "Why couldn't you obey me? I could have used you to gain complete power. Your greediness for power will cost me more precious years in gaining control of this world, especially if the communists come to power."

Chapter 24

It was another Saturday, and Samson preached fervently in the auditorium. He preached about God's love and how God would protect His flock of believers. He preached about Jesus becoming king of the whole world.

Occasionally a fervent worshiper would scream praises, causing the whole congregation to become even more excited with spiritual fervor.

During the middle of his sermon, everyone in the congregation suddenly heard the distant clapping of hundreds of helicopter blades. Ominous quiet filled the auditorium, and dread filled everyone's hearts.

Samson said with a worried voice, "Brothers and sisters, just to be on the safe side, I'll end this sermon now, and have everyone go to our bomb shelter. Please don't panic. It's probably just a military exercise and has nothing to do with us. Please walk in an orderly way to the exit now. Don't run or push. Remember, God will protect us."

People stood up, and amid curious jabbering, walked to the exit.

As the sounds of the aircraft drew even closer, the jabbering grew louder. People crowded together, wanting to get out of the auditorium even more quickly.

When the explosions began, they pushed against one another in panic. Some were knocked down and trampled. Some of the women and children screamed in fear.

"Brothers and sisters," Samson cried out over the commotion, "please be calm! Please don't scream! Please don't push! Please walk out in an orderly manner! God will take care of us. God will save us. God..."

The screams and explosions overshadowed Samson's words, so he ran over to Lemuel and ordered loudly, "Follow me! We'll have to take the back exit and gather together the pilots. We're probably going to have to make a last stand! We'll have to activate our antiaircraft batteries, as well. Perhaps they'll be able to destroy most of the enemy!"

Pamela clutched on to Lemuel's arm as she whimpered with fear. "What can I do?" she asked.

"You'll have to go hide in the bomb shelter," Lemuel said with concern. "We'll need you there to help care for the children and any wounded."

Before leaving, he bent over and kissed her on the forehead. "I love you, Pam, and I always will."

He then left quickly with Samson leading the way. They did not even look back. Pamela was stunned with shock. After a moment passed, she came to her senses and stood up. "Please wait," she whispered, but they were already gone.

"Please wait," she repeated as tears streamed down her face.

Instead, Samson and Lemuel ran out the back entrance. They ran like gazelles to the main headquarters.

Running breathlessly inside, Samson hit the loudspeaker alarm. The alarm would gather the militia together to where they were supposed to be. The antiaircraft batteries would be activated, and the pilots would congregate by the helicopters. Samson would direct the battle from the ground.

When Larry, Lemuel's pilot, arrived at headquarters, they jumped on motorcycles that were parked outside. They then sped off to the helicopter pads. They rode past explosions, making it quickly to their pad.

Lemuel and Larry jumped in together, and Larry quickly started the helicopter up. Within five minutes, all the choppers were manned with blades twirling. When the others watched Larry rise off the ground, they followed.

When Larry confronted the enemy, Lemuel's heart fluttered with fear. Before him flew larger and better-equipped helicopters. He estimated several hundred flew directly in front of him. A couple hundred against their twelve. He knew it was a losing battle. The odds would be approximately twenty to one.

Since their crafts were smaller, he assumed they would be easier to maneuver. Swallowing his fear, he told Samson over the radio about the enemy's superior numbers and how best to defeat them.

Samson took his advice and ordered the all the outnumbered pilots, "Fly into their midst and play chicken with them. Let them shoot each other down as you dodge them. Also shoot them down at close range."

Leading the way, Larry flew deep within the enemy's formation, with the others following close behind.

Cain's superior numbers were caught off guard. Some of them exploded in large billows of flames and smoke, with metal parts from destroyed copters hurtling violently against the intact ones, causing others to crash also.

Cain screamed with frustration over his radio, "Forget about destroying their buildings. Destroy the attacking enemy with your heat-seeking missiles!"

Cain's forces let loose missiles with loud whooshing sounds. The smaller craft exploded into smithereens, but the missiles destroyed more of Cain's forces, because the smaller choppers moved quickly aside, leaving the missiles to destroy the much bigger ones. For every small one destroyed by the missiles, three large ones were destroyed.

Cain did not care. He knew his forces vastly outnumbered Lemuel's, so he was willing to pay the sacrifice. He knew three-to-one odds were in his favor.

The air became thick with noxious black smoke from the explosions. It caused a metallic taste to linger in everyone's mouths.

After a few moments, Lemuel saw the battle was lost. Their forces were whittled down to just his helicopter, so he decided to do a kamikaze before meeting death.

"Fly at the bird where I think the main leader is!" he screamed at Larry. Larry hesitated in panic, but when Lemuel slapped him out of his hysteria, he obeyed. His hesitation might have saved Lemuel's life. Instead of hitting Cain's helicopter head-on, their blades only hit it, immediately tearing off and swirling their craft around and around. Turning upside down, it fell like a heavy rock straight to the earth.

Lemuel and Larry both watched the ground rush up to meet them. They both screamed with terror while covering their faces with their arms. When they crashed, immediate blackness shrouded their consciousness.

Cain watched triumphantly as the last enemy helicopter hit the ground. The enemy craft caused his little damage when the blades hit, and he was relieved he had a pilot who was good enough to avoid an outright crash.

He picked up the microphone on his radio and spoke directly with Joseph, who was in another helicopter, "Pope, I want you to help destroy this compound. After we land, we'll split up into two companies. Help me find the survivors, and kill them all but Pam. If you find her first, hold her as prisoner. Bring her to me at the American Embassy in Jerusalem after this is over."

"Are you sure you want them all killed but Pam?" Joseph asked.

Cain breathed a deep sigh of impatience as he said, "Yes, I want them all killed but Pam. Now you finally know what I plan on doing to all the religious fanatics in the world, starting with these. Since they never accepted the nano chips under their skins, they're enemies of the world. They're rebelling against us, so they need to die. Don't worry about any political attacks afterward. I'll program the public to agree with my genocidal program, so don't feel like you're the only one doing it. I'll be doing it, and I'll give orders to the world to destroy everyone who refuses to obey me, especially the religious fanatics."

"As you wish," Joseph said with reluctance.

After all of the choppers had landed, they engaged the resistance on the ground. Most of the male survivors on the compound fought stubbornly.

Cain felt exhilarated as he engaged in the fight, eagerly killing a few himself with his automatic weapon. He looked at it as a hunting expedition, with humans being the prey, the most dangerous of all.

Cain's company fought their way into the underground bunker and went from room to room, killing everyone who stood in their way.

Most of the survivors fought back with a tenacious resolve, holding each room to the death, usually killing three times their number before finally being killed in a hail of bullets from Cain's superior numbers.

The last room was the biggest, full of women and children. There were hundreds of them, and they huddled together in fear.

Cain ordered his soldiers to herd them outside and have them all killed.

As they were forced outside under guard, Cain's heart pumped excitedly when he recognized Pamela.

Pamela recognized him, and she resisted when they brought her to him. She tried to fight back, to kill him with her bare hands, but Cain was much stronger. He slapped her brutally, knocking her to the ground.

He then had her taken to his private suite at the American Embassy in Jerusalem...

Because of his own devious plans, Joseph avoided the armed conflicts inside the buildings. Instead they killed all the wounded they could find outside the buildings.

Eventually Joseph happened on the unconscious body of Lemuel.

Lemuel's pilot, Larry, had died in the smoldering ruins of the crashed helicopter, but Lemuel had been thrown clear and survived.

Joseph decided to secretly rescue Lemuel and keep him hidden at the home of the Israeli prime minister in Jerusalem. Since the fraudulent prime minister was still under his control, he knew it would be the perfect place to hide Lemuel.

He felt sure he would be able to convince Lemuel to kill Cain in order to rescue Pamela. She would be the perfect bait to cause Lemuel to kill Cain, leaving himself as the most powerful man on earth. He would then blame everything on Lemuel and have him killed. Lucifer would not be able to blame Joseph for Cain's death, since Lemuel would be the culprit...

After Lemuel regained consciousness, Joseph told him about Cain abducting Pamela, and even where she was being held prisoner.

Several days passed after Cain's attack.

Lemuel sat in the Israeli prime minister's home. He was determined to rescue Pamela, and he would attempt to do so that day. He did not trust the pope, but he believed what he told him concerning Pamela's abduction. Lemuel felt weary after many eons of strife against Cain, and he decided it was time to end it. He was ready to break the ancient mandate that no hybrid would be allowed to kill one another, for the sake of Pamela and for the sake of the world.

The dark clouds left a hint of melancholy in the Jerusalem morning air. The rays could not penetrate through them. They left the city looking dull and gray.

He checked his pass again. The pope had obtained the pass for him, and it would be easy to get into the American Embassy with it.

He pulled out his sharp, double-edged dagger and checked the sharpness. Both sides were razor-sharp, and they drew a drop of blood from his finger. Grasping the ornate handle, he carefully placed it inside his jacket and walked out of the home to the nearest bus stop.

A city bus stopped where he waited.

He walked up the steps and past the open bus doors.

The doors closed with clattering abruptness, and the driver released the air brakes with a long hiss.

Lemuel paid the bus fare and staggered to the back of the bus, as the bus' jerking acceleration jarred him back and forth. After he made it to the back, he sat down relieved.

His mind became clouded with memories of Pamela. He

remembered when they'd first met in Mexico City. The times she laughed when they played around with each other. The first time they'd made love. The bus hit a pothole, snapping him out of his reminiscence with a loud thud and a bone-jarring jerk.

He then began reviewing his plan. To distract attention, he would wander into the American Embassy with other guests. Since he had been in the embassy before, he would be able to easily find Cain's suite. He felt sure he would find Cain and Pamela there. He would then kill Cain and rescue Pamela. He would do the world a favor and rescue the woman he loved, even if it meant sacrificing his own life.

Lemuel's rational mind thought it was a plan based on foolishness. He knew after living for thousands of years, he was acting out of love, not common sense, but he knew the end of the world was drawing nigh, and the love he held for Pamela blinded him to all the dangers he would encounter.

The bus finally made it to the American Embassy and stopped, opening its doors automatically.

He stood up and walked out.

He waited outside the embassy gate until another person walked up to the gate. He quickly stepped behind him, and when his turn to show his pass came, he showed it with a relaxed smile. The guard allowed him to pass, and he numbly made his way to the outdoor rest area, walking nervously to some benches.

When he sat down, he picked up a discarded newspaper and pretended to read it with calm patience. He needed to go into the embassy with more than one person, so as to draw attention away from himself.

Fluorescent pigeons flew over. After they landed in front of him, they pecked hungrily at his feet, cooing for the bread crumbs they were accustomed to receiving from the many visitors who had sat on the same benches before.

Suddenly he jerked his head up, causing the pigeons to fly up with fearful surprise, leaving behind floating bird down as their beating wings flapped away.

Lemuel gazed on the tour bus that had stopped in front of the gate. American vacationers were disembarking and walking through the embassy gate. They chatted excitedly among themselves with pleasant smiles and curious eyes.

Lemuel stood up and laid the newspaper back on the bench. A slight breeze blew a page over as he walked over to the vacationers.

He watched a tour guide stand in front of the group, telling them about the American Embassy. The guide then pointed toward the embassy while the group muttered with fascination.

As they walked toward the embassy with mesmerized eyes looking toward Cain's suite, Lemuel slipped in behind them and with quick strides followed closely. He blended in with them as the tour guide showed the embassy guard at the front door their passes. Afterward, they all walked in unmolested.

Nervous excitement filled Lemuel's heart as they walked into the embassy. His plan was going as anticipated. He stayed behind the group as the tour guide spoke about the visiting president.

Everyone became so fascinated by what the tour guide was saying, they began chatting with excitement among themselves.

Lemuel found it the perfect time to drift off from the group. No one noticed him as he discreetly slipped away.

Determination filled his heart as he walked past many rooms. The closer he came to Cain's private quarters, the more his heart filled with anticipation. He would finally do something he should have done thousands of years ago.

After Cain brought Pamela to his suite, he stripped her clothes off and chained her naked to a bed with arms and legs spread out, each limb cuffed to a corner post of the bed. He only unlocked her cuffs whenever she needed to use the adjoining bathroom. He always accompanied her, and after she finished, he would cuff her back to the bed. He fed her by hand.

Because of his enormous ego, he did not have sex with her against her will, and he refused to use the aphrodisiac medication he had used before. He wanted to charm her into having sex with him. He wanted her to give herself willingly.

After a few days of continuous resistance, it became obvious she would never have sex with him willingly. He decided then it was time to have her implanted with the nano chip.

He had improved its functions with the aid of scientists. Not only could it control a user's thoughts, but also its basic life functions and hormonal functions.

The hour had arrived when he would use her as a sexual experiment.

As he sat at his desk, he typed instructions into a nano chip. He programmed in it commands for her to enjoy sex with him. Her resistance had become a thorn to his ego, so he decided it would end one way or another.

After typing in the instructions, he stood up from his chair with anticipation.

Picking up the syringe that had the nano chip in it, he walked in the bedroom where Pamela lay with handcuffs still around her wrists and ankles.

"Hey, sexy, I've got a little treat for you. It's a gift that will help you enjoy sex with me, and this time I promise you it's no kind of medication," Cain said gloatingly.

Pamela stared hatefully at him as she said, "I'll never enjoy having sex with you because I hate you with all my heart."

Strolling over to her, he put the syringe next to her forehead and pressed the button. The syringe hissed as the nano chip penetrated her skin, resting firmly next to her bony skull.

No bigger than a grain of mustard seed, the implant never left a protrusion. While inside, it released instructions to her brain by way of electronic impulses. It gained control of her life functions, hormonal functions, and thought functions.

When sexual feelings assailed her, she opened her eyes wide with surprise, as her face flushed red with passion. She struggled internally against the chip's program, but hormones betrayed her by activating her sexual desires.

Cain gazed on her flushed face and laughed in triumph. "I knew you'd come around. I'm too handsome to resist indefinitely."

"What have you done to me?" she asked in alarm.

Cain appeared hurt as he said, "I told you I wouldn't use any medication on you, and I haven't. Why can't you just accept the fact that you're attracted to me?"

With all the willpower she possessed, she spat out hatefully, "Death would be better than being your sex partner!"

With a spiteful smile, he stripped off his clothes while saying, "Oh, you still want to lie and hurt my feelings, even though I can tell you want me."

As she watched him strip his clothes off, sexual heat pumped through her with each heartbeat. Her nipples grew elongated, and she opened up, wanting to be filled. She shook her head with resistance, trying to overcome her physical passion with sheer willpower, "No! I don't love you, and I don't want you! I'm Lemuel's woman now, and I'll always be his!"

He lay beside her and looked into her eyes with amusement. "Lemuel's dead. All you have left is me."

Fighting against her own feelings, she screamed defiantly, "I don't believe you, and even if it's true, I'd still rather be dead than be your woman!"

"I don't think so," he said seductively while touching her wetness, causing her to gasp with inflamed lust while raising her hips reflexively.

Smiling with satisfaction, Cain said, "See, you're ready for me now."

"No!" she screamed with all the willpower she possessed, as her body cried out a silent yes, betraying her resolve.

"Sure," he said with a mischievous smile. "Sure, you don't." Moving over her, he positioned himself between her spread legs. She moaned ecstatically.

Her body trembled with mindless passion.

Somewhere deep inside, she found a small remnant of resistance. She grabbed tenaciously to it and struggled against her traitorous body.

Even with feminine whimpers of sexual pleasure, she struggled.

Shaking her sweat-streaked head from side to side and rasping out words of resistance, she struggled, "No... Can't... Oh... No... Can't... Oh..."

Suddenly, like in a dream, she saw the door burst open and Lemuel rush in with raised dagger.

Cain quickly turned his head around with surprise, just in time to see Lemuel sink the dagger into his back. As blood spurted out from his mortal wound, along with the immortal vapors of vibrant life, he shrieked in terror, then passed out from shock.

Lemuel heard distant voices. He quickly rolled Cain's body off the bed onto the floor and under the bed.

"You're alive!" Pamela exclaimed with joy. She then asked with astonishment, "How did you get in here?"

"I don't have time to explain," Lemuel said impatiently. "Where are the keys so I can unlock your cuffs?"

She understood the urgency of getting out of a dangerous situation as quickly as possible, and she spoke quickly, "They should be in Cain's pants pocket."

Lemuel rummaged through Cain's pockets as he heard the voices draw nearer. He found the keys and raised up, quickly unlocking each cuff.

Running to the closet, he grabbed a bathrobe and tossed it to her. "Quick," he said urgently, "put this on. We have to leave before security arrives!"

While slipping on the robe, she asked with fear, "Where are we going?"

"We'll have to go into hiding since I don't trust the pope or the prime minister. Now that Cain's dead, we'll have everyone looking for us. We'll worry about that later, but right now we have to leave! I'm sure a few people heard Cain scream out before he died, and they'll be here any second."

He then wrapped an arm around her shoulders and led her out. She cuddled close to him while walking, as shame filled her heart.

(PAST)

Adolf Hitler felt intoxicated with the power he possessed. He attributed all his success to the wise counsel his aide, Cain, had been giving to him. Because of his advice, France had been taken easily and was now fortified with German earthworks and soldiers. Hitler felt sure the Allies would never break through.

Most of Europe already belonged to him, and he felt sure that after Europe was conquered, the world would follow. He promised to make Cain second-in-command if they did conquer the world.

The day felt chilly, with dark clouds floating in the sky. The inclement weather did not dampen Hitler's feelings of power. As he was driven to the extermination camp in his prized Jeep, he anticipated watching a ghastly show of Jews being exterminated.

Cain had advised him to exterminate all the Jews since they were to blame for all of mankind's troubles. Hitler had agreed. He also loved to see people killed, and so he had been looking forward to the show. Watching people killed made him feel even more powerful.

Cain drove him to the guard shack at the extermination camp. The guard stood at rigid attention and saluted stiffly.

Hitler smiled while saluting back.

Cain then drove him to the camp's headquarters, and the commander stood at rigid attention beside the door. He yelled with a respectful salute, "Heil, Hitler!"

"At ease," Hitler said as he stepped out of the Jeep.

His muscles felt sore from all the bumps and jerks he had

endured along the rough terrain. After stretching his arms out with a contented grunt, he said happily, "I just came over to inspect the efficiency of our new gas chamber. I've heard it works even better than the others."

The commander became alarmed when he observed Hitler with just one bodyguard, who was Cain.

"Sir, it's dangerous to have just one bodyguard."

Hitler brushed his concern aside with a careless wave of his hand. He then said with confidence, "Most of my enemies are either dead or ready to die. Besides," he said as he patted his gun holster with even more confidence, "I came armed with a powerful German Luger. The best handgun in the world."

The commander nodded with agreement while saying, "Very good, sir. Please follow me. We have a batch of Jews ready to be exterminated already."

Hitler and Cain followed him into a large metal building that smelled sterile. They walked into a room with a two-way mirror on the wall. From it, they gazed into a large chamber bare of all furniture, with air vents placed high on the walls beyond human reach.

The commander said reassuringly, "We look out this mirror to watch them die, but they can't see us."

Hitler nodded with understanding as he gazed into the chamber. It was already crammed tight with thousands of Jews who were terror-stricken. Some mumbled incoherently with denial, while others screamed occasionally, shrieking with terror.

The commander pushed a button on his desk, and they watched the vents spew clouds of deadly green gas.

Both Cain and Hitler watched with perverse glee as most of the victims screamed with absolute terror. The screams reverberated against the walls. They watched with excitement as the victims gasped and coughed. They watched with perverted delight as the victims fell to the floor, shaking with convulsions. They watched with satisfaction as the victims' lives twitched away.

"Very good. Very good," Cain mumbled vindictively as he watched some of the seed of his age-old enemies die a miserable death.

Chapter 25

Joseph woke up and found himself in an extraordinary room. Gazing around with astonishment, he looked on objects made of thick lights, so thick they appeared to be physical in composition, yet still made of thick, colorful lights.

The luminous objects were three-dimensional and consisted of different textures of brilliance, depending on the objects.

There were statues of different life forms, many not from Earth.

There were decorative vases filled with shimmering flowers of living light.

The pulsating walls and floor shone brilliantly with their own radiant materials of light.

In the center of the room, a radiant throne of light sparkled like a giant diamond. Built in the throne were rich veins, resembling ruby, sapphire, and emerald. The veins of color added to the throne's majestic splendor by bestowing a glorious halo of red, purple, and green around it.

Delicious aromas of cinnamon, myrrh, and lavender permeated the room with aromatic vapors that smelled so strong, he could easily taste them.

As he continued staring with astonishment on the room of light, his peripheral vision caught a movement, and he jerked his head back to the empty throne.

In awe, he watched a humanoid creature materialize on the throne.

The creature's body consisted of a solid yellow light shining so radiantly that it surpassed all the other objects in its brightness. The creature of light shone so brightly, it was difficult to recognize any features on its face.

Joseph fell prone with his face immersed in the colorful floor of light. He trembled with terror while realizing he had just looked on the face of God. After a few moments of intense tremors, he begged with a frightened voice, "Please, God, have mercy on me. Please don't destroy me."

Loud laughter, sounding like deep rumbles, echoed throughout the room. A deep voice then bellowed out humorously, "My name's Lucifer, not God! You've met me before, remember? You don't recognize me because I'm much more beautiful in my own domain, with a beauty that's practically blinding. I'm also more glorified here with a glory that shines out unhindered by Earth's atmosphere. You're now in my kingdom of light." With fake gestures of humbleness, he continued with a meek tone, "You have nothing to worry about from me. I'm as meek as a lamb. It's more than I can say about God."

Joseph rose off the floor weakly, and with stuttering fear, said, "I re-re-remember you. You're Sa-Sa-Satan, the devil."

Lucifer bowed his head with deceiving sadness, and said with pretended hurt, "Yes, humans have called me that, but I assure you I'm not a liar, or a murderer. I've been working at saving humanity for thousands of years now, which brings me to the reason I've summoned you here. I thought you were on my side. I made a deal with you, remember? If you wouldn't harm Cain, I'd help you eventually rule the world. Why have you killed him?"

Joseph pretended ignorance as he said, "I don't know what you're talking about. I never killed Cain. That's the truth."

Lucifer replied back with a menacing outburst, "Stop lying to me! You didn't kill him personally, but you plotted his death, and you helped Lemuel kill him!" Quickly smiling, as if he had not just been upset, Lucifer said, "I'm not holding you liable. I forgive that dastardly deed because I'm merciful. All I ask is for you to repent, and to resurrect Cain. You must resurrect him soon and never have him killed again. Those are my only requirements. If you don't do what I've requested, I'll destroy you the next time we meet."

Joseph sputtered with frustration, "Bu-bu-but, I've no idea how to resurrect Cain! I don't have the power to do that."

Lucifer laughed at Joseph's stammer, then said, "Of course not, but I do. I'll give you the power to resurrect him. There's a war going on against the Creator now. I was forbidden to resurrect people, but since I'm at war against Him, I don't follow His orders any longer.

"You must resurrect Cain soon after I send you back. Arrange a ceremony in Jerusalem for the now-deceased Cain. I want the stadium to be full of people, and for the event to be telecast worldwide. I want the stage to be covered with real soil, trees, and other transplanted plants. I want it to look like a miniature earthly paradise. I even want wildlife in it to give it a more realistic appearance.

"I then want you to resurrect Cain from the soil that's on stage, with my help, of course. You'll tell people that since Cain is the Messiah, he can't be killed. You must then worship me through Cain, and tell everyone to do the same.

"If you do this, I'll spare your life, and forbid Cain to harm you. I'll even give you the ultimate power you crave after this war's over. It really depends on whether you follow my orders from now on."

"I'll do it!" Joseph said quickly, hoping Lucifer would not change his mind and have him destroyed anyway.

Lucifer then said with pride, "I'm full of wisdom and perfect beauty. In the Garden of Eden, every precious stone was my covering. I'm the anointed cherub, the most beautiful of all creations. I'll always be perfect in all my ways. Rejoice, Joseph, and worship me, for I'll lead all of mankind to eternal life and happiness."

Joseph bowed down in worship while saying reverently, "Praise Lucifer, the light of the world."

Lucifer then giggled in an uncontrollable way. Laughter burst forth all around him, as if thousands of invisible creatures laughed together. The room slowly dissolved, and Joseph found himself back on Earth in bed, with eyes wide open, wondering if it had been a dream.

Several days later, on stage at a stadium in Jerusalem, Joseph stood in front of tens of thousands of people as he chanted repetitiously over a piece of the ground that had been placed on the stage, along with trees and other vegetation. Wild animals were brought in to give the stage the realistic appearance of being a small oasis in the middle of the stadium.

As he continued chanting, a blue jay perched on one of the trees cocked its head sideways with curiosity as it watched dust swirl around on the ground. A flying black crow cawed excitedly at the sight, and a hyperactive brown squirrel scurried up a tree to observe the anomaly in safety.

The swirling dust gradually settled until it came to a halt. It settled over a human body of a young adult male who lay completely naked.

A buzzard with a red bald head circled around a few times out of curiosity, until the human chest jerked unexpectedly. The newly created human gasped air in greedily with a loud wheeze, causing the hungry buzzard to fly away in disappointment. The surprised blue jay twittered fearfully, and the frightened squirrel froze in place, hoping not to be seen.

The human eyes opened wide, unblinking. After a moment of uncertainty, the newly created human stood up on wobbly knees, causing the audience to gasp with wonder.

At six foot, six inches tall, the human's muscles appeared well proportioned, like an aesthetic work from a professional sculptor. He possessed snow-white hair, sapphire-colored eyes, and a face that appeared chiseled from delicate marble.

Cain sighed with relief. That last thing he remembered was Lemuel plunging the dagger into his back. He felt so overjoyed to be alive, tears of happiness rolled from his eyes, leaving streaks of wetness on his face. With curiosity he looked around at the landscape and felt surprised with how beautiful it all appeared.

Delicate flowers carpeted the ground, surrounding thriving trees. It appeared like a small chunk of paradise made just for him. He gazed on the large audience who cheered with exuberance. He could not understand how such a small oasis could be surrounded by so many people.

Joseph came over and said, with what appeared to be happiness, "Welcome back, Mr. President. You've been resurrected by your father."

He then hugged him close, causing the crowd to cheer loudly.

When Joseph released him, he turned to the crowd and cried, "Ladies and gentlemen, please let me speak."

After the cheers subsided, he said with pretended excitement, "You've seen it with your own eyes! President Cain has been resurrected with a new body! Since he's our Messiah, who can destroy him? Even when someone tried by taking his life, he still came back. He has already given eternal life to everyone who accepts it, and now he has come back a third time to rule the whole world! He only wants your obedience and love. Love him and worship his father through him!"

Joseph then fell to his knees and began worshiping Cain's father fervently by saying, "Blessed are you, son of the living god. Praise your father, the most beautiful, most holy creature alive. Praise your father..."

Everyone in the stadium did the same.

As their worshiping voices intermingled together, Cain smiled a happy smile. Finally he would rule the whole world after thousands of years of elaborate plans and futile attempts. Power coursed through him like an intoxicating aphrodisiac.

Since Lemuel did not trust the pope or the prime minister, they remained hidden at a hotel in Jerusalem. He saw no feasible way of escaping out of the city, but he became alarmed one day while watching the news. It was the day Joseph resurrected Cain. Lemuel knew then they had to flee from Jerusalem soon.

He became even more alarmed when the governments began imprisoning all those who would not consent to getting their hands or foreheads marked with a digital sensor. The governments explained that the sensors were essential in helping lower crime and expanding world markets. No one needed cash or financial cards any longer. Crime did go down, and the markets prospered, but personal freedoms suffered.

By then, Lemuel had decided what to do and where to go. They would disguise their appearance and return back to Megiddo. Perhaps some of Samson's converts had escaped and would aid them in staying hidden. He also had other, more important reasons for going there, which he did not want to share with Pamela.

As they sat in a restaurant near the bus depot awaiting their bus to Megiddo, Pamela asked with nervousness, "Are you sure we should leave today? Cain has been resurrected for a while now, and he hasn't found us yet. Maybe we'd be safer if we just stayed where we're at."

Lemuel felt famished. After eating a couple more spoonfuls of soup, he said with frustration, "I killed him! You saw the knife. I stabbed him in the back, and it hit his heart. Why did the pope resurrect him, and how did he have the power to do that?"

Pamela nodded with understanding as she tried to answer Lemuel's questions. "Maybe the pope's working for the devil, and maybe the devil gave him the power. Maybe Cain has no more desire to search for us now. It appears he's finally in control of all the governments, so maybe he's too busy to worry about us."

"Oh, he has a desire, alright! Remember what he was doing to you before I killed—"

When her eyes filled with hurt, he stopped himself abruptly. With an apologetic grunt, he cleared his throat and said sadly, "I'm sorry, Pam. I know you weren't willing, and I know you're still having to deal with that traumatic experience. I'm sorry."

A tear trickled down her face as she said, "It's okay, you're just upset. I know you didn't mean to hurt me."

He nodded with agreement, then said with determination, "Enough of that. We'll still need to leave as soon as our bus arrives. If we stay here, I'm sure Cain will find us soon. Perhaps we can get some help in Megiddo."

Reminiscing, Pamela remembered having a conversation with Professor White when they first met. She still remembered a conversation they'd had concerning the city of Megiddo. He wanted to tour the city because archaeologists had unearthed one of the oldest Christian churches there. With that in mind, Pamela said excitedly, "Of course, you're right, Lemuel. We should go to Megiddo. We should make a vacation out of our visit this time. We can tour all the ancient landmarks, especially one of the oldest Christian churches ever to be excavated. When he was alive, James wanted to go see it. He often talked about it."

Lemuel thought about it for a few seconds, and he also remembered James talking about it. He felt relieved that Pamela had decided to cooperate, so he said with a big smile, "Pam, you're a genius. Of course we should make a vacation of it. After all we've been through, we deserve a vacation."

Pamela smiled proudly.

Cain sat in the Israeli prime minister's office.

The imposter prime minister sat behind a desk and gazed at Cain with an inquisitive tilt of his head. He wondered how Cain felt after having been dead. He wondered how the pope had managed to resurrect him. He also wondered why.

Cain was not interested in what the prime minister was thinking. After gaining more worldly power than ever, he was about ready to apprehend Lemuel and Pamela.

He had been kept informed of where they were. It had been easy since Pamela transmitted information to the super computer via the nano chip. The chip had become an integrated part of her. Whatever she saw or heard was transmitted to the computer. Because of that, Cain could have apprehended them on the day he was resurrected, but he needed to consolidate his worldly power first.

He needed to tie up all the loose ends on the political world stage. He had been successful with all but one, Israel. He needed to somehow convince the Israeli prime minister that serving him was mandatory, and then convince him to betray the pope.

Cain felt the pope controlled the prime minister in some way, but he could not prove it. Since Israel was the only country he did not yet have control over, he felt the pope had something to do with it. If he could convince the prime minister to admit to it, he could then have the pope killed without retaliation from Lucifer. Cain still hated the pope about as much as he did Lemuel.

The Israeli leader said with a smirk, "I'm glad you were resurrected. Being killed must have been a traumatic experience for you."

Cain was not fooled. He said with a frankness he hoped the Israeli leader respected, "Sure, you are. I'm positive you wished I would've stayed dead. Come now, Mr. Prime Minister, let's stop playing games. I know you're working for the pope. He's been seen with you a lot in secret. Just admit it, and I'll make sure he brings you no harm.

"You should know I'm in control of every country in the world but yours, so you need to stop being so stubborn and relinquish your power to me also. If you don't, you could have a deadly accident. It could even happen at your home."

The Israeli leader appeared flabbergasted as he sputtered out insecurely, "I d-d-don't know what you're talking about, but I'll have to investigate my staff now to find out who's been lying to you.

"As far as me handing over power of the Israeli government to you, I wouldn't feel like a civilized human being if I did that. I know you'd have a lot of our citizens killed, or even worse."

Cain then decided to use blackmail again. He would use the other copy of the video he had held back secretly when he had blackmailed him the first time. It was a copy of the Israeli leader engaging in homosexual activities. It had worked before, and he felt sure it would work again. With that in mind, Cain said threateningly, "You're making a dreadful mistake. You've left me with no other option but to go to the worldwide press in order to show them your homosexual tendencies."

The Israeli opened his eyes widely with frustrated surprise. "You told me last time you gave me all the copies."

"I lied," Cain said with a smirk.

The Israeli leader replied back with frustration, "Mr. President, I see you're a very unscrupulous man, and impossible to trust. I refuse to be blackmailed by you anymore. Now it's a matter of principle. Of course, I don't want my reputation ruined, but it's not worth being one of your minions, so I'll not help you. You can even send that video to my wife.

"Before you do, though, I want you to know I'll not be going down alone. I'll let the Israeli press know exactly what kind of president you are, and I'll implicate you in rape, kidnapping, and murder.

"By the way, thank you for telling me about the deadly accident I may have. I'll immediately have my residence guarded with maximum security, so good luck in trying to break in with your CIA." With a firm resolution, he picked up his phone and called an Israeli general.

As he talked on the phone, Cain felt rage surge in his heart. With a flushed face, he clenched his jaw muscles, while controlling himself. He wanted to kill the prime minister. He wanted to kill him so badly, he could taste it. He wanted to stand up and grasp him around his scrawny neck and strangle him to death. As he slowly stood up, his video cell phone rang. He flipped it open with his index finger and looked in the face of his head scientist.

The scientist said with concern, "Mr. President, I hope I haven't disturbed you, but you told us to call if there were any changes concerning the status of Lemuel and Pamela."

"What is it?" Cain asked with impatient anger as some of his pent-up rage came spilling out.

The scientist said timidly, not wanting to upset Cain anymore, "Mr. President, Lemuel and Pamela left Jerusalem and have just arrived in Megiddo."

"Continue keeping me updated," Cain said curtly as he closed his phone with a loud click.

He still felt like killing the prime minister, but he decided the time had not yet arrived. He wanted to make sure his control over the other countries remained strong. He decided to take his rage out on Lemuel and Pamela instead. The time had finally arrived to apprehend them.

Looking at the still talking Israeli leader, he said with a disgusted grimace, "Don't worry about me attacking your home right now. I've more important things to do."

Cain then turned around briskly, leaving the Israeli leader worried. He decided to deal with the last defiant government later. He needed to release some stress by torturing Lemuel to death and ravishing Pamela.

Several hours after their arrival, Lemuel and Pamela sat outside on the patio of a Megiddo restaurant catering to American tastes. Before them sat a large pan full of juicy New England pot roast, covered with steamy white potatoes, orange carrots, and yellow onions. It sent forth redolent scents of roasted beef simmering in a cornucopia of fresh vegetables.

Pamela spread soft white butter on her bread while smiling with satisfaction. "This kind of food reminds me of home. Does it you, Lemuel?"

Lemuel agreed with a nod. It did remind him of home in America, but he had hundreds of homes in hundreds of cultures in his thousands of years of existence. He knew New England pot roast had become as American as baseball and Coca-Cola, so he said, "Yeah, it reminds me of home in America, and I miss it. Maybe someday we'll get back and everything will be alright again."

He then placed a forkful of juicy pot roast in his mouth and chewed hungrily. After swallowing the tender meat, he said, "You should eat more of this roast, Pam, it's absolutely delicious."

She laughed at his eagerness to consume the roast as he cut off another big piece and plopped it on his plate. She then said while raising her eyebrows quizzically, "I've eaten so much already, I don't know if I can fit anymore in, but I'll try for old times' sake."

She reluctantly reached over and began cutting off a small piece of the dark brown roast. Looking up, her eyes widened in terror and her hand froze in place with the knife still in the juicy roast.

Smiling with glee, Cain walked in the direction where they sat.

Lemuel turned his head to where Pamela stared. He immediately jumped up when he saw Cain with two burly bodyguards walking toward them. "Stand up, Pam!" he exclaimed loudly.

She sat there as terror froze her to the chair like an icicle. Lemuel rushed over to her, shielding her body with his own.

Cain and his two bodyguards soon stood within a couple feet of them.

Cain said with a touch of superiority infecting each word, "My, my, my, look who we have here. Mr. Jackass and his little slut."

"How di-di-did you find me?" Lemuel stuttered with puzzlement.

Cain replied back with a menacing tone, "I have my ways. The real question is, did you and Pamela actually believe you could hide from me?"

"You'll never take me back alive!" she said with venomous hate dripping from each word.

Cain retorted back spitefully, "Oh, but I will. I'll take both you and your man back alive. I'll then torture your man while I screw you like the little slut you are. It'll be exhilarating, and I'm sure you'll enjoy it, too." Looking at his two bodyguards, he motioned them toward the stunned couple with an order of disgust. "Arrest both of these idiots."

Suddenly a beam of transparent light surrounded the couple.

Everyone looked up into the sky and saw an amazing sight. Above their heads flew a transparent UFO with a barely discernible outline. Inside the UFO sat a creature that appeared to be made of thick, purple light. The beam of light originated from the UFO.

"Get them anyway!" Cain demanded with frustrated anger.

One of the bodyguards cautiously moved his hand forward and touched the beam of light. His fingertips singed against the beam, causing him to clutch his hand quickly to his chest and scream in agonizing pain, leaving behind a little tendril of smoke curling in the air, along with an odorous smell of burnt flesh.

Cain then heard Lucifer's voice deep in his mind, though no one else could hear, "An angel's protecting this couple. You'll not be able to touch them. The only way you'll be able to apprehend them is to start a war against it. Tell the world they're being invaded by aliens. The ship's proof enough. Mobilize a great worldly army, and we'll end this once and for all."

Cain stared with hatred at the couple as he said with frustration, "It appears you're safe for now, but not forever. I'll be back, and I'll have the largest army this world has ever seen." He then turned around and walked away with his bodyguards following close behind.

The beam of light vanished, though the UFO continued to hover protectively above Lemuel and Pamela.

Other bystanders stopped in their tracks and looked up astonishingly into the sky, pointing at the hovering UFO.

"What is it, Lemuel?" Pamela asked with awe.

Lemuel smiled with reassurance as he said, "It appears to be an angel in his ship. Apparently he's going to be our bodyguard from now on. Come on, let's go to our hotel room."

As they walked off, the UFO slowly followed them, causing people to watch with openmouthed amazement.

(PAST)

President Kennedy asked, bewildered, "So what do you think about the situation, Lemuel? It's not enough they've helped Cuba turn communist, now the Russian bastards are placing nuclear weapons there so they can nuke us if the urge hits them."

Lemuel replied back with a serious tone, "You must dissuade them, Mr. President, starting with threats."

President Kennedy laughed as he said, "You're a rabid dog with your advice."

Lemuel smiled respectfully as he said, "I've been known to bite occasionally, Mr. President." Brushing his hair back with worry, he added, "Seriously, Mr. President, you can't allow those nuclear weapons in Cuba. That's too close to the mainland of America, and it poses a serious risk to our security."

Kennedy sighed with frustration as he said, "Of course, you're right, Lemuel. I'll have word sent to them immediately that I'll consider it an act of war if they don't remove those weapons from Cuba."

Lemuel sighed with relief as he said, "I'm sure it would work, Mr. President. I'm sure they'll not take a chance in going to war with America."

"Enough of that," Kennedy said with a wave of his hand. "Have you heard about my rocket and satellite plans?"

Lemuel smiled with excitement as he said, "Yes, Mr. President, I've heard about them, and I think it's a great idea."

Kennedy asked with pride, "Do you know why I'll put a satellite up there?"

Lemuel put his finger to his lips and mumbled with curiosity, "Mmm, to show the world we're smarter than the USSR? Perhaps to show the world we're the greatest country on earth? To help our prestige?"

Kennedy agreed with silent nods to each of Lemuel's answers, but he added proudly after Lemuel finished, "Yes to all those answers, but those aren't the only reasons. The satellite I'll send up has extra-powerful telescopes and cameras attached to it. It'll be able to see things as small as vehicles. We'll be able to keep track of our rivals, such as their hidden nuclear weapons."

Lemuel said with surprise, "Oh."

Kennedy replied back with disappointment, "Is that all you have to say?"

Lemuel smiled apologetically as he said, "I'm sorry, Mr. President, I'm just a little surprised. I thought your idea of controlling populations with subtle commercials was an excellent idea for propaganda purposes. I just hope these satellites don't take away the freedoms America is so proud of."

Kennedy chuckled as he said, "Lemuel, I hate to break the news to you, but America isn't as free as you think. Our government already owns everything. Remember, every year Americans must pay taxes on the land they own. If they don't, our government will eventually evict them. In effect, everyone is just paying rent to the government. I could go on and on about the supposed freedoms and rights America enjoys, but it would take all day. In reality, freedom is just an elaborate illusion."

Lemuel knew the president was right, up to a certain point.

Kennedy then cleared his throat in order to change the subject, and asked politely, "Why don't you come out on a double date with me, Lemuel?" He added with anticipation, "I have two gorgeous blondes lined up, and I need to get out of this rat hole for a while."

Lemuel shook his head with mild disapproval as he said, "I'm sorry, Mr. President, I don't have time for dates at this time. Besides, I don't want to conspire with you in cheating on your wife, Jackie. I'm sure she wouldn't appreciate me encouraging you to commit adultery."

Kennedy laughed as he slapped Lemuel on the back. "Don't worry, she'll never find out. It'll be our secret."

Chapter 26

The Christmas morning air in the city of Megiddo felt cool and crisp, with a mild breeze blowing off the great sea.

Everyone in Megiddo was worried. Within the last few months, the city had become surrounded by an enormous army of over two hundred million men.

Cain had convinced the world an alien invasion would be coming, starting at the city of Megiddo. He used the lone UFO as proof.

Since it hovered constantly over the city, most people in the world felt threatened, so they prepared for an alien attack by sending the vast majority of their armies to Megiddo.

The city also became home for thousands of jet fighters from all the world's air forces, with hundreds of jets flying around the UFO constantly, some of them playing hazardous games of chicken with it. Since it never moved aside from them, a few of the jets exploded in blazing infernos against its force field.

The UFO refused to go past the city limits, so Lemuel convinced Pamela it would be better if they remained put. He did not want to give up the invaluable protection it gave them.

Cain sent undercover agents after them more than once, but whenever they attempted to apprehend them, they would be repelled by a beam of light. No matter if they attempted to apprehend them inside buildings or outside, the results were always the same.

For some unknown reason, the nano chips ceased functioning on all who resided in Megiddo. Cain sent a multitude of messages to Pamela's nano chip ordering her to leave the city, to no avail. He knew somehow the angel who protected them made the nano chips obsolete for all who resided in the Megiddo.

On Christmas morning, Lemuel and Pamela ate breakfast at their favorite restaurant. As they sat at their favorite table with a red checkered tablecloth, they ate their food quietly, becoming engrossed with personal thoughts.

As she took a drink of her cinnamon-laced eggnog, the redolent smell of cinnamon triggered thoughts of her childhood holidays. She picked at her yellow omelet, which consisted of small chunks of red tomatoes and green bell peppers. Visions of green Christmas trees with twinkling red and yellow lights flashed through her mind. She had always loved Christmas, and she missed the Christmas spirit that always filled her heart during the season.

Lemuel felt revulsion as Pamela cut up a slab of ham. He did not eat pork, but he knew Pamela loved it. As Pamela savored the salty yet tart pieces of juicy ham, Lemuel withdrew in his mind to a private spot. He refused to watch Pamela eat food considered unclean and taboo.

After she finished with her succulent breakfast, she gazed forlornly into Lemuel's averted eyes and asked sadly, "Lemuel, when will we be allowed to return to America?"

Lemuel did not know how to tell her, but he knew he had to tell her somehow. His appetite deserted him as he slowly chewed on a piece of corn beef. Swallowing it, he said with dread, "I don't know when we'll be going back to America. I didn't want to tell you this, but I guess the time has arrived. Megiddo is the shorter name for Armageddon."

"Oh, my God," she said with horror highlighting her surprise. "How long have you known?"

Lemuel looked away with discomfort as he said, "I've known about this city for more years than you'd believe. I knew the end of our present civilization was drawing close. Since Revelation said this would be the place God would fight the final battle of this civilization, I knew God's attention would be focused on this place, so I intuitively knew God would protect us here."

"What do we do now?" Pamela asked, in a mild state of shock.

Lemuel shrugged his shoulders helplessly as he said, "We can't do anything but pray and hope to be preserved."

Pamela cocked an eyebrow with suspicion as she asked, "Are there any more secrets you've kept from me?"

Lemuel sighed with reluctance as he said, "Just one. I'm immortal, and I'm four thousand, five hundred and sixty-three years old."

Looking confused, she said, "I don't believe it. You're human just like me." Lemuel sighed with disappointment as he said, "Not full-blooded."

"I don't understand," Pamela said with puzzlement.

He looked away sadly as he said, "I didn't want to tell you because I've kept it a secret for many years. Since the end of this civilization has finally arrived, I see no harm in telling you now."

"I don't understand. You're talking like you're an alien or

something," she said with exasperation.

Lemuel looked at her, and with shame he said, "No, I'm not an alien, but my father is. He was among the angels who rebelled against God and mated with human women thousands of years ago. I'm a hybrid, half-human and half-demon, at least that's what some people call the fallen angels."

She shook her head firmly in denial while saying, "No, you're not a demon! Stop being so cruel. You're my man, and you're human. You're starting to scare me now. Have you lost your mind?"

Lemuel smiled gently as he said, "I assure you, Pam, I've not lost my mind. Yes, I'm a demon, at least half-one anyway. Not only that, but I'm a bastard also. The demons took whatever woman they wanted, and some of them didn't marry, either. Cain's mother didn't marry his father, and neither did my mother.

"If it's any consolation, I'm not rebellious like my father and his peers were. I hate wickedness, and I love righteousness. I'm an oddity for my race.

"I feel God has big plans for me since I am a lover of righteousness. I feel God will use me for the benefit of mankind. I think that's another reason I came here when I saw the end of this civilization drawing near, so God can use me to help usher in His heavenly kingdom.

"No matter what happens, though, always remember that I love you with all my heart. You're the most precious, beautiful woman in the world to me."

Tears flowed from her eyes as happiness filled her heart. "Do you really love me that much? Am I really that precious to you?"

With a sexual tone, he said huskily, "Yes, my sweet woman, I really love you that much, and you really are that precious to me."

She jumped up and rushed to him.

He stood up in time to catch her in his arms.

She rested her head against his chest and wept happily with all her heart. He wrapped his arms around her shaking body, resting his face against her head, lovingly comforting her with a tender embrace.

On the outskirts of Megiddo, Cain stood on a platform in front of hundreds of generals. There were generals from every country in the world. All the powerful men on earth feared Cain. Except for Israel, no country in the world dared go against his orders. Indirectly he had become the world's dictator.

Because of the vast network of people he controlled by the nano chips, he had insidiously infiltrated every government in the world. Because of the super computer and the technology it generated, no wars between countries existed and hardly any more crime. His super computer helped produce a flourishing economy, which in turn eliminated famine and poverty. Almost everyone partook in his serum, and it bestowed on them eternal life. Most people believed they were on the path of eternal life and prosperity.

Except for Israel, every capital of each country erected a life-sized statue of white marble in Cain's image. He became the most famous, loved man on earth. The statues became symbols of his supposed benevolence. Most people accredited all the good things in society to him, so when he said the earth was being invaded by aliens, most believed him.

Looking over the crowd of generals, Cain said with a heartwarming smile, "Generals, it's an honor to address you all at the same time. Thank God English has become the universal language, or we'd have a problem."

Everyone laughed at Cain's humor.

Cain smiled and waited for the laughter to abate before he continued. "Generals, one of the reasons I'm having this meeting today is to update you on the attempts I've made in contacting the alien invader. I'm sorry to say, I haven't succeeded. I've tried languages, sound waves, light waves, microwaves, air motion waves, and any other kind of wave you can think of with no apparent success. The alien refuses to communicate with me, or anyone else for that matter. After I exhausted every option, I've come to the conclusion that there's no other option but to fire on it and knock it from the sky. Are there any questions?"

A multitude of generals raised their arms. Cain chose one from Germany.

The German general cleared his throat and said loudly for all to hear, "Mr. President, we've already seen what these alien ships can accomplish when they decimated the Chinese armies. Our weapons are useless against their invisible force fields. How do you propose we knock that ship out of the sky without getting our armies destroyed in the process?"

Cain smiled as he said, "That's a good question, General, and one I'd be happy to answer. Scientists from around the world have joined together and developed a weapon that will destroy it and any other ship that may come to its aid. We call them light cannons, and I've been placing them in position for the last week.

"Since it's Christmas, I've decided to start our attack at 12:00 p.m. today. I've a thousand light cannons spread all around the city in case other alien ships appear. Make sure there are always men on the cannons in order to keep them operational.

"Your conventional weapons are obsolete, so don't waste your missiles, bullets, or jets. The cannons are our only defense against these creatures."

More of the generals raised their hands eagerly in order to be called on. Cain chose one from Iraq.

The Iraqi general said with worry creasing his forehead, "Mr. President, how can we use the light cannons when we don't know how?"

Cain chuckled lightly at the Iraqi's question, which caused a lot of the other generals to laugh.

After the laughter subsided, Cain said with confidence, "There's nothing to fear. A child could easily learn how to use these cannons in a matter of seconds. They're so easy to activate and use, it's hardly even worth telling you. All you have to do is turn it on, sight it on the alien ship with a scope that's attached, and press the green button on the side of it. A thick laser will then shoot out from it. It will disable every alien ship it hits.

"Please make sure all your men have these simple instructions on how to operate these cannons because the alien will probably fire on your men after it comes under attack, so we'll need plenty of men keeping the cannons operational if more alien ships decide to join in."

Cain then gazed impatiently on the crowd as he asked, "Are there any more questions before I adjourn this meeting?"

Because of Cain's apparent impatience, only one hand from the crowd rose. General Love boldly raised his hand and asked with frowning uncertainty, "Mr. President, what happens if a large alien force aids the lone UFO? What happens if some of the aliens survive the crash and start attacking our forces by hand? How do we kill them since conventional weapons will probably cause them no harm?"

Cain smiled with confidence as he said, "Let's hope that doesn't happen, but if it does, turn the light cannons on the ones on foot, as well. It should destroy them."

A fearful murmur rose from the crowd of generals.

Lucifer stood in front of his large congregation of demons. They stood behind the worldly human armies that camped around Megiddo. Unlike the human armies, they were unseen and could not be heard.

Looking at them all, Lucifer said with a solemn voice, "Comrades, I called you all here today because this will be the day we win Earth's independence from a cruel God. No more will He be a God to mankind. Instead, we'll be their gods, just like we were in days long ago. Once more we'll be worshiped by them, except this time we'll be worshiped without interference from a meddling God.

"We'll help our human servants in the coming battle. Our job will be to walk among them, and after they shoot down a ship, to apprehend the angelic pilots.

"We'll bind them and hold them as prisoners. After the battle, we'll use them as hostages to bargain with God, in case He attempts to reclaim the earth."

All the demons murmured their approval.

Lucifer screamed angrily, "Silence! I've not finished yet. If we do lose on this day, I want you all to destroy humanity as quickly as possible. No human must be allowed to live. It'll be our ultimate victory over God, even if we lose the war. If humans can't be our worshipers, then all must die.

"If we lose, I'll destroy all the live humans in Megiddo. Each of you chose a town and a city to destroy. After all the humans in the cities and towns are slain, kill all the people in the rural areas. With that said, please take your positions among the human soldiers."

The light cannons were activated at 12:00 p.m. with a thousand cannons focusing lasers on one UFO, causing it to wobble for a second, then plunge to the earth, smashing the town municipal building with a loud crash.

Immediately some of the townspeople saw an alien made of thick purple light climb out of its destroyed vehicle. At ten feet high, it stood higher than any human. Its humanoid-shaped body appeared to be naked. It also appeared sexless.

The creature looked in all directions, but before it took a step, ten yellowish-colored creatures materialized beside it, surrounding it.

The threatened pilot spun around, going faster with each revolution, until it was a blur.

Each time a yellowish creature attempted to apprehend the threatened pilot, it was hurled on its back.

They finally decided to act in harmony, and lunged at the spinning pilot the same time with outstretched arms. Each grabbed a hold of the whirling mass.

The pilot was forced to stop twirling with an abrupt jerk, swinging all ten of the abductors around once. The pilot then struggled against them with all its might, but resistance was futile. The attackers quickly restrained the pilot with restraints it could not break free from, then dragged the struggling pilot away.

Since they all stayed visible, every human they passed opened their mouth wide with amazement.

Suddenly the sky became filled with thousands of UFOs. If the ships had not been nearly transparent, the sun would have been hidden because of their imposing numbers. As it were, the sunrays passed through them, with just the skeletal lines of each ship visible. Because of their transparency, it diffused most of the sunrays into a spectrum of multiple lights twinkling everywhere. Every human on the ground rubbed their eyes, thinking something was lodged in them.

The generals ordered the cannons to fire on the alien ships. There were so many of them, they did not even have to aim. They just shot up into the sky, immediately hitting a ship.

The ships fought back with their own lasers of annihilating light. Men screamed briefly in torturous agony as thousands of lasers hit into their ranks. As soon as a laser enveloped a man, he would scream in terrified torment for a second before vanishing in a puff of smoke. The smoke smelled like putrid human flesh, corrupted with decay.

The cannons continued discharging their own lasers of light, and the angelic craft continued dropping from the sky like oranges being shaken off trees. As soon as one crashed to the ground, yellowish demons materialized around the fallen ship, dragging out a struggling orange angel and restraining it.

Angelic aircraft continued falling at a steady rate, but the human armies were being decimated at an alarming rate. Soldiers began running away in panic, with the translucent ships following them, destroying them as they ran.

Soon thousands of ships began landing. Lucifer did not have enough demons to apprehend them all. Soon the angels were apprehending the demons.

Lucifer screamed in a language all demons and angels understood, "Retreat! Retreat and destroy every human you find! Destroy all humanity!"

The demons slowly began to disappear, but the angels were quicker. Before the demons completely disappeared, a swarm of angels pounced on each, binding them with manacles of light within split seconds.

Lucifer watched his strategy disintegrate before his eyes. He screamed in anguish as a swarm of angels apprehended him.

Cain knew his plan of ruling the world had dissipated before his eyes, with the millions of tendrils of smoke rising throughout the battlefield. With beams of lasers all around, it felt as if he were walking through a giant laser game. His rage drove him toward Megiddo in a sprint. With a M16 rifle in his hands, he felt determined to survive long enough to kill Lemuel. He blamed his defeat on him.

He soon found himself in Megiddo with people screaming and running in panic everywhere. He ran past the residential area into the business district. He knew which way he needed to go. His informants had earlier confided in him by telling him where Lemuel and Pamela were. He felt that since the angels were engaged in a massacre, they would not be guarding Lemuel or Pamela. He clutched his M16 closer to his chest as he chuckled in a psychotic way.

Lemuel and Pamela sat holding hands at their favorite restaurant when Cain came bursting in with a maniacal expression on his face.

Both stared at him with surprise. Since everyone in the city ran around panic-stricken, they did not expect anyone to be coming into their favorite restaurant.

"At last," Cain said with a triumphant, crazed grin. "At last I'll have the opportunity to kill you both!"

He then aimed his M16 at them and fired a rapid round of shots, laughing with a deranged look.

As soon as Cain pulled the trigger, Lemuel lunged over the table in a split second, right onto Pamela, knocking her to the floor with his body protecting hers.

Cain sent splintery wood flying all around as he rapidly sent one bullet after another into their upturned table. Quickly the ammunition cartridge became empty, so he took it out with lightning speed and threw it to the side of the room. He frantically searched for another full cartridge in his camouflaged uniform.

"If only you'd have been cooperative, I wouldn't have to be doing this. If only you'd have joined me, perhaps we would've become good friends."

Lemuel had no interest in ever becoming good friends with Cain.

After being his mortal enemy for thousands of years, he only wanted him dead. While Cain searched for a full cartridge of ammunition, Lemuel grabbed Pamela by the wrist. He pointed frantically to the back entrance.

She nodded fearfully with understanding.

He pulled her off the floor, and together they ran bravely toward the back, as Cain pushed the second cartridge into his weapon's chamber with a loud click.

"Hey, I'm not finished with you two yet!" Cain screamed in a frenzied rage.

He ran after them, running at a sprint across the restaurant and through the open back door. By the time he made it out the door, he saw them run around the right corner of the restaurant, thus causing him to lose sight of them.

He sprinted toward the right corner and stopped abruptly at it. Taking a deep breath of air, he looked around the corner cautiously. He watched Pamela running in front of Lemuel. He would have to shoot Lemuel in the back before he could shoot Pamela.

As the couple ran across the dusty ground, Cain took careful aim and shot Lemuel in the back with a quick burst of six shots. Every one of the bullets found their mark and burst out of Lemuel's chest in a stream of red blood.

Pamela screamed in terror at the sound of the M16 rifle. Turning her head, she watched Lemuel's body fly in the air toward her with an expression of agony on his face.

His body flopped to the ground face-first with a loud thump.

As he lay facedown on the dusty ground, Pamela stopped running away and ran over to his broken body.

Red blood spread out around his body, nourishing the parched ground.

She turned him over on his back with tears clouding her vision. Moaning with despair, she said, "You can't leave me now, Lemuel! We're getting married. Remember? Oh, Lemuel, my sweet Lemuel, I love you more than life."

After no response, she rested her head against his bloody chest and wept with deep cries of sorrow. Her body trembled with each mournful cry. She wept with every ounce of strength she possessed.

Cain walked over to the scene. As he looked down at them, he said vindictively, "See, if you'd have listened, we wouldn't have to be going through this. If only you'd have obeyed me."

Pamela looked up with hatred in her eyes, and she spit a

mouthful of saliva on his pants. "Go to hell!" she screamed with rage.

"You first," Cain said with a contemptuous smile as he aimed his M16 directly at her head.

Suddenly a laser fell from the sky onto Cain. When it enveloped his body, he screamed agonizingly for a second, then his body disappeared in a puff of putrid smoke, adding to the foul smell already permeating the air.

Pamela looked up and saw a translucent ship floating beside a white, puffy cloud. She then screamed in anguish at the top of her lungs, "Why, God? Why have You allowed my man to be taken from me?"

Suddenly dust began swirling around Lemuel's dead body.

She watched with stunned bewilderment as the dust covered Lemuel completely. After the dust ceased swirling and settled lightly on him, she looked at him with wonder. His body appeared completely intact and healthy. He looked perfect and flawless. She gasped with delight when he opened his eyes and gazed lovingly into hers.

Rising to a sitting position, he asked with curiosity, "Is it over? Am I in heaven?"

Tears of joy filled her eyes as she said, "No, my love, we're not in heaven. I think God wants us to make this earth into a paradise first."

He smiled as she bent over and kissed him with joy and love in her heart.

Cain swirled around and around in a black, seemingly endless funnel that appeared to go into infinity. Finally his senses became shocked with a bright light so blinding he had to shield his eyes from it. After his eyes became accustomed to the light, he opened them wide with fear. A golden throne made of light appeared before him, with a spiritual Being consisting of beautiful lights sitting on it. God stared at Cain and those who were with him with a disgusted look on His face.

Cain looked around and saw Lucifer and millions of his demonic followers. All had their heads bowed with respect and terror.

God spoke with a deep, thunderous voice, "Because all of you have disobeyed My orders and become embroiled in human affairs, I have no option but to sentence all of you to one thousand Earth years in prison. A prison I have prepared at the very core of the Earth."

Looking directly at Cain, He added with disgusting disappointment, "Since you followed them so faithfully, I have decided to give you a taste of what your superiors are like. You shall also be cast in their prison for a thousand years!"

With a wave of His hand, a lingering stream of magical powers resembling zillions and zillions of colorful dots of glitter floated around them.

It picked them all up at once and hurled them back down the pitch-black, seemingly endless funnel of infinity. All of them screamed with absolute terror the whole way back...

Thousands of miles deep inside the Earth, Cain walked with terror to Lucifer's hellish cave. When God first imprisoned him there, terror became his only friend. He knew then he was in the hell the Bible spoke of.

The sky consisted of a gigantic cavern roof stretching for thousands of miles in every direction. Dark caves, large and small, hung down from the cavern roof like ugly giant wasp nests, with stone walkways leading to each cave. Under the walkways, a giant lake of molten lava spewed forth large, streaming billows of noxious smoke, with smells of sulfur and brimstone rising out continuously.

Even though reason told him he should not be able to feel the heat because of having only a spiritual body, he still did, so he remained out of the seething lake of lava as much as possible. He still became exceedingly thirsty every time he looked on the fiery lake, which was unusual since spiritual bodies had no need of physical nourishment. He attributed his physical feelings to the common lore of losing a physical arm and yet still feeling it.

When he first accidentally fell into the burning lake, he screamed with agony and insanity for over a week. After he came to his senses and noticed the demons on the stone walkways laughing hilariously at his insane screams of terror, he realized all he had to do was pull himself out with the aid of a stone walkway that ran just above the lake.

After that realization, he had pulled himself out and found a cave to live in. There were millions of caves, so he had no problem finding an unoccupied one.

A few demons reluctantly aided him by teaching him how to make furniture and other objects made of light. He eventually possessed a bed, a couch, a chair, a desk, and other luminous possessions. He kept busy writing out plans on what to do when rejoined with physical society. He knew his prison sentence was only for a thousand years.

He felt miserable where he was. Each day seemed to stretch

indefinitely, with the same activities every day. The demons also treated him as an inferior, with no respect or kindness. They laughed at him, hit him, kicked him, and even raped him at times. Occasionally they would even blame him for the bad predicament they were in.

Lucifer rarely saw him. Cain could only see him by appointment. In the first year of being incarcerated, he only saw Lucifer twice, so he felt nervous when he stood at Lucifer's majestic abode, one of the largest caves around.

"Father Lucifer, it is I, your son Cain," he yelled out in a trembling voice. "Come in," an irritated voice bellowed out.

Mustering up his courage, Cain forced himself to walk into the very large cave with armed demons standing at attention alongside the wall like statues made of thick, yellowish light. Soon he found himself standing in front of a throne made of red light that appeared to vibrate with awesome power.

Lucifer sat with a musing expression of disgust on his face. Staring at Cain in silence for a moment, he finally said with a nauseating tone, "My demonic brothers are becoming bored with this imprisoned life, and they want to use you and the other inferiors as amusement, maybe once a month for a day or so, with all the inferiors taking their turn.

"They liked you better when you were screaming with terror. Remember when you first arrived? After you accidentally fell into the burning lake, you screamed insanely for a week straight while splashing helplessly in it. We all thought it was a hilarious sight, and it brought us lots of laughs. You gave all our miserable lives some enjoyment then.

"Because of that, I'm allowing them to cast you and the other inferiors here in the lake of fire for around a day or so each month. Everyone will have their turn, starting with you."

Terror filled Cain's heart as he pleaded, "Father, no, please! Not me! Cast the other inferiors instead! Please, I'm your son! Please, Father..."

"Take him away," Lucifer said with disgust resonating off his unmerciful face. High-pitched screeches of glee filled Lucifer's cave as demons pounced on Cain, who screamed with futile horror as they dragged him out of the cave...

Cain screamed with insane terror and excruciating torment, as he frantically splashed around in the bubbling lake of fire. His mind became so clouded with dementia, he could barely hear the great multitude of demons laughing at his terrifying, torturous ordeal.

Chapter 27

The alien ship flew high over the Earth beside the puffy white clouds. It flew over a world whose land and waters were free from all pollution. Beautiful trees of assorted colors zoomed past with amazing speed.

Looking down, Michael the archangel observed with his perfect vision light brown lions, black apes, red parrots, gray elephants, and colorful peacocks. All tame and all friends. He saw beautiful homes with stunning lawns, colorful vegetable gardens, fruit orchards, and nut trees.

Eventually he came to a large metropolitan area known as New Washington, DC. In the center of the city sat the American governor's estate. He landed his ship on the parking area of the estate. The top of the ship lifted up, and he got out.

Stretching his arms out with a whimper of ecstasy, he took a deep breath of the alfresco air with satisfaction. It smelled and tasted clean, crisp, and fresh, with scents of honey, perfumed flowers, and rich soil intermingling to cause invigoration, as if breathing in a pleasant health tonic. He loved the atmosphere. Each breath brought him feelings of exuberance.

As he walked toward the large government building known as the New White House, he listened to beautiful Earth sounds of melodic birds, roaring bears, howling wolves, and other vibrant animal sounds. They all lived free and unhindered throughout the cities and countrysides of Earth since they posed no danger to anyone.

He soon found himself by the New White House's front door. He cautiously pressed the doorbell. He always felt afraid he would break it. Humans were so fragile and weak in comparison to his people.

At ten feet in height, Michael possessed a humanoid-shaped body, but that was where the resemblance ended. His body appeared to be made of pure purple light. His thick body of solid light appeared to be in constant motion, like a giant humanoid-shaped cup filled with thick grape syrup. The creature wore no clothes and appeared hairless and sexless. He also possessed two large white wings protruding out from his back, also made of thick light.

The door opened with a human servant looking at him with awe and respect. "May I speak with the governor please?" Michael said politely.

"Right away, sir!" the servant said quickly with awe. He opened the door wider as he continued, "Governor Lemuel gave me explicit orders to allow you in unescorted. He said you'd know the way."

Michael smiled and nodded a silent yes as he walked past the awed servant. Soon he stood in front of the door to Lemuel's living quarters.

He knocked on the door.

The door opened with Governor Lemuel and his wife, Pamela, looking at him with warm smiles.

Governor Lemuel appeared around twenty-one years of age and in perfect health, with a rosy glow to his cheeks. At six feet in height, he weighed a healthy two hundred pounds. His muscles appeared as lithe as a cheetah's. His face possessed a square outline that gave him a manly appearance. His dark brown eyes appeared soothing, with curly black hair extending down to his shoulders.

His wife, Pamela, also appeared around twenty-one years old and in perfect health with glowing, supple skin. At five feet tall, her weight appeared perfect at one hundred pounds. She possessed a body well-proportioned in all the right places. Her breasts were small but firm, with voluptuous thighs and buttocks. Her face possessed a beautiful, feminine look with brown eyes and straight black hair framing her lovely face with a picturesque beauty.

They both wore comfortable robes.

"Hello," Governor Lemuel said with an amiable tone. "It is good to see you again, Michael. Are you doing your yearly rounds?"

Michael nodded.

Lemuel then asked, "How do you like my new servant? The last one I had decided to quit so he could devote his time to growing a large garden."

Michael smiled while saying, "I love him."

Lemuel smiled with a mischievous twinkle in his eye as he said, "Still not very talkative, I see. Well, come on in, you big purple slug, and fill me in on any new information you may have. Hopefully it's more exciting stuff than last time."

Lemuel and Pamela escorted Michael to their private office.

The office appeared cluttered with antique furniture, historical pictures, and other decorations. It also possessed one giant guest chair made specifically for Michael. It sat in the center of the room.

The room also possessed an antique desk that past American presidents had used, along with a comfortable antique chair. Official papers lay scattered haphazardly on the desk. By looking at it, one could safely assume that Governor Lemuel spent a lot of time in the office doing governmental tasks. He also used it for God's main ambassador, Michael.

Lemuel sat in his comfortable office chair, with Pamela sitting snugly on his lap. He then said hospitably, "Please, Michael, make yourself comfortable."

Michael sat down in the giant purple chair and appeared to blend right in like a giant chameleon. So much so that Lemuel barely noticed the solemn expression on his purple face.

"What's wrong, Michael? Why the long face?" Lemuel asked with concern.

Michael sighed with resignation as he said, "God gave me important orders to give to all the governors of this world. God has decided to start resurrecting people who have died, starting today. He'll continue to resurrect them for the next nine hundred and ninety years. Of course, by then tens of billions of people will be alive, from Adam and Eve on down.

"Your job will be to help find those people who have been resurrected in the province of America homes to live in. You must also teach them how to live righteous lives. Of course, you may enlist the aid of other people in this endeavor.

"Governors in every province will be doing this, so don't feel like you're alone. We have to help the resurrected ones get started the right way by helping them to love righteousness, and hate wickedness.

"King Jesus has already implemented God's plan in the province of Israel. You must do so in America."

Lemuel sat stunned. They were not prepared. They needed to build a lot more houses, grow a lot more food, and train a lot more teachers. He wondered why God had not at least given him a year's notice so he could have been prepared for the first ones who would be resurrected. He felt completely at a loss for words, and his emotions were mixed with a vast array of confusing questions.

"By the way," Michael said with a sense of humor, "happy anniversary. It has been ten years since the old system of mankind passed away. Just nine hundred and ninety years to go before God liberates the demons, and those with them, in order to use them to test how righteous this new world really is."

Lemuel did not look forward to that year.

At the center of the Earth, Cain had to rely on the demons to tell him what year it was since he never saw the sun. He still found it hard to believe only ten years had elapsed since his incarceration. It felt as if he had been incarcerated for at least a hundred years, since days appeared to pass so slowly in hell.

In those ten years, he had met other evil hybrid humans who had been killed in the Great Flood during Noah's time. He also met some of the most wicked humans who ever lived.

The demons took turns picking human hybrids and regular humans to toss in the lake of fire for short amounts of time. All the human and human hybrids had to endure the burning lake's tormenting lava. There always seemed to be a lot of unfortunate ones screaming in torment at all times in the lake of fire. It was the demons' favorite recreational activity, to watch the inferior humans and human hybrids squirm with anguish and screaming torment.

One day Cain stood on a stone walkway near the great lake of fire. The reddish lake of fire bubbled with intense heat unceasingly. Billows of thick, noxious smoke of sulfur and brimstone rose throughout the cavern, giving it a continuous hazy appearance.

Thousands of hybrids and human spirits screamed in agony in the lake of fire, their resonant screams reverberating against the caverns with echoes of torment.

Cain knew exactly how they felt. Soon it would be his turn again, and he would be in torment along with the ones chosen. He remembered vividly how the lake sent pinpricks of intense pain piercing into every part of his spiritual body, and how his famished thirst would intensify even more. Visions of icy glasses of refreshing tea or lemonade would then bombard his mind in an unmerciful onslaught of deprivation, causing his tormented spirit to suffer even more. He dreaded being thrown into the lake with every second he remained out. Soon his turn would arrive again.

Suddenly someone tapped him on the shoulder, which caused him great surprise. "Who has the audacity to disturb my last day of peace before my turn arrives?" he mumbled with self-pity as he turned around and gazed on a spiritual Joseph smiling at him. "What do you want, idiot?" he asked angrily.

Joseph feigned hurt as he said with a mocking whine, "I'll pretend you didn't say that. In fact, I'll even forget you probably had me killed before Armageddon. Yeah, I know Rosa worked for you. She told me so before she shot me to death. Don't worry about it, though. All that's in the past. To answer your question, I came to tell you how we can get away from this burning lake for a while."

With suspicious eyes, Cain asked, "Why would you want to help me if you're so sure I had you killed?"

"Simple, really," Joseph said with a casual shrug. "Since Lucifer's your father, we might be able to get away with it."

Cain gazed around and watched thousands of human and hybrid spirits swimming frantically in the burning lake, screaming with absolute torment and anguish. Demons stood on the stone walkways beside the lake with pitchforks made of light, hoping for a chance to poke someone trying to escape. Whenever a desperate human or hybrid attempted to escape, a sadistic demon would run over with excitement and cruelly stab the unlucky person back into the inferno while shouting with sadistic glee, "Your turn's not up yet! I'll tell you when it is."

Cain looked hopelessly away as he said, "Not possible."

"That's what everyone thinks," Joseph said excitedly, "but I've heard of a way out! I've been talking to a man who could be our ticket out of this part of the cavern for a while, to a part where there's no lake of fire, just a lot of caves.

"This man told me he found a demon friend who used to possess him when he was alive in human form, and so the demon became fond of him. Sometimes the demon takes him to the caves far away from this lake and leaves him alone in peace for a while. If we can get his demon friend to take us, it would be a good vacation for us occasionally."

Hope filled Cain's spiritual heart; maybe it might work, he thought with excitement, maybe I could just stay there for good. I've lived down here for a while, and I know how to make things of light. I can make tools, furniture, and so on. I could start a spiritual human community far away from this wretched hellfire. A place where people don't have to worry about floating in a lake of fire. Controlling the excitement he felt, he said encouragingly, "Okay, Joseph, I believe you. Introduce me to that demon."

Joseph led him thru a maze of stone walkways, until he arrived at the cave he wanted. He walked in with Cain close behind.

Cain saw a man lying on a bed of light.

Joseph motioned for him to remain at the entrance as he walked over and spoke with the man, who nodded with agreement.

The man rose out of bed and walked out of the cave, with Joseph following close behind.

Cain followed Joseph.

After thirty minutes of continuous walking, they arrived at a cave where a demon lived.

Joseph and Cain stood at a distance as the man spoke fervently to the demon.

The demon occasionally shook his head with an angry refusal, but the man continued pleading with the demon even more fervently. Finally, the demon grew weary and appeared to cooperate with reluctant nods of his head. The demon then walked over to Joseph and Cain.

The demon said with disappointment, "My friend here's Jack the Ripper. He has convinced me to escort you both to my secret hiding place where there's no lake of fire. It takes three months to get there. After we arrive, you may stay for one week, then you must follow me back here."

"Why?" Joseph asked.

"Because that's the way I say it is!" the demon exclaimed angrily. After taking a deep breath to calm his nerves, he continued in a more rational tone, "I don't want to stay gone too long because someone might figure out you're gone. Besides, the only way we can receive a little happiness around here is by watching you worthless inferiors suffer in the lake, so I'll not be taking you there that often."

Cain knew demons possessed large amounts of pride, so he would use their weakness to his advantage. With desperation, he said, "What if I told you that if you took Jack, Joseph, and me there and left us there, we'd worship you as a god?"

With an incredulous expression, the demon broke out in loud laughter. After his laughter subsided, he said with sarcastic humor, "Wow, I'd be a great god with just three worshipers."

Cain replied, "You could have thousands of worshipers." The demon looked at him with curiosity as he asked, "How?"

"Simple, really," Cain said with confidence. "Just escort other humans to where you'll escort us, and leave them there, too. We'll build a large community in the caves away from this place, and you could live among us as our god."

The demon liked the sound of Cain's offer. He loved the idea of being worshiped as a god, even if it would only last during their incarceration. He then fantasized about being greater than Lucifer.

Concern creased his brow as he said, "Since I can only escort six at a time so the others don't become suspicious, it'll take me at least a couple hundred years to secretly obtain enough worshipers to make it worthwhile."

With anticipation, he began doing calculations on his demonic fingers, attempting to estimate how many worshipers he could obtain in a couple hundred years...